Praise for
The Personal Librarian

The Instant *New York Times* Bestseller!
A *Good Morning America* Book Club Pick!
Named a Best Book of the Year by NPR!
Named a Notable Book of the Year by the *Washington Post*!

"Historical fiction at its best. . . . *The Personal Librarian* spins a complex tale of deceit and allegiance as told through books."
—*Good Morning America*

"Benedict, who is white, and Murray, who is African American, do a good job of depicting the tightrope Belle walked, and her internal conflict from both sides—wanting to adhere to her mother's wishes and move through the world as white even as she longed to show her father she was proud of her race. Like Belle and her employer, Benedict and Murray had almost instant chemistry, and as a result, the book's narrative is seamless. . . . I became hooked."
—NPR

"An extraordinary tale that is both brilliant historical fiction and an important and timely commentary on racism. By holding up an unflinching mirror and illuminating this little-known chapter in American history, these two gifted authors have penned a work that is a must-read."
—Pam Jenoff, *New York Times* bestselling author of
The Woman with the Blue Star

"A marvel of a story. This unflinching look at one woman's meteoric rise through New York's high society is enthralling, lyrical, and rife with danger. Belle's painful secret and her inspiring courage will capture—and break—your heart. Serious kudos to Benedict and Murray for bringing this true story to life."
—Fiona Davis, *New York Times* bestselling author of
The Lions of Fifth Avenue

"A fascinating story."
—*Real Simple*

"*The Personal Librarian* illuminates the extraordinary life of an exceptional, intelligent woman who had to make the impossible choice to live as an imposter or sacrifice everything she'd achieved and deserved. That Belle denied her true identity in order to protect herself and her family from racial persecution speaks not only to her time but also to ours, a hundred years later. All that glitters is not gold. This is a compelling and important story."

—Therese Anne Fowler, *New York Times* bestselling author of *A Good Neighborhood*

"As richly depicted as the lush world of art and literature Belle da Costa Greene presided over . . . an immersive, sweeping delight as well as an intimate, moving, and powerful portrait of Belle's personal and professional life. An unforgettable, captivating read!"

—Chanel Cleeton, *New York Times* bestselling author of *Our Last Days in Barcelona*

"Meticulously researched, heartbreaking, and inspiring . . . a fascinating look at a very public figure fighting a deep private battle, whose story still resonates with surprising power and immediacy today."

—Kristin Harmel, *New York Times* bestselling author of *The Book of Lost Names*

"A stunning and timely novel about a woman who, in forging a path for herself, had to battle constantly against the limitations society tried to place upon her due to her gender—and who also had to hide her true identity from a racist world. . . . Both a triumph and a fitting tribute to Belle's courage, her fierce desire to protect her family, and her personal struggle to be both the woman she was and the woman she was not allowed to be."

—Natasha Lester, *New York Times* bestselling author of *The Riviera House*

"An intimate and extraordinary conversation with the past. . . . As Belle da Costa Greene achieves her dreams by forsaking an identity, we wonder if we would or could do the same to irrevocably alter the literary world and our family. A novel abundant with culture, art, literature, and romance—the beauty and recklessness of love are revealed with astonishing clarity."

—Patti Callahan, *New York Times* bestselling author of *Surviving Savannah*

"An untold story that is simply amazing. It's timely and impactful."
—Brenda Jackson, *New York Times* bestselling author of
One Christmas Wish

"Upon starting this novel, be prepared to do nothing else until you've reached its poignant, reflective end. Through brilliant pacing and with painstaking care, Benedict and Murray paint a vibrant portrait of a woman whose accomplishments, relationships, and secretive history were as complex and intriguing as the collections she helped curate. . . . A timely, provocative read perfect for book clubs. I loved it."
—Kristina McMorris, *New York Times* bestselling author of *Sold on a Monday*

"From the moment I picked up *The Personal Librarian*, I was in awe of Belle da Costa Greene. My heart went out to her as she navigated the life she lived and the one she hid. . . . Belle's story couldn't come at a more fitting time as our country faces a united path forward."
—ReShonda Tate Billingsley, national bestselling author of *Miss Pearly's Girls*

"From the opulent Gilded Age ballrooms of New York to the fiercely competitive auction houses of Europe, *The Personal Librarian* is a poignant story of race, class, and one woman's struggle to live authentically."
—Renée Rosen, author of *The Social Graces*

"The story of Belle da Costa Greene is timely, universal, and enduring. Through it, Benedict and Murray raise questions that are as important now as they were a hundred years ago—questions to which a true historical answer may be less important than the fact that we are continuing to face them in contemporary ways."   —*Pittsburgh Post-Gazette*

"This fictional account of Greene's life feels authentic; the authors bring to life not only Belle but all those around her. An excellent piece of historical fiction that many readers will find hard to put down."
—*Library Journal* (starred review)

"A powerful take on the accomplishments of J. P. Morgan's librarian. . . . Benedict and Murray do a great job capturing Belle's passion and tenacity as she carves a place for herself in a racist, male-dominated society. This does fine justice to a remarkable historical figure."
—*Publishers Weekly*

"Every element of this blockbuster historical novel is compelling and revelatory, beginning with the bedazzling protagonist based with awe-struck care on Belle da Costa Greene. . . . A novel of enthralling drama, humor, sensuality, and insight. . . . [A] resounding tale of a brilliant and resilient woman defying sexism, classism, and racism during the brutality of Jim Crow. Benedict and Murray do splendidly right by Belle in this captivating and profoundly enlightening portrayal."

—*Booklist* (starred review)

"Kept me intrigued, fascinated, and mesmerized throughout. . . . Everyone should know about the woman who took risks, carved her own path, silenced the naysayers, and forged ahead to becoming one of America's most prominent librarians in history. Definitely a must-read."

—The Nerd Daily

"An engrossing, well-researched read."   —*The Christian Science Monitor*

The
PERSONAL
LIBRARIAN

Marie Benedict
and
Victoria Christopher Murray

BERKLEY
NEW YORK

BERKLEY
An imprint of Penguin Random House LLC
penguinrandomhouse.com

Copyright © 2021 by Marie Benedict and Victoria Christopher Murray
Readers Guide copyright © 2021 by Marie Benedict and Victoria Christopher Murray
Penguin Random House supports copyright. Copyright fuels creativity, encourages diverse voices,
promotes free speech, and creates a vibrant culture. Thank you for buying an authorized edition of
this book and for complying with copyright laws by not reproducing, scanning, or distributing any
part of it in any form without permission. You are supporting writers and allowing Penguin
Random House to continue to publish books for every reader.

BERKLEY and the BERKLEY & B colophon are registered trademarks of
Penguin Random House LLC.

ISBN: 9780593101544

The Library of Congress has catalogued the Berkley hardcover edition of this book as follows:

Names: Benedict, Marie, author. | Murray, Victoria Christopher, author.
Title: The personal librarian / Marie Benedict and Victoria Christopher Murray.
Description: New York: Berkley, [2021]
Identifiers: LCCN 2020045266 (print) | LCCN 2020045267 (ebook) |
ISBN 9780593101537 (hardcover) | ISBN 9780593101551 (ebook)
Subjects: LCSH: Greene, Belle da Costa—Fiction. | GSAFD: Biographical fiction.
Classification: LCC PS3620.E75 P47 2021 (print) | LCC PS3620.E75 (ebook) |
DDC 813/.6—dc23
LC record available at https://lccn.loc.gov/2020045266
LC ebook record available at https://lccn.loc.gov/2020045267

Berkley hardcover edition / June 2021
Berkley trade paperback edition / June 2022

Printed in the United States of America
1   3   5   7   9   10   8   6   4   2

Book design by Nancy Resnick
Title page photo by Triff/Shutterstock

For the two sides of Belle:
Belle da Costa Greene
and
Belle Marion Greener

CHAPTER 1

The Old North bell tolls the hour, and I realize that I'll be late. I long to break into a sprint, my voluminous skirts lifted, my legs flying along the Princeton University pathways. But just as I gather the heavy material, I hear Mama's voice: *Belle, be a lady at all times.* I sigh; a lady would never run.

I release the fabric and slow down as I weave through Princeton's leafy Gothic landscape, designed to look like Cambridge and Oxford. I know I must do nothing to draw any kind of extra attention. By the time I pass Blair Arch, my stride is quick but acceptable for a lady.

It's been five years since I left our New York City apartment for this sleepy New Jersey college town, and the quiet is still unnerving. On the weekends, I wish I could return to the energy of New York, but the sixty cents for a train ticket is outside our family's budget. So, I send money home instead.

As I duck under a crenellated tower, I moderate my pace so I won't be breathless when I arrive. *You are at Princeton University. You must take extra care working at that all-male institution. Be cautious, never do anything to stand out.* Even though she's nearly sixty miles away, Mama insinuates herself into my thoughts.

Pushing the heavy oak door slowly to minimize its loud creak, I pad as quietly as my calfskin boots allow, across the marble foyer before I sidle into the office I share with two other librarians. The room is empty, and I exhale in relief. If sweet-natured Miss Mc-Kenna saw me arrive late, it would have been of no import, but with hood-eyed, nosy Miss Adams, I could never be certain she wouldn't mention my offense at some future time to our superior.

I remove my coat and hat, careful to smooth my rebellious curly hair back into place. Tucking my somber navy skirt beneath me, I slide onto my chair. Within minutes, the office door flies open, slamming against the wood-paneled wall, and I jump. It is my only dear friend, fellow librarian, and housemate, Gertrude Hyde. As the niece of the esteemed head of purchasing for the library, Charlotte Martins, she can breach the quiet of the library's hallowed halls without fear of repercussions. An ebullient twenty-three-year-old with ginger hair and bright eyes, no one makes me laugh as she does.

"Sorry to make you jump, dear Belle. I guess I owe you two apologies now, instead of the single one I'd intended. First, we abandoned you this morning, which undoubtedly led to your lateness," she says with a mischievous smile and a glance at the wall clock, "and now, I've given you a fright."

"Don't be silly. The fault is mine. I should have put aside that letter to my mother and walked to campus with you and Charlotte. Miss Martins, I mean," I correct myself.

Most days, Charlotte, Gertrude, and I walk together from their large family home on University Drive, where I have a room and share meals with Charlotte, Gertrude, and the rest of their family who live in the house as well. From the first, Charlotte and Gertrude have welcomed me into their home and social circles with warmth and generosity and have provided me with abundant guidance at work. I cannot imagine what my time in Princeton would have been like without them.

"Belle, why are you fussing about what to call Aunt Charlotte? There's nobody in here but you and me," Gertrude mock scolds me.

I don't say what I'm thinking. That Gertrude doesn't need to assess every single moment of every single day against societal standards to ensure her behavior passes muster. She has no need to analyze her words, her walk, her manner, but I do. Even with Gertrude, I must act with care, particularly given the heightened scrutiny in this university town, which operates as if it lies in the segregated South rather than in the supposedly more progressive North.

The distinctive clip of Miss Adams's shoes sounds in the hallway outside my office door, and Gertrude's skirt rustles as she moves to leave. She has as much fondness for my office mate as I do, and she'll skedaddle before she can get locked into a conversation.

Before she exits the office altogether, she turns back to me, whispering, "Are you still free for the philosophy lecture tonight?"

Since Woodrow Wilson assumed the presidency of Princeton University three years ago and instituted all sorts of scholastic reform, the number of lectures open to staff and members of the community has increased. While Gertrude and I revel in being included in the academic life of the campus, I loathe certain of Wilson's other decisions, such as maintaining Princeton as a whites-only university when all the other Ivy League schools have admitted colored folks. But I would never voice aloud these views.

Instead, I say, "Wouldn't miss it for the world."

The quiet of the stacks wraps around me like a soft blanket. I relax into the subdued hush of patrons turning pages and the scent of leather bindings. My long days spent in the company of medieval manuscripts and early printed books calm and delight me. Imagining the labors of the first printing press users as they memorialized the English language and broadly disseminated its literature through the meticulous work of placing the type letter by letter, transforming empty pages into beautiful text to inspire worshippers and readers, transports me beyond the limitations of this time and place, just as Papa always believed. To him, the written word could act as an invitation to free thought and the broader world, and nowhere was that more true than in the dawn of the printed word, where—for the first time—that invitation could be made to the masses instead of a select few.

"Miss Greene." I hear a soft voice from beyond the stacks.

Two simple words, but my visitor's modulated tone and distinctive accent give him away, and anyway, I've been waiting for him.

"Good day, Mr. Morgan," I reply, turning in his direction.

Even though I'm talking softly, Miss Scott glances up from the circulation desk with a disapproving scowl. It isn't so much the volume of my speech as the pleasantness of my relationship with the fellow librarian and collection benefactor that vexes her.

While Mr. Junius Morgan is ostensibly a banker, he has generously donated dozens of ancient and medieval manuscripts to the university, which is why he also holds the titular position of associate head librarian. I'm convinced that Miss Scott thinks any sort of relationship between us—even the cordial, professional one we share—is beneath him.

A slight man, with wispy brown hair and a kindly expression behind his circular glasses, materializes. "How are you today, Miss Greene?"

"Well, sir. And yourself?" My tone is professional and reserved. He's twenty minutes later than the time we'd mentioned, and I'd begun to think he'd forgotten about our appointment. But I would never dare mention his tardiness.

"I was going to take a gander at the Virgils, as we discussed yesterday. I wonder if you'd still care to accompany me. Assuming your duties and your interest permit, of course."

Mr. Morgan, whom I think of as Junius in the privacy of my thoughts, knows that my zeal for the library's most valuable collection is nearly as intense as his own and that none of my other tasks will stand in the way of the private viewing he has promised.

We share a passion for the ancient Roman poet Virgil. The library houses fifty-two volumes of his poetry. My discussions with Junius about the dark voyages in *The Aeneid* and *The Odyssey* are some of the brightest moments in my days. While Junius admires Odysseus, I identify always with Aeneas, the Trojan refugee who desperately tries to fulfill his destiny in a world that holds no place for him. Aeneas was driven by duty, sacrificing for the good of others.

"I have cleared my schedule, sir." I smile.

"Wonderful. If you'll follow me."

My skirts swish the oak floor as I follow Junius to the small, elegant room where the Virgils are housed. I have to inhale and restrain my foot from tapping as I wait for him to fish out a heavy key ring from his pocket.

Finally, he pushes the door open to reveal the glass cases holding the precious collection of rare books. There are only about one hundred and fifty printed books of Virgil's poetry in existence. These volumes were all printed in the fifteenth century. Most of them have been donated by Junius.

I've seen these books only a few times before, while in the company of the restoration team. This is a holy moment.

Mr. Morgan's voice worms its way into the sanctity of my thoughts. "Would you care to hold my favorite?"

Junius is carrying the Sweynheym and Pannartz copy of Virgil, the rarest of all the books. German clerics Conrad Sweynheym and Arnold Pannartz were two of the first users of the printing press in the fifteenth century, and the book he's proffering is one of their press's very first editions.

"May I?" I ask, incredulous at this opportunity.

"Of course." His eyes are bright behind his spectacles. I suspect it's a thrill for him to share his prize with one who cares equally about it.

I slide the proffered white gloves onto my hands. The book is heavier than I expected. I sit before its open pages. *How Papa would have relished this moment.* I think of my father, who introduced me to the rarefied world of art and manuscripts when I was only a girl.

One day, the beauty of your mind and the beauty of art will be as one, Papa had said once.

The memory of Papa's words makes me smile as I turn the yellowed pages. I examine the hand-detailed letter *T* that marks the beginning of a page, marveling at the luster of its gold leaf. I am oblivious to Junius's presence near me until he begins talking.

"I saw my uncle last evening."

Junius doesn't need to identify who his uncle is. Everyone at the library knows he is the nephew of the infamous financier J. P. Morgan, which is exactly why I never mention him. I want Junius to understand that I appreciate him for his erudition alone.

"Ah?" I answer politely, never moving my eyes from the page.

"Yes, at the Grolier Club."

I know the club he speaks of, by reputation anyway. Founded about twenty years ago, in 1884, the private club consists of moneyed bibliophiles whose main aim is to promote the scholarship and collection of books. I would adore a peek behind the closed doors of its Romanesque town house on East Thirty-Second Street. But as a woman, I'd never be admitted, and to those men, my gender would not be my only sin.

"Were you attending an interesting lecture?" I attempt to continue making small talk.

"Actually, Miss Greene, it wasn't the lecture that was interesting." Junius's tone contains a quality unusual for him, bordering on playful.

Curious, I turn away from the Virgil. Junius's placid face, always pleasant but always serious, has cracked open wide with a smile. It is a bit disconcerting, and as I lean away a little, I wonder what on earth is going on.

"No?" I ask. "The lecture wasn't good?"

"The lecture was fine, but the most fascinating discussion of the evening was with my uncle about his personal art and manuscript collection. I advise him about it from time to time, as well as the new library he's constructing for it right next door to his home in New York City."

"Oh, yes," I say with a small nod. "Is he considering an intriguing new acquisition?"

Junius pauses for a moment before he answers. "In a manner of speaking, I suppose he is in search of a new acquisition," he says with a knowing chuckle. "I have recommended that he interview you for his newly created post of personal librarian."

CHAPTER 2

DECEMBER 7, 1905
NEW YORK, NEW YORK

As the Broadway line trolley lurches its way uptown and nighttime New York City unfolds around me, I'm almost happy that Mr. Richardson's late-afternoon appearance in my office forced me to delay my train departure to seven o'clock. The sky is a moonless midnight blue, and yet New York City is bright and alive. I watch nattily dressed couples with linked arms saunter down the streets alongside young male students returning from the library or heading to the pubs, and newsboys calling out headlines as they try to sell their papers. Although I should be inured to the nighttime bustle after living in the city for over ten years before decamping to drowsy Princeton, the nocturnal vividness surprises me every time I return home.

Home. That word stops all of my thoughts. Is New York City really my home? I've lived here since I was eight years old, but it is the place that I remember before our relocation to New York that fills me with the warmest memories.

As the trolley chugs up Broadway, I fall back into the past, smiling at the little girl I see in my mind. I imagine my younger self on the front lawn of my family's two-story row house on T Street NW in Washington, DC. On either side of our house lived Mama's family. Gramma Fleet to the right, who lived with Uncle James and Uncle Bellini, and to the left, Uncle Mozart, his wife, and their son. There, I always felt safe, good, even whole.

I recall a too-warm summer day where I found welcome shade in a cherished spot under the elm tree. Long ago, I'd claimed the elm as mine, and no one dared deny it to the grandchild most beloved and cosseted by Gramma, the family matriarch. On that day, I leaned back against the tree trunk and flipped open a page of my sketch pad to draw the tree's intricate web of leaves. The roots were in Gramma's front yard, but the branches stretched far across our yard toward Uncle Mozart's house. But before I had the chance to sketch more than a few lines, I heard Mama, calling me to come inside for dinner.

I ignored the summons twice before I dropped my sketch pad and pencil on the lawn and scurried inside. Even at my age—five or six back then—I knew that if Mama had to call a third time, I would have broken one of the rules that governed the behavior of the Fleet family: never were we to raise our voices, and never were we to do anything that would make any of the adults have to raise *their* voices at us. That was just one of the many tenets that we lived by. To be a Fleet was to be well educated (all of my aunts and uncles had gone to college) and hardworking (the women were all teachers and the men, all engineers). Fleets were understated in dress and presentation, connected to the community, mannerly in demeanor, and always dignified, no matter what treatment we encountered outside the bubble of our small world.

"There's my baby," Gramma said when she saw me, as always. She opened her arms and wrapped me inside her embrace. With my nose pressed against her apron, I smelled the delicious aroma of the yeast rolls that always lingered in the cloth. The way Gramma held me, I could have stayed in her arms forever.

"Now, go take your seat," she said and pointed to the table.

I sat down and relished this special time of the day, especially since Papa was home, a rarity because he was always so busy with things that I didn't understand. Once we settled at the two tables—one that sat ten for the adults and a smaller one that I shared with my sisters, Louise and Ethel; my brother, Russell; and our cousin, Clafton, Uncle Mozart's son—Papa said grace, and then, with his glass raised high, he stood.

"To the Fleets, may you always know prosperity and peace in our little Eden. To my dearly beloved, Genevieve, who has been my constant source of strength and forgives me for my eagerness to save the world, may you always know how much I love you. To my dear children, who will never be able to understand how much they are loved, may each of you thank the good man above for his bounty and for his sometimes capricious ways."

Everyone laughed and I did, too, even though I had no idea what was so funny. But then, Papa leaned over and kissed Mama, which he did at any and every opportunity. I giggled and covered my eyes, even though the way they held hands and kissed made me feel warm all over.

A rumble of the trolley jolts me out of my reveries, and I sigh. Almost two decades have passed since that time, and though we returned occasionally for holidays in the beginning, it has been ten years since our last visit. Now, my only connection to Washington, DC, is the birthday cards we all receive from Gramma Fleet and an occasional letter from Uncle Mozart. Mama's brother used to visit us when we first moved to New York. He and Papa were good friends, and Mozart had even introduced my parents. But he hasn't made the journey in a long time, and all I have now are my memories. Although these recollections are old and a little blurry around the edges, I cherish each day that I remember, and I know DC will always be home.

The streetcar jerks, and I glance out of the window. This is my stop. After I disembark from the trolley, I still have to walk four blocks to my family's apartment as the winter wind whirls and wraps around me. With the temperature hovering around freezing, a carriage from Grand Central Station would have been welcome, but given the unplanned nature of this trip, the family finances cannot accommodate it.

I try to pick up my pace, but my satchel, packed with my finest gray work dress and my newest lace-up shoes, the ones with the heels, is heavy. Turning off Broadway onto West 113th Street and working with frozen fingertips, I try to unlock the front door to the brownstone bearing the number 507. But when the lock doesn't click, I realize that it is broken again and the key isn't necessary. I wish that we could move someplace where everything worked.

Inside, I rub my gloved hands together, then start up the stairs to the first-floor landing. A single globe-shaped light fixture dangles above me; at least the broken light has been replaced. Mercifully, the key slides into the doorknob with ease, and I slip into my family's apartment.

This is where Mama and my siblings moved over two years ago when my older brother, Russell, started an engineering graduate program at Columbia University. Before that, my family lived farther downtown in the West Nineties in a pleasant middle-class neighborhood chock-full of carpenters, police officers, bookkeepers, and shopkeepers, if they were men, and seamstresses, clerks, and teachers, if they were women, mostly of German, Irish, and Scandinavian descent. This new neighborhood brims with students, professors, and workers of all backgrounds that service the university, and we were able to find an apartment in one of the least expensive buildings that is a mere three blocks away from Columbia. There, my brother pursues multiple graduate degrees in mining, electrical engineering, and steam engineering, an endeavor that will bolster the economic wherewithal of my entire family. We are unreasonably proud of him.

I expect the apartment to be dark, with the two bedroom doors shut for the evening and Russell asleep on the sofa, since they all have to rise early: Louise and Ethel for their work as teachers, Russell for his classes, and my youngest sister, Theodora, for her own school day. Instead, I find Mama sitting in the parlor, in her rocking chair next to a tiny table lamp. She looks like nothing less than a bouquet of hothouse flowers, perfectly arranged, with her ankles crossed and her hands folded and resting on her lap. Like a flower, her features are delicate and lovely: high cheekbones, a straight, narrow nose of which I've always been jealous, and rosebud-shaped lips. Only the streaks of gray in her dark brown hair hint at her fifty years of age. As usual, she wears her embroidered silk robe, a gift to her from Papa from before I was born.

"Evening, Mama," I whisper. I don't want to waken Russell.

Her hazel eyes flutter open, and it takes a moment for her to register my presence. "Ah, Belle Marion," she answers sleepily, though her voice is as low as mine, "you're finally home."

I must have awoken Mama from the deepest of sleeps for her to call me by my first and middle name, the name often used in my childhood. She has forbidden anyone in our family to use Marion since I moved to Princeton. I must *be* Belle da Costa Greene, she is wont to remind me.

I give her a gentle kiss on her cheek. "You shouldn't have waited up for me, Mama. It's late." I glance at my brother, though he hasn't stirred.

"Not too late to greet my daughter." Mama pulls out her pocket watch and says, "My goodness, it's after eleven o'clock. I hate to think of you out alone on the city streets at this hour."

"I had hoped to arrive earlier. On that five o'clock train. But I had to finish an assignment before I could leave."

"I'm just happy to see your beautiful face now, Belle. You've got a big day tomorrow." Even in the low light, her eyes glimmer. It's an important day for my entire family. What benefits one of us, benefits us all.

Mama stands, and I follow her across the room to the kitchen. As quietly as she can, she pulls back a chair from the table, and I squeeze into one next to her. Even with just the two of us, the kitchen is crowded. The table, which seats six, is squeezed in front of a cupboard that barely fits between the icebox and the stove. The entire two-bedroom apartment feels crammed. It is too small for the five of them, but it is all we can afford. My sisters' teacher's salaries and the little bit that Mama earns offering hourly violin lessons to school-children is just enough to cover the bills and pay for Russell's education. I send home what I can, but because I have to pay my own room and board in Princeton, it isn't much.

"So." Mama is all seriousness. "Tell me about your preparations for the interview."

I'd been so happy to see Mama, but now I am annoyed. Her question and tone imply I may not have properly readied myself. Even though I publicly subtract several years from my age, I am, in fact, twenty-six years old with a successful professional career—despite the fact that librarians don't make as much as teachers—and yet Mama insists on speaking to me as if I were nineteen. But we were raised in the language of respect, and I would not consider expressing my irritation.

"Junius—" I correct myself. "Mr. Morgan." Mama wouldn't approve of the familiar use of his name. "Mr. Morgan, the younger, has helped, of course. He's given me a list of Mr. Morgan's collection, and I've done research on his artwork, books, and artifacts, with an eye not only to cataloging it properly but also to cohesively adding to it. And I've been studying the architectural drawings of the new library, so I can offer suggestions as to how he might display and store his collection."

"Good, good, I'm glad to hear you're prepared to discuss his new building and holdings. Assuming he doesn't find that presumptuous, of course, since he hasn't hired you yet. But that's not all he's going to ask you. You know that, Belle," Mama says. Her normally slight Southern lilt intensifies, a signal that she's in earnest.

"What do you mean?"

"What are you going to tell this Mr. J. P. Morgan when he asks you about your education? He has his pick of librarians, most of whom hold mightily impressive degrees, I'm guessing. You're going to have to prove yourself." Mama's right eyebrow lifts as it always does when she's anxious or skeptical.

I hate to admit it, but Mama has an uncanny ability to point out a key item I've overlooked. I hadn't considered how best to present my formal instruction, because no specific education is required to become a librarian, and no one has asked me about my schooling in the five years I've worked at Princeton. "I did attend Teachers' College."

"Are you applying for a teacher's position?" Mama folds her arms as if she's the one interviewing me.

"No, of course not." I struggle to hide my irritation, knowing she's preparing me for every eventuality, but her tone reminds me of the conversations we had six years ago. Mama argued that I should take the same safe path that my demure sisters Louise and Ethel had taken. *You need a career like teaching that you can pick up at any time, no matter what setbacks you face*, she had said. But when a classmate mentioned that there was an opening at the Princeton University Library, I couldn't be dissuaded from interviewing for it. After I got the job, Mama was far more conciliatory.

"So if you're not applying for a teacher's position, what might you say instead?"

My mind is blank, but then an idea comes to me. "I know exactly what I'll say—my time at Princeton has been the best education in the world."

Mama laughs in delight, then presses her fingers against her lips as Russell stirs on the sofa. "Well, if that isn't threading the needle, I don't know what is," she whispers. "That's just about perfect. And since the young Mr. Morgan will be there, he'll love the mention of his alma mater and sing your praises all the more to his uncle."

We nod at each other, then Mama's brow furrows again. "What if he asks you about your teachers and your training at Princeton? Your 'education,' as you've described it? After all, it is a college for men."

I am on safe territory again. "I'll describe the extensive training I was given by Mr. Richardson, the head librarian. And the instruction from Miss Charlotte Martins, the librarian in charge of the purchasing department. And of course, there is always my apprenticeship in the New York Public Library system and my bibliography course at

Amherst College's Fletcher Summer Library School, if he really presses."

"Excellent, darling." She lets out a sigh that sounds almost like a low whistle. "Imagine. The opportunity to work directly for Mr. J. P. Morgan. He's the most important man in New York, maybe the country." She shakes her head in disbelief, and I think that after Mama's interrogation, my interview with Mr. Morgan might seem easy.

Before she opens her mouth to speak again, I know what she's going to say. "This is precisely why we chose this path," she begins as if, once again, she has to not only explain but convince me as well. "A colored girl named Belle Marion Greener would never have been considered for a job with Mr. J. P. Morgan. Only a white girl called Belle da Costa Greene would have that opportunity."

Her words make the past wash over me, and I am no longer a grown woman but a seventeen-year-old girl. It was early evening, and I could smell the warm baking bread and the chicken stew. We'd moved from DC about ten years earlier when Papa got his new job at the Grant Monument Association, and I'd learned to enjoy the city, especially our apartment on West Ninety-Ninth Street, right around the corner from Central Park. My brother and sisters and I were thrilled when we moved into the expansive space. With four bedrooms stemming off a long corridor that poured into the living room on one side and the kitchen and dining room on the other, the house felt as big as the park.

That night I was sitting at the kitchen table helping Teddy with her homework when we were interrupted by the sounds of shouting. I assumed the noise came from our loud next-door neighbors, a salesman and his wife and their five young towheaded boys, who were often raucous.

"I should have known this was your goal. From the beginning, I should have realized this was what you wanted." My father's voice boomed. "From the moment you chose this neighborhood and misled the landlord to get this apartment, I should have known."

"Everything I've done, I've done for our children and for you and me." My mother's voice, normally a cultivated note just above a whisper, was almost as loud as my father's.

It was shocking to hear them this way. Of course, I'd noticed that with each passing year, there were fewer loving gazes, less hand-holding, and an absence of stolen kisses. The tension between my parents had mounted, but I assumed it was because my father was often away fundraising for the Grant Monument Association and giving speeches in support of equal rights. But I'd never heard them raise their voices. Fleets didn't yell.

I froze. Until Teddy shifted in her chair. When I glanced across the table, my ten-year-old sister was shaking. She rested her elbows on the table and covered her ears. I gave her a quick hug and then made my way across the hall to the dining room so I could hear my parents more clearly.

"Next, it was the children's schools," my father continued. "You only wanted them in all-white schools."

"Because I want the best for them," she cried.

"No, Genevieve, this was all about you. This is the life you've always wanted."

"How can you say that to me?" Her voice quivered with distress. "This is not what I've wanted. This is what I had to do. I am a Fleet; I'm proud of my heritage."

My father's laughter was bitter. "*Your* heritage! Ah yes, you are a daughter of the great Fleets, while I am just the lowly grandson of a slave. You married a Greener, a man far below your station in life."

"Richard, please don't say that. You know how much I love you."

"Do you?"

"Yes, I do. And I know you love me. That's why I want you to understand. You're accusing me of walking away from who I am, and that's not what I'm doing."

"Yes, you are." I heard the rustling of papers, and then my father shouted, "The evidence is right here. You reported our race to the census workers as white."

My father was furious, but I didn't understand his anger. What difference did it make how Mama had reported us to the census since our skin was as fair as everyone who lived in our neighborhood? And we were quite a bit fairer than the newly arrived immigrants I'd seen in lower Manhattan, those of Italian and Mediterranean descent who were presumed to be white, although a low sort of white. I was sure that Papa didn't want us to live in the neighborhoods where the colored folks were crammed together—the Five Points, Greenwich Village, the Tenderloin, or Harlem. The conditions in some of those crime-infested tenements were notoriously unsanitary, disease broke out with regularity, and some places didn't even have toilets or running water.

So what was the harm in reporting ourselves as white, when we lived as whites? But then, the issue had never been discussed, at least not among the children. I'd learned long ago, among my many etiquette lessons as a Fleet, that race, like politics and religion, was never to be discussed in public and only very rarely in private.

Mama's words were muffled. I could not discern anything clearly until Papa spoke again.

"How can you not understand that this has enormous ramifications, Genevieve? You have made official our status as whites. After all the work I've done to advocate for the equal rights of black and colored people. After how hard I've argued in courts and in newspapers and journals and on stages that all citizens should be treated the same—whether they are black, white, or colored. That we should not be defined by how many drops of African blood run in our veins, but by our character and our deeds. That we should not be ashamed of our heritage and we all, blacks and coloreds alike, should unify in our fight against prejudice. Your act goes against everything I stand for and everything I've worked for—"

I heard the sound of sputtering, but was that my father? How could a man renowned for his oratory skills—*the* Richard Greener, first colored graduate of Harvard, former professor at the University of South Carolina, and former dean of Howard University School of

Law, who gave speeches all around the country—be now, it seemed, rendered speechless?

"I am doing what's best for all of us, Richard, don't you understand? Especially here in New York. This city is not like our protected neighborhood at home. And even there, the laws are changing. DC is no longer safe. Here, assimilating will give our children the best opportunities." Her voice was calm and clear now, as if no oratorical maneuver or logical presentation could sway her.

"Assimilating? That's not what you're doing. You're not just trying to fit in—to provide a better education for your children and cleaner accommodations for your family—you're trying to *be* white!" I had never heard my father so angry. "Do you realize what you're doing is the reason why my fellow activists are avoiding me? Do you understand your actions are the reasons why the Republican Party's Western Colored Bureau in Chicago is second-guessing their decision to hire me to cover the campaign to elect McKinley as president? Rumors are flying that because I live in a white neighborhood and have been working exclusively with white people on the Grant Monument Association that I'm trying to cross the color line. They think I've become cozy with the whites and abandoned my own people. If anyone ever got wind of the fact that you listed us as white in a census document, they would consider me a traitor, and no one would hire me or have me speak or write on issues of race ever again. And *that* is my life's work, Genevieve."

"Family should always come first, Richard. Me. Your children. We should be paramount," Mama replied, her own voice rising.

"When will you realize we are part of a larger family, Genevieve?" His voice was nearly a howl. "The colored community? You should have the same pride in that as you have in being a Fleet. You should understand how important it is to raise up that family alongside our own."

Papa, so fair that folks often mistook him for white no matter his words and actions to the contrary, must have composed himself, because his tone was more regulated, though his voice was still raised, when he continued. "Reporting yourself and our children as white is like turning your back on your own people. Turning your back on yourself." There was a long pause before he spoke again, but when he did, it was barely above a whisper. "And turning your back on me, most of all."

A sob escaped my mother's lips. "The fight for equality is over, Richard. You lost it. *We* lost it fifteen years ago when the Supreme Court overturned the Civil Rights Act that would have given all black and colored people the equal rights we deserve. Yet you continue to think something is going to change for the better. But the time for hope is past; things are only going to get worse. There is only black and white—nothing in between—and they will always be separate, but never equal. Segregation will take care of that."

There was resignation in Papa's voice. "That may be true, Genevieve, but that does not mean we should surrender. We need to keep fighting, and to keep proving what we are capable of."

"I disagree. It *is* time to surrender. The forces that are against equality are too great to overcome. But we have an advantage. We have our fair skin, Richard. It is a gift that God has given to us."

"You think our pale skin is a gift from God?" Papa's fury was evident. "Don't you ever think about the reason we are light-colored? Does the violence that white men perpetrated upon our ancestors never cross your mind?"

I gasped at his words. Of course, I knew about such matters, but no one dared speak them aloud in our house.

But Mama's reply was every bit as firm as her initial pronouncement. "In this country, as colored people, we have to use every advantage. Our pale complexions give us a choice." She paused before announcing, "I choose white for the children and myself. I can't make that choice for you, Richard, but please. Please make this choice with me. Make it for us. For us and our children."

In the quiet, their tension seeped from the living room, floated into the kitchen, and rested over me.

I held my breath until I heard the sound of heavy footsteps echoing through the hallway as Papa passed by the dining room in a blur of motion. He was like a smear of gray and black and ivory, his clothes indistinguishable from his skin. The front door opened with a squeak and then slammed shut, leaving me with an overwhelming sense of confusion, anger, and childlike longing that has never really left me.

With that act, the deed was done. I would no longer be called Belle Marion Greener, proud daughter of Richard Greener, a lawyer, an advocate for equality, and a member of the talented tenth, and of Genevieve Fleet Greener, part of the elite Washington, DC, community of free people of color. No. Shortly thereafter, I accepted my mother's decision as if it were my own and I became the white woman known as Belle da Costa Greene.

CHAPTER 3

DECEMBER 8, 1905
NEW YORK, NEW YORK

I s that a Rembrandt?" I ask Junius, my foot hovering over an exquisite framed etching.

The luminous golden portrait of a grizzled old man sits atop a stack of books, one of many scattered around the intricately inlaid marble floor underneath the rotunda. I have to step over it to follow Junius across the grand entryway. Junius had told me that Mr. Morgan had over one hundred and fifty Rembrandt etchings in his collection, purchased in 1900 from a single collector, Theodore Irwin, but this couldn't possibly be one of them. No one would leave a priceless piece of art sitting on the floor.

Junius examines the etching. Then he guffaws, a sound I would never have believed could emanate from the mild-mannered antiquarian. "I believe it is, Miss Greene. Only Uncle Pierpont would toss a Rembrandt on the floor like it was yesterday's newspaper." Junius takes every opportunity to refer to Mr. Morgan as the familiar Uncle Pierpont; indeed, he may be the only person in the world who calls the titan of industry by the name he prefers—Pierpont—instead of the nickname J. P.

We'd entered Mr. Morgan's new library through a set of impossibly ornate bronze doors on Thirty-Sixth Street. I'd been overwhelmed by the lavishness of the entryway rotunda. The walls and the marble floor were modeled after the Vatican gardens, according to Junius, and they burst with color from varying shades of marble and lapis lazuli. Paintings of classical figures, urns, and acanthus foliage decorate the blue-and-white-stucco ceiling that vaults up three gilded stories to a rotunda, although a ladder still stands in one uncompleted corner. Even unfinished, the entryway to the Pierpont Morgan Library, as it will be known, is breathtaking.

A voice like thunder echoes throughout the rotunda, ricocheting from pillar to pillar as if lightning seeking an object to strike. I jump, and I wonder from where the sound is coming. Three closed doors lead off the entryway—to the east, west, and north.

Junius glances over at me. "Not to worry, Miss Greene. It's only Uncle Pierpont."

But I do worry. The financier and steel, railroad, and electrical-power magnate is reported to be mercurial, and I'd hoped to find him in good spirits for my interview. As the roar continues, I realize that it originates from behind the western door, Mr. Morgan's study, I believe, and it certainly isn't the sound of a man in a fine mood.

"How many times have I told you?" the voice booms. "I don't want to see any papers about U.S. Steel while I'm here at the library."

There is a mumbling, words that I cannot discern from another man, before the thunderous voice vibrates again.

"Unless I specifically ask for them, those documents are to be kept at my Wall Street office."

As we wait for the tirade to end, I wonder if I even want to continue this interview. I cannot imagine working for a man who speaks to anyone this way. At last the door opens and out slinks a tall bald man who doesn't look in our direction. I hardly notice him, though, overwhelmed as I am by my first glimpse of Mr. Morgan's gorgeous two-story study.

I follow Junius inside, my nerves momentarily forgotten as I take in the majesty of what is before me. The disorder that prevails in the rotunda has been largely tamed here. The hints of disarray that remain—a few piles of leather-bound books seemingly destined for gaps in the deep walnut bookshelves that line the room and two Renaissance Madonnas leaning against a wall—go almost unnoticed. It's difficult to register anything but the vibrant crimson silk-covered walls. Scarlet blankets not only the walls but the velvet sofa and wing chairs, the marble rimmed windows, and even the imposing chair that presides behind Mr. Morgan's ornate desk like a throne. The room veritably pulsates with red and makes me feel woozy. Until I take in the man at the room's center, puffing a cigar.

Leaning against the edge of a fireplace so vast he could fit inside is Mr. J. P. Morgan. From beneath his heavy black brows, he stares at us with eyes as bright, piercing, and forbidding as a highly polished blade—and so intense I don't even notice his notorious bulbous nose, the focal point of countless political cartoons about him.

The two Mr. Morgans could not be more different. In other circumstances, the disparity may have been comic—the junior, so slender and average in height; the senior, barrel-chested and strikingly tall. But this situation holds no humor for me. Too much is at stake.

Junius clears his throat before he speaks. "Uncle Pierpont, it's my pleasure to introduce Miss Belle da Costa Greene." He nods toward me with a glimmer of pride.

"It's an honor, sir." I smile and gather my skirt to do the small half curtsy I'd practiced this morning as Mama lectured me on the finer points of the behavior that might be expected from me this morning. Mr. Morgan tilts his head in my direction but isn't quite ready to acknowledge me.

Instead, he turns back to Junius. "Did you have a chance to research the Rembrandt etchings that the Vanderbilts have offered to sell me?"

"I did, Uncle Pierpont."

"Well, let's hear it. I cannot promise that your research will make me want to accept their offer, but I am always willing to listen." Mr. Morgan begins pacing around his enormous study.

As the uncle and nephew discuss the merits of Mr. George Vanderbilt's print collection of 112 Rembrandt etchings, I study the senior Morgan to get my own measure of the man. No matter his reputation for brusqueness, and the shouting I'd just witnessed, Mr. Morgan is polite to Junius, even solicitous of him throughout his—to my mind—overly long recitation of his research.

"Uncle, I do believe that Rembrandt captures more of the humanity of his subjects in his etchings than in his paintings, and in that way, they are uniquely valuable and not only in monetary terms—" Junius says.

Mr. Morgan is visibly bored with his nephew's long-winded musings, and he pauses behind his desk before he turns to me. "Let's take a look at your Miss Greene, Junius." He puffs on his cigar.

Stand tall, square shoulders, glance steady, never waver outwardly. Under Mr. Morgan's gaze, I respond to Mama's directives as if she were in the room, and I return his stare. Mr. Morgan must understand that I will not be cowed. And no matter what he thinks he sees in my skin tone or my nose that is a bit broader than my siblings', he must believe I am a confident, competent white woman.

Mr. Morgan rounds his desk, and I don't speak as he pauses in front of me. He begins to circle me slowly, as if he's assessing an expensive rococo painting. I repeat Mama's words in my head and maintain a self-assured silence in the face of his inspection, understanding this is part of the test.

As if to himself, he says, "So petite."

This is a rather obvious observation. He is over a foot taller than me, with hands so wide a single one could span my waist.

When he stands in front of me again, he stares, although the corner of his mouth turns upward under his mustache as he does. "Such unusual eyes. Gray, somewhere between a smoky and silvery shade. Very compelling."

I do not respond. What would I say?

"A real beauty." Again, he speaks as if he's appraising artwork, and I'm not sure if the known philanderer is considering me as a woman or inspecting me as a librarian. His comment does not invite a reply, so again, I say nothing. But then, he adds, "Da Costa. An unusual name."

Repeating my practiced line, I say, "It's my family name. My grandmother is Portuguese."

"Ah." He nods, but his eyes remain fixed on me. I inhale, and focus to maintain my confidence in the face of his scrutiny.

Then suddenly, he turns away. "I've heard what Junius thinks about these etchings, but I wonder about your view, Miss Greene. What do *you* think of acquiring the Vanderbilt Rembrandts?"

I exhale, grateful for the sudden shift and the opportunity to prove my expertise to Mr. J. P. Morgan.

I gather myself, draw from the extensive files in my mind. "Unlike his contemporaries, Rembrandt did all the work of the etchings for the prints himself—from incising the lines on the copper plate with various needles to submerging the plate in the necessary chemicals afterward. He thought etchings should be an important artistic medium, not simply an easy means to publicize his more expensive oil paintings, as most of his contemporaries did. From this perspective, Rembrandt's etchings are masterworks by the genius himself, with a greater range of subjects than his more famous oil paintings." I pause. "The etchings are remarkable. As the Pierpont Morgan Library will be, if *I* am placed in the position of librarian."

In my peripheral vision, I see Junius flinch.

Mr. Morgan drinks me in, and for a long moment, I feel as if he sees *all* of me. Then, his mustache twitches, and I see a hint of a smile beneath the shadow cast by his swollen, misshapen nose and the downward turn of his thick black mustache. For a brief moment, the suggestion of a grin and the confidence he exudes remind me of my father. Lulled by the transitory resemblance, I am about to return Mr. Morgan's expression when his face turns stormy.

I glance over at Junius, who is frozen, awaiting his uncle's judgment. I'm reminded that Junius is my ally—and, dare I say, my friend—and it is critical that I realign with him and demonstrate the affinity in our views.

"Echoing the sentiments of Mr. Morgan, if you acquire Mr. Vanderbilt's collection, you will possess the world's largest collection of Rembrandt etchings. Presented all together, they will give scholars and collectors an unprecedented opportunity to study the evolution of the great master's style and skill. It would bring a unique level of renown and attention to your collection." This last statement is brash. This is Mr. Morgan's private library, and he's never publicly indicated he intends to open his institution to scholars. But I hope to hint at what might be possible, while appealing to his pride.

The only sound in the vast two-floor study is the deafening tick of the gold clock on that enormous stone mantelpiece. What does this silence signal? Appreciation? Or, more likely, anger at my pre-sumptuousness? Will he explode at me the way he erupted at that gentleman just before I entered his office? Before my thoughts wander too far to the other side, Mr. Morgan bellows, "Why do you think that I should hire you for my personal librarian, over all the other contenders I've interviewed, many of whom are older and more experienced than you? How will *you* make the Pierpont Morgan Library unparalleled?"

I take one step toward him. "Mr. Morgan, I am glad you pointed out that your other candidates are different from me, in experience, age, and"—I pause for emphasis—"gender. It is that exact divergence between my characteristics and everyone else's that makes me the *perfect* candidate for the Pierpont Morgan Library. My relative inexperience means that I do not arrive with any staid, old preconceptions that hamper what the Pierpont Morgan Library can become; instead, my vision and ambition for the library are limitless. My youth means that I have boundless time and undivided energy to devote to you and your collection. My passion for rare manuscripts and incunabula means that I will be relentless in acquiring the ideal items to make your collection incomparable, learning from your expertise in negotiation and the marketplace as I do so, of course. And the fact that I'm a woman means that every time I enter a room, I will have everyone's attention, which is exactly what the Pierpont Morgan Library deserves."

He nods. "And how would you make my library incomparable?" But before I can answer, he continues, "I hope acquiring Thomas Malory's *Le Morte Darthur* by the printer William Caxton is on your list of targeted accomplishments." He peers at me as if he's waiting for a reaction, and I am certain that I see a bit of a smirk on his face. "Because that Caxton is what *I* want."

"It's an extremely rare incunabulum, one of only two copies, if I'm not mistaken." Surprise fills his eyes. "But I will do everything in my power to bring that to your collection, if given the opportunity."

His smile is unmistakable now. This volume was printed in 1485 by the famous printer and publisher William Caxton, who is credited with bringing the printing press to England. Entitled *Le Morte Darthur*, it recounts the legend of King Arthur and the Knights of the Round Table and their quest for the mythical Holy Grail. Is the acquisition of this particular elusive book Mr. Morgan's own sacred quest?

"You are impressive, Miss Belle da Costa Greene."

Once again his eyes roam over me, but I stay focused. "Mr. Morgan, if given the chance, I will ensure that your library is unrivaled. And I will make the Pierpont Morgan Library itself the masterpiece you deserve."

CHAPTER 4

What on earth have I promised? I think as I climb the wide steps to the gleaming, multi-paneled bronze doors of the Pierpont Morgan Library. As I stand before them, I realize I must make good on my word. Beginning today, I have to prove to the famous *and* infamous Mr. J. P. Morgan that I can take his world-class manuscript and art collection and the breathtaking building he's constructed to house it and turn them into a place of legend. Me, a *colored* librarian.

I feel a wave of irrepressible laughter take hold of me, a blend of excitement at the prospects lying before me and the preposterousness of my promise. But I can't let it out. I force myself to think about Mama and my siblings back in the apartment. I focus on the calculations I've been doing since I received the letter from Mr. Morgan offering me the position with its salary of seventy-five dollars a month, an extravagant nine hundred dollars a year. After our monthly rent of sixty dollars, Russell's tuition, the groceries, the other bills and incidentals, and of course setting aside some money for the new clothes that I will surely need in this position, we will have just a little room to breathe between my salary and my sisters' teaching income—forty dollars a month—for the first time since Papa left us. In fact, my salary will allow Mama to stop working as a music teacher.

But my hope isn't just for our financial situation. I anticipate that this role with J. P. Morgan will provide me with access to a higher level of society, one that will cement our status as white beyond what living and working as whites has done so far.

Composure restored and veneer of self-assurance in place, I stand on my tiptoes and knock my gloved hand on the central panel of the right door, which Junius told me was once attached to a medieval Florentine villa. Only a limp tap sounds out, hardly enough to signal a butler or maid, so I remove my glove and rap my knuckles hard on the cold metal surface.

As I wait, I wonder who will respond. Does Mr. Morgan have a colored staff? Mama's words come to me. *If you see any colored people, stand tall, don't make eye contact. If eye contact is made, only acknowledge with a nod and then turn away. And never, ever enter into a conversation.*

The door opens, and a tall, bald, dour-faced older *white* man, wearing the well-cut woolen suit of a secretary, not a butler, greets me. He scans me up and down, and then finally speaks. "You must be Miss Greene."

"I am indeed."

I'm guessing he is the man Mr. Morgan addressed on the day of my interview, but I receive neither a pleasant salutation nor an introduction, so I cannot be certain. "We've been waiting for you." His tone is curt.

Waiting for me? Am I late? Junius's most recent note said that his uncle wanted me to report at eight o'clock, and glancing at my pocket watch, I see that it is seven fifty-nine. I am precisely on time.

Following the man inside, I see the ceiling's frescoes, which had been underway on my earlier visit, are finished, and the entry shines with the gilt-trimmed ceiling paintings and the variegated red, white, and tawny marble and lapis lazuli floors and pillars. A few stacks of books remain on the periphery, but the space appears largely complete. Has the entire library been put in order? What work will there be for me if the institution has already been organized?

"Please follow me," he instructs.

Taking his lead, I pass through the rotunda into what I assume to be the library proper. Once inside, I gasp. The sumptuous room—which seems to be as wide and as long as a ballroom—is lined with three balconied stories of floor-to-ceiling walnut bookcases, all empty and waiting for me to fill. A carved marble fireplace topped by a medieval tapestry dominates the right-hand side of the library, so large that it dwarfs the vast hearth I'd seen in Mr. Morgan's study. I assume its purpose is decorative, as no single fire could warm a chamber this immense. The ceiling glimmers with gold leaf and an intricate series of painted lunettes and spandrels, which appear to have two distinct themes: great historical figures and their muses in the lunettes, and the signs of the zodiac in the spandrels. I feel like I'm standing at the center of a jewel box.

The as-yet-unnamed gentleman clears his throat. He gestures to the wooden crates stacked in the center of the room, which I hadn't noticed before, too distracted by the dazzling periphery. "You are the expert, of course, and Mr. Morgan is a man who knows his own mind, but if I had to guess, one of your first tasks will be to catalog and organize the books inside the crates. Before you decide where they are to be shelved," he says, pointing to the vast bookshelves, "there are more crates in the vaults downstairs, because the library will only house a portion of the collection. I assume you'll rotate the treasures?" he asks, but before I can answer, he continues. "And there are crates in your office as well."

My office?

I expect the gentleman to lead me next to a small cubby with a shaky little walnut desk, but instead, he indicates a hidden closet where I can store my coat and hat. "I assume you'll want to begin working right away, Miss Greene," he says, and leaves without another word.

As the door closes, I spin around in disbelief that this magnificent chamber is my workplace. I'll have to find my little cubby later.

An open crate awaits, and I start there. Reaching for the blank cataloging notecards from my bag, I pull out the first leather-bound book. Examining the exterior, I write down on my notecard that the book has some minor cracks in the green morocco and does not bear a title. Gently opening the book to its first page, I realize that it is a rare eighteenth-century copy of *Don Quixote* in what looks like Spanish. Just sitting here on the floor, in a crate.

"My God," I say and lose myself in its ancient pages.

"I see you've found *Quixote*," a deep voice says, followed by a laugh. At least I think the sharp barking sound is a laugh. "I bought it as part of the Toovey collection in 1899. They never really understood the value of what they owned."

Startled, I look up into the blazing eyes of the towering Mr. Morgan. "Sir, my apologies. I, I started—" I stammer, but he interrupts me.

"Never apologize for intellectual curiosity or the appreciation of fine art, Miss Greene."

"Yes, sir," I say, and I have to stop myself from a curtsy. What am I doing? Where is my confident demeanor? I've already decided that Mr. Morgan needs to be kept on his toes with a mix of light deference and engaging banter. I'll have to find ways to achieve that tone as I craft an entirely new sort of relationship with this man, one perhaps he's never had—especially with a woman.

"I see that King introduced you to the library." His pride is evident and well deserved. "I apologize for him if he was brusque. My business secretary is a jealous sort and doesn't like the notion that you and the library might steal me from him and our business commitments."

"That would never be my intention, sir." I venture a small tease. "At least not at first."

Do I see a return smile?

"Of course not, Miss Greene," he says. Then he definitely smiles. "Still, it might be a natural upshot of our time together."

Do I hear the hint of innuendo in his words? *Stop*, I think, *you are simply reading his reputation into his tone.*

"I bet King didn't show you to your office, did he?"

"No, although he did mention it."

"That sounds like him. He's such an old curmudgeon. If he didn't have such a head for numbers, I would have fired him long ago." He pauses, never taking his eyes off me. "Well, not to worry, once we are settled, you will not have to see King every day. He'll float between my business offices and the library depending on where I need him. We will have our own full staff here, of course, two maids, a serving girl for meals and drinks if necessary, and security guards to protect the collection; in time, you'll have your own assistant."

I try to keep my expression calm, as if I'd expected to have my own assistant all along. "That sounds wonderful, sir. No less than your collection deserves."

He pivots and leaves the room. I understand that I'm meant to follow. Scurrying after him, I catch up as he exits through the library, back out into the rotunda, and through the door next to his study. When I reach his side, he asks, "So do you like our McKim, Mead, and White design? Lucky that we worked with McKim instead of White, isn't it?" He glances at me, and his right eyebrow is raised like a question mark. I surmise this is another test.

But it's not a challenge to pass it. McKim, Mead & White has been the focus of every recent news story. The famous architect, the crazed millionaire, the famous actress. It had every element of scandal a journalist would desire. Stanford White, the architect who was famous for creating the Washington Square Arch, was dead. Harry Thaw, the crazed ex-husband of the beautiful Evelyn Nesbit, shot three bullets into him in Madison Square Garden. Of course, Junius hadn't told me the name of the architectural firm who designed the Pierpont Morgan Library. I am sure Junius thinks that the facts of the Stanford White murder trial are unseemly for a woman's ears. Apparently, Mr. Morgan holds no such view on women's delicacy.

"It is fortunate indeed that you worked with Mr. McKim," I reply without a beat.

He nods, sweeps into the center of the room, and pivots back toward me, staring at me again with his sharp eyes. A little unnerved, I turn away from his gaze and focus my attention on the walnut-lined two-story chamber. Nine exquisite Renaissance-style paintings of the Greek gods and goddesses are set into a gilded stucco ceiling. An Italianate stone fireplace, complete with ornamental cherubs, presides over the enormous room.

"This is *my* office?" The question slips out, and I wish I could swallow back the words. The audacious librarian I presented to him at my interview would not be surprised by the bestowal of this office.

A full-blown grin appears on his face, the corners of which extend past the reach of his mustache.

"Do you think it will be acceptable?"

I regain command of myself. "Mr. Morgan, I believe this will be the perfect base from which to launch the inimitable Pierpont Morgan Library."

CHAPTER 5

I feel like skipping up the flight of stairs to my family's apartment, hardly aware that I am shivering from my chilly walk from the trolley. True, the hour is late, well past the six or seven o'clock I thought I'd return home. Yes, I'd stayed at the Pierpont Morgan Library after everyone left for the day, except the security guard assigned to protect the library's treasures every evening. Even so, I'm not tired. The very notion of sitting on my velvet chair behind that expansive carved-walnut desk—directing the priceless manuscript and art collection of Mr. J. P. Morgan—fills me with an irrepressible lightness and energy.

I can hardly wait to tell Mama and my siblings every detail of my first day.

After my usual fumble with the key, I push open the door, expecting to find Russell at the kitchen table studying for one engineering exam or another, or to discover Louise and Ethel on the sofa preparing their lesson plans for the next morning.

However, the entry and parlor are pitch-black, with not even a glint of light from the kitchen or bedrooms. I'm disappointed; I cannot believe Mama and my siblings aren't waiting to hear about my day.

Then, a gaslight illuminates, and the cry of "surprise" sounds out. Mama, Louise, Ethel, Russell, and Teddy are standing behind the dining room table, gathered around a store-bought cake, a rare treat.

Squeals of delight and congratulations fill my ears as a tangle of arms wraps around me. The air is festive as my siblings speak one on top of the other, their enthusiasm bubbling over like champagne.

"What was he like?"

"Is he as scary as his photos in the newspaper?"

"What does his nose look like?"

I laugh, so happy that I can relax in the refuge of my family and celebrate my excitement, something I've had to refrain from all day.

"Does he really have all of that money?"

"Did you see any of his money?"

"Hold on," I say. "First, let's start with what is he like." As Louise doles out slices of the cake and we settle into seats, I try to do an impression of Mr. Morgan's booming voice and unsettling gaze. It's terrible, of course, but good enough to make my siblings laugh.

Then I turn to the Pierpont Morgan Library. Now, they are quiet, and with wide eyes, they gobble down the details as quickly as they devour the sugary cake. Neither can satiate them quite enough, but despite their appetite to know everything, I withhold certain salient particulars.

Never would I want them to know that my excitement has been tempered by anxiety. All day I had to quiet the voice inside my head filled with insecurities about my readiness for this task and my ability to work with a man as volatile and mercurial as Mr. Morgan.

I don't want to share my fears with them, as they've already plotted out how their lives might change based on the money I will be adding to our household. I must carry that burden of consternation alone.

"Will you be too fancy to share a bedroom with me and Mama now?" Teddy half whispers. Although she smiles, I see the seriousness of the question in her eyes.

In some ways, I've missed the space and independence I enjoyed in Princeton, as well as my friendships with Gertrude and Charlotte, with whom I enjoyed a strong intellectual connection as well as so much laughter. But one of the pleasures of returning to a shared bedroom in a cramped New York City apartment is the proximity I now have to my little sister. Of all of my siblings, I've always been closest to Teddy. Seven years older, I was the one who helped Mama feed, change, and dress the newborn when she first came home. To me, she was a live doll, and I would hold her, sing to her, and watch her sleep for hours. And our closeness has not diminished over the years.

"Don't be silly, Teddy," I say. "You didn't see me come home in a crown, did you?"

"No, of course not." She giggles. Her skin is as pale as the vanilla frosting on the cake. Not so the rest of us; Louise and Ethel can reasonably be described as fair, but not Russell or me.

"I'm still the same old me." I giggle with her.

It is only then that I notice how quiet Mama has been as the rest of us indulged in cake and chatter. She's the one who usually has the most questions, but tonight, she only has one. She wipes the corners of her mouth before she asks, "You're still *Belle*?"

"Yes, I'm still Belle." I wish Mama hadn't asked that question, because now everything has shifted: my siblings' eyes, their energy, the entire mood of this celebration. Even the air feels heavier with the burden that always comes with a reference, however oblique, to the passing we must all do.

The laughter is gone as my brother and sisters avert their eyes and instead study the pieces of cake in front of them. Except for the sound of forks scraping the last crumbs from our plates, the kitchen remains silent.

I feel my siblings' frustration and their sympathy, especially from Louise and Ethel. All of my siblings, even Teddy to some extent, know that although we all live in this world that doesn't belong to us, no one bears the brunt of that decision more than me.

I stare at each of my siblings in turn: Louise and Ethel, such hardworking teachers, a matched set of pretty, compliant, and otherwise invisible girls, so skilled are they in the art of blending in. Russell, my determined, bright, soon-to-be-an-engineer brother, with his slightly darker good looks mirroring my own complexion and features, although these prove less of a hindrance to overcome for him as a man than me as a woman. And then Teddy, the fairest of us all, quite literally, and baby to everyone. All of us, under the ever-proper, ever-watchful, always lovely Mama.

She is the gatekeeper, the one who transformed us, although I wear the scars of the greatest conversion. The extent of the transformation in my sisters' lives has been nothing more than the simple dropping of the *r* from our last name. But the change from Greener to Greene has been much more involved for me. Like Russell, I had to add the Portuguese da Costa to my last name—after dropping Marion—because the ties that bind us to Africa are plainer in the shade of our olive complexions. So Mama invented a Portuguese grandmother for us in order to deflect suspicion and obviate any need for further examination. But I have to do even more—operate seamlessly in a rarefied white world.

Yet, the color of my skin isn't why Mama asks if I'm "still Belle." It isn't why she stares at me as though I'm the weakest link to our whiteness, despite the fact that I move within that world better than anyone and my new position could lift us into an unassailable echelon within that realm. Her concern stems from the fact that I'm the most like our father—headstrong and bold. Although I've never questioned my mother outright about her decision, she can see my doubts and uncertainty about the world we've chosen to live in. Most importantly, she can feel the longing I still have for my father.

And I'm certain today reminds her of another surprise party, when we all gathered around a much larger table in a much grander apartment for a celebration like this.

Blow out the candles," Louise, Ethel, Teddy, and Russell shouted around the kitchen table, after they'd scared me senseless wishing me happy birthday. As my siblings jumped and chanted, I tingled with excitement. The ten candles flickered, and the flames colored the air gold.

"Blow them out," my siblings continued chanting.

They hungered for the momentous birthday event, but I wanted to linger, to count the candles, make my wish, and with a long breath, blow out every candle. I finally acquiesced, only because the candle wax was dripping onto my favorite icing. In the split second of darkness before Mama lit the gaslight again, my sisters and brother clapped, but no one applauded louder than my father.

"What did you wish for?" Russell asked.

"She can't tell you that. It's a big secret," Papa teased my brother. Then, he wrapped his arms around me and pulled me into a hug. "I can't believe you're ten years old, my Belle Marion."

I giggled as I always did when Papa showed me special attention.

"Richard!" I heard the reprimand in my mother's tone. She didn't like it when Papa made such a fuss over me.

A flash of anger crossed over Papa's handsome face at yet another admonishment from Mama, but then he reared his head back and laughed. It was a hearty guffaw that made all of us—except for my mother—laugh harder, even though we weren't sure what he found so funny. Finally, he said, "Oh, Genevieve, let's celebrate our Belle's birthday. Our beautiful girl who has such a lovely face and a lovely mind and one day will be the belle of the ball."

My siblings clapped while I beamed beneath the attention and approval of my father. "It's time to open your cards and gifts," he declared as everyone enjoyed their cake.

He handed me an envelope first, and I grew excited when I saw it was from Gramma Fleet. She'd sent me a card for my birthday for the last two years, and I knew there would be a dollar inside. Already I was thinking about what toy I could buy at the Schwarz Toy Bazaar.

Next Papa handed me a present wrapped in beautiful blue paper. As I peeled off the corner, I saw that it was a book, but I didn't comprehend its magnificence until I fully removed the paper: *The Venetian Painters of the Renaissance* by Bernard Berenson. I inhaled as I turned the pages; the book was as exquisite as the paintings Papa and I studied on weekends when we went to the Metropolitan Museum of Art. Papa had a way of revealing the meaning of a painting and the life of the painter who created it, and when I listened closely, I felt as though I were traveling back in time to the moment of its inception.

Without Mama's watchful eye, I learned more about my father as well as the art we viewed on those museum trips. I heard stories about his attendance at Phillips Academy and then Harvard University, where he'd been part of an experiment that opened the door for other colored students of the Ivy League school. I watched him chuckle as he told me tales about rowing down the Charles River with his friend Oliver Wendell Holmes. But I saw sadness in his eyes, too, because I knew that most of his youth had been spent hustling for money and opportunities after his father—a free black born to former slaves—left the family for the gold mines of the west. If he ever discussed such topics at home, particularly about his writing and speaking alongside other equal-rights advocates like the famous Frederick Douglass, Mama would shoo us children away to our rooms, as if she didn't want our young ears to be defiled with the business of the country.

"Thank you, Papa." I closed the book, then wrapped my arms around his neck.

Papa smiled. "We will read this book together. I know that some of the paintings are actually at the Metropolitan. Belle, I want you to remember this author. Mr. Berenson is *the* expert on Italian art."

I nodded and opened the cover once again. On the inside page there was an inscription: "For my beloved Belle Marion on her tenth birthday. One day, the beauty of your mind and the beauty of this art will be as one. All my love, Papa."

"It seems like such an advanced book for a child," Mama said, looking over our shoulders at the volume. I closed it quickly; I didn't want her to see the inscription. My present was controversial enough.

My father shook his head. "Not this child." He pinched my nose, making me giggle. "Our Belle Marion is going to be an art scholar or a historian one day. She has the knack for appreciating and understanding art, especially the history of art, and this book is just the beginning for her."

I nodded because if Papa thought I should become an art scholar or historian, then so be it.

But my smile faded when I glanced up at Mama's frustrated face. "Why are you filling her head with this, Richard? Belle Marion will not be any kind of art scholar. She's a colored girl. She needs to focus on a proper career, like teaching. She will become a teacher." She announced this as if the matter had been discussed and resolved.

"Oh, no, Genevieve." Again, he shook his head. "Wait and see what our Belle is going to do." He winked at me, then said, "Now, who wants some more cake?"

My sisters and brother are staring at me, undoubtedly wondering if I will continue to share stories of Mr. Morgan. But I have nothing more for them tonight.

It has been eight years since we became the six Greenes, yet the absence of the seventh one has stayed with me every day, and in this moment I miss my father more than usual. When I glance at Mama with her arms folded and her lips pressed together, I yearn for Papa even more. I want him here not only to protect me from the scolding eye of Mama but to celebrate. After all, it was Papa who made this prediction and who laid the groundwork for me to become Belle da Costa Greene, personal librarian to Mr. J. P. Morgan.

Balancing the books in my hands, I close the bedroom door behind me, then tiptoe past Russell sleeping on the sofa. I settle at the kitchen table and pull out a book from the teetering stack. Turning to the marked place in my lesson, I spread *The Latin Primer* wide. While Mr. Morgan has not made it a part of my job responsibilities, I've taken it upon myself to learn Latin, among other languages, because many of the texts that I'll be acquiring for the library are written in these languages. In order to assess their authenticity, I need to know what I am reading. So tonight will be my first lesson.

But before I begin studying, I hear the door to the bedroom that I share with Mama and Teddy open. I am surprised as Mama approaches me; I thought she was asleep when I left the room. Her face is scrubbed, her hair is pulled into a long braid that ends at the center of her back, and she's wearing only her sky-blue ankle-length nightgown. It is unusual to see Mama dressed in her nightclothes without her embroidered dressing gown on top. She hardly ever leaves the bedroom without it.

I smile, but Mama's lips are pressed tight; her expression hasn't changed from earlier tonight. "I wanted you to see this," she whispers.

I take the envelope from her hand, but before I can ask any questions, Mama turns away from me. With her head high and her shoulders back, she returns to the bedroom. I glance down at the letter addressed to Mama, and right away, I recognize Uncle Mozart's handwriting. I am surprised, because while I know Uncle Mozart writes separate letters to Mama as well as me and my siblings, never before have we shared our letters.

Slipping the paper from the envelope, I begin to read.

> *My Dearest Genevieve:*
>
> *I suppose I should start this letter as usual, with all of the news of our family and how all is well at home. But the news I must deliver is pressing. I wanted you to hear about Richard from me and no one else. I believe I told you that President McKinley, before he was assassinated, appointed Richard to a diplomatic position in India. Richard didn't go because of the bubonic plague, but since then, Richard was transferred to*

*Vladivostok, which I think you know. But what you don't
know is what's happened in Russia, Genevieve. Richard has
taken a Japanese woman as his common-law wife and
together, they have two children . . .*

My hands and my lips are trembling as I place the letter on the
table without reading the rest. Papa is married? Living in Russia?
With children? How can this be? In all of his letters to me, Uncle
Mozart never mentioned Papa's overseas appointments, although it
seems he kept Mama abreast of some of Papa's developments. I guess
Uncle Mozart couldn't be silent about this, though, because he
wanted to protect Mama from the blow of finding out from someone
else.

Now I understand Mama's sadness tonight and why she questioned me as she did. I turn to the bedroom and wonder what Mama
is doing behind that closed door. Is she sharing her sorrow with her
pillow, sobbing quietly so that she doesn't awaken Teddy?

My eyes burn with tears as I remember Mama and Papa together,
holding hands and stealing kisses. Even though eight years have
passed, I know Mama still loves Papa; I have always believed that is
why she never pushed for a divorce. Perhaps there was a part of her
that held that door open, one that is now forever closed.

Pushing myself up from my chair, I want to run to Mama and
hold her. But then I slowly lower myself back down. I know my
mother. While she wanted me to be aware of this news, she will not
want to discuss it. I am meant to bury this information deep within
myself, as I have with so many other things. I suspect she will share
this news with no one but me.

I wipe away a tear that has trickled down my cheek and stare at
the books before me. These lessons are even more imperative now.
Tonight, Mama made clear that there is no longer even a shred of
hope that I can return to being Belle Marion Greener, not that I ever
seriously believed I could. The well-being of this family now depends

upon my rising up and fully claiming Belle da Costa Greene as my own.

Lifting *The Latin Primer*, I pause when Russell stirs on the couch, then I quietly open the pages when my brother settles down. The news of my father has exhausted me, but I cannot rest. Before, I had a desire to be successful, but now, it can no longer be a simple desire; success must be my commitment.

CHAPTER 6

Miss Greene." Mr. Morgan's voice makes its way across his study, through the rotunda, and into my office. By the time his bellow fully reverberates in my ears, I've already smoothed down my hair, straightened my new jade-green dress, and grabbed my paper and fountain pen. I've learned to calculate, almost to the second, when I will be summoned.

There's no trick to it, really. Mr. Morgan's call for me is always preceded by the distinctive scrape of his chair pushing back from his desk, a slow, thoughtful graze of that lion's paw walnut foot on the marble floor. The noise resounds throughout the entire building, giving me enough time to separate from the mountain of work on my desk and prepare for whatever Mr. Morgan might need. If I were so inclined, I could even make my way through the rotunda and appear at his door just before he actually yelled for me, as if I were some sort of vaudevillian illusionist, but I won't. Even though my success rises and falls on his whim, it wouldn't do to appear too eager. Instead, I rise in anticipation, and wait until I hear my name; then will I materialize in front of him.

"Miss Greene!" he shouts again, before he realizes I'm standing against the doorframe to his office.

"Yes, sir," I answer, knowing that—as always—he will look up at me with a startled expression, marveling at my quick arrival on his literal doorstep. The repetition of his reaction after these months in his employ amuses me. What I find less amusing is the toll each encounter with Mr. Morgan takes on me, as I attempt to strike the correct demeanor for every interaction and ready myself for the increasing array of tasks he demands. Whether I'm required to catalog and organize his treasures, advise on purchases, retrieve art and books on loan to various institutions, deal with requests to visit the collection, meet with dealers visiting Mr. Morgan, or correspond with those dealers afterward, it seems as though my responsibilities grow alongside his appreciation of me. I had believed that my years of hiding my true identity in plain sight—with all the attendant vigilance and self-modulation to ensure I blend—would prepare me for whatever changing demands Mr. Morgan might have, and to a certain extent, they have. But the quick-witted, talented, capricious Mr. Morgan is unlike anyone I have ever met, as are his needs.

He composes himself and barks out, "Have you made any progress on that damned Caxton yet?" Before I can respond, he continues, "When will you bring that to my collection?!"

Along with all of his other demands, Mr. Morgan questions me periodically about the Caxton *Le Morte Darthur*. While I know he truly longs for this elusive item, I also sense—because his inquiry usually emerges when he's irritated with me about something—that he brandishes it about as a means of reminding me who is in control by drawing my attention to this unfulfilled task.

"I continue to make inquiries of all the major incunabula collectors and museums to try and ascertain its location," I say, then add, "If it indeed still exists, I will find it."

From the curl of his lip and the narrowing of his eyes, I can tell he is not pleased, but at least he moves on and asks, "Have the boxes arrived from the Lenox Library?" Before he built the Pierpont Morgan Library, Mr. Morgan loaned much of his art and book collection to museums around the world, as a means of storage, among other things. Now, I have the unenviable task of retrieving some of those objects, arranging for their safe return to the library, and then finding them a home here or elsewhere.

"I'm told they'll be here tomorrow, Mr. Morgan."

He lets out a dispirited snort that bears an uncanny resemblance to a horse's whinny, and says, "Is it really so much to ask people to return your belongings in a timely fashion?" Pointing to the sole spare corner of his bookshelves, he continues, "There is a large gap there I'd like you to fill with the books I loaned to the Lenox Library. I have a—" He pauses. "Special friend visiting here tomorrow, and I'd like my study to look picture-perfect."

I don't need to know the identity of his special friend, as I've learned these particular "friends" are interchangeable and the friendships short-lived. He has a few "special friends"—currently, his mistresses consist of two wives of prominent New York businessmen, as well as the widow of an English financier—and I have grown used to their rotating presence at the library. This urgency to make his study appear even more flawless suggests a new paramour may be on the scene, and I wonder if there is truth to the rumor I read in the gossip columns about a competition between Mr. Morgan and Diamond Jim Brady for the famous actress and singer Lillian Russell. I may even break my rule on not telling Mama about Mr. Morgan's female visitors if the famous Miss Russell should pop into the library.

"What time is your appointment, Mr. Morgan? The head librarian tells me that the engravings were so delicate that they necessitated specially constructed boxes for shipment, but even still, they should arrive tomorrow morning."

"She should be here around—"

The word "Papa" reverberates in the entryway, interrupting him. Silencing him, really, as the voice belongs to his youngest child, his thirty-two-year-old unmarried daughter, Anne.

Mr. Morgan's affairs are not exactly secret—occasionally he even recruits a reluctant Anne to travel with him and his mistress as cover—but open discussion of his relationships is discouraged. Discretion is the order of the day, so I know this part of the conversation will end for now.

"Papa!" Anne calls to her father again.

"In the study!" he yells back.

While Mrs. Morgan rarely makes an appearance at the library even though it is quite literally situated next door to her home, the four Morgan children are a different matter. Alongside their sister Anne, the beautiful Juliet and the favorite, Louisa, both married, can be found underfoot with regularity. But it is the son who visits almost daily when his father is at the library. John Pierpont Jr., who prefers the nickname Jack, is beginning to take control of the family business and consults frequently with his father. On the odd occasion I happen to overhear their exchanges, I find myself wincing at their strained relationship—Jack always deferential and Mr. Morgan always domineering and often judgmental.

Although Juliet, Louisa, and Jack have come to accept me and my access to their father as critical to his work as an art and book collector, and have proven to be quite pleasant, Anne is tolerant but not welcoming of her father's female librarian, even after these months of proving myself useful to Mr. Morgan. Her coldness has surprised me, given what I've learned of her efforts to support other women. She is part owner of the Villa Trianon near Versailles to assist in promoting the interior decorating career of her friend Elsie de Wolfe. She helped organize the very first social club for women in New York City, the Colony Club, and lately, she's developed an interest in supporting female workers of various industries and the cause of women's suffrage. Perhaps her exposure to her father's infidelity makes her chary of most women in his orbit, or perhaps she's jealous that another woman besides her occupies so much of her father's time during the day.

Anne steps into the study, her black eyebrows, so like her father's in color and thickness, rising and her dark eyes blazing. The first word that came to mind when I met Anne, just days after starting at the library, was "sturdy." She is a tall woman with broad shoulders and wide hips, yet somehow she manages to make even the most expensive fashions look stately. Today, for example, she is wearing a high-collared white blouse with puffy sleeves and a black skirt slightly nipped at her waist that likely cost more than my monthly salary, and still the ensemble appears rather drab on her. And yet none of her matronliness detracts from her formidable nature.

"Ah, you are with Miss Greene," she says to her father as a means of greeting me. "Am I interrupting?" She draws out the final word, opening it to any number of interpretations.

"We are discussing the matter of the Lenox Library loan, but you are always welcome, as you know," Mr. Morgan says, his tone cautious yet solicitous. Of all his children, Anne is the one he treats with the most care; her political sensibilities have begun to border on the liberal, even unorthodox, and thus they contradict Mr. Morgan's view.

I sense his fear that she might break with the family, and he is desperate to keep her close.

She smiles at her father, although the light around her dims when she glances at me. "Mama was wondering if you were joining us for luncheon with the Vanderbilts, and if so, if you'd like to return to the house with me."

He glances at the clock on his mantelpiece. "I believe I told your mother over breakfast that I'd be attending the luncheon. But the Vanderbilts won't arrive for over an hour, Anne."

In the silence that follows, I know Mr. Morgan is waiting for an explanation about why he should arrive an hour early for a luncheon party. However, Anne stands her ground, unwilling to explain; I've learned that they are similar in their stubbornness and strong personalities, among other things. I wonder if this silence is because of me. Does Mr. Morgan understand the unspoken request? Whether it pertains to his professional or personal realm, I often feel as though

I'm stepping midstream into his world, without an understanding of the origins or nuances of the exchanges I witness.

He sighs, a leaden sound that makes the room feel heavy. "I'll join you at the appointed hour for lunch, but not before." Gesturing to me, he says, "Miss Greene and I have business to tend to before I socialize."

"Business?" she says in a tone that challenges his words. When he adds nothing, her eyes narrow. "As you wish, Papa."

His refusal has injured her in some manner. She prepares to leave, but before she passes through the study door, she says, in an unmistakably caustic tone, "I wouldn't want to keep you from your precious Miss Greene."

She exits, and for a long moment we are quiet as we listen to the sound of Anne's heels echoing across the rotunda. Just as I begin to wonder whether I should retire to my office, he says with a sigh, "Read to me, Miss Greene."

This is not a new request, although it is not one I anticipated when I undertook the position. I walk over to a small pile of books assembled on top of a shelf. "What would you like to hear today, sir?"

The first time he'd asked that I read to him, I was taken aback. The nearly seventy-year-old financier is perfectly capable of reading to himself, and librarians typically do not read aloud to their patrons, unless they are children. However, I'd obliged, reading from one of his Bibles, on that day the story of Joseph, the man who'd gone from prison to a prince. It had soothed him, and he now entreats this of me regularly, often having me read aloud to him from either the Bible—typically a rare incunabulum—or one of the books he's considering for purchase.

"Let's have the Bible. Perhaps the Jonah story?"

While I'm tempted to select the early thirteenth-century Moralized Bible, a sumptuous, gilt-illuminated work, I know it will not contain the story he seeks. So I pick out a relatively innocuous eighteenth-century Bible—a focal point in anyone else's collection, but not here—and settle into the chair facing his desk.

As I read the ancient tale of the man who refuses his calling to be a prophet and consequently faces a fierce storm from a vengeful god, Mr. Morgan's eyes flutter and close. I continue, regardless of whether he's awake, until I finish the narrative of Jonah's survival inside the belly of a whale and his ultimate acceptance of his role.

There are a few silent seconds before Mr. Morgan utters, "Some days I feel I might only survive my family if a whale swallows me whole." If I were anyone else, the mention of his family could be an opening, a reason for me to ask about the undercurrent between him and Anne today, but I would never. I must content myself with speculation.

His eyes suddenly fly open. "That's a lovely dress."

"Thank you," I say, pleased that he noticed. Managing my salary carefully, I have been able to add a couple of dresses to my wardrobe, and today I'm wearing what the salesgirl at B. Altman's told me was a princess gown with a bolero waist, apparently one of the latest new designs for the spring.

When I first began working in my position and Mr. Morgan complimented my appearance, I wasn't sure how to take his words, and thoughts of his reputation always ran through my mind. But as time passes, I have come to understand that Mr. Morgan sees me through a paternal lens, in part at least.

"You have quite a sense of style." I smile because his tone conveys a better mood. "If only Anne would consent to go shopping with you."

This is not the first time that Mr. Morgan has suggested that Anne and I socialize in some way. But it is apparent to me that Anne and I are not destined to be friends.

Mr. Morgan switches topics again. "We have half an hour before I leave. Tell me what you think of this manuscript from Leo Olschki."

From the belly of the whale to women's clothing to the Florentine publisher and dealer. This sharp shift from one subject to another is one of his most constant qualities, and I've had to adapt.

A few days ago Mr. Olschki's assistant delivered an extremely rare copy of Cicero's *De Oratore* from 1468, printed by Pannartz and Sweynheym no less, for Mr. Morgan's potential acquisition. I'd examined the volume and was thrilled to have the exquisitely typeset and illustrated book to myself for a long study. I also spent considerable time assessing the accompanying letter setting forth the dealer's price.

"Well, both the binding and the interior pages are in excellent condition. A Pannartz and Sweynheym is nothing to sniff at, of course, and it would certainly round out that part of your collection," I say with the borrowed confidence that has come from the months that I've been with the self-possessed Mr. Morgan, who has made my status as his *white* librarian secure by never questioning my heritage— with either overt queries or subtle glances. So I am confident to a point, yes. But comfortable, never.

"True enough." He nods appreciatively.

"Your nephew donated a fine example of a Pannartz and Sweynheym book to Princeton, of course, which has garnered him accolades," I comment.

"Yes, yes it has. The Virgil," he says, his eyes narrowing as he watches my assessment. "You have some objection, though, Miss Greene. Don't be shy. Tell me what you think."

How well he's come to know me, I think with amusement. "Compared to the market, the price that Mr. Olschki requests is ridiculous. And insulting to you."

I carefully choose the word "insulting" because my patron prides himself on always paying asking price and never bargaining—he finds haggling to be "demeaning," so merely flagging Olschki's price as bloated would not move him. But Mr. Morgan is not a man to tolerate an insult.

He sits upright in his chair. "What do you mean?"

"Eight thousand francs?" I say. "He is only demanding that obscene amount because you are J. P. Morgan, known for your wealth and generosity. But . . ." I allow myself a slow intake of breath so my words sound calm and self-assured. "If you give me the opportunity to act as gatekeeper, he shall not have the same audacity in the future.

And you'll still get your Pannartz and Sweynheym's *De Oratore*. We will build you into a modern Medici, and not only in your bibliophilic holdings—and you'll get your Caxton."

A smile flits across his lips. I see that the idea of a young, petite librarian standing guard for the infamous hulk of a man known as J. P. Morgan humors him. But it pleases him as well, as does the comparison to the renowned Florentine Renaissance banking family.

"All right, then, Miss Greene, if you want to protect me and my collection as it grows," he chuckles to himself, then continues, "then you've got to know my enemies. You must come to the upcoming ball in four days at the Vanderbilt home. It is there that you'll find my adversaries in the form of dealers and experts and collectors alike."

At first, all I can hear is his acquiescence. This expanded role at the library is exactly what I have been aiming for. But wariness grows in equal measure to my euphoria when I realize that he has just invited me into his social realm, a sphere populated with not just his family and friends but also his adversaries. I will have to tread carefully as I enter the home of one of the richest families in America. Enemies can be especially dangerous for a colored girl named Belle Marion Greener as she crosses the threshold into the wider white world as Belle da Costa Greene.

CHAPTER 7

MAY 28, 1906
NEW YORK, NEW YORK

As I step into the vestibule of the Vanderbilt mansion, I am surrounded by women in extraordinary gowns with bodices gleaming with crystals and pearls, and men in white-tie formal wear, and I must force myself not to gape. Already I feel like a shadow, the dark presence over which the eye skims while seeking the light, and I am not even inside the ball yet.

I present my invitation to the first of the two Vanderbilt butlers, a man with chestnut hair dressed in a white waistcoat, who squints and peers at me as if his deep brown eyes have special lenses. His stare makes me tense, and I scroll through my mind for Mama's instructions: *Stand tall, square shoulders, glance steady, never waver.* I believe I am meeting all of her expectations, but clearly something is wrong.

The butler's eyes stay on mine as I hand him the gilt-edged, embossed card. My heart pounds as his gaze shifts from me to the invitation.

Be cautious, never do anything to stand out.

Have I done something? Or is this the moment I brace myself for almost daily, the moment when my secret will be revealed? I wait for the question and prepare myself for the righteous indignation I will give him in response.

"You've come alone?"

I blink, then I breathe. He isn't concerned about the color of my skin. But my relief is swept away when he repeats his question.

"Yes," I say, not pleased that my voice sounds hesitant. What is behind his question? What have I done wrong?

He shakes his head with clear disapproval, but then he motions for me to enter. I rush in, away from his silent reproach. I can almost feel whispers trailing behind me as he shares my indiscretion with the other butler. At least the whispers are about my social ineptitude and nothing more.

Only once I'm inside the great hall do I feel safe from the butler's glare. Why didn't Mr. Morgan tell me that I'd need an escort? What else do I not know? From a passing waiter, I accept a crystal flute of champagne, hoping this will calm my feelings of inadequacy. But while the golden effervescent liquid helps me ease into the room, I am now faced with trying to mingle with people I do not know whose stations in life soar above mine. Can I make a leap so fine and wide?

I wonder what glitters more, the ladies with their gemstones or the gilt-framed medieval masterpieces on the walls. I have never before been in the presence of such luminance—animate or inanimate— not even in the Pierpont Morgan Library.

I stop myself from glancing down at the gown that Mama, Teddy, and I spent hours modifying. I wonder why I had bothered insisting on adding intricate lace cap sleeves to this old emerald silk dress, even arguing with Mama that the sleeves were fashionable and not inappropriately garish. These sleeves that I fought for look positively dowdy in this room with gowns cut so low that the ladies' décolletage serves as another form of adornment. At least Teddy had the genius idea for me to wear a tall feathered hat. It definitely rescues my outfit a bit and gives me confidence.

Where, I wonder, *do these peacocks live by day?* Or do they strip off their feathers and wander the streets unadorned and unrecognized? That thought makes me chuckle, and I hold up my glass as another waiter fills my flute with more champagne. How could I have ever thought I'd have a gown worthy of a Vanderbilt ball? No finery I have ever owned—or likely will ever own—could be deserving of this event. Not unless I suddenly stumbled onto great wealth and spent a goodly portion of it on clothing. The best I can hope for tonight is invisibility, which seems to be happening anyway, since no one has yet spoken to me.

For a moment, I imagine what Papa would think of this night, and then I pause and take a deep breath. It's been months since I read Uncle Mozart's letter to Mama, and my anger and sadness remain. But at the same time, my love for my father hasn't waned, and I still long to share this experience with him. He is the reason I'm here.

I push thoughts of my father aside and decide this is a fine time to wander through the mansion. Surrounded by dozens of couples chatting and laughing, I saunter through the grand five-story Caen stone foyer with two sweeping staircases and square footage that is larger than my family's entire apartment. Next, I enter the breathtaking solarium, which showcases the gardens. To one side, I see the first colored people here tonight, servers weaving their way through the guests, and I quickly avert my eyes. It is then that I spot Anne Morgan engrossed in a conversation with her sister Juliet. I am relieved when they glance my way.

Juliet waves, and I follow suit. She looks lovely in a frothy mauve gown encrusted with matching crystals, particularly standing next to Anne in her more severe gray gown. I smile as I move toward them. Anne glares at me before she tugs at Juliet's arm, pulling her sister in the other direction, through the enormous arched double doors.

The warmth of embarrassment surges through me as I absorb this slight. I glance over one shoulder and then the other, but there is no one among the fifty or so people in this room who has even looked my way. In this moment, I am grateful for my invisibility. As if it were my intention all along, I continue moving through the grandiose space, trying not to ask myself which was worse: my interaction with the butler or the snub by Anne.

I push the ostracism from my mind as I'm distracted by the wonder of this vast and luxurious house. Exiting the solarium, I enter the Vanderbilts' library, nowhere near as grand as the Pierpont Morgan Library, of course. Still, this single room is impressive with the dark English paneling, white marble carved fireplace, and floor-to-ceiling bookshelves filled with thousands of books. I then float from the gallery, where portraits and landscapes hang from the purple velvet walls, to the dining room, which could likely serve thirty people at once, and finally into the marble-lined music room; each space vies with the next for the most sumptuous. It seems that the mansion's primary purpose is to telegraph not only the wealth but the assumed nobility of its owner. No great surprise given the bootstraps-like rise of the Vanderbilts from newly rich upstarts to the inner circle of New York City society—the so-called Four Hundred—who'd held a firm grip on their ranks since the seventeen hundreds.

By comparison, Mr. Morgan shows no real passion for grand real estate. His home, a lovely brownstone on the corner of Madison Avenue and Thirty-Sixth Street—which I've visited only once, when he asked me to pick up an etching inadvertently left behind—is comparatively modest by the standards of his contemporaries on Fifth Avenue. Although, of course, Mr. Morgan has his indulgences—women, his art collection, and his three-hundred-foot oceangoing ship, the *Corsair III*, which needs a crew of seventy. The Morgans live in luxury and comfort, but not showiness, which seems the order of the day with the new breed of Fifth Avenue millionaires. But then, Mr. Morgan's wealth and stature got their birth generations ago in Boston, which also explains his disdain for artwork and manuscripts with any hint of modernity.

I make my way into the two-story gilt-laden ballroom, where most of the guests have congregated, either dancing or engaged in animated conversation. The concept of a ballroom inside a home astonishes me, but I try to remain unimpressed, a difficult feat given the magnificence and massiveness of the space. White gilded chairs line the room's edge, while heavy gold brocade curtains hang from the windows, and countless chandeliers swing above us. This room, more than any other in the mansion, feels overwhelming; whether it is the lavishness of the decor or the gregariousness of the guests, I cannot say for certain. I only know that I feel utterly alone and insignificant.

Moving to the perimeter, I survey the room in search of Mr. Morgan, but it is difficult to see past the couples waltzing across the dance floor. The other guests move through this world with ease.

I decide to study the guests' mannerisms and the way in which they interact. As I examine the women, I realize that their speech is accompanied by gentle touches—the flick of a fan on a man's shoulder, or the light touch of a gloved finger on a gentleman's arm—and pointed glances, often sidelong. These women—old and young alike, available and taken—are flirting. Mama would never approve of these exchanges, but I see that, in order to fit in, I may have to adapt.

One of the women catches my stare, and I know I must move away. I make my way through the room in search of Mr. Morgan. Where is he? Did he use the invitation as a front for a rendezvous with one of his special friends? If that is the case, how am I meant to meet his enemies without formal introductions?

Suddenly, I feel as if there are eyes on me, and I turn around. I smile, expecting to see Mr. Morgan. Instead, I lock eyes with a serving-woman. It is more than her simple white-collared black dress with a full white apron that separates her from the crowd. It is her deep brown complexion that makes her stand out yet simultaneously renders her unseen to the guests.

Although my instinct tells me to turn away, I am drawn to her, and our eyes stay fixed on each other, even as I hear Mama's warning: *If you see any colored people, stand tall, don't make eye contact. If eye contact is made, only acknowledge with a nod and then turn away.*

My glance lingers too long, and in the ephemeral connection we've made, I can see that *she knows*. For the second time this evening, my heart beats wildly and I try to read what I see inside the woman's eyes. Does my deception anger her? Will she reveal my identity to the host? To my boss? Will I lose everything I've worked toward in this single instant because I didn't heed Mama's warnings? Can I plead with her not to reveal my secret? Make her understand that this fall wouldn't be just about me but would affect everyone I love?

Those questions roll through my mind as she approaches. Then, before I decide what to do, the servingwoman grins. A broad, delighted, *proud* grin. Relief courses through me. This woman, defined by her skin, the shade of a new penny, and by the debilitating laws of segregation dividing our country and our people into two halves, seems proud that one of her own has wriggled free from the restraints still inflicted upon some, like the chains that bound our ancestors.

She nods at me. It takes a moment for me to catch my breath and nod back. She tops off my flute of champagne before she breaks our gaze and moves on to other guests. But my eyes remain with her, and I have a new understanding. With the gift of the position I now hold, I am responsible to many more than just Mama and my siblings. The world I inhabit may not know that I am colored, but there will be some, like this woman, who will discover my secret, and I wish that, in some small way, my achievements will give them hope.

As I watch her weave through the guests, seen yet unseen, without even a nod of acknowledgment, the taste of the fine sparkling wine in my mouth sours and I feel a sense of sadness, tinged with anger. Now I can think only about the serving hands that poured it. Those hands are cracked and swollen from heavy lifting and serving, while mine are covered in satin opera-length gloves. Why does she serve while I am served? Why is it that the relative whiteness of my skin has given me this chance at privilege? It seems incomprehensible, but it is thus.

These thoughts make me want to depart from this decadent place. My time would be better spent with my private studies or back at the library finalizing the catalog. I pivot away from the crowd, but just as I'm about to step over the threshold of the ballroom, I hear my name.

"Why, Miss Greene, is that you?" Behind me, a voice calls out. "It is Miss Greene, isn't it?"

I turn and face Mr. Smythson from J. Pearson & Co. He is a fine arts dealer with whom Mr. Morgan occasionally does business and oftentimes squabbles. We have met at the Pierpont Morgan Library on two occasions. "It is indeed, Mr. Smythson."

"Pleasure to see you out of the library."

"It's a pleasure to be out of the library, I don't mind saying."

His glance roams over me, and with a look of surprise upon his portly, florid face, he says, "You look lovely. Nothing at all like a librarian."

"Just because I'm a librarian doesn't mean I have to dress like one." The insouciant sentence tumbles out of my mouth before I can stop it. It is the sort of jaunty remark I might toss out to one of my sisters. But never, ever to a near stranger. I can feel Mama's disapproval.

He laughs, a deep, melodious sound that causes party patrons to glance over at us. I can almost read their faces.

Who, they wonder, *is the young woman delighting Mr. Smythson?*

"In this moment, you *certainly* don't look like a librarian," he says.

Lowering my eyes, I glance up at Mr. Smythson through my lashes. "Well, you know what they say."

His eyebrows rise in anticipation.

Stepping closer, I do my best imitation of the other women in the room, by touching my finger to his shoulder, tossing my head back, and saying, "Looks can be deceiving. There is certainly more to me than meets any man's eyes."

He chortles, and for the first time this evening, I feel at ease and have an epiphany. This is how I must behave in order to fit in. Mama has admonished me to be cautious and blend, but I realize now that she was wrong. In order to assimilate with this crowd, I must be bold, daring to hide my differences in plain sight.

Other men join Mr. Smythson and me, gathering around to meet the young woman who seems so delightful and share in the merriment. As I'm introduced to each one, I accept their pleasantries and compliments in turn, retorting to the final one that "I don't doubt you've said that to every woman you know, but I like it just the same." The men erupt in laughter, and for a fleeting moment I think of Mama again. She would be appalled, but I will myself not to care. This, too, is necessary to become part of Mr. Morgan's world.

By the time I spot Mr. Morgan, quite a circle has formed around me. He's in the company of an unfamiliar woman who fits the mold of a "special friend." He notices me, and with a brief word to his friend, he leaves her in his wake and strides over, cigar dangling from his mouth. The circle around me parts before him, and I am struck anew by the palpable nature of his power as I witness him outside of the library.

"Ah, Miss Greene, I see you're conversing with several of my enemies." His glance drifts from one man to another before he settles on Mr. Smythson. "And this one in particular." Mr. Morgan's voice booms, but his tone is surprisingly pleasant.

Mr. Smythson sputters at the label. "Mr.—Mr. Morgan, I've always thought of you as a trusted friend and occasional client."

Pulling himself to his full, towering six feet two inches, Mr. Morgan arches one of his magnificent eyebrows and half-jokingly asks, "Do you try to swindle all of your 'trusted friends'?"

I see the game he is playing; Mr. Morgan knows he must maintain relations with all the key dealers to have full access to the artwork and manuscripts that come to market, but the slipperier ones need to understand that he won't tolerate exploitation. If we are to meet our goal of creating America's foremost manuscript collection—equal to Europe's finest—then we have to scoop up entire collections, and we cannot do that by alienating any key dealer. Hence, the warning wrapped in the quip.

"Swindle?" Mr. Smythson looks confused, then terrified. Lesser accusations by Mr. Morgan have ruined men.

"Oh, is this the gentleman that offered you the flawed Mozart musical manuscript?" I say coyly. As if I weren't entirely certain that it had been a Pearson's dealer who'd tried to pass off a handwritten copy of a Mozart concerto by one of his students as the original composed by the master himself.

With a nod, Mr. Morgan says, "He's the one."

"Ah." I look at Mr. Morgan. "You needn't worry that you'll be faced with such deceit again."

"No, Miss Greene? Why is that?" he asks, as if we'd rehearsed this exchange.

I shift my gaze from Mr. Morgan to the art dealer. "Because the next time we do business with Mr. Smythson, I'll be on hand to verify the authenticity of any antiquity that comes through the doors of the Pierpont Morgan Library. And should an item that doesn't pass muster arrive—which could, of course, be through no fault of Mr. Smythson . . ." I pause, wanting the dealer to see how I have provided him with an excuse for his past reprehensible behavior. "Then we will resolve the issue before it ever reaches your desk, Mr. Morgan."

"Excellent, Miss Greene," Mr. Morgan says.

"Isn't that correct, Mr. Smythson?" I ask sweetly.

Mr. Smythson looks simultaneously concerned and relieved; he's been both accused and exonerated. "It would be my honor to do business with you again, Mr. Morgan, and, and—" He sputters again. "You as well, Miss Greene, in whatever manner you see fit."

"Good. Come, Miss Greene," Mr. Morgan says, dismissing Mr. Smythson and the others with those simple words.

I give Mr. Smythson a short nod, and then together Mr. Morgan and I walk away from the slack-jawed dealer.

"You played him very well," he says quietly.

"I simply asked myself what my employer would do, and then followed suit."

Mr. Morgan lets out a laugh that sounds like a bellowing seal. "You speak to me as no one else, Miss Greene. Not even men well above you in station. Certainly not my son."

His bright hazel eyes narrow as he assesses me in the same way he did the day of my interview. This time, though, I have no doubt that his appraisal is of me as a woman. The music plays and guests mill around us, yet for just a split second, it all becomes silent; we are alone. I feel a shift between us. He is no longer a paternal figure; he is no longer my boss.

Instead of unease, I feel a pull—a frisson of attraction. Goose bumps rise on my arms, but then I hear the music again and I return to the ball. The moment passes, and Mr. Morgan offers me his elbow.

"Let's circulate around the ballroom," he says casually, but his voice is thick. He, too, felt that surge between us. "I have some other enemies I'd like you to meet."

CHAPTER 8

MAY 29, 1906
NEW YORK, NEW YORK

T he front door to the apartment opens before I can even slide my key in the lock. I nearly tumble forward, but then the steadying arm of Teddy clasps me.

"What are you doing up?" I ask, in a mock-scolding whisper. The hour must be past midnight.

"I heard your footsteps coming up the stairs"—she keeps her voice low—"and I couldn't wait until morning to hear about the party." Her excitement makes her sound like a girl, even though she's a young woman of nineteen.

I should have guessed she'd stay awake. Out of all of my siblings, Teddy is the one most interested in my life with J. P. Morgan. She reads the society pages of the city newspapers as if she were going to be tested on them; the *Ladies' Home Journal* is her study guide for how to dress. Despite my modest sleeves, her tips actually proved helpful with my dress tonight, particularly her suggestion about my hat. After what I observed this evening, I'm going to need all my sister has learned about fashion.

"Where's Russell?" I ask when I take in the empty brown sofa.

"He's out with friends from his program," Teddy says, waving her hand as if she can wave my question away. There is only one thing she wants to discuss right now.

"Well," I begin as we sit side by side on the sofa. I pause as a yawn overtakes me. Morning is not that far away, and I wonder why the wealthy entertain on weeknights. *Silly,* I chide myself. The rich have no obligation to rise early. They can sleep until noon if they wish.

"Would you rather hear about the house or the dresses?" I ask. "They were both magnificent."

"Oh, the dresses, of course."

Even with only the gas lamps from the street for illumination, my sister's prettiness shines. Her light brown hair is straight and silky, so unlike my coarse, wavy hair, which I force into submission daily with elaborate updos and a mountain of pins. Her hair swings, framing her sweet, fair face.

"My favorite was a gown of a blue so dark it nearly appeared obsidian—" I start.

Teddy interrupts. "A black dress was your favorite?" She is horrified that a somber mourning shade should be preferred.

"You didn't let me finish. The gown was a midnight, inky blue, and all around the skirt and train were crystals and colored gemstones in the pattern of the constellations."

Teddy gasps.

I continue, "And when the woman danced, it looked like the night sky."

My sister presses her hand against her chest. I understand her reaction; I almost did the same when I saw the dress swirling on the marble ballroom floor in time to the symphony. I describe other gowns that I know Teddy will appreciate. I report the trend of jewel tones and the prevalence of crystals and pearls on the gowns' bodices.

Of the two moments that stand out from the night, I avoid any reference. I say nothing about those seconds of attraction between Mr. Morgan and me. Similarly, I make no mention of the colored servant and the impact of our connection. Teddy wouldn't understand. She has inhabited Mama's white world for nearly her entire life. She was barely a year old when we left DC, and once we were in New York, we basically lived as whites even before Mama changed our names and revised our past.

Sometimes when I look at Teddy, with her light hair, alabaster skin, and pale eyes, I wonder if she knows about the violent origins of our white skin. What does she remember about Papa, or are her lessons all from Mama?

As if I summon her by thought, Mama emerges from her bedroom in a blue nightgown. Once again, she is without the silk dressing gown that Papa had given to her, the one she always used to wear. Her eyes are puffy with sleep, and her mouth hardens into a stern line seeing the two of us whispering on the sofa.

Even before Uncle Mozart's letter about Papa, Mama had to toughen herself. Being in New York is often a struggle, beyond our finances. Keeping our true identity a secret is a burden that grows heavier with time. Every day there is more to lose as the world around us becomes increasingly unaccepting. While segregation is the law of the South, the tentacles of Jim Crow have stretched into New York, too. So many policies reinforce discrimination and relegate the colored to the worst neighborhoods and to employment with the lowest pay and station. Since Papa left, we have been living on the edge, but as whites, we surely have lived a better existence than if we'd lived the truth—and that is because of Mama.

Before she can lecture us, we say, "Sorry, Mama," in unison, and then giggle at our little rebellion.

"Night, Belle," Teddy says, giving me a quick kiss and then scooting into the bedroom.

"I should get ready for bed myself," I say. "I'll tell you about the ball tomorrow."

Mama doesn't say anything, but glances at the dining room table. My stack of language texts has spilled over. Is she angry that I left my workbooks out?

"Don't you have your daily studying to do? I don't believe you had time between work and the party, and you don't want to lose the ground you've gained in your languages."

My eyes widen with surprise. I've been diligent in my studies but surely, since these lessons are my choice, I can miss one evening. "It's past midnight, Mama. I think it can wait for tonight."

"Are you certain, Belle?" It's not a question. "You told me how critical your facility with Latin, German, and French is for your position. Do you think another J. P. Morgan will come knocking on your door if you fail?"

Fail?

We lock eyes as we momentarily lock wills. Just for this evening, just this one time, I want to be simply her daughter, as precious and tenderly cared for as Teddy. Or even as steadily regarded as Louise or Ethel, who have much less far to fall should they disappoint. I want her to tell me to go into the bedroom so that I can lay my head and my burdens down.

"Come." My mother beckons me before she moves toward the dining room table.

I pause. Every night, I've sat at that table alone, studying until my eyelids drooped and begged for rest. As I follow Mama to the table, I wonder what she's doing. Until she sits in one chair, then motions for me to take the other.

Spreading out my ball gown around me like my nighttime blanket, I open my Latin textbook and turn to the chapter on subordinate clauses.

"Where should we begin?" Mama asks.

She knows nothing about Latin, but I am grateful that she will sit with me. Her tending to me may not resemble what she does for my siblings, but it is caretaking nonetheless. I know Mama really does still see me as her daughter.

CHAPTER 9

NOVEMBER 4, 1906
NEW YORK, NEW YORK

In the ten months since I've become part of Mr. Morgan's world, I have transitioned from cataloging his collection and organizing his shelves to advising on acquisitions and attending operas, dinners, parties, and balls at his behest with social luminaries and art experts alike. I've become comfortable chatting companionably with the Fricks about Renaissance painting, talking to Metropolitan Museum director Caspar Purdon Clarke about the finer details of decorative arts, taking a turn on the dance floor with John D. Rockefeller, or sitting in between the Carnegies and the Phippses at the opera. Given all this, why is it still daunting to walk across the rotunda into Mr. Morgan's office and ask him to focus on a pressing matter?

I find excuses to walk past his office, hoping to discover that he has turned his attention to the catalog I placed on his desk over two hours ago. But there it lies, still open to the page I've folded wide. I cannot think of a single urgent thing that's arisen today, and yet the catalog sits unattended while the deadline on remote bids for the Boston auction looms.

While Mr. Morgan has come to rely on me to present potential prizes for his consideration, he makes decisions at his own pace, and frequently asks me to consult experts for second opinions. Nor can I always access art and manuscripts coming to market, because there are several dealers who won't work with me or do so only because they believe they can dupe me. Just last week Mr. Pryce wrote to Mr. Morgan complaining about "that woman in your library" when I refused to purchase a manuscript on the grounds that its condition was far poorer than he'd represented.

Mr. Morgan wrote a scathing reply in support of my assessment and referred Mr. Pryce to me for all future negotiations, but it is hardly the only such missive he has received. Even though I spend my evenings at the opera and theater and dinners with the society collectors, dealers, and curators in Mr. Morgan's circle, it isn't enough to secure an equal position in the ranks of my peers.

On this lap around the rotunda, I pause at Mr. Morgan's study. He sits on his lion's throne, as I like to call his ornate desk and chair, reading the newspaper.

The delay frustrates me, but I cannot show it. Mr. Morgan reacts poorly to nagging and wheedling. I step into the room. The *New York Daily News* does not lower. I slip into the chair opposite his desk and clear my throat.

Finally, he looks up. "What are you doing in here? I don't remember calling you into my office, Miss Greene," he snaps.

I've grown accustomed to the empty bluster of sharp comments, and do not allow them to disturb me. "Sir, have you had a chance to study the catalog?"

"I do have other matters to attend to than your lust for art, Miss Greene," he yells.

It no longer intimidates; it is simply something to be managed. "Mr. Morgan, this is *your* collection, not mine. I only want to help grow it so that it rivals the best European institutions—royal and private alike—and this acquisition is a step toward that goal. Am I wrong in assuming you share my objectives?"

I've had to say these same words to him many times, and Mr. Morgan rarely maintains his stern facade when faced with my temerity. Usually he breaks into a smile, making me think of him some-times as being all thunder and no lightning. Not that he cannot be intimidating and fierce. I've seen his rage at the parade of financiers, industry leaders, and art world principals who pass through his door—even at Jack for asking questions Mr. Morgan deems stupid. But his real fury does not manifest as a roar—it manifests as silence. An eerie, terrifying quiet that I avoid at all costs.

"Of course I share your objectives. They are my damned objec-tives, after all—including getting that damned Caxton *Le Morte Darthur.* Have you found it yet?"

"I am working on it, sir." I always get a queasy feeling in my stom-ach when he brings up that particular Caxton. Of course, securing it has been a priority since my first day, but it has proven maddeningly elusive.

"It's why I hired you, that and your impeccable eye for ancient manuscripts and medieval art." His rant slowly deflates until he set-tles back into his chair. Reaching for the catalog, he says, "Well, if I can't have my Caxton right now, let's look at your precious Bible."

"Shall we read the description?" I ask. I've brought my own copy of the auction catalog into his office.

He agrees with a grunt.

"Please turn to lot number sixteen," I say, waiting until he's fo-cused upon the pertinent entry. "There you can see that the Bible was printed by the University of Cambridge's printers in 1638. It goes on to say that it was King Charles the First's own copy, and as a result, it was bound in red velvet embroidered in silver thread with the king's initials and crest, and said crest is inlaid with silver and gems. The catalog notes that it is in a perfect state of preservation. I've been tracking down the provenance of the Bible, and this seems to be the authentic copy."

"Buy it," he announces and picks up the newspaper again. For him, merely saying the words will make them happen. *How magical it is to be Mr. Morgan.*

Relief and delight wash over me. I consider the English king who prayed for the safety of his kingdom—or perhaps for himself when he was overthrown and charged with treason—with that Bible between his palms. I imagine holding the ancient book, opening its crimson velvet cover, turning its thick pages to read the sacred words within, and allowing its history to course through my own hands. And I think about the printer who painstakingly laid out all the letters for the printing and then fashioned its exquisite binding, all in an effort to bring God closer to the king through the Bible's sacred words.

"Wonderful, Mr. Morgan. I'll fill out the paperwork and notify the auction house." I am about to rise when an interesting approach occurs to me. "Or would you rather circumvent the auction altogether and offer the seller a large preemptive bid? I could arrive at a number that is fair, but would be tempting enough, and approach the seller privately."

He asks me to repeat myself and his eyes shine. "Clever, Miss Greene. I like that tactic, and we'll use it in the future. But for this particular volume, let's use the traditional auction process."

"Yes, sir." I stand and take a deep breath, gathering my courage. "There is one way I can be certain that we will be the buyer."

"What's that?" he asks.

"I could attend the Boston auction and do the bidding myself."

He doesn't speak for a long moment.

"If you leave shortly"—he glances at the mantelpiece clock—"you could make it to Boston by nightfall."

He's giving me permission? I can't believe it. My mind whirls at the preparation I'll have to undertake. But no matter. It will be a terrific adventure and the biggest, most public imprimatur of Mr. Morgan's support to date, one that will register with all the major players in the art world. If I succeed, it has the potential to inexorably change my place in this exclusive world.

I can't help the grin plastered on my face. "Thank you, sir. I will not disappoint you. What limit would you like to place on my bidding?"

"I said I want the thing, Miss Greene," he snaps, "and that means there is no limit. Do you understand?"

No limit.

"I understand. Even still, I will not allow you to overpay should the bidding escalate beyond what I think is fair."

Chuckling, he says, "Oh, I don't worry. Except perhaps about your competition. I almost pity them." He pauses, and his tone changes. His voice is softer when he adds, "They have no idea the fierceness that lurks within your petite frame."

The intensity of his gaze makes me inhale. I've seen this expression before—at the Vanderbilt ball—and this time, there can be no mistake. His glance is filled with appreciation. But then, he clears his throat, and his tone and his words are businesslike. "Don't forget, when you are assessing the item in person, look into the eyes of the man selling it to you. You're judging the seller nearly as much as the object itself."

I nod, feeling a little unsettled at Mr. Morgan's uncharacteristic admiration. In the almost six months that have passed since the moment we shared at the Vanderbilt ball, I have done everything to maintain the professionalism between us. And Mr. Morgan has reciprocated, making me believe sometimes that I imagined our brief attraction.

Hoisting himself to a standing position, he asks, "Shall we toast to your success?" He doesn't wait for my response as he decants an amber-colored liquid from one of the crystal bottles on his side table and hands me a glass. "To Belle," he says, "a ferocious adversary who hides her strength behind a beautiful smile."

I pause, wondering if there is more coming. But his expression is back to one of being my employer, and so I raise my glass to him, but I know I did not imagine what happened this time.

"And, Belle," he says, "let us now give a toast to the both of us. To our little conspiracy. Together we are saving the past for the future. With my fortune and your gifted eye and hard work, we are rescuing and protecting the most beautiful and important treasures that history has to offer—those artifacts and manuscripts that memorialize the physical history of the book."

I touch my glass to his. I'm too embarrassed to ask what kind of liquor he has poured, but whatever the type, I take a sip. It burns as it travels down my throat and I cough. Of course, this is the precise moment when Anne—the ubiquitous judgmental daughter, the occasional ambassador of her mother, the only one who shares her father's external steeliness—arrives at the library.

"A little early for a drink, isn't it?" she asks as she surveys the scene. Today, Anne is wearing a deep plum dress with a matching jacket and a white fur tossed over her right shoulder. Very fashionable, and still, she manages to make the outfit look matronly.

When neither her father nor I respond, she repeats her question. The condemnation in her voice is clear. I cringe. Sometimes when I am in Anne's bright, quick-witted company, I think we could have been friends. But most of the time, too much tension exists between us. I do not know if it's jealousy or simple dislike, and every effort I make to bridge the divide is met with coldness.

"Anne, don't be such a wet blanket," Mr. Morgan scoffs. "We're just drinking to Miss Greene's triumph at the Boston auction tomorrow." Then, he amends, "Anticipated triumph, that is," before he takes a sip.

"You're not sending King?" she asks, and her thick eyebrows rise high on her forehead in surprise. In years past, Mr. Morgan's secretary attended auctions in his stead. "Or cousin Junius? I thought *he* was your art expert."

Like Anne, I have wondered why Junius hasn't been summoned for more consultations or auctions, and I have worried that his marginalization would create animosity between us. Fortunately, my letters from Junius do not reflect any jealousy or sense that he's been displaced from his uncle's affections, only pride that "his protégé" is working at his uncle's side. Maybe he's relieved that he no longer has the pressure of advising Mr. Morgan with such frequency.

"It is Miss Greene's job, and she will be securing a Bible once owned by a king." His tone makes clear he will brook no further discussion on the matter. But when he continues, he adopts the softer quality he tends to use with his youngest daughter. "It'll be perfect for the collection, don't you think, Anne? Rounds out the Gutenbergs."

She turns away from her father and addresses me directly. "That's quite a coup, Miss Greene, standing in for my father at an auction. Your people will be delighted, no doubt, at this opportunity."

I flinch, but only on the inside. *Strange*, I think, *for her to reference "my people."* I keep my face expressionless. She has never inquired about my background before. Nor has her father for that matter. It's always seemed enough that I am here because of Junius and her father.

Keeping my expression even as my heart rate speeds up, I answer, "Yes, I am sure they will be."

Her face is painted with innocence, an obvious effort, as she asks, "Remind me of who your people are again?"

There is no need for a reminder; she knows well we have never discussed this. Still, without hesitation, I answer. "We hail from Virginia, Miss Morgan, but my immediate family lives here in New York City."

Anne tilts her head. "And before that?"

I say a silent prayer to a God I've largely ignored and continue with my story. "My grandmother was from Portugal, although that is about as interesting as my family heritage gets." Then, in an attempt to make her point for her, I add, "Nothing as esteemed as your own family." I half laugh as if I'm embarrassed by such a common heritage.

Her eyes narrow. "Really? I thought I heard something about you having tropical roots," she says as her father walks away to get himself another drink.

Rage rises up within me. I'm not going to allow this jealous daughter to banish me by brandishing around what she thinks she may know. "Don't believe everything you hear, Miss Morgan. I would certainly ignore any chatter about you." I meet her stare.

I would never speak aloud the rumors I heard at a recent opera. During intermission, I was sipping champagne with renowned art dealer Mr. Jacques Seligmann, one of the most important antiquarians and art dealers in Paris and New York.

When Anne passed us by, she glanced my way, but didn't speak a word. She was chatting with her two close friends, the interior designer Miss Elsie de Wolfe and the literary agent and producer Miss Bessie Marbury, who represents Oscar Wilde and George Bernard Shaw among other luminaries. But I knew Anne was pointedly ignoring me, the way she had at the Vanderbilt ball and every other time since when I'd seen her in public.

Mr. Seligmann turned to me and whispered, "Don't let Miss Morgan's coldness bother you. Everyone knows she only has time for Elsie and Bessie, who—they say—are all in a Boston marriage together."

I laughed with him as though Boston marriages were commonplace in my world, but in truth, I'd never met a woman who was in a romantic relationship with another woman, let alone two.

"I'm not certain how such a thing works," Mr. Seligmann continued. "But they've made it abundantly clear that there's only room for those three. And those they've designated as particular friends."

I'd taken another sip of my champagne, keeping my eye on Anne, Bessie, and Elsie from across the room. The constant companionship of the three women now made sense. They'd cloaked their personal relationship behind their professional partnerships at the Villa Trianon at Versailles and the Colony Club. They were hiding in plain sight, and I knew a little about that.

That memory is in my mind as Anne and I lock eyes. She blinks first and pivots, turning to study a painting she's seen thousands of times. I take her silence as a victory.

Drink in hand, Morgan approaches us. "Enough of this banter,

Anne," he says. "Miss Greene has to get ready for her trip." Once again, he raises his glass in my direction before quaffing it down. "To your prowess," he declares as his daughter watches with a wary expression.

I sip at the liquor, and it eases my nerves. Anne may think she knows something about me and she may be awaiting my missteps, but I'm the one going to Boston tonight. And I will not let her ruin my evening—or my chance at success. Anne has built a life for herself, and I plan to do the same.

CHAPTER 10

NOVEMBER 5, 1906
BOSTON, MASSACHUSETTS

I leap into the cold, dark waters of the auction. My fellow bidders are a white-capped sea of men in charcoal-gray and midnight-blue suits. *How best to enter these waters?* I wonder. Should I wade in with ladylike circumspection, taking the temperature as I go deeper? Or should I dive?

Be cautious, never do anything to stand out, I can hear Mama say, but I've learned how important it is to be bold.

I decide to plunge headlong.

Identifying one familiar face in the crowd of about one hundred white men, I gather my skirts in my free hand and walk across the marble entryway toward the group with whom Mr. Edwards is conversing. This gentleman, if a dealer of his shady reputation can actually be called a gentleman, has a business purchasing and selling Italian Renaissance artwork. One evening at the opera, I was introduced to him by Mr. Morgan, who privately described him as one of his key "enemies," and I marveled at the way in which a notoriously picky industrialist welcomed the dealer into his opera box as a guest despite the rumors that he'd sold forgeries.

As I approach, I think how, like the men, I dressed for this occasion. While packing yesterday, I'd debated between my new jade-green gown and the more sensible pin-striped gray dress, which Mama advocated. I'd settled on the gray dress, thinking that it might bring me the same luck it had bestowed when I wore it to my interview with Mr. Morgan. But now I wonder whether the more daring gown would have better matched my purpose. I suppose it doesn't matter; these men are determined to scorn me regardless of what I wear.

The little band of five men closes ranks as I approach. They are clearly aware of my presence but are ignoring me.

"Mr. Edwards," I call out, knowing that even a cad cannot ignore the direct appeal from a lady.

Slowly, he turns toward me. "Is that you, Miss Greene?" he asks, making a show of looking down and squinting at me. As if my presence hadn't registered the moment I passed through the heavy oak doors of the auction house.

"None other," I reply with a wide smile.

Propriety leaves the group no choice but to part. But they step aside just enough to allow me a glimpse at their faces; there is not enough space for me to actually join their coterie. Among them, I recognize a dealer who works with the famous collector Isabella Stewart Gardner.

"I am surprised to see you here. I would have expected Mr. Morgan's secretary. Or perhaps his nephew?" Mr. Edwards says with a forced laugh and a knowing glance to his cadre, who join in his laughter.

"I don't know why you would have expected that." As I reach up to tuck a wayward curl back into my hat, I allow a gloved finger to graze Mr. Edwards's shoulder and give him my own forced laugh. Then, glancing at him through my eyelashes, I add, "I am his *personal* librarian, you know."

His eyebrows rise a bit, and now his chuckle is genuine. "Personal, you say? Just how personal?"

That is exactly the question I wanted him to ask. "I am *personally* responsible for making important acquisitions as well as being in charge of his collection. I am *personally* authorized to make the decisions and purchases all on his behalf." I pause. "Entirely as *I* see fit."

He smiles, nods, and once again glances at his group of friends. "Sounds like a big job for a little lady."

I sigh and lower my eyes. "Yes, it is an awfully big job. And being a woman, I know that I must do my job twice as well as any man to be thought half as good." I glance up with a broad smile and add, "Lucky for me, that won't be too difficult." I laugh, then slip my vivid red scarf from around my neck and let it trail behind me sinuously as I turn away. "Have a good day, gentlemen."

A ripple passes through the men, indiscernible and inaudible but undeniable. Over my shoulder, I hear a bevy of farewells and "nice to meet you, Miss Greene"s, but their voices are soon drowned out by the sound of a gong, and I am already on to my next task of choosing that all-important auction seat. I've read Mr. Morgan's volumes on the auction rules and probed my colleagues about their practices. Auction-goers have clear preferences. Some seek out seats in the front row to be seen or in the rear so their bids can only be seen by the auctioneer. Those more interested in displaying their finances and their power choose the center. I know precisely where to be.

I wait until most of the crowd has settled into their chairs, and then I walk down the aisle. Once I am certain all eyes are upon me—not difficult, given that I'm the only woman in the room—I take the last seat on the aisle in the very center row.

The auctioneer takes his post and raps his gavel on the podium. "Today, we are honored to be handling the estate of Robert Wilkinson, the esteemed collector whose passion for books and manuscripts sent him back and forth across the Atlantic Ocean every year as he sought out the rarest exemplars from both America and England. As many of you undoubtedly know, the collection of the late Mr. Wilkinson was assembled over the course of many years from private sales as well as the divestiture undertaken by famous libraries, including those of kings and queens. Mr. Wilkinson was known for his keen eye, his vast knowledge of books, and his acumen in the field, and his heirs are loath to disband his collection. But the unfortunate circumstances of pending levies and taxes—with which most of you are intimately familiar—require it."

The auctioneer waits for an audience member to finish a ragged bout of coughing, and as we sit idle, I remember a rumor I'd heard about the auction. Supposedly, there was talk of shipping the books to England for sale given their Anglo content and provenance, but with the additional layer of customs payments, the decision was rendered to sell them here.

The gong sounds again. "We begin today with the category of rare Bibles and important works by early church fathers." A somberly dressed assistant makes his way onto the stage, displaying a wooden box, inlaid with patterns of pearls. He pauses, then lifts the lid to reveal the leather Bible that lies within. "I draw your attention to lot number one," the auctioneer says.

My Bible will not emerge for another fifteen lots, so I take this opportunity to study my fellow bidders. The ways in which the men signal their bids vary widely—from the slight lift of a hand to the circumspect wave of a rolled-up catalog—and I wonder if gestures reflect some key quality of the bidder.

A parade of sumptuous priceless volumes appears on the dais until the auctioneer finally reaches lot sixteen. "The King Charles the First Bible, certainly one of the prizes of this auction, even though, of course, Mr. Wilkinson's collection contains many valuable items. As is detailed in your catalog, this Bible was not only owned by King Charles the First in the seventeenth century, but it is also considered the finest example of its kind. Shall we open the bidding at one thousand dollars?"

I itch to raise my scarf, having decided to use it as my bid signal, but I know I must wait. My competition needs to reveal itself before I make clear my intentions. I watch as two unfamiliar men bid in hundred-dollar increments until the Bible's price reaches five thousand dollars. It is then that I raise my scarf high, a flash of crimson against the backdrop of stormy grays and blues.

"Did she just jump in at the five-thousand mark?" I hear one man whisper to another behind me.

His neighbor replies in a low tone, "Who the devil is she?"

"What is a woman doing in here anyway?"

"And an olive-skinned one at that."

I flinch but keep my focus on the auctioneer's announcement that he'll adjust the bidding to five-hundred-dollar increments. At this point one of my two opponents drops out with a quick shake of his head. But the other gentleman continues, matching me dollar for dollar. Soon we've moved past ten thousand dollars, and then, in what feels like a dream, I bid fifteen thousand dollars.

As I lower my scarf, a quiet settles on the room. I realize that my competitor has not responded. I have won.

The gavel slams down on the podium. "Lot number sixteen has been sold, to the gentleman—I mean the lady—with the red scarf in the center row." He and I exchange brief nods, and then he turns his attention to the next lot.

As prices are named and hands fly up, I stand and walk slowly down the aisle. Leaving the auction midway is not the usual protocol, but I want everyone to understand that the Pierpont Morgan Library and its librarian are singular.

CHAPTER 11

FEBRUARY 9, 1907
NEW YORK, NEW YORK

The sunburst chandeliers illuminate the Metropolitan Opera House, and their light reflects off the famous gold damask stage curtains that have just been lowered. I blink as the lavish theater materializes before me at intermission, finding that I am loath to leave behind the captivating world of *Aida*.

Russell's hand is on my elbow, though, and I allow him to slide his arm through mine as we rise from our luxurious red velvet seats. We push past the curtains at the back of Mr. Morgan's box and exit into the lobby area, which is reserved for the owners of the exclusive boxes that ring the upper level of the opera house. As we walk toward a waiter holding a tray of champagne, my brother and I chat about the first and second acts.

Ever since my social blunder of having attended the Vanderbilt ball alone, I make sure that I'm accompanied, especially when I come to the opera and theater. In the past, when I wasn't with Mr. Morgan, either Louise or Ethel would accompany me. However, Mama had insisted that Russell escort me tonight.

"Please, Belle," she'd said. "Your brother is going to need a job in a few months."

"But he's not going to find one at the opera, Mama. That's not how it works."

"I don't expect him to sit down and have an interview there, but he can meet people of importance who can help him secure an engineering position once he graduates."

What Mama does not understand, and what she does not want to hear, is that the opera box attendees operate at a level so much higher than the one to which Russell aspires that a chance encounter would have little effect on his prospects. But that is not the only reason why I prefer to attend these events with my sisters. Standing next to the fairer Louise and Ethel never brings forth questions of my ancestry. It is always different when I'm with my darker-skinned brother. Yet, as I often do, I gave in to Mama.

In the lobby, I am greeted with kisses by Mrs. Hamilton and Mrs. Phipps, and several acquaintances of theirs who'd asked for introductions. In the wake of the Boston auction three months ago, the *New York Times* had seized upon the story and written an article about the pretty young librarian wielding the power of the legendary J. P. Morgan—maker of markets, banker to presidents and kings, savior of the United States economy—and the image of me captured the public's fancy. Mr. Morgan delighted in the publicity and in the incongruity between us as presented in the article. While the article was innocuous enough, it prompted gossip column mentions of my attendance at society events—linking me with men I've never met— and I am wary of the notoriety that could bring additional scrutiny. While there is little I can do about the gossip pages, I've decided to manage the public coverage by denying the dozens of requests that have come in for personal interviews.

Still, Mr. Morgan's pleasure at this public success has yielded several benefits that have offset some of my worries. He awarded me my first raise, which allowed my family to finally move to a three-bedroom apartment near Central Park, where Russell now sleeps in a proper bed in his own bedroom. And Mr. Morgan has given me greater latitude in identifying pieces for acquisition, and I have turned this into a series of small victories, securing masterpieces and then collections in their entirety for the Pierpont Morgan Library. Although I have yet to acquire the Caxton *Le Morte Darthur*, as he likes to remind me.

The lights flicker to indicate the end of intermission, and Russell and I down the remainder of our drinks. We press through the crowd toward the box and nearly reach it, when I hear a distinctive, high-pitched voice call out, "Miss Greene? Miss Greene, is that you?"

If I had been alone, I would have ignored that call, and I make an initial attempt at escape by continuing toward the box, but as I knew he would, Russell grabs my arm.

"Belle, I think that woman is calling you," he says, in an effort to be helpful. My brother is innocent of the machinations of which the elite are capable—from petty gossip to malevolent long-laid plans of economic destruction.

I do not have time to educate Russell. All I can do is turn toward Elsie de Wolfe with a wide smile.

"I thought that was you, Miss Greene," she says with a kiss on each of my cheeks. "So lovely to see you here." With her soft hair gathered high upon her head into a loose topknot and a welcoming twinkle in her eyes, the esteemed interior decorator—the person who veritably created the profession—seems kindly, and the light, brightly colored interiors for which she's become famous would certainly suggest a blithe temperament. But I have reason to be wary. Over the past months, I've confirmed the closeness of her relationship with Anne—and what Mr. Seligmann told me, in part at least. In fact, according to several others, Elsie does live with Bessie at a Sutton Place residence in a Boston marriage that seems to involve Anne in some capacity as well, even if it's simply as a friend.

"It's a pleasure to see you, Miss de Wolfe," I say, hoping my tone doesn't sound false. I know everything about this exchange will be reported back to Anne, so my behavior must be impeccable. "I hope you've been enjoying *Aida*."

"I certainly have been," she says, and then stares directly at Russell.

Reluctantly, I make the requisite introduction. "Will you do me the honor of meeting my brother, Russell da Costa Greene?"

"It is a pleasure, Miss de Wolfe," Russell responds, then asks, "You are friends with my sister?"

I groan inside. How little Russell understands this world to assume that, because people are acquainted, they are friends. This elite realm holds many gradations and types of relationships, and only a few of them contain actual friendship.

In her offhand way, Miss de Wolfe explains. "Friends? Well . . . so, you are Belle's brother." She peers at his symmetrical features and light gray eyes. "Yes, I definitely see the resemblance."

As Russell and Miss de Wolfe exchange pleasantries focused upon his education and prospects, just as Mama would have wanted, I become increasingly uneasy. As a designer, Miss de Wolfe is famous for her keen visual sense, and I wonder what she'll see as she studies Russell and me side by side. This is the exact situation that I wanted to avoid.

"Well," I begin, already moving toward the box and hoping Russell follows my lead. "It was good to see you."

But Miss de Wolfe continues speaking, holding my brother hostage with her conversation. Russell will never step away while she holds court; lessons in etiquette prevent such transgressions from politeness.

"Yes, you are siblings. The same skin tone and your features? Interesting." From her concentrated expression, I see that the real inquiry is coming. "Where are your people from again?"

I stiffen. It's the same question Anne asked me during our last encounter. It seems Miss de Wolfe is on a fishing expedition for Mr. Morgan's daughter.

My well-trained brother automatically says, "Our grandmother is from Portugal."

"Yes," she says, her eyes holding as much doubt as her tone. "Portugal. That's what I've been told. But I would have thought you had tropical roots."

There is no doubt now; Anne and Miss de Wolfe have spoken about me. But to what end are these questions?

"I would have thought your people were from someplace more like Cuba, maybe?" Miss de Wolfe continues.

I know what she's intimating by offering Cuba for our origins. I press my hand against my chest to calm myself and pretend it's a gesture of amusement. "Cuba?" I chuckle as if I'm delighted by her words even though inside I seethe. "Oh, no. But I would certainly love to visit that country one day."

"Are you sure you have no Cuban heritage?" she says, openly doubting my words. "I've heard so many rumors."

I cut her off with a wave of my hand and more laughter, because I'm unsure how far she will go. Nor am I certain how Russell will withstand the ongoing inquiry. "Don't believe everything you hear, Miss de Wolfe."

"It can be challenging, Miss Greene, when the rumors are so persistent." She holds firm.

"Well, I am certain you—of all people—understand how stubborn rumors can be, how hard to shake. I find that can be particularly true with rumors about strong women—such as ourselves. But don't you think we owe it to other women to push aside slander and gossip about one of our own?" I do not expect an answer, but I do anticipate a reaction. "I certainly ignore the chatter I hear about you and Miss Marbury."

From the frozen expression on Elsie's face, I've achieved my goal. By appealing to her stated commitment to women's interests—while subtly hinting at the whispers about her own life—I have boxed her in. How can she persist in her persecution of me at the same time she publicly espouses support for women, especially given that she now knows I'm aware she has secrets of her own?

It's time to take my leave. "Good evening, Miss de Wolfe. Enjoy the rest of your night."

This time, I take my brother's hand and firmly lead him into the box. As the chandeliers dim for acts three and four, I whisper, "You see what she was doing, don't you?"

"I do now. Sorry."

The orchestra begins, and we sit in frozen, fitful silence. I do not need to inquire about my brother's thoughts; I know precisely what he is thinking. In some ways, we are the most similar of our siblings, particularly because our appearances don't always give us the same room to breathe as our sisters. We are on a tightrope, trying to keep our balance, and I must reconcile myself to the fact that the suspicions about me will never disappear.

CHAPTER 12

OCTOBER 1–NOVEMBER 2, 1907
NEW YORK, NEW YORK

The slow pace of acquisitions that began at the Boston auction turns into a fast ride, and my successes continue to grow. Mr. Morgan and I decide that the Pierpont Morgan Library will become more than America's greatest collection of incunabula and illuminated manuscripts—a living history of the written word and printed books—worthy goal though that is. It will contain the pinnacle of objects owned or created by rulers, royals, artists, and inventors in every category. Napoleon's watch. Da Vinci's notebook. Shakespeare's folios. Catherine the Great's snuffbox. George Washington's letters. When I place the Medici jewels in the vault, I feel their legacy passing from them to Mr. Morgan and his library, advancing his evolution into a modern-day Medici, as I'd promised.

But life can change suddenly. Previously inflated items drop in price on rumors of a pending economic crash. The newspaper headlines report dire circumstances and predict worse. The New York Stock Exchange falls daily, and fear mounts about the impact on banks. I overhear conversations from Mr. Morgan's study that detail excessive stock speculation in railroads, mining, and copper; overinvestment in

ill-regulated trust companies that are teetering on the edge of sol-
vency; bank loans backed by shaky stocks and bonds as collateral.

It seems our economy is a house of cards, but Mr. Morgan assures
me that there is nothing to be concerned about. In fact, he suggests
that we should keep spending despite the economy. Then he asks *me*
why I think he's making this recommendation.

He has been slowly educating me in financial matters. He has
shown me balance sheets and profit and loss statements and has suggested I read the business columns in the papers.

I muse on the question—which feels like a test—for a long moment. I contemplate the way he values companies and investment
opportunities, and I finally say, "We should be examining not the
current value of books and art, but their future worth, which we've
assessed as enormous. And given their low price compared to their
soaring futures, the artwork and manuscripts on the market present
unique opportunities and excellent value. We should proceed," I finish, awaiting his verdict.

Smiling, he says, "Ah, Miss Greene, you see that to which everyone
else is blind."

But even our opportunistic spending cannot withstand the con-
tinual downturn of the financial marketplace. By the beginning of
October, the newspapers are reporting the collapse in copper shares,
which takes down other stocks like dominoes. Alarm sets in when
people realize that stocks serve as collateral for a large percentage of
the bank and trust loans, and then the fears come true. Lines form
outside banks as people empty their accounts. I see them on the way
to work, and Mama and I have secreted a small carryall of cash under
her bed. When Mr. Morgan decides we should forestall purchases
and doesn't even ask me about his precious Caxton for weeks, I wonder if I should have Mama join her bank's line and withdraw all our
savings.

The moment I step into the rotunda the morning of October 10,
Mr. Morgan calls out to me. This is peculiar, since he'd been sched-

uled to leave the night before for the Episcopal Convention in Richmond, Virginia. Not to mention, I usually arrive before him.

Before even removing my coat, I walk into Mr. Morgan's office. He's slumped over in his lion's chair, not enough for others to notice, but the hours I've spent with this man have made me aware of even subtle shifts in his posture, and his eyes do not have their usual hawklike gleam.

"Yes, Mr. Morgan," I say.

He averts his gaze before responding. "Please sit down."

Anxiety rushes through me. I already know what he's going to say, and questions overwhelm me. Will Teddy have to drop out of college? Will Mama have to return to teaching again? And what about our new apartment? We've only been there for a year. My only hope is that I will be able to find a new job, return to Princeton, perhaps.

"A friend from Boston committed suicide."

His words stun me, but I do not speak.

"Last night," he continues. "In San Francisco. His investment company was already on the brink of financial ruin. But the crisis sent his company plummeting over the edge. His poor wife found him with the gun."

He shakes his head before lowering his eyes, and I know this is my signal to leave. "I'm terribly sorry, sir," I say before heading to my own office, where I sit at my desk, trembling from the news. In part, I feel relief; I still have my job at a time when many are out of work. But I push that selfishness aside as my eyes fill with tears for a man I've never met and his family.

Although he does indeed leave for the Episcopal Convention that evening, before he goes, Mr. Morgan has had a shift in his thinking. He no longer believes this crisis will pass, and no one else does either.

Three tense weeks later, Mr. Morgan—the man who saved the gold standard in 1895, and the American economy along with it, by controlling the flow of gold in and out of the country, the man who created the world's largest steel company and first billion-dollar entity by financing the merger of Andrew Carnegie's steel company with his two biggest competitors—answers the country's calls for help, and is summoned back from his convention. Once he reaches New York City by his private railroad car, he assembles a committee of young bankers to investigate and audit the various players.

By the time he strides through the heavy bronze doors of the library on the morning of November 2, he looks ten years younger than the man who left. With an invigorated step, he gives me a nod before he leads ten men into his study for a meeting that he says he hopes will end the crisis. I feel his strength and now know in my very bones this economic crisis will be solved. However, within the hour, my office door swings open wide.

I jump at the sound, surprised to see that it's Mr. Morgan. "Sir? Can I help you or your guests with anything?"

He crosses the room with uncharacteristic speed, and settles himself into the chair opposite my desk. "How I wish you could, Miss Greene."

"You know I'd do anything to help."

"How about knocking some sense into the bankers and trust men I brought into the library today?" His tone is gruff, filled with more frustration than anger.

I chuckle at the thought. "If I could, I would, sir."

"You might be the only one who could," he says with a rueful laugh. "I haven't had much luck so far."

"I don't know about that," I offer. "You managed to get the government to pledge twenty-five million dollars to help the brokerage houses, and you assisted in raising thirty million dollars to help New York City meet its expenses. Not to mention your request that the city's religious leaders preach calm in last week's Sunday services. If I may, sir, that was nothing short of brilliant. There's no doubt it slowed the liquidation of holdings in the market and the banks."

He smiles, pleased by my assessment. "Small mercies, Miss Greene. What we need is a miracle."

I am not moved by his uncertainty, and anyway, I know he needs encouragement. "You've managed miracles before, Mr. Morgan, and

I don't doubt that you will again," I say, holding his gaze. He needs to be confident in his ability to fix this catastrophe, because if he can't, who can? "What is your plan?"

He's pensive for a moment. "Well, I've had the front doors to the library locked, after having enough provisions brought in for the duration, because I told those damned financial men we aren't leaving until this matter is resolved. I put the bankers in the library and the trust men in my study, so I'll be holed up here with you until I get word they've got some proposals."

"It will be my pleasure, sir, to keep you company. If you have a few minutes now, I wouldn't mind learning the latest developments."

He leans across my desk and begins mapping out what's happened thus far, leading up to the discussions this morning. I am fascinated by his passion and his desire to do what's best for the country. Just as he finishes running through the potential scenarios, a rap sounds at my office door. I rise, opening the door to the astonished face of a silver-haired businessman.

"Um," he begins before he glances over his shoulder, then returns his eyes to me, "I was looking for Mr. Morgan?" His statement turns into a question. "I must have knocked on the wrong door."

As he backs away, I gesture for him to enter. "No, you are in the correct place. This is my office, but Mr. Morgan is here."

Stepping inside, he cannot disguise his awe. Even in the midst of disaster, my opulent two-story office has the capacity to overwhelm. "This is *your* office?" he asks, sounding incredulous that a woman—a young woman—should preside over such a grand space.

Mr. Morgan calls out, "This is my librarian, Miss Greene. And she deserves every inch of this room, for God's sake. Why are you wasting her time and mine by interrogating her?" His tone is filled with impatience. "You should be offering me a plan of action."

"We don't have one yet. Just a question."

Mr. Morgan stands and faces the man. Very quietly, very calmly, he says, "Don't come back in here until you and your damned trust men have a solution to this crisis. Do you hear me?"

"Sorry, Mr. Morgan. Sorry, Miss, Miss—" He stumbles over my name; he has clearly forgotten it.

"Her name is Miss Greene!" Mr. Morgan yells, collapsing back down onto his chair, and the man exits without asking his question.

"Bumbling idiot," he mutters.

I sit down, trying to ignore how peculiar it feels to preside behind the desk while Mr. Morgan faces me in the supplicant's chair, which can barely contain his girth. After studying him for a moment, I say, "You already know the solution, don't you? Could you simply share it with them?"

"I can say this only to you." He inches toward the edge of his chair. In a low voice, but not the near whisper of his fury, he says, "I honestly don't know what we should do. I feel the hint of an answer in the far reaches of my mind, but it hasn't taken full shape. When the bankers and the trust men begin to sketch out possible solutions, the resolution will come to me."

I nod, knowing he would have never spoken these words to anyone else. Not his son nor his daughters and certainly not his wife or any of his mistresses. Today, I am more than his librarian; I am his confidant. "I'm certain it will."

He leans back. "In the meantime, help me pass the time."

"Would you like me to read to you?" I am halfway out of my chair to fetch a volume before he stops me.

"I'm too wound up for that. Let's do this." Reaching into his pocket, he pulls out a deck of cards.

"Oh," I say with surprise.

"Do you play bridge, Miss Greene?" he asks as he shuffles the cards.

His question brings a smile to my face and a memory to my mind. "A little. I used to love watching my grandmother and her friends play bridge when I was younger in—" I stop right before I say Washington, DC, but it is already too late.

Mr. Morgan's eyes are filled with curiosity when he says, "Your grandmother? The one from Portugal?"

Did I actually just mention Gramma Fleet? My heart pounds, and I can't believe my mistake. I can only explain the slip by a combination of surprise at the cards and being far too comfortable with my employer.

Before I can respond, he continues, "For some reason, I thought your grandmother lived in Portugal. I didn't realize she was here."

"No, I mean, yes. I mean—she lives in Portugal. You are correct. It was just one time, when I was younger, and she visited." I stutter my way through an explanation.

Throughout my tenure with Mr. Morgan, I've been confident and steady handed, but the way he looks at me now tells me that I appear shaken.

After a long second, he says, "Well, you need four players for bridge, unless you do a modified version. What about bezique?"

Only when he leans forward to deal the cards, instructing me as he does, do I exhale. How could I have been so careless?

The clock strikes two, then three. By the time it chimes four bells, Mr. Morgan says, "Maybe you should read to me, Miss Greene."

From my shelf, I pick up Dickens, and begin to read aloud from *Great Expectations*. We keep on in this circular pattern of playing cards, then reading, then discussion as the clock continues its rotation, and the daylight, which shines blue through the colorful stained glass of my medieval window, turning my walls violet, transforms into the golden light of early evening and finally into the pitch black of a moonless night. Our routine is interrupted only when one of the gentlemen seeks a word with Mr. Morgan or one of the maids delivers sustenance and drinks.

After midnight, Mr. Morgan suddenly rises from the chair without a word and exits for the first time since he's entered. When he returns forty minutes later, he is beaming.

"You've solved it," I exclaim, leaping up from my chair and clutching his arm.

"I have indeed," he says, and I hear his pride. "I've found a way to bolster the frailer trusts and companies, thereby stopping the cataclysmic effect on the entire market if they fail. I've arranged for U.S. Steel to acquire Tennessee Coal and Iron, and that should shore up a substantial share of the faltering companies and trusts which hold its stock as collateral."

I frown. "Will that not cause a problem with the anti-trust laws?"

"Smart question, Miss Greene." His smile broadens, and his pride is now directed at me. "I got Roosevelt to agree to the deal. The federal government will not file suit."

"You did it!" Without thinking, I stand on my tiptoes and embrace the great hulk of a man.

He pulls me closer to him. "With you at my side, I feel I can do anything, Belle."

I lean away, astonished at my own misstep. Mr. Morgan and I have had these moments of attraction, but we've never touched in this way. Yet, who can deny this frisson has been building between us?

What am I doing? I cannot succumb to this man—this notorious philanderer, more than forty years older than me. I begin to pull away just as Mr. Morgan abruptly lets go. Glancing down, I berate myself for my impulsiveness, when I feel his finger under my chin.

Tilting my face toward his, it takes me a moment to look up, and I see that tender expression again, although today, there is something else in his eyes as well. It is more than an appreciation for my femininity; it is a longing. He whispers, "My romantic entanglements always end badly, and I could never stand to lose you, Belle. You mean more to me than any woman, even more than my own family most of the time. I want you at my side—as my partner, my confidant, and my librarian—until the end."

I nod because I can't speak. Only after he spins around and walks out of my office can I finally breathe.

CHAPTER 13

We board the train with dozens of other New York passengers bound for Washington, DC, settling ourselves in the last, unobtrusive row of the train car, where we find six empty seats near each other. Melancholy has beset my family since we received word of Gramma Fleet's passing two days ago, and for the first half hour of the ride, we sit in silence.

As I look out the window, I feel riven between the joy at my accomplishments at the Pierpont Morgan Library and my overwhelming sadness. On one hand, I'm proud of the important acquisitions I've orchestrated and the increase in the library's standing under my direction, for which Mr. Morgan has rewarded me with a second raise. And I've been pleased with the new rhythm we've found in our work in the four months since that moment in my office, the night he saved the country from financial ruin. We have never spoken about that time again, although it is settled that, no matter the attraction between us, we are best as employer and employee.

On the other hand, the pleasure I feel from my work is weighed down by this staggering loss. Despite the fact that I haven't returned to DC in over a decade, the passing of time has not lessened the connection I feel to a place imbued with love and family, the tie I feel to a different sort of life. But I wonder what it will be like without Gramma, the woman whose warm embraces I can still remember as if her arms are wrapped around me.

"We should do something," Ethel finally says and pulls a deck of cards from her handbag. She shuffles them, and starts dealing cards on the table among the four seats where the five of us have squeezed in. I glance at Mama across the aisle to see if she'll frown upon this small entertainment in the midst of our mourning, but her eyes are closed and I suppose the rumble of the train has lulled her to sleep.

We take our turns silently in the beginning, until Louise whispers, "It feels strange returning to DC, doesn't it?"

"It does," Ethel echoes. "When was the last time we were back?"

"At least ten years," Russell replies.

"It's been twelve years," I say with a nod. "I was sixteen the last time we went for Christmas. We used to visit more for holidays and family get-togethers, but then we stopped going."

"Why?" Ethel asks.

How can she not know why we no longer go to Mama's home? She's only a year younger than me, but sometimes, with her obliviousness and her blind obedience to Mama, she seems much younger. I guess this is her way of coping with our life.

"Because Papa left," I answer, when no one else seems willing to chime in. "And we couldn't really afford it once he was gone. Some nights it was hard for Mama to feed the five of us, after all. Don't you remember how we struggled, before you, me, and Louise started earning salaries and before Mama's career as a music instructor got going?"

"Not really," Ethel murmurs. "I guess I try not to think about those times."

Louise says, "I remember those days. They were awful, and Mama wasn't strong like she is now. She was weepy." Tears well up in her eyes.

I decide to let the conversation end with Louise's words, although all of us, with maybe the exception of Teddy, know the real reason these trips stopped, even though money troubles certainly played a part. Once Mama made the decision that we would live as white, we no longer traveled to DC. Mama decided that, even though the Fleets were part of the upper class and living well in the district, they were still colored. We could not take the risk. Only her mother's death could warrant crossing the color barrier.

More silent seconds pass until Louise says suddenly, "I wonder where Papa is now."

"I don't care where the hell he is," Russell blurts out, his pale gray eyes flashing. He is a little too loud, telegraphing his anger at Papa. Mama stirs, and we shush him. The last thing we need is to awaken grieving Mama with a harsh statement about Papa.

My sister's question and my brother's reaction make clear that Mama shared the news of Papa's posting in Russia and his new family only with me, as I'd suspected she would. And just like Mama expected, I had buried that revelation and had no intention of bringing it up now. While I'd hidden that truth about my father deep inside, I hadn't been able to do the same with my feelings for him. I yearn for a day when I can see him, thank him, and maybe even have the chance to forgive him for leaving. Or ask him to forgive me for following this road that Mama has forged for us. But given that he lives in Russia now with a new family, I suppose that meeting will never be.

We play the next few hands, again returning to silence, keeping our focus on the game, until Teddy says, "I don't remember DC at all, and I have only a few strong memories of Papa."

We digest her remark, and I feel nothing but sadness for Teddy. Louise, Ethel, and Russell have memories of Papa that they've chosen to push aside, but Teddy's situation is different. Her absence of recollections is not by choice.

I wish Teddy had had the opportunity to know Papa better. I will always treasure my afternoons with him at the Metropolitan, studying art and listening to his stories of the past. But I cannot re-create for her a lifetime of memories with him, so it is best that I say nothing to my little sister.

After the train stops in New Jersey, Philadelphia, and a couple of cities in Maryland, the whistle sounds, awakening Mama, as we pull into the station in Washington, DC. We hurriedly gather up our belongings. Russell begins to exit out of the front of the train car, but Mama stops him. She gestures to the back of the car and leads us through a rear door into another, connected car—the one for colored people. As we pass into this car, fellow passengers staring at the fair-skinned trespassers in their realm, I notice that the seats are the same size, but that is the only similarity to the white train car. There is no upholstering on the hard wooden seats; no tables are installed; the absence of luggage racks forces passengers to store their bags around their feet; and the smell emanating from the tiny bathroom—really nothing more than a bucket—makes me gag as we walk by. *How strange is the power of geography and law that we could leave New York City as white people but arrive in Washington, DC, as colored.*

Walking down the rickety steps from the train and into the station, we search for the route to the carriages for hire. Signs are posted throughout the station demarcating where colored people—such as we have just declared ourselves to be—may pass. The route takes us around the back of the train station, through the rubbish and piles of discarded coal, to an alleyway that appears to empty out onto a side street.

"Why do we have to walk here, Mama?" Teddy protests as we all pick our way through the narrow passage, littered with broken bottles, half-opened bags of trash, and a discarded shoe. "It's just filthy."

"Keep your voice down," Mama hisses. "I told you why before we even got on the train in New York. If we were to pretend to be white here and then be called out as colored, the ramifications could be fierce. What if I should run into someone I know in the train station and our situation was revealed? We could get arrested or worse. While we are here, we will be who we are. We will be colored."

Teddy's cheeks flame red. She knows about our heritage, but she neither remembers living this way nor really understands the consequences we could suffer if we were discovered to be living as white. She doesn't read the newspapers that I do every day at the Pierpont Morgan Library. She hasn't heard of the hundreds of lynchings that happen every year, including one of a college student who'd been caught passing.

We emerge from the dark passageway onto the side street near the station, blinded like moles by the bright afternoon light. A line of ramshackle carriages for hire is assembled, and we join the queue of colored folks. Russell signals a driver when we reach the front, and we load into the open carriage, jostling along the rough streets. Washington, DC, isn't recognizable to me, until our carriage pulls up to the familiar tangle of Fleet homes on T Street. Then all the strangeness falls away and I'm an eight-year-old girl again, playing in my grandmother's front yard under my favorite tree.

Quiet tears stream down my face as I exit the carriage with my carpetbag in one hand and a leather satchel in the other. I am finally home.

The door to Gramma Fleet's house opens, and Uncle Mozart exits with his arms open wide. "Welcome," he says.

Even though Uncle Mozart writes regularly, he hasn't visited New York in at least ten years. His warm smile is the same, though there is a lot more salt in the color of his hair than I remember.

He hugs Mama first, then he embraces my sisters and brother and me. Uncle Mozart takes Mama's bag, but just before he steps over the threshold into the two-story row house of our childhood, Mama asks, "Is it all right, Mozart? For us to stay here?"

Uncle Mozart's smile fades. "Genevieve, all will be well. Trust me. You have to do this."

I frown, not understanding the exchange until we step into Gramma's home. A man whom I recognize as Uncle Bellini stands at the front door, though his greeting isn't as warm as Uncle Mozart's. The burly, silver-haired man nods as Mama walks in, and though he doesn't embrace any of us, I reach for him. His arms are stiff, and he releases me quickly. But before I can think too much about that reception, I'm inundated with the residual scent of Gramma's cooking, and the memories of gathering around her table at mealtime.

We follow Uncle Mozart into the parlor, and although much is familiar, the furniture seems worn and weathered now. But everything is still in its place: two sofas sit on opposite walls, one crimson, the other brown, and they face the round wooden parlor table. Then I see Gramma's rocking chair in front of the fireplace, and for a moment, I can almost hear it creak as she beckons me to come sit in her lap.

Then, I blink and notice the two gray-haired women sitting close on the crimson sofa, both with grim expressions and arms folded. When I recognize Aunt Adalaide and Aunt Minerva, I smile; they do not.

My mother stands in front of her sister and Uncle Mozart's wife. "Minerva, Adalaide," she says to both of them in greeting. There is a pleading in her tone, but they give her no words, only a nod of acknowledgment.

Finally, Uncle Mozart says, "Sit your bags down and rest a bit. I know it was a long train ride."

"Yes, sir, thank you," my sisters and I mutter. I can tell that my siblings feel the tension in the air.

"Yes, Genevieve." Aunt Minerva finally speaks her first words to her sister. "Sit. If that brown sofa over there isn't too dark for you."

We all freeze, and Uncle Mozart snaps, "Minerva!"

It is only at this moment that I realize what is going on. I have never considered what Mama's family thought about our decision to live as whites once Papa left. It has never occurred to me that it would anger anyone in our family. Why should it? Didn't they understand the advantages Mama was trying to give us?

"Well, what do you expect me to do, Mozart?" Aunt Minerva asks. "We just gonna sit here and ignore the fact that our own sister has turned her back on us?"

"That is not what I've done!"

Aunt Minerva raises her eyebrows in mock surprise. "It's not?"

"No," Mama cries. "I am still a Fleet."

"You don't act like one," Minerva huffs. "You won't even let Mozart come to see you when he's in New York because now you're the *Greenes*."

She says our name with disdain, but that is not what's most shocking. Is that why Uncle Mozart stopped visiting? I thought it was because he'd always come to see Papa, but he'd stopped because of Mama? Because she didn't want him to be seen with us? I think of the times when I prefer to be with Louise or Ethel, rather than Russell, because the fairer shade of their skin validates mine. Is that how Mama feels about her brother, too?

"I am proud to be a member of this family," Mama says, ignoring her sister's words.

"You don't act proud. Look at your children." Every eye turns toward us, and even though I am twenty-eight years old, I stand stiffly, as if I'm about to be scolded. "They have no idea who they are. They think they're white; they certainly don't know anything about being Fleets."

There are tears in Mama's voice when she says, "You just don't understand, Minerva. I'm a mother who was abandoned with five children."

Now I suck in air. Louise and I, and even Ethel and Russell, were hardly young when Papa left. But is that how she felt? Abandoned? My heart aches, because if Mama felt abandoned, I realize now that she was alone. Her family felt just like Papa. None of them, except for Uncle Mozart, understood, and now it seems as if they don't even want us here.

Mama continues, "I did what I had to do to give my children the best opportunities, the best life." Her sister and sister-in-law exchange long glances, which makes her say, "You don't know what it's like in New York. It's the North, but as colored, we wouldn't have had the life there that we had here."

"And as I've always said," Minerva responds, "you could have come back home. We would have welcomed you with open arms, Genevieve."

Mama sighs as if that decision has been a weight she still carries. "As I've always said, this neighborhood, this place that was created for people like us, it isn't going to last." She shakes her head. "DC is still the South, and with the way the country is moving, I expect that soon, segregation and blatant attacks on colored folks will snatch this all away."

The silence makes me want to grab our bags and run. This isn't the welcome I'd expected; this isn't what home is supposed to feel like.

Finally, Mama adds, "And without . . ." She pauses before she speaks Papa's name. Then, she straightens her shoulders and stands taller. "I've done what I know is best for my children. To be colored in America is a burden that I don't want them to have to shoulder."

Mama has spoken as eloquently as I've ever heard her. Can't her siblings understand that she is right? This part of DC has remained unscathed so far, but the vise of segregation has been tightening and oppression has been escalating. Every week I read another newspaper article about mobs of white men terrorizing colored neighborhoods, dragging black men from their homes on the word of white women who have made accusations. The Atlanta Massacre happened two years ago, but the city is still reeling and recovering from the two days of race riots that started with four allegations of rape by white women and ended with more than twenty-five colored men dead. No one is exempt from the denigration that accompanies this deep-seated racism. Even President Roosevelt faced the contempt of the Southern Democrats when he tried to welcome Booker T. Washington into the White House, an invitation that yielded threats by senators to lynch hundreds of coloreds. Segregation is really just slavery by another name, lynching is one of its proponents' weapons, and we would be subjected to segregation and threatened by lynchings if we lived as colored anywhere in this country.

Aunt Adalaide unfolds her arms with a sigh. "I don't agree with what Genevieve has done," she says, looking around at everyone. "But all of you know, Mama Fleet wouldn't have allowed this kind of unpleasant talk in her house. She would have wanted us to come together. To support each other, even if we don't like the decisions that we've made." Pushing herself from the sofa, she walks to where my siblings and I have been standing, too afraid to move. She wraps her arms around Louise first, and then continues down the line. When she hugs me, I exhale.

"You have all grown up so beautifully," she says when she finally releases Teddy. Standing back, she takes in the sight of us all together. "Genevieve must be doing something right."

She smirks at Mama, and for the first time since she heard the news of Gramma's death, I see my mother smile.

Uncle Mozart says, "Adalaide is right. These next few days should be all about Mama and all about her family. Let's keep our focus on that. Let's focus on what we have in common and not on the differences that have pulled us apart."

When everyone nods, I am relieved. Especially when Uncle Mozart changes the subject. "Belle, I've been reading all about you. We hear that you are indispensable to Mr. J. P. Morgan himself."

"Yes, Belle," Aunt Minerva says, accepting the truce. "What's he like? Is he as heartless as all the papers make him out to be?" She motions for all of us to sit down. "Come on in here and tell us everything."

"Yes, Belle. Come in here. But I don't want to hear anything about him. I read in one of those gossip columns that you were among the guests at the Marjorie Gould and Anthony Drexel wedding. Is that true?" Before I can answer Aunt Adalaide's question, she keeps on. "The pictures I saw of that white satin gown were something else. I bet it was expensive."

"Yes." I smile. "Her gown was exquisite and expensive, but it didn't come close to the half-a-million-dollar Fifth Avenue mansion that her father gave her as a wedding gift."

My aunts fill the room with oohs and aahs, and it's as if the air has been released from a hot-air balloon. We gather around, and I answer all of my aunts' questions. There is still some tension—the smiles are a little forced, the laughter is a bit fake, but all of the Fleets are trying. All for Gramma's sake. About a half hour later, Uncle Bellini, who hasn't spoken a word, now says, "Genevieve, there is one thing you can do that will go a long way in helping me to forgive you."

The room quiets, and Mama stiffens at her brother's words. "What is it, Bellini?"

He pauses, and I hold my breath as my uncle looks around at each of us and then says, "Do you still know how to make Mama's sweet potato pie? 'Cause it seems she only taught you, and I'm gonna need a piece of that pie before you leave."

For a few seconds, there is silence, then genuine laughter fills the room. All of the tension is gone now and for just a moment, I think, *Finally, I'm home.*

I step outside to the porch, letting the screen door slam behind me before I secure the belt on my jacket, tightening it against the chill of the March air. The street is early-morning quiet; it is just a little after seven. Having been back in New York for more than two years now after my time in Princeton, I'd forgotten about the peace that comes at this time of the day.

Behind me, a wave of laughter floats through the screen door, and I smile. Over the last three days, Mama and her siblings have come to a place of understanding, if not reconciliation. Last night, as Teddy and I slept in Gramma's bedroom, Mama and her brothers and sister sat in the parlor talking until the early hours of the morning.

I sigh. This time that we've spent here laying Gramma Fleet to rest has been bittersweet. After the initial reception, it has been good to connect once again with my aunts and uncles and cousins, whom I've loved so much, even from afar. But the bitter—my eyes fill with tears as my glance roams from the left to the right. I want to soak it all in, the three family homes, the lawns where we used to run and jump and play. When my eyes settle on Gramma Fleet's front yard and my favorite tree, a tear seeps from the corner of my eye. I am filled with so many emotions. I've thought of this place as home for as long as I can remember, but now I know that this is likely the last time I will ever be here.

When I hear the screen door open and close behind me, I wipe my tears from my cheeks, and smile when I turn to Uncle Mozart.

"Everyone in the house was looking for you," he said. "But I knew you would be out here." He chuckles. "I'm just surprised I didn't find you sitting under that tree."

"I'm surprised you remember that."

"Of course I do. I remember everything. And one thing I remember is how close you and your dad were." I tilt my head when I look at him, surprised that he mentioned my father. "I wanted to tell you that Richard is back from Russia."

My eyes widen at that announcement.

He adds, "Genevieve told me that you know about his new family, and though I didn't think it was my news to share with you, I'm glad you do." He leans closer, and even though we're alone, he lowers his voice. "You know you were his favorite."

Together we laugh.

I say, "I'm really glad that you stay in touch with him, Uncle Mozart."

"Richard and I have been friends for a long time, way before I introduced him to Genevieve, and even though I was so mad at him for leaving my sister and you kids," he says as if I'm still ten, "I get it. It took me some time, but the desire to make America equal burns within him. He loves the United States, and because of that, he's challenging every aspect of this country to be better. By the time he's done, I have no doubt he will accomplish his goals; we will be a better nation. We will have the equality we deserve."

That makes me proud. For a moment, I think of asking Uncle Mozart for my father's whereabouts. Do I dare try to connect with him after more than ten years? But instead, I say, "Would you mind letting me know from time to time what's going on with him?"

He shakes his head. "Wouldn't mind doing that at all. I only hear from him once or twice, maybe three times a year. But I'll let you know when I do." After a long pause, he adds, "You know, he's really proud of you."

My question comes quickly. "Did he say that?"

Uncle Mozart tilts his head back and looks up, as if he can't decide how to respond. Finally, "We don't talk about Genevieve, or any of you." His voice is downcast. "That was an unspoken deal that we made. But I know your father, and I'm sure he's following you, just like we are. He's proud," he says with certainty.

Once again, I feel tears, but I'm not sad.

"We're all proud of you, Belle, but . . ." He pauses. "I want you to be careful."

"What do you mean?"

"All of you, up there in New York, you're taking a big chance."

Uncle Mozart doesn't have to explain further. I know what he means. My eyes are on my favorite tree when I say, "I understand the risks. Every morning when I wake up, I prepare myself, knowing that once I walk out that door, I'm on a stage and playing a role. And I'm careful."

"Careful?" The way he says that makes me turn to him.

"I don't think you can be careful enough, Belle. You're working for J. P. Morgan. Some people say he's one of the smartest men in the country. I don't know about that, but I know he's one of the most ruthless. What would happen if he finds out that you're colored?"

"He won't." I shake my head emphatically. "I've been very careful. But even if he were to say something, Mama has it planned out with all of us. That's why I use the name da Costa."

He smirks. "Yeah. I heard you had a Portuguese grandmother out there somewhere. I'm glad Mama never found out about that."

His words make me hesitate. That was something I hadn't considered. How would Gramma Fleet have felt about that? The ramifications of our decision to live as white spread wide.

Uncle Mozart says, "I know all about the stories you've prepared in case someone questions your ethnicity and the precautions you've taken so that won't happen, but the stakes are high, Belle. It's one thing if Louise or Ethel is caught passing. They're teachers; they'll be fired and that will be the end of it. But with you—I'm afraid there will be a higher price to pay for your deception."

I press my lips together.

"I'm not trying to scare you, honey. I'm trying to save you by reminding you that you're playing on a level where the consequences of being outed will be much higher. Just be careful. Just remember this is J. P. Morgan you're dealing with."

After a moment, Uncle Mozart hugs me. "Let me go in there and get everyone together. We've got to leave in the next ten minutes or so, in order to make sure you have time to settle in at the station."

Uncle Mozart has left me breathless. Is the risk I'm taking too high? Of course, I've thought about the consequences, especially with a man like Mr. Morgan, but to hear my uncle voice his concern out loud makes the stakes even more real. It's too late to go back now, though. The money that I'm earning has changed our lives. We're living in a comfortable home, have more than enough money for food and to cover all of our bills, and Mama and my siblings can enjoy life a little.

Yes, the risk is high, but so is the reward. I will have to be even more careful and even more driven in my success so that our family's whiteness is unquestionable. I allow myself one final glance across the lawns before we assemble and begin our journey north—to the only home we have left.

CHAPTER 14

Miss Greene"—I hear my name called the moment I step over the threshold of the gallery—"I thought you'd never come."

Edward Steichen rushes toward me, and I take his outstretched hand. A lock of his dark hair flops onto his forehead, and as he brushes it away in irritation, I wonder if it gets in the way of his work as a photographer.

"Oh, Mr. Steichen, you should have known that I wouldn't miss your gallery show for the world," I say with a playful touch on his shoulder. "I would have come earlier, but I was at the Carnegies', and you know how difficult it can be to extricate oneself from a soiree with the rich and powerful. They believe *their* time is precious, but *ours* is best spent on their whims, however long—or short—that might be." I wink.

He laughs at my veiled reference to his photography session with Mr. Morgan. Five years ago, Mr. Steichen had been hired by the painter Fedor Encke to take a few pictures of Mr. Morgan in preparation for a portrait the painter was undertaking. Mr. Morgan, who was willing to sit for a total of three minutes for two photographs only, was so delighted by Mr. Steichen's work—and his brevity—that he paid him five hundred dollars on the spot.

As Mr. Steichen recounts the story of those three minutes, I laugh, thinking how pleasant it is to chat with someone closer to my age and station than is usual for me these days. He lifts his hand almost imperceptibly, and another man appears at my side. "Miss Greene. I'd like to introduce you to my partner in the gallery, Alfred Stieglitz."

The fellow, who has a thick mustache that makes him look older than his thirty-odd years, gives me a quick bow. Steichen and Stieglitz joined forces a few years ago to create not only this gallery—dubbed 291 for its address at 291 Fifth Avenue—but also the Photo-Secessionist movement to promote photography as a fine art. Both men are committed to elevating the reputation of their craft, in which they use a variety of painterly techniques to imbue their subjects with specific moods and meanings. But recently, they decided to display the latest modern art from Europe alongside photography, and when Mr. Steichen invited me to tonight's exhibit, he promised a most scintillating show, "one I couldn't miss," he told me.

"Welcome to Two Ninety-One." My host gestures to a room crowded with guests. The walls are lined with a paper somewhere between silver and taupe and accented with matching fabric skirting the bottom half. While I assume the rather plain neutral walls were chosen to offset the art, the room seems very stark in comparison to the crimson realm of the Pierpont Morgan Library. "Tonight, we have a rare treat in store for you, Miss Greene. Two Ninety-One is proud to host the American launch of *two* very important European artists—the French sculptor Auguste Rodin and the French artist Henri Matisse."

Mr. Steichen walks me around the space, in which photographs are hung alongside black-and-white drawings he identifies as Rodin's work. I know Steichen and Stieglitz hope to elevate the perception of photography by juxtaposing it with other, already accepted forms of fine art, and while I admire the atmospheric photo images, I am more captivated by the exquisite charcoal drawings.

"With a few spare lines, Rodin somehow manages to convey movement and intention all at once," I say, marveling at the manner in which the sculptor shares so much with so little.

Mr. Steichen, who bursts with energy despite the fact that his work as a photographer must require long periods of stillness, beams at me.

"With a few words, you've managed to capture the essence of the sculptor's vision," he replies, and it is my turn to smile. "How I wish you could see one of his finished sculptures in France, in their intended locations in all their three-dimensional glory."

"Why, Mr. Steichen, are you inviting me on a naughty Parisian getaway?" I tease, and to my delight, Mr. Steichen's cheeks flame red.

"Oh, Miss Greene. I'm so, so—sorry," he stammers. "I wouldn't dare to suggest—"

I laugh. "I am only having a bit of fun, Mr. Steichen," I assure him, and then just as quickly, I turn the conversation back to the study of art. "Rodin's approach is very different than the classical and Renaissance sculptures I'm more familiar with."

The two men linger behind me, fielding questions from other gallery guests, while I study each sketch. I know they want me to admire the photographs and artwork alike, although what it might mean to have the imprimatur of the Morgan librarian, I don't know exactly.

"Shall we move on to the Matisse room?" Mr. Stieglitz asks.

As I follow him down the corridor, I notice that a couple trails behind us. They share the same studied expression, as if they are casually strolling around the gallery, but I can see that they're staying close, listening to the gallery owners as they talk about Rodin and Matisse.

When I step into the adjoining gallery room, I freeze. From the opposite wall, a single, vivid painting of a woman stares at me. In pulsating oranges, pinks, and greens, Matisse shows a forest with a lone nude figure. The landscape jettisons the hard-won three-dimensionality rediscovered in the Renaissance to create a strangely engaging two-dimensional image rife with patterns. I am mesmerized and confused all at once, because I have never seen anything like it.

Mr. Stieglitz blurts out, "What do you think?"

"Alfred!" Mr. Steichen chastises his partner.

I laugh. "It's fine, Mr. Steichen," I say. "There's no need to stand on ceremony with me, gentlemen. As I think you should know by now."

"So? What *do* you think?" This time, it's Mr. Steichen who asks.

I turn back to the painting. "As an art expert, I feel like I should comment on the groundbreaking way Matisse approaches the very traditional subject matter of the pastoral landscape—one I've seen over and over in classical and Renaissance paintings, but . . ." I pause.

"But what?" the men say together.

I turn to them. "To answer your question, I don't believe Matisse wants me to *think*, but to *feel*."

The men give each other a relieved, hopeful glance. "It seems you understand," Mr. Steichen says.

"I do. Perhaps one day we will imbue the Pierpont Morgan Library with some of this modern feeling," I say, thinking how 291 is only a few short blocks from the Pierpont Morgan Library, but very far away in the manner in which art is perceived and valued.

"We'd like nothing more," Mr. Steichen says.

After an hour lingering in the company of Matisse's other paintings and drawings, I thank the gentlemen for their invitation and time, and take my leave. It is after nine o'clock, and normally, I would be catching the trolley or the subway home. But ever since our return from Washington, DC, I've been working even longer hours. Uncle Mozart's words have stayed with me, and though I am convinced that the precautions I've taken have been enough to protect my secret, I am equally persuaded that massive success is a safeguard as well. And so, since I have returned from Gramma Fleet's funeral, I have worked on investigating key collections and forging relationships with important dealers so I can continue building Mr. Morgan's holdings, often not returning home until nine or ten o'clock, or later, if a social engagement requires it or I return to the office after an evening out.

Since I am just blocks from the library, I begin walking up Fifth Avenue. Even with the late hour, the streets are filled with couples strolling and friends moseying, everyone enjoying the warm spring evening.

But then, I hear, "Miss Greene, Miss Greene."

Startled, I turn to see Mr. Stieglitz calling out and running toward me. "I am," he pants, "so glad that I caught you." He presses a rectangular object in my hand.

"What is this?"

"A photograph of one of Rodin's sculptures. For one day."

I thank Mr. Stieglitz before I continue on my way, never saying aloud what I think. That "one day" will never come.

Even though I worked till after ten last night, I've been at my desk for at least two hours by the time Mr. Morgan arrives at the library. "Good morning, sir," I call out as usual.

Instead of poking his head into my office and regaling me with a vignette from the remainder of the evening at the Carnegies', from which I slipped out last night to attend the gallery event, he storms through the rotunda into his office without even a gruff greeting. He slams his door, something he's never done in the two years that I've worked with him.

What on earth is wrong?

I know better than to rush into his office. On those occasions when a business associate or an art dealer has angered him, Mr. Morgan prefers to be left alone and given time to let his fury abate.

So I return to the work piled high on my desk. Today I have to make a decision about an upcoming auction, and I turn my attention to this as I wait for Mr. Morgan to call me into his office. But an hour passes. And then another. Mr. Morgan does not surface or even appear at my door with a query, as is his wont. Even when the security guard knocks on his door to admit a delivery, Mr. Morgan does not answer. By the time the lunch hour passes, I am nonplussed. I cannot imagine what is going on.

I have a dilemma. Mr. Morgan and I were to speak today about the auction, and I cannot really put that discussion aside. Perhaps my presence will help him work through whatever or whoever has triggered his anger, and allow him to focus on library business.

Rising, I gather my papers and straighten my wool skirt before I cut across the rotunda to his office. Just as I lift my hand to knock on the intricately carved wooden door, I pause, feeling a sudden rush of anxiety wash over me. Could the "whoever" causing his anger possibly be me?

I cannot think of a disagreement that's simmered between us recently, so I shake the unsettled feeling away and knock. "Mr. Morgan? May I have a minute of your time to discuss the Sotheby's auction?"

There is silence.

There have been times when he has bellowed a "don't come in" to King, or even to one of his children. But what if Mr. Morgan isn't answering because he cannot? What if he's hurt in some way behind this closed door? I quickly push it open.

Mr. Morgan sits behind his desk on his lion's throne, his head down as if he's engrossed in a newspaper. I exhale, not realizing until that moment that I'd been holding my breath. He's fine; he's just chosen not to respond for some inexplicable reason.

I wait for him to look up, to acknowledge me in any way, but he does not. He doesn't even admonish me for entering his office without permission. Fear begins to take hold.

"I'm sorry for interrupting, Mr. Morgan," I say, after a few silent seconds pass. "It was so quiet in here that I became concerned about you."

"You were?" he asks, without looking up.

I frown. "Yes, of course. You've been behind closed doors all morning and we were supposed to discuss the Sotheby's items."

In a voice so low it's nearly inaudible, he asks, "Why should I meet with *you?*"

I don't understand his question, but I do know that something's very wrong. Mr. Morgan doesn't have a problem with an art dealer or a business associate or anyone else. His problem is with *me.*

You're playing on a level where the consequences of being outed will be much higher. Just remember this is J. P. Morgan you're dealing with.

My heart pounds. Over the last months, Uncle Mozart's words have haunted me, but I've pushed his warning aside. I believed I'd taken enough precautions and erected enough safeguards, but now I feel like I'm falling headlong from a great height. Did Mr. Morgan find out?

The room is eerily quiet, and I tremble because silence is a clear signal of Mr. Morgan's fury. I stand without moving, not wanting to utter a word. My thoughts race and swirl. What can I offer to defend myself from the rage and accusations that are coming? Through the years, Mama has given me several ways to deny the truth about my race, but at this moment, I can't remember a single one.

Finally, he speaks. "I've spent the morning searching the newspapers to see if I can find another article about you."

Did he discover my deception from a newspaper? Did Anne reveal my secret to a reporter so the whole world would know—including her father? Perhaps that was her goal after all.

I cannot open my mouth. I cannot speak to offer more lies about my background or to give him excuses for lying. I know I should just confess, apologize, and beg for his forgiveness and mercy. But fear has rendered me immobile.

"I'm usually a good judge of people," he says.

He finally meets my gaze. I try to swallow the lump that has formed in my throat.

"But it seems that I've misjudged you, Miss Greene."

Miss Greene. He hasn't called me that in months.

He holds out the newspaper to me, but I do not want to even touch it, let alone read it. Maybe I should just tell him the truth and try to convince him to spare me and my family, even though I doubt any words will turn the tide of his fury. While Mr. Morgan has been kind to me, I've overheard him in conversations disparaging everyone from Jews to Italians to the new Polish immigrants. And while I've been spared any overt disdain he may have for the colored in this country, I can't assume he doesn't have the same feelings about my people as he does for so many others.

"Take this," he orders, and I obey. The paper flutters in my trembling hands. "Read what's on page seven. In the middle column."

My breathing is shallow, but I must face this situation and take my punishment. As I focus on the article, I almost cry thinking of Mama and my siblings. All of their lives will be destroyed because of me. Louise and Ethel will lose their jobs, Russell and Teddy will have to drop out of school, and Mama—I cannot allow myself to think about this any further. Not right now.

I hold my breath as I read the brief article:

Is J. P. Morgan becoming a modernist, or worse, a Photo-Secessionist? A little birdie told this reporter at an exclusive event at 291 last night that the ultra-traditional titan of industry is considering branching out from collecting the medieval and Renaissance treasures for which he's famous. Bells chimed and cash registers chinged throughout the city at the heady notion of an Henri Matisse finding its way onto the Pierpont Morgan Library walls!

I blink and resist the urge to wipe my eyes to make sure I am seeing properly. This isn't good, of course, but it isn't the article I expected. Not at all. This article—little more than a gossip column about art rather than an exposé about my race—I *might* be able to survive.

"Who the hell do you think you are?" Mr. Morgan's voice is little more than a whisper.

I feel sick at his question and his voice, but I remind myself that at least he's not asking me that question literally. "Mr. Morgan, I have no idea why this is in the newspaper. Please believe me. I did not say this."

"You were at that blasted Two Ninety-One gallery last night, weren't you?"

"Yes, sir."

"I knew that reference to 'bells' in the column was a clever allusion to you."

"Yes, sir. It likely was." No sense denying it.

"They didn't pull this story out of thin air. Where the hell did it come from, if not you?"

I think about the gallery last night and cannot imagine Mr. Steichen or Mr. Stieglitz leaking a story such as this. But the gallery was filled with other people, and any one of them could have been a reporter who twisted my words enough to write this story. Even though I never said this.

"Someone must have overheard me, and taken my words out of context. I am so sorry, sir."

He doesn't seem to hear me, or perhaps what I say in this moment doesn't matter. He needs to rail. "The Pierpont Morgan Library is a preeminent traditional institution. And I will not have even an intimation that modernist garbage will hang on its walls, do you understand?"

Instead of denying it again, I say, "Yes, sir. And I'm sorry. It was a mistake to—"

He interrupts me. "You don't have the luxury of making mistakes, Miss Greene," he says without realizing how true his words are. "Not as long as you are my ambassador and you work for me."

Again, I say, "Yes, sir. I understand."

His eyes are dark when he peers at me. "There is something that you must never forget."

I nod.

"It is *my* name that is carved above this library's doors, not yours. And I never want to have to remind you of that again."

CHAPTER 15

It seems impossible that in seven months I've gone from the 291 incident to my first transatlantic trip. I step out of the carriage, past the bustle of elegant, somberly dressed Londoners, and walk into the opulent Langham lobby, with its gilt-topped marble pillars and its towering sprays of exotic flowers more lavish even than the *Mauretania*, the beautiful ocean liner upon which Mama and I sailed from New York to London. When I spin around to see Mama's reaction, she is beaming as a bevy of bellmen descend upon her to assist with her bags. She's impressed, and that makes me smile. Despite my initial misgivings, I know I've made the right choice by inviting her to be my chaperone on this important trip.

In our suite, we collapse on our plush beds in laughter at our luck. I think how girlish my mother seems. Her face looks lighter, younger even, as the deep mourning that had settled upon her has lifted.

But the familiar Mama resurfaces in a flash as she rises and orders me to work. "Let's get your new dresses out of these trunks before they wrinkle any further."

Together, we unfold and shake out the dresses. Before the trip, I had splurged on three new gowns, knowing that if I was to impress the English dealers, collectors, and curators, I must look the part of Mr. Morgan's representative, in these meetings more than any other.

As we hang the dresses in the armoire, I reflect on the last seven months with Mr. Morgan. I've logged countless hours at the library and amassed a trove of delightful acquisitions—never the wished-for Caxton, though—but I wasn't certain that I'd worked my way back into his good graces until he asked me to take this trip to pick up several items he'd purchased during his annual trek to London. How grateful I am to have his trust again.

Still, I am fixated on performing well here. Not only will I bring back Mr. Morgan's pieces, but he has given me license to make purchases on my own initiative. I have targeted a rare, stupendous collection of Caxtons that are to be auctioned this coming week. It does not contain *Le Morte Darthur*, but still, it will turn Mr. Morgan's Caxton collection into one of the largest in the world and, more importantly, make Mr. Morgan proud. And I plan for it to be a surprise.

Mama smooths and hangs the vivid violet dress, which I especially adore. While it bears fashionable lace trim detail, I had instructed the dressmaker to otherwise use a streamlined classical style—without any bulky layers or fussy features—making it, I hope, versatile for both work and social occasions. "I don't know why you choose these audacious colors, Belle."

"Mama, I will never blend in with my peers. Those men will always perceive me as different, as an outsider. Because I am a woman, or . . ." I trail off, then take a deep breath before I continue. "I've come to believe that the best path to success is by embracing my gender, Mama. Flaunting it even"—those words make Mama flinch—"rather than trying to hide. Then once I have their focus, I demonstrate my skills and knowledge."

Mama's expression grows alarmed. "Should you really draw so much attention to yourself, Belle?"

"It's not as if I can hide the fact that I'm a woman by wearing dowdy dresses."

"But if you invite their stares, what else might they scrutinize?"

Uncle Mozart and the scare I had with Mr. Morgan have filled me with enough anxiety; I do not need Mama to add her worries. I know I'm walking a tightrope, but what else can I do? I'm committed to this pathway. "They see the shade of my skin no matter what I'm wearing. And strange as it might sound, dressing boldly is like hiding in plain sight. Because no one can imagine that a colored girl would be so brazen."

She shakes her head. "I'll never understand your approach, Belle. But then I don't understand the fascination you and Mr. Morgan have with all of these old books. Maybe I can appreciate those illuminated manuscripts the monks labored over, but not those printed volumes—the Caxtons—that you've come to London for."

I explain to Mama that in the late fourteen hundreds, an English merchant and diplomat named William Caxton used the new printing technology invented by Johannes Gutenberg twenty years prior to make the first English-language books. "After all," I point out, "Caxton not only made available a larger range of texts to English speakers but unified the English language. His books are important for not only historical and literary significance but also linguistic."

"I guess it does make some sense, Belle. But why do you need so many of them?" she persists.

"Mama, if we can combine the sixteen Caxtons on offer at the auction with the volumes we already have, it will go far in establishing the institution's preeminence."

As soon as I make plain that my planned purchase will heighten the library's standing—and therefore my own—she understands, and asks no more questions. Nothing is more important to her than her children's success, after all.

But I don't tell her about my unorthodox plan to bring the Caxton trophies home to New York City, a scheme that requires I woo the wealthy Lord Amherst with a compelling proposition. It is a daring scheme that would trouble my rule-abiding mother. But in order to continue to build back my worth to Mr. Morgan, I must take risks I wouldn't have chanced before.

Even though Mama and I have only two hours between unpacking and my first appointment, we are determined to see something of the city. We undertake a brisk stroll on Bond and Oxford Streets to orient ourselves and get a brief taste of London; Mama and I feel giddy at the very idea that we are in Europe.

What I expected most from this trip was to be astonished by the centuries-old history that courses through its buildings and streets and rivers like blood pumping through veins. I'd readied myself for the amazement I'd experience taking in the vast art collections, layered with medieval masters and Dutch geniuses and gifted modern portraitists. I'd even planned to be awestruck by the wealth and privilege of the English capital and its citizens, understanding that no amount of time with the Morgans and the affluent of New York City could serve as an adequate preparation for the British.

But I could not have guessed London's greatest gift. Here, as I walk the streets, I don't feel the same assessment of my color that I routinely experience, and constantly anticipate, in America. Perhaps London's citizens don't have the same need to categorize us by race as they do in America.

Is this because slavery has been illegal in Great Britain for over seventy years, and thus the sort of formalized segregation we are beginning to experience in America does not exist? Or is it because the entrenched nature of the British class system means that one's status is more important than one's race? Since Mama and I look the part of well-heeled society women, will we be accorded that position automatically here, even though our skin isn't as fair as most English citizens'? I don't know the answers, but I feel a sense of relief and freedom to which I'm not accustomed.

By the time Mama and I stroll back to the Langham Hotel, I feel emboldened for my crucial meeting with Lord Amherst. Rather than gathering at his London home, where the power will tip in his favor, I organized teatime in the hotel dining room, with Mama joining us for the first pot of tea, and then excusing herself as I order the second. Propriety dictates that a chaperone be present, at least for part of our meeting.

As Mama and I enter the dining room, we receive appreciative glances from the male guests. I imagine we make a handsome pair; I'm in my striking new violet gown, and Mama wears a complementary plum-colored tailored skirt suit with a waist-length jacket, which I purchased for her for this trip.

We follow the maître d' to the table where Lord Amherst awaits, and I think how different Mama is here. Not only is the doleful expression of her mourning gone, but she laughs. Not only does she speak, she chats. I even heard her humming this morning, something I do not recall ever hearing her do before. And when we talk, her words aren't constantly filled with reprimands and warnings about my behavior or regrets about Gramma Fleet. I sense that, like me, Mama is enjoying the freedom London offers.

The maître d' gestures to a table where a silver-haired, distinguished-looking gentleman is waiting for us, and I see that Lord Amherst is precisely as he'd been described to me, extremely proper in his demeanor and manners. We exchange pleasantries about our transatlantic trip and the London weather before discussing business. From the start, even in our innocuous exchanges about the auction, he is defensive about having to sell off his library. The gossips whisper that financial reasons necessitate the sale, though I have also heard that he is spending his vast fortune on Egyptian antiquities.

After I order the second pot of tea, Mama excuses herself. I sip my chamomile, and then remark, "I understand that it must be hard to part with the Caxtons."

He looks down at his empty cup. "Yes, Miss Greene. It certainly is."

"I hope you understand, Lord Amherst, that if the Pierpont Morgan Library should be the lucky purchasers of your Caxtons, they would be a treasured part of our collection."

"Is that so?"

"Yes, in fact, together with the Caxtons that the Pierpont Morgan Library already owns, they would be a centerpiece."

"Mr. Morgan is rumored to have a vast and varied collection, and it is hard to fathom that the Caxtons would be so central."

"Oh, but they would." I meet his eyes. "Lord Amherst, since I was a young girl, I've been entranced by early books. The sight of them, the smell of them, the wonderful feel of their covers and pages, and the thrill of the places to which they've traveled and the barriers they've crossed. And no early book holds as much magic for me as the Caxtons."

He holds my gaze. "What do you propose, Miss Greene?"

"Lord Amherst, I would be delighted to offer you an excellent price for the Caxtons right now before the auction even begins. And if we could reach an agreement, then you needn't put them in the auction at all. I imagine that might be easier for you."

I place the carefully worded offer I've prepared in front of him. He doesn't make a move to pick it up, and I hope I haven't made a mistake.

You don't have the luxury of making mistakes, Miss Greene.

I shake Mr. Morgan's words from my mind. I do have one more ploy to try, no doubt an audacious one, but paired with the very generous offer I just made, it might work.

"I would hate to have traveled all this way only to return home empty-handed. In fact, I might become so despondent that I would be unable to attend the auction at all," I say, my eyes downcast.

He has many objets d'art and books listed in the catalog. The recusal of the Pierpont Morgan Library would affect the ultimate amount paid for those as well. Mr. Morgan is known for bidding high on many objects, and the others at the auction will likely assume I'll do the same, thereby artificially increasing the prices.

He pauses, speechless. Suddenly he reaches across the table for the piece of paper I offered him and stands. "I'll telegraph you my decision, here at the hotel." Then he storms out of the hotel dining room.

I sign the bill, then I retire to my hotel room. I may seem calm, but I refuse to attend the theater with Mama as we'd planned. I do not want to miss Lord Amherst's telegram. But the hours tick by without a messenger. I wait until noon the following day before deciding to keep an appointment at the Victoria and Albert Museum. There, along with Mama, in the company of an all-male cadre of scholars, dealers, and curators, I converse with fellow art realm professionals who, for once, seem interested not in my gender or the nebulous shade of my skin, but instead in my opinions.

"How do you think the painters of these portrait miniatures would feel about their images being separated from the handwritten books they were meant to illustrate?" Mr. George Durlacher, of the prominent dealer Durlacher Brothers, asks as we tour the Victoria and Albert's renowned collection of portrait miniatures.

"I think that painters knew that the portraits might be taken apart from the book itself and used for other purposes, such as making introductions to one another or as a sign of favor. A luminary like Simon Bening might not like it but must have understood it came with the territory." I gesture to a long case brimming with gorgeous miniatures. "But perhaps we might display them with their original books for context. It might be more illuminating for the visitors."

"Interesting thought," Arthur Banks Skinner, director of the museum and our tour guide, says. "You must return for a tour of the new building when it is complete this summer—the Aston Webb building. I'd welcome your thoughts on the way the portrait collection is displayed within its structure."

"I'd like nothing more. Be careful what you offer, however; I might just take you up on your invitation," I say with a flirtatious laugh. "But it wouldn't be fair to share my insights only on one side of the Atlantic, would it?"

In the days that follow, I jettison the notion of waiting for Lord Amherst's reply, and instead inform the Langham of my daily whereabouts in case the elusive telegram arrives. My days are filled with invitations to collections and lunches and dinner parties with dealers I know only by reputation or letters—Mr. George Williamson and Mr. Joseph Fitzhenry among them—and curators like Mr. Charles Hercules Read, keeper of the British Museum's Department of British and Mediaeval Antiquities. Befriending these gentlemen is a professional necessity, but they make me feel welcome in a way that New York City dealers and curators never do, and even offer insights on how to manage those "crass" art men from New York, particularly since some of the dealers have opened branches in New York. I know these men will go to any length to outbid me at auction. But they understand that I'll do the same, and we arrive at a professional camaraderie regardless.

On our second-to-last evening, the night before the auction, Mama and I dine with the gentlemen. Having received no word from Lord Amherst, I've given up hope that he will sell me the Caxtons directly; I'll have to cast my lot with the others at the auction. I conclude that I have taken my newfound confidence a few steps too far with Lord Amherst, and while I will learn from my misstep, I cannot let the failure clip my wings. And anyway, even without the Caxtons, the trip has been a success in other ways—I've procured all of Mr. Morgan's artwork to bring back to New York, and I've made all of these important connections.

I enjoy myself, watching Mama open up more tonight and charm the gentlemen with her slow, elegant drawl and manners. How enticing she must have been to my father as a young, cultured woman.

What would he think of Mama now? What would he think about me? Would he be proud of my success? Or would he lament my passing as white, feeling that I'd let down not only him but all our people?

"What are your plans for the auction tomorrow? Has your famous Mr. Morgan given you a long shopping list of items to procure?" Fitz asks, interrupting my slightly maudlin musing.

When Mr. Joseph Fitzhenry first requested I call him by the nickname all the dealers use for him, Mama had bristled at the idea. But as our London days progressed and she witnessed the importance of my social connections to my work—and the attendant importance of equal treatment in their ranks—she acquiesced. Indeed, she began calling them by their Christian names as well.

"Let me guess," George W. interjects. Given that we have two Georges in our group, Mr. George Durlacher and Mr. George Williamson, a consensus has been reached that we should call them George D. and George W. "Mr. Morgan wants you to secure the Mazarin Bible?"

It is an excellent guess, given Mr. Morgan's well-known predilection for collecting Gutenbergs. The Mazarin Bible to which George W. refers, printed by Gutenberg in 1450, was found in the Mazarin Library in Paris, hence the name.

"Ah, the Mazarin Bible is a treasure indeed. I wish that he sent me here to bring it back to New York. But alas, no, Mr. Morgan is satisfied with his current inventory of Gutenbergs. For the moment, anyway."

"How casually she speaks of her Gutenberg Bible collection!" George D. exclaims. The other men chuckle.

Of the 180 copies of the Gutenberg Bible printed, each different from the other, only fifty remain. The fact that Mr. Morgan owns two is legendary.

"How I wish he wanted a third," I answer.

Chatter about the auction overtakes the room, each dealer talking about his clients' or his institutions' interests. Everyone wants to know what everyone else will be bidding on, a way for each to begin to strategize, I suppose. The waiters clear the final dinner course and begin pouring coffee and tea in preparation for dessert. The maître d' walks over to our table, an envelope in his hand.

"Miss Greene?" he asks.

"Yes, that's me," I answer.

"I have a telegram for you." He hands me the envelope.

"Last-minute instructions from New York?" Fitz asks, a glimmer in his eye. I've become quite fond of the portly dealer, who is as funny as he is fierce.

I answer only with my smile and wait until he's engrossed in another conversation to slice open the envelope with a silver knife. My hands shake in anticipation, and the telegram flies out of the envelope, nearly falling on the floor before I catch it.

It is from Lord Amherst. He accepts my offer.

"Intriguing instructions?" George D. inquires.

"Something like that," I say, and have to prevent myself from beaming.

Glancing at the group to ensure they aren't listening, he drops his voice nearly to a whisper. "Will you promise me something, Miss Greene?"

"How many times have I asked you to call me Belle?" I tease him. Something about his ruddy cheeks and wiry, unkempt gray hair endears him to me. "After all, your lot has insisted that I call you by your given names."

"True enough, Belle." He struggles with the name, and I can see the familiarity doesn't sit well with the proper Englishman. "Back to that promise I was going to extract from you."

"Of course." I turn my attention to him. I only hope the request will not be of a romantic nature. While I've found that a bit of flirtation helps ease business dealings, particularly since I cannot smoke cigars and drink after-dinner brandy to establish a rapport like my colleagues can, I like this Englishman and don't want to have to reject his advances.

"Will you promise you won't bid against me for the Caxtons at the auction tomorrow?" His tone is pleading and his eyes beseeching, and if I hadn't been so ambitious and didn't have this compulsion to succeed—and if I hadn't already swept the Caxton collection out from under the auction—I might have been persuaded.

How to reply? I cannot reveal my triumph, but I've grown to respect these men, and would prefer not to lie or demur. Then suddenly, the perfect response strikes me.

"Yes, I promise not to bid against you *tomorrow*," I say, with emphasis. And it is true.

I will not break my word to Lord Amherst or this gentleman. I will be at the auction, and only there will he discover that I have no need to bid against him because I've already won the auction's prize—and, I hope, Mr. Morgan's full trust along with it.

CHAPTER 16

The carriage races down the crowded city streets, which seem dirtier and more ragtag after my days in London, jostling over the bumpy mix of materials that comprise its surfaces. I clutch the heavy box containing the Caxtons, knowing that I cannot risk damage to this bounty before I can show it to Mr. Morgan. I am so eager to return triumphant to the Pierpont Morgan Library, trophy in hand.

As the carriage pulls up to the library, I imagine this is how it must have felt to be a Roman emperor who paraded in triumph with overflowing carts piled high with gold and marble plunder trailing in his wake. Despite the heaviness of the Caxtons' crate, I stride up the wide stairs to the heavy bronze doors that stand guard, feeling as though my power is no longer borrowed from Mr. Morgan but my very own. I believe this prize in my hands will deliver it to me.

Before I even bang the door knocker, the bronze door opens. "It is our returning warrior!"

It is Mr. Morgan. I don't think I have ever seen him answer the door himself.

Striding into the marble foyer as if I've grown accustomed to having one of the most powerful men in America open the door for me, I say, "I come bearing gifts. The spoils of war, if you will."

"Of course! I read your telegram," he says, referring to the wire I sent him just before Mama and I boarded the *Mauretania* to return home. Mr. Morgan rubs his hands together in expectation. "Let's have a look at your prize."

We walk side by side, our heels clattering against the variegated marble. Even though I've examined the elaborate foyer ceiling hundreds of times, it catches my attention because the gilt edging around the ceiling fresco seems to gleam particularly bright and the colors look unusually vibrant. Strange how new and fresh the library seems after spending time steeped in the history-laden streets and buildings of London, and how incongruous the pristine library is against the grittiness of New York.

He gestures to a place on the floor for me to put down the box and begins to clear his desk. In seconds, I wrench off the lid and spread out the Caxtons on his desktop. "Holiday presents, if you like," I say calmly, though that is not how I feel; my victorious return has made me feel relieved and elated.

Lifting the *Recuyell of the Historyes of Troye* Caxton, he studies the cover, and then opens to the first page. His breath catches as he examines this first example of a printed book in English.

His eyes are shining. "I feel like we should be heralding your return with a ticker tape parade."

"I'm so glad you're pleased," I answer modestly. Mr. Morgan rarely expresses delight on this scale.

"Pleased?" He laughs. "I'm thrilled by your coup." Then he arches an eyebrow at me. "Even though it's not the Caxton that I want." He smiles. "In you, I have many things, but among them is an agent capable of dealing with the most challenging of owners—an aristocrat down on his luck. Not to mention, in you, I also have an agent capable of outwitting the trickiest of dealers. Those London dealers may seem the essence of politeness, but underneath it all, they are consummate swindlers, more masterful than any on our side of the pond."

"Maybe dealers on both sides of the pond have finally met their match."

He guffaws and asks for details of my dealings with Lord Amherst and my time with the London dealers and curators. I had, of course, written him extensively on both topics, but he wants the tales firsthand. I regale him with the story of my appointment with the Caxtons' owner, my museum visits and meals with the dealers, and my favorite moment, that final dinner in which I received the telegram and the promise I had to concoct for George D. about bidding at the auction.

"Well, this certainly explains the glowing letters I received from the dealers as you sailed home."

I froze. Was he being facetious? "They weren't angry?"

"To the contrary. They would've liked the Caxtons, of course, but they respect your prowess. How did Fitz put it?" He pauses. "Ah yes. He said that I finally have a worthy representative, who shares my skill in the art of negotiation. One that taught the old British dogs some new tricks."

We beam at each other, and when he reaches for my hand, I clasp back. "You are no mere librarian, Belle," he whispers.

I glance up at the towering figure, and when he pulls me closer, the confusion in his eyes matches my uncertainty. It has been a year since we had that moment in my office, and although I have caught him giving me lingering glances, we've neither mentioned nor shared another, similar moment. *Is he rethinking the nature of our relationship? Am I?*

My heart hammers as our lips inch closer. But then, voices echo throughout the foyer, reverberating into the study. I release his hand and step back. "Who is here?"

Taking a deep breath, he says, "I nearly forgot about them." He clears his throat, and his authoritative tone returns, although he is speaking quietly. "It is only Mr. and Mrs. Bernard Berenson, here from Italy to visit the collection."

"They were in the library this entire time?" I ask, wondering what they might have overheard. The acoustics in the Pierpont Morgan Library are such that the sounds from one room are perceptible in another. But then, the frisson that passed between us was of a visual, physical nature, not audible.

"Yes, engrossed in the objets d'art, I hope."

Appeased, the names of the guests reappear in my mind, and I ask, "Bernard Berenson, the writer? The Italian art expert?" The book Papa had given to me on my tenth birthday, *The Venetian Painters of the Renaissance*, was written by an author of the same name. And through the years, another book on Florentine painters in the Renaissance period that had fueled my love of the art and books of that era was also written by a Bernard Berenson.

"The same. He's also a curator of sorts, helping guide collectors with their purchases"—he grins—"not unlike you, although you have many other talents, of course. His main patron is that irritating Isabella Stewart Gardner in Boston, where he's from, and he styles himself as the preeminent authority on Italian Renaissance art."

Mr. Morgan has had little actual exposure to Mrs. Gardner, but it was enough that she had a private art collection that people were discussing favorably. He does not like competition.

"Why is he here if his most important patron is in Boston?"

"I believe he is trying to scrounge up new business. Ostensibly, though, he and his wife are giving lectures in the region and seeing important collections."

"His wife is a writer, too?" I'm surprised to find another woman in this realm.

"No, but she has some artistic expertise about which she lectures. Damned annoying woman, though, if you ask me. No charm." He sighs. "But Anne attended a dinner with them recently and arranged for Mrs. Berenson to give a speech at the Colony Club. No surprise she invited them to call on us and see the library. What could I say?" he asks with a slight shrug.

I am not surprised. Given the ever-growing divergence in political and social views between Anne and Mr. Morgan, he's always looking for common ground and ways to please his youngest child.

"I guess I could have raised the rumors to Anne as a means of objecting to this meeting," he says, almost to himself.

"What rumors?"

He leans closer to say, "A few years back, when we were searching for a new head of the Met"—Mr. Morgan sits on the board of the Metropolitan Museum of Art and is involved in major decision making—"Berenson's name came up. But there was some scuttlebutt about his ties to a forger. By the time the allegations were largely disproved, the decision about the director had already been made. Maybe that explains why Berenson has been critical of a few of my purchases, the Raphael in particular. But I'm trying to put all that aside today. For Anne. Berenson would have never worked out as the head of the Met anyway," he adds.

"Why?"

His eyebrows furrow. "Because he's a Jew," he spits in a tone that I've heard from him before. "Or is rumored to be one anyway, though that is not what Berenson claims."

Inside, I sigh. Anti-Semitism is as rampant as racism against the colored in this country.

The voices escalate in volume, as does the clatter of footsteps in the foyer. A woman's voice calls out for Mr. Morgan, but he doesn't respond. Finally, a man steps into the study, full of apologies for the interruption. He is a thin, handsome man of average height, with gray-green eyes that are covered by tiny circular glasses, and a closely trimmed chestnut-colored mustache and beard. I am struck with an overwhelming, inexplicable sense of familiarity. The sensation disappears when I am distracted by the entrance of a smiling woman, larger than the man but with the same intelligent, curious mien.

Mr. Morgan takes one small step toward them, and says, "Mr. and

Mrs. Berenson, I'd like to introduce you to my personal librarian, Miss Belle da Costa Greene. She has just returned from a victorious trip to London, where she stole a cache of priceless Caxtons out from under the nose of Lord Amherst himself." His expression resembles nothing so much as that of a proud parent, and I think how wildly our relationship vacillates within the span of a few minutes.

Mrs. Berenson greets me first, and then her husband follows. "Miss Greene," he says, taking my hand, "it is truly a pleasure to make your acquaintance. Even across the Atlantic, we have heard tales of your acumen with manuscripts and your formidable skills as a negotiator."

"Your reputation precedes you as well, Mr. Berenson," I respond, delighted to meet one of my favorite authors.

Mrs. Berenson chimes in before her husband can even speak, "Oh, Bernard has developed quite the expertise in Renaissance art on both sides of the Atlantic. He's too modest to describe his successes and credentials, but I'm always delighted to share them."

Her statements sound practiced, and I wonder if this is their usual, falsely humble way of introducing Mr. Berenson's prominence into conversations. She sounds more like a business associate than a spouse.

"So I understand," I say. "But that is not the renown to which I am referring. I was actually introduced to Mr. Berenson and his prowess when I was gifted his first book as a little girl."

"You read my Venetian art book as a child?" He looks genuinely surprised.

"I did indeed."

"Well, even though that makes me feel quite old," he chuckles, "that's quite impressive, Miss Greene. Those theories and observations are rather sophisticated."

"What can I say?" I shrug. "I was precocious."

Mr. Berenson and I smile at each other, and he holds my gaze. For a moment, it feels like Mr. Berenson and I are alone, and then Mr. Morgan clears his throat.

I look away, feeling embarrassed at allowing my eyes to linger on a married man in the presence of his wife. *How mortified Mama would be.*

A somewhat awkward silence settles onto the room, and I must change the tenor. I force a laugh and say, "Well, Mr. Berenson, it seems as though this isn't exactly an introduction. Apparently, I've known you since I was ten."

CHAPTER 17

I stare around the room, thinking how much fun it will be to share every detail of this affair with Teddy. A Red Party. Who could dream up an entire evening dedicated to the color red? Women wear elaborate gowns in every shade of red—vermilion, crimson, deep maroon, coral, even delicate rose—myself among them in an unusual cerise gown I bought in London. With its high-waisted, swathed bodice, squared neckline, and just enough of a train to draw attention, I feel quite striking in it.

When I first received the invitation from the well-known art dealer Joseph Duveen and his wife, I'd assumed the vast expanse of red would stop at the women's attire. How wrong I'd been. Every object in the room, from the carpet to the newly hung silk wallpaper to the furniture, the china, the flowers, and the food, is a shade of red. Even the paintings hanging on the damask garnet walls feature primary reds.

How I wish Mr. Morgan were at my side. We would laugh together over the overabundance of red, much as we occasionally chuckle over the layers of vermilion in his office. But while I wish for his companionship, I no longer need his presence or an escort; I now have my own cadre of acquaintances with whom I can and must mingle. My own enemies, as Mr. Morgan likes to refer to them.

Archer Huntington and his mother, Arabella, wave to me, and I make my way around the periphery of the dance floor to the side of the fabulously wealthy widow of the American industrialist Collis Huntington, who pioneered western railroads. As I move, I leave a trail of stares and whispers in my wake. The guests don't think I see or hear them, but it is impossible not to *feel* their curiosity and sometimes even their disdain. Two years ago, this would have had me glancing over my shoulder or wondering what they were questioning: the dusty tint of my skin or the strangeness of my clothes?

Tonight, I still feel it, but I have no cares. With the help of Teddy's magazines, my own developed fashion sense, and a sizable budget for clothing that comes from my increased salary, I'm as well dressed as any of these peacocks, with my own unique sense of style. As for my complexion, after that scare with Mr. Morgan, I am now more confident that my secret is safe. He believes me to be white, therefore I don't care about others' conjectures. No one would dare utter a word of their suspicions and risk Mr. Morgan's ire. Only Anne has dared to challenge his verdict, but I've had no more of Anne's suppositions as of late. After all, she's a woman with secrets, and just like me, she should be careful throwing stones.

"How are you, Belle?" Mrs. Huntington asks when I reach her and Archer. Mrs. Huntington, sometimes described as the richest woman in America, is a rabid collector of paintings, antiques, rare books, and jewelry. I often face her representatives in fierce competition across the auction house floor, but we manage to shed that combative approach in social settings.

Very few are as knowledgeable about art as this still-beautiful woman in her middle years. I enjoy exchanging art world gossip with her, and we respect each other.

"Can you believe this crimson extravagance?" she asks with a scoff. Her disdain is curious as her beribboned gown may contain more shades of red than anyone else's, and from her ears to her neck to her wrists, she is covered in rubies. Not to mention that her son's suit is a deep oxblood. "In my day, none of this display was necessary. People knew other people's worth without a show."

"Or by the art on people's walls and shelves," I add.

"Exactly," she agrees with an emphatic nod. "Your Mr. Morgan understands that."

"He does indeed."

She pivots the conversation toward a rumor she's heard about our host and his brother Henry, joint owners of Duveen Brothers, powerful, aggressive art dealers with offices in New York, London, and Paris. Gossip, it seems, has been spreading throughout the ladies' teatimes about a possible forgery that Duveen Brothers sold to a widow in Mrs. Huntington's set.

As I share my plan to continue to do business with the Duveens, but to be cautious of any possible duplicity, I see Mr. Berenson. He is deep in conversation with Joseph Duveen himself.

Only now do I realize I've been searching for him from the moment I arrived, hoping that he would be attending. He seems different than during our brief encounter at the Pierpont Morgan Library. There, he'd appeared familiar and intelligent, a fellow art lover and collector, but diminished somehow in proximity to Mr. Morgan. Here, he shines with a vividness that sets him apart even in this sea of crimson. He alone wears the traditional black-and-white evening suit, with only a red silk pocket square as his nod to this evening's theme. He's not the tallest or most handsome man in the room, but something about him captivates. Could it be all those childhood days spent in the company of his words, laid out so eloquently on the pages of his art books?

Even though I turn my attention back to Mrs. Huntington, I watch Mr. Berenson in my peripheral vision. He and Mr. Duveen are standing quite close, almost gesticulating in each other's faces. Mrs. Berenson is leaning so far in, she is nearly touching the two men in her efforts to listen.

I've been curious about the Berensons from the moment we met, and over the last few days, I've uncovered quite a bit about the couple. They've been married for eight years, since Mrs. Berenson's first husband died, although she'd been separated from him for years and it was rumored that she'd been having an affair with Bernard during the entirety of that separation, which I found intriguing. Her only children, two daughters, are from her first husband, Frank Costelloe. I also learned that Mr. Berenson, the Boston Brahmin, Harvard-educated aesthete, is not Jewish, as Mr. Morgan claimed; he is Roman Catholic.

Mrs. Huntington breaks into my thoughts. "Shall we partake of the red feast?" she asks, a glint of disapproval mixed with curiosity in her eyes. As usual, her son nods but adds little to the exchange.

We turn away from the Berensons and Duveens toward the walnut dining table, so enormous that it could seat forty people. An extraordinary repast spreads before us. However, I have no idea what to select because I cannot discern one dish from the next except by shape, and even then, it is a challenge. Every object on the table—the meats, the breads, the vegetables, the fruits—has been dyed red.

As I listen to Mrs. Huntington guess at the real nature of the scarlet foodstuffs, I feel rather than see someone draw close to me. A shiver passes through me, and before I even turn around to ascertain the newcomer's identity, I know who it is.

"A pleasure to see you again, Miss Greene. And so soon," Mr. Berenson says.

His eyes, a glimmering shade almost like grisaille, have an extraordinary effect on me, and I feel pulled into his gaze. It takes me a long beat to look away, and I answer with as blasé a tone as I can muster, "It's nice to see you as well, Mr. Berenson."

As he bows toward me, I study him. His fastidious evening suit and well-groomed, aristocratic features are background to the intensity of his intelligent eyes, and I find this disparity peculiar. In my, albeit limited, experience, patrician gentlemen are rarely deeply curious; the softness of their lives dulls the possibility of a more academic nature. The blue-blooded Mr. Morgan is an exception, and perhaps this Mr. Berenson is as well.

"You look lovely this evening. The cut of your dress is unusual, simple and yet eye-catching," he says, making an unusually astute observation about clothes for a man. Although, I suppose, Bernard Berenson is known for his uncommon eye.

I've received many compliments from many men, but none have made my cheeks warm this way. "Thank you."

"It was a delight to see you in your natural habitat," he adds, "the Pierpont Morgan Library." He says this with a grin, and if he were a single man, I would say he was flirting with me. But he is a married man, with his wife in this very room, so I'm not certain how to read his manner or his words. Even the most lascivious society men I've encountered obey the unspoken rule to remain proper in their wives' presence.

"I wasn't sure if you would be here tonight. Or your wife, of course," I say, stepping away from the dining area and taking my leave of the Huntingtons. Mr. Berenson follows me, and we stand together.

He nods. "Yes, we try to take in as many attractions as we can when we're in the States. There is so much this country has to offer, such as this madcap celebration of a single hue. I can think of many Renaissance artists who would have adored this display—Sandro Botticelli for one. He loved a deeply saturated carmine shade." He smiles at a private memory, then asks, "Have you seen the sumptuous red paint he uses in his *Primavera*?"

His smile is warm and engaging, and I can't help but grin thinking of the legendary Renaissance master Sandro Botticelli strolling through this room, gawking at the parade of red. But before I can respond that I've never seen the famous Botticelli painting in the flesh—or confess that I've never even been to Italy—Mr. Berenson changes the subject. "The Pierpont Morgan Library has amassed an impressive collection of manuscripts."

"It has been my honor to continue what Mr. Morgan started," I say with a societally expected deference that I don't really feel. I know the value I've added to the library collection.

"You don't give yourself enough credit. I am aware of the scatter-shot manner in which your patron amassed books and manuscripts before you became his personal librarian—a Gutenberg Bible here, a common Elizabeth Barrett Browning book there. You have swooped in and expanded the disparate volumes into a formidable collection that has the potential to rival the best museums." He nods as if his declaration has become fact. "It is most impressive, Miss Greene."

My cheeks must be the color of the gowns circling this room, they are so hot from his praise, so unlike the usual superficial compliments I receive. Bernard Berenson is the very man who practically reignited the current interest by collectors and museums alike in Italian Renaissance artwork. His words are high praise.

"I hope I've done justice to the treasures in my care."

He chortles. "No need for false modesty with me, Miss Greene. You've done much more than justice to the volumes you've acquired and those you've inherited in your role as librarian. You've united them so they tell a cohesive story about the importance of the written word—the Caxton purchase, in particular, was genius. When I think back to my days as a boy at the Boston Public Library, marveling at the thousands of volumes at my disposal and imagining how those books could change my life, I know that none of that would have been possible without printers like Caxton who made the written word available to the masses. The Morgan book collection—in your care—will tell that story."

I am moved by his deep comprehension of what I'm trying to accomplish, all the more so because, in this moment, his words and tone and message sound like my father's. It is an understanding of my work that I've never heard anyone articulate, not even Mr. Morgan, and I feel *seen*. His sentiment softens the criticism of my patron implicit in Mr. Berenson's compliments, statements I find strange because it would serve him well to gain Mr. Morgan's favor.

He nods in appreciation of me, and then his voice grows thick and quiet as he continues. "Mr. Morgan is fortunate to have you at his side. But you must make sure he doesn't get in your way as you turn the book collection into a scholarly masterpiece that has a critical narrative to tell not only experts but the common man, if the collection is ever made available to them. I'd hate to have him hinder you with the books as he has with the paintings."

No matter Mr. Berenson's flattery, I can no longer ignore the critique of Mr. Morgan; it is too blatant. He and I have grown even closer over the last few months, and I cannot bear to have him denounced in any way. I am the library's protector, after all, which means that I have to protect *him*. "What do you mean, Mr. Berenson?" My voice is as hard and cold as ice, and any flush of warmth left on my cheeks from Mr. Berenson's praise disappears.

My reaction to his words registers, and he says, "I didn't mean to offend. The library certainly has its masterpieces."

"Yes, it does. The luminosity of the Francesco Francia *Madonna and Child* is undeniable."

"True enough. But the Pratovecchio *Virgin and Child*? The perspective doesn't have the same expertise as other Renaissance paintings. With your eye, you could ensure that the library artwork echoes Mr. Morgan's Renaissance-inspired walls and decor. I'd love to see a Perugino or Botticelli on those red walls, so the paintings match the quality of the book collection you've assembled. You deserve to be surrounded by art equal to your talent." He pauses. "And beauty."

I am perplexed by Mr. Berenson's frank speech; most art world experts talk about Mr. Morgan in reverential tones. Since Mr. Berenson's work focuses, in large part, on giving acquisition advice to wealthy collectors, I imagine it would behoove Mr. Berenson to forge a relationship with Mr. Morgan, but his comments about the library flatter me alone. Is he trying to woo Mr. Morgan by appealing to my expertise? Or does he assume that he will never work for Mr. Morgan because of his relationship with Mrs. Gardner, and thus is he simply trying to woo me? Regardless of Mr. Berenson's motives, he is correct about the library's paintings—even though I'd never admit that out loud—and I've often found myself having thoughts similar to those he's espousing. Somehow I feel alive in his presence, as if all things are possible.

He continues, "How I would welcome the opportunity to tour you around the countryside of Italy, to show you the true masterpieces of the Renaissance in situ—"

Just then Mrs. Berenson appears, the very moment I'd begun to imagine myself in the Italian countryside on her husband's arm. Her long-chinned face is open and eager, and she seems pleased to see me, making me feel terrible for the scene I'd just envisioned. She is wearing an elegantly cut cherry-red gown. With its high collar and long sleeves, it is a modest dress that would surely meet with Mama's approval.

"What a delight to make your acquaintance twice in the span of one week, Miss Greene." With her thick waist and booming voice, she is the polar opposite of her finer-boned, slender husband.

I smile graciously. "Yes, it certainly is. I've heard from Miss Morgan that your lecture at the Colony Club about Florentine paintings was masterful. She thinks the world of you."

Actually, I had heard nothing of the sort from Anne directly. At the library, she acts as though I'm invisible; yesterday, in fact, she stood right next to me but spoke only to Mr. Morgan. Still, I could hear her, and I'd learned she'd been quite impressed with Mrs. Berenson. So much so that she speculated it was Mrs. Berenson and not her husband who wrote his famous art books.

"You flatter me," she says with a slight flush in her cheeks. "The people of New York have been uniform in their welcome, and we are eternally appreciative. Bernard and I hail from Boston, although we now live in Italy, and we hadn't expected such a reception. It seems we are faddish at the moment."

I lift up the glass of Burgundy I'd taken from a passing waiter. "Here's to the moment." We clink glasses, all smiles and ebullience.

After a sip, Mrs. Berenson says, "We were honored that Mr. Morgan gave us copies of the catalogs of his collection."

I'd been astonished when he'd given a set to the Berensons. His catalogs, which contain details of his manuscripts and artwork, their provenance, and several reproductions, are highly sought after and rarely distributed, as with all renowned collectors who prefer to keep the particulars about their collections private. "He obviously values your opinion and scholarship," I say, rather than admitting my surprise.

"He values yours as well, and I understand why," Mr. Berenson responds.

I have to keep my eyes on Mrs. Berenson, because her husband's words and glances unsettle me. But I say, "I've worked hard to prove my worth to him."

"Well, we hope to be of service in whatever way we can, and to prove *our* worth," Mr. Berenson says, "to Mr. Morgan and to you."

"I will recommend you to Mr. Morgan," I say with a nod to him and Mrs. Berenson. The differences in their statements about Mr. Morgan make me wonder if they are of like mind in their approach about him.

"That would be lovely." Mrs. Berenson smiles at me and changes the subject. "Will we see you at the dinner hosted by Mrs. de Acosta Lydig next week?"

"I'm afraid not. Duty calls," I reply, but the truth has nothing to do with work.

Rita de Acosta Lydig, married to a banker and Wall Street broker, is a fixed part of New York City society, despite the fact that her parents are from Spain. This fact, paired with her "exotic beauty," might have made her a social outcast, except that her Spanish lineage has aristocratic ties. I avoid Mrs. de Acosta Lydig whenever possible and would never attend one of her events, although I'm always invited. I simply couldn't stand next to her and have the parallels between us—

the similar last name, the darker shade of our skin—explored with any depth. My noble ties would come up lacking, and I cannot give those who wonder about my heritage more material.

"Ah." She gives me a nod of sympathetic understanding. "I'm sure Mr. Morgan isn't an easy boss. The demands on your time must be great."

As I had with Mr. Berenson's comment about Mr. Morgan, I bristle at the implicit denunciation. "It is an honor to work for Mr. Morgan. The demands he makes are ones I'm happy to fulfill."

Realizing her misstep, Mrs. Berenson blanches. "Oh, I didn't mean to—" she begins, but before she can finish, a woman in a bloodred gown interrupts.

"Excuse me." She looks between the three of us and then settles her eyes on Bernard. "Would you mind if I borrowed your wife for a moment? There is someone I must introduce Mary to."

Mrs. Berenson is pulled away and I am left alone with Mr. Berenson. Before I can decide what to say—whether to return to the thread of the significant conversation we'd been having before his wife's arrival—he offers me a smile along with his arm, and says, "Shall we perambulate around the room and part it like Moses and the Red Sea?"

His offer makes me laugh, and I put down my glass before I accept his arm. As I slide my arm through his, a charge surges through me.

"Do you see how everyone is looking at you? You are as singular as the art you acquire." Whether he intends it or not, his lips are so close to my ear that I feel the warmth of his breath. When I turn toward him, I find that, because of his height, our faces are close, very intimate.

I have learned to flirt with ease, but my visceral and intellectual reaction to this man is robbing me of my usual banter. Is it because—for once—I feel understood? It is as if I am naked before him, without the armor of wit and humor I usually wear to these occasions. I don't allow myself to back away, but I try to wrest control of our intimate exchange and steer it back to a more usual course. "I'm sure their eyes are on you, not me. You are visiting from Italy and are a novelty for this insular group. Do you have parties like this in Boston? Or Italy?"

He laughs, and I am not sure if that is a response to my subject change or my actual question. "Oh, no. Boston social gatherings are staid affairs, even in the exquisite home of my patron, Mrs. Isabella Stewart Gardner. And in Italy, well, its traditions and rituals are too rich with history to embrace an event like this."

I'm calmer now, having maneuvered the conversation to a safer space. "What do you make of this?" I ask, assuming—with his discriminating taste and fine eye—he'd find the vivid show of red gauche.

His eyes wander for a moment as he takes in the great wave of red cresting around us. "I quite like it. There's something liberating in the uniform wash of red, don't you think? How freeing it would be if we could all be the same color."

My breath catches in my chest. Why would he associate all of this with skin color? Does he know about me? We stop moving as his glance returns to me. He clarifies, saying, "I mean, not all of us share the same economic circumstances or the identical blue blood background, and yet here, awash in red, we are all the same. This party is a great equalizer." He sounds almost wistful. "Because of that, I quite like it."

We begin walking again, our arms still linked together, and I wonder about Mr. Berenson's words, what his phrase "a great equalizer" tells me about him. He'd mentioned his childhood days at the Boston Public Library—a clear hint at the lower economic station of his family—and perhaps the financial situation to which he'd been born preys upon him amid such lavishness. I can certainly relate to his sentiment about being an outsider.

Although I am not quite certain how to respond, I need to tread lightly and not reveal too much in my reply. Settling on an innocuous response, I say, "It can be quite overwhelming to be always in the presence of great wealth."

"Yes," he says, then looks straight at me, "but here, for a moment, we are equal."

Even though we are surrounded by chatter and music, we stay silent. I don't know what he's thinking, but my only thought is this: *I must get to know this man.*

CHAPTER 18

MARCH 24, 1909
NEW YORK, NEW YORK

Belle!" I glance up from my desk to see Mr. Morgan standing at the threshold of my office. "Do you have any plans for this evening?"

I smile the way I always do when Mr. Morgan asks me this question; it happens at least once a week when he's in New York. In actuality, his question is a command to stand in his stead at an event that he's forgotten or that interferes with his private plans with a mistress. It is my job to attend.

"Where would you like me to be, Mr. Morgan?"

"At the opera."

"Which art dealer or collector would you like me to entertain?" These events are typically quests for information about a dealer's upcoming offerings or a collector's future plans.

"Rachel Costelloe." I recognize the name, and when my smile fades, Mr. Morgan frowns. "Is something wrong?"

"No, I'm just surprised. I assumed that you wanted me to meet with someone who had something to do with the library."

"I do. Do you know who she is?"

I wonder how to answer the question without revealing too much, so I simply say, "I've never met her."

"Anne was meant to attend the opera with her tonight; Miss Costelloe is her acquaintance, after all. But Anne informed me that she has an important engagement with the Colony Club." He waves his hand in the air as if he is irritated, as if his daughter's plans matter not at all.

"So you want me to step in?"

"Yes, Miss Costelloe is the stepdaughter of Bernard Berenson, and I need some information." I knew who she was, but hadn't wanted to admit it. I worried that the knowledge could have revealed my fascination with Bernard. He adds, "I want you to see if she knows anything about the upcoming acquisitions of her stepfather's patron, Isabella Stewart Gardner."

Ah, this is all about competition. Mr. Morgan wants to be certain his private art collection is unmatched.

How strange that Mr. Morgan is the one to provide me with the opportunity to learn more about the man I've been orbiting for the last three months. At a private dinner at Delmonico's, during the intermission at a Broadway showing of *King Lear*, throughout the Hudson-Fulton exhibit of Dutch art at the Metropolitan Museum, Bernard Berenson and I exchanged stolen glances and hidden smiles. To anyone on the outside, these encounters have been nothing more than any number of opportunistic flirtations I've had with men in the art world over the past few years. Flirtation is my device, nothing of note or consequence to anyone—except, this time, for me.

Each time I've seen Mr. Berenson, I haven't been able to make sense of my desire. Not only is Mr. Berenson close to two decades older than me, but he is a married man, and for all of my flirtations, I would never become involved in such a dalliance. Yet, I yearn to spend more time with him.

Could it be that I'm attracted to his inscrutable demeanor? Or am I drawn in by the sense that we both have secrets that force us to operate furtively—yet seamlessly—in a world that isn't our own? A world riddled with bigotry and racism. I have had no opportunity to discover the answers because his work has taken him away from New York for weeks—to Boston, Providence, and Philadelphia—consulting on such esteemed collections as Peter Widener's. I've been waiting for his return and his promise of "a special evening."

Within minutes of meeting Miss Costelloe—or Rachel, as she asks me to call her—in the lobby of the Metropolitan Opera House to see *Il Barbiere di Siviglia*, I realize she knows nothing about her stepfather's business affairs. Still, the twenty-one-year-old Rachel is delightful, bubbling with her commitment to the suffrage movement. When we break for intermission, she chats about the accomplishments of women activists, even as they continue to fight for the right to vote. She is an articulate advocate for the movement, and I am amused when she tells me, "Belle, it would be so wonderful if you came to one of the meetings with me. You would be so inspiring."

"I'm not sure about that. I'm ashamed to say that I know little about the movement."

"That's okay, the movement knows all about you."

Her words astonish me. "Really? Me?"

"I don't know why you're surprised. This is about so much more than just fighting for our right to vote. How could we not know about you? You're all around the city, attending all the balls and soirees, but you're also conducting serious business in the art world. You're living a life of equality, and that's what we're fighting for. Whether it's in your work—like you—or in your personal life—like my mother, who's chosen not to conform to the traditional constraints of marriage."

"What does that mean?" I ask before I can stop myself.

"My mother is a woman before her time," Rachel explains. "She is progressive in her attitudes about work—she undertakes projects right alongside Bernard—and she is forward thinking in her attitudes about relationships. She and Bernard love each other, but they are free to pursue other romantic affairs; she doesn't believe people should be hampered by preconceived notions and expectations. Their marriage is very cosmopolitan, wouldn't you say?" she asks with a grin.

The lights flicker, the sign that we are to return to our seats, and I am relieved. I need to be alone with my thoughts. By the time the opera reaches its conclusion, I've begun to realize what Rachel's disclosure could mean for me.

Marriage is not something that I've really considered. I've always known that, because of my heritage, a traditional relationship would not be possible for me. Not only because of my family's financial dependence but because a marriage means children, and that is something I cannot hazard. Without the fairer skin of my siblings, I could never risk bearing a child whose skin color might reveal my deception.

Perhaps Bernard's unique marriage could allow me to experience the man I desperately want to know better, without the danger that he'll expect more from me than I can give. Don't I deserve to experience the same emotions and grand passion as other women? Perhaps with Bernard, I might be able to have a taste of the type of romantic relationship most women take for granted.

The carriage jostles over the cobblestones, and my nerves jar along with it. I've been waiting for weeks for this moment with Bernard, but now that it has arrived, I am anxious. Rachel's disclosure has conjured possibilities I'd previously believed impossible for me, but tonight, all that speculating could become reality. Am I ready?

After stepping out of the carriage, I smooth my windswept hair and the skirt of my emerald wool dress before I step into the Great Hall of the Metropolitan Museum. Today I take no notice of the magnificent classical beaux arts entry. Normally its soaring limestone dome and arches impress me, but the vast space also perplexes me. How can two million square feet look so friendly and welcoming? But today I'm distracted as I search for Bernard.

A few visitors straggle, adjusting their hats as they ready to leave, but I don't see Bernard among them. Did I get the time wrong? Our tour is planned for after hours. We are going to have a private viewing of a recently acquired sculpture.

"Miss Greene, Miss Greene!"

I spin until a familiar face, perfectly round in shape with a distinctively curled mustache, appears at my side. "Here you are, Miss Greene. Lovely to see you again." He extends his hand without introducing himself.

I know we've met, though I cannot place him. "Wonderful to see you as well," I answer, shaking his hand, and in that instant, his name finally comes to me—Mr. Johnson.

"Follow me, if you will, Miss Greene. Mr. Berenson and our Greek statue await," he says, setting off through the diminishing crowd.

At first he ducks and weaves through them so quickly that I struggle to keep up. We leave the lingering visitors in our wake and progress down the dark hall housing ancient Greek and Roman art. Mr. Johnson continues to lead me through the warren-like hallway—until I spot a Roman sarcophagus that I know well. The coffin dates from the imperial Roman era, anywhere from the first century BC to the first century AD. Its vividly colored wood surface makes it stand out among the marble and alabaster from which most of the objects in this room are made. It isn't only the brightness of the sarcophagus that captures my attention but also the realistic portrait found on its lid. This Fayum portrait, as this rare type of ancient art is called, depicts the people of its place and time as they actually looked—dark skin, curly black hair, and deep chocolate-brown eyes—and challenges the commonly held perception that ancient Greek and Roman people were blond and blue-eyed. The Fayum portrait was a particular favorite of mine and Papa's during our visits to the Metropolitan Museum. Only here did we see people who looked like us.

"Miss Greene," Mr. Johnson calls, waking me from my reverie, and I hasten to catch up. Suddenly, we veer right into a small room branching off the primary hall, passing by several glass cases holding pieces of ancient jewelry and pottery, until we approach a door hidden in the fabric on the wall.

"Nearly there, Miss Greene." Mr. Johnson glances over his shoulder with a grin.

Finally, he leads me into a room where we step into another world. We no longer inhabit halls with carefully curated exhibits and perfectly arranged displays of precious artifacts and artwork, but instead are standing in a sprawling half-finished storage room lined with wooden crates. It is as if we've stepped behind the curtain of a Broadway play to the ragtag mess backstage, losing the illusion in the process but gaining an understanding of how the magic is created.

There, in the center of the room, stands Bernard, staring up at a striking white alabaster sculpture of a man's torso. To my eyes, he appears just as extraordinary as the art. He turns toward me when he hears my footsteps, and I am rewarded with a beaming smile.

"Ah, Miss Greene, so glad you were able to join us."

"So glad you extended the invitation, Mr. Berenson," I reply, losing the battle to hold back an embarrassingly wide grin of my own. I am filled with such joy at just the sight of him.

Access to the inner sanctum of the Metropolitan Museum is strictly limited to insiders, usually academic sorts only. When he learned about my interest in the new statue, Bernard cashed in a favor from Mr. Johnson. Bernard understands that a behind-the-scenes glimpse at my favorite museum is far more romantic than any lavish present or dinner date might be.

"If you'll join me over here," Mr. Johnson says, taking a position at the front of the torso. "I'd like to introduce you both to the newest addition to our collection of Greek sculptures." It's only the torso of a boy, but this boy's chest thrusts out with power; it commands attention.

Mr. Johnson begins his lecture. "Look at how his torso is turned. You can see the remnants of arrows here"—he points to the right shoulder—"which indicates he was being pursued and was running away from danger. We believe this is a depiction of one of Niobe's royal children. If you remember your mythology, Niobe bragged that she was a better mother because she had borne more children than Leto. A very angry Leto exacted revenge against Niobe by sending out her children, Apollo and Artemis, to kill Niobe's children. As I'm certain you both know, sculptures showing Niobe's children trying to escape the deadly arrows of Apollo and Artemis were often depicted through antiquity. The ancients wanted the people to know that hubris can be a deadly crime," he adds with a small smile.

"It's a lesson some modern-day folks could still use," I retort.

As the men laugh, I ask, "What date do you give this statue?"

"We estimate that it was created in Greece somewhere between 425 and 400 BC."

Bernard and I circle the statue, catching glimpses of each other as we do. "It's really quite lovely. The craftsmanship in the torso's movement particularly," I comment, but Bernard—famous art scholar and critic, known for his insightful, occasionally biting assessments—is strangely quiet.

"I think you're quite right in your identification of the subject, Mr. Johnson," Bernard says finally. "This is likely one of Niobe's children." He pauses, placing a finger on his pursed lips. "But are you certain that it's a Greek original? That it isn't a Roman copy?"

A strange gurgling noise escapes Mr. Johnson's mouth, a cross between a laugh and a cry. "I think we'd know a Greek from a Roman statue around here, Mr. Berenson."

I stand back and watch Bernard. His question is not an unfair one. Very few Greek statues have survived, but the copies made by the ancient Romans have fared far better.

Bernard approaches the statue, bending down so he's eye level with three curious striations I'd noticed. "Do you see these light diagonal cuts along the lower torso? The chisel marks here and there?"

Mr. Johnson crosses his arms at first, refusing to draw nearer. A long minute passes before he acquiesces.

"Those are the markings of a sculpting instrument that wasn't in use until the first century AD in Rome," he says in a voice that bears no hint of triumph. It seems to pain him to correct the attribution of this sculpture, but he knows he must.

Mr. Johnson's cheeks flame red. "I believe your specialty is Renaissance art, Mr. Berenson," he snaps. "That hardly makes you an expert in dating antiquities."

I have no wish to alienate a Met curator, but I cannot sit by and allow him to insult Bernard. "Mr. Johnson," I say. "As you undoubtedly know, Renaissance artwork was the rediscovery of classical design and art, particularly that of ancient Greek and Roman origin. In order to become expert in his field, Mr. Berenson had to become an expert in both Greek and Roman antiquities, and given that he makes his home in Italy, I am guessing that he studies ancient Greek and Roman art in situ."

"I spend a significant amount of time in Italian churches, where I have the opportunity to examine statues that were reappropriated by the church."

His last words are the ones that make Mr. Johnson's cheeks lose their fire, and as his shoulders slump, a sickly pallor takes hold. He realizes the museum has made a mistake in its acquisition. And that, given Bernard's observations and his expert status, the museum's newest treasure will not soon be viewed by the public.

The sun is setting by the time we leave the museum, turning the building's limestone facade a golden pink. The March air is refreshingly crisp after the stuffiness of the Met's storage rooms. I inhale as Bernard and I step down onto the sidewalk bordering Fifth Avenue. The street overflows with carriages of gentlemen returning home from their day's labors and couples heading out for the evening's entertainment. The clop of horses and the low murmur of passersby obviate the need for conversation at first.

In the quiet between us, I tighten my coat around me. Bernard breaks the silence. "You are quite the defender, Miss Greene. While I appreciate your efforts, I do think I could have protected my honor without you." He beams at me, and his teeth gleam in the low lamplight.

I smile back. "I've never been one to mince words or suffer fools, Mr. Berenson."

"I have noticed. I've also noticed that you continue to call me Mr. Berenson, when I thought I asked you to call me Bernard."

I counter smoothly, "And I noticed you continue to call me Miss Greene when you promised over and over again that you would call me Belle."

His bark of laughter makes my insides warm. "Touché, Belle." He grins. "How about an agreement? When we are in the company of others, we use the more socially acceptable 'miss' and 'mister.' But when it is just us two, we call each other by our given names." He pauses for just a moment, as if he wishes to make sure I hear his next words. "And I do hope there will be many times when it is just the two of us, Belle."

I nod, impossibly happy. I thought I was sure about his feelings before, but now, I have no doubt. But then I am struck by a wave of sadness. Because I know with absolute certainty that Bernard would not deign to talk to me if I were introduced to him by my actual given name. The famous art scholar and critic Bernard Berenson would never stand side by side laughing and conversing about art on the streets of New York with a colored girl.

But as he peers at me, my sadness washes away, until he says, "I'm leaving."

Leaving? Again? What does he mean? Back to Italy? I have questions, but I'm too scared to ask them. Instead, I stand still, listening to the sounds of the city as I try to tease out a single thought from the many swirling through my mind.

"I'm returning home to Italy," he explains, before I have the courage and wherewithal to ask. "In three days."

My heart sinks, but I tell myself it is for the best. Not only is he married—never mind the incomprehensible arrangement he shares with his wife—but what makes me think a few flirtations are tantamount to real emotion? Especially since his unconventional marriage allows him to pursue relationships with whomever he wishes?

As we wait for our carriages, standing so close that I inhale every breath he exhales, I cannot meet his eyes. Part of me wants to prolong this moment, and part of me wants to leave, taking my feelings with me. Bernard challenges the barricade to romantic feelings that I just recently realized I'd erected years ago, as a way to protect myself and my family from a connection I should not—in fact, cannot—forge.

"I know it's not much time, but I want to see you, Belle, before I depart." I finally meet his gaze. "Do I dare hope that you will join me for dinner, just the two of us?"

Before I answer, I think that even if he would not ask such a question of Belle Marion Greener, I am relieved and excited that he's asked Belle da Costa Greene. And even though I know many young women would blanch at the idea of dining alone with a married man, I am not most young women.

"Yes, Bernard, I will join you."

CHAPTER 19

MARCH 26, 1909
NEW YORK, NEW YORK

My hand hovers in the air, in front of the door of this suite at the Hotel Webster, an establishment only a few blocks from the library. Even though the society men and women around me regularly engage in this sort of scandalous behavior, it goes against every rule of acceptability I have been taught. I do not have the money and family name that protect them from besmirched reputations. I have responsibilities to my family; my work secures their white existence. I cannot become like Lily Bart in *House of Mirth* and allow myself to be destroyed by society's judgment. And yet, I agreed to meet Bernard.

Just this morning, as I sat at my desk at the Pierpont Morgan Library, I was plagued with doubts. Hourly encounters with Mr. Morgan, in which he solicited my opinion on a proffered manuscript and asked for my guidance on a tricky trust question, solidified those worries. How could I dream of attaining a station in life like this without Mr. Morgan? If he ever discovered my relationship with a man he barely tolerates—a relationship I am sure Mr. Morgan would perceive as a betrayal of the undivided attention and affection he believes he is owed from his personal librarian—I am certain I'd be fired and he'd seek out someone else for the job. I had almost decided to cancel our engagement when a letter arrived for me at the library. The envelope contained a single page, with the words "For Belle" scrawled on top followed by excerpts from a poem. His words undid my resolve.

Finally, I knock on the door leading to Bernard's suite of rooms, and when he opens it, I cannot bring myself to meet his eyes, so I step inside without a word. The elegant little parlor is lined with celadon-green damask wallpaper; a pair of matching wingback chairs sits before a crackling fire. A table for two is set with a white linen tablecloth, a floral spray of local buttercups and bloodroots, a silver candelabra, two place settings of china, each with a silver dome covering the meal, and a bottle of wine, already uncorked. Bernard has arranged the intimate space both welcomingly and carefully to ensure that we will remain alone.

As I face the fire, I feel so young, so inexperienced. Then Bernard's hands are on my shoulders, and I shiver expectantly. He slides my coat off in a single movement, steps away, and hooks it on the bronze rack.

Then, he speaks the first words we share. "Shall we?" He gestures to the table.

A wave of relief passes through me that I've been directed to an activity, because I have no idea how one is meant to behave in situations such as these. *Is there a script one follows when engaging in peccadilloes?* I quickly banish the thought. I don't want to think of our encounter in base terms, because in truth, my feelings for him are soaring.

He pulls out my chair, and I sit down with shaking legs that I hope are hidden by the skirt of the deep azure silk gown I chose for the evening. When he lifts the bottle of Burgundy, I have to take a deep breath in order to hold up my glass steady enough.

I take a long sip. It warms me from the inside out, softening the nerves that have plagued me. He removes the silver domes from our plates, and we begin to eat the delicate quail, scalloped potatoes, and early asparagus he's ordered for us.

I feel suddenly shy. Intimacy, of both the physical and the emotional variety, is a place I have not visited with any man.

Sensing my discomfort, Bernard takes up the conversation. "Do you think Mr. Johnson will inform his fellow curators of the dating error of the sculpture?"

I exhale at the comfortable issue he's raised. The image of a florid Mr. Johnson explaining the attribution error to the self-important curatorial staff—who had undoubtedly called in several experts for verification—tickles my imagination, and I giggle. Bernard laughs along with me, and soon we are overtaken by tension-breaking merriment.

Easy conversation follows, and I listen as he talks about how he became enamored of Italian Renaissance paintings and drawings. This love affair, he reveals, did not occur immediately, but in stages over time.

"One captivating bust led to the next exquisitely rendered painting until I lost my heart," he says. "The rich Renaissance artwork, with its freshly hewn three-dimensionality and deep allegorical meaning, transported me away from myself and my reality to a time and place where true genius was possible, a time like and yet unlike our own. And I knew I had to help transport others in turn. That's why I first began writing. I didn't think the wealthy alone deserved to have access to this understanding." His tone is confessional. "I wanted people like me—" He stops before finishing and finally says, "I wanted people like me, who were not born with that easy connection to art and its experts, to have that access as well." Once again, he's revealing his position on the periphery of our world.

But it is his talk of art that mesmerizes me. *He is seducing me*, I realize. I allow myself to be drawn in by this slow dance. First, leaning closer to him across the table, then easing to the edge of my seat, and not long after, sitting on his lap on one of the wingback chairs before the fire. Before I even feel his lips upon mine, I breathe in his scent. His heady, musky smell, distinct from the cologne he uses to mask his natural fragrance, sends a shiver through me, and when he leans in to kiss me, I surrender. I am twenty-nine years old and this is my first real kiss. I savor the moment and the warmth that rises within me.

Suddenly, his hands are on my back and in my hair, and when his fingers find their way to my breasts, I can barely breathe. But when his hands begin working at the row of tiny buttons on the back of my gown, I pull away.

"What is it, my love?" he asks, his voice thick with the same desire that fills me.

My heart clenches at the endearment, and I realize just how easily I could surrender to him. I will myself to remain steadfast. "I want to give myself to you"—I glance downward—"but I don't dare."

For some reason, he feels my words are an invitation, and his fingers are once again on my buttons. "If you are concerned about Mary, you needn't worry. We have an understanding."

"It isn't that, Bernard." I put a hand on his chest, and he stops. "I've already been told about that."

He raises a brow at my knowledge, and I answer his unspoken question. "Rachel."

"Ah," he says in understanding. "What then, my love? Is it that I'm not currently free to marry?"

How can I tell him that a woman like me with a life-altering deception can never marry? A relationship with Bernard, attached and yet in some ways free, beguiles in a way that nothing else ever has. And yet, I am scared. If I take this enormous risk, it must be worth the dangers.

Finally, I respond, "It isn't that, Bernard. Marriage has never been my plan." I hesitate. "It's that I—with you—I could be lost forever."

"What is wrong with that?"

"Nothing. And everything."

He groans, not out of frustration but from desire. "You cannot know the effect you are having on me, Belle. I want you for my own."

"And I want you." I speak the truth. "But I need to know your feelings are not fleeting and that, if I give myself to you, our affair will not be just another dalliance."

He takes my hand and kisses my palm, and then with his index finger he draws circles in the same place where the feeling of his lips on my hand lingers. The surge of passion that those two simple gestures cause almost breaks my will. Almost makes me lean forward and kiss him deeply.

"All right," he says. "We will wait until I prove my devotion to you, my love. You will see that my adoration is unwavering, and then we will arrange a rendezvous worthy of that emotion." He pulls me closer and kisses my forehead, then my eyelids, my cheeks, and finally my lips. I slip into the sensations arising within me, and I am almost adrift on the waves of this passion.

Then he whispers into my ear, "You are my Belle."

With his words, I am awakened to myself, and yet I know I am lost forever.

CHAPTER 20

My time with Bernard that evening, however brief, rouses something within me. I am no longer satisfied with this endless pretending, this charade of a life I lead. I've made an authentic connection, and I want more of these.

Bernard is gone but our bond remains, and I am inspired to be more myself. I dress even more audaciously in the brightest of colors; I speak boldly, saying whatever is on my mind at dinners, operas, and parties. To my surprise, the normally stiff society folks and art world luminaries find this exhilarating; it seems I'm saying aloud what they've only entertained in the privacy of their thoughts.

One evening, after a discussion of the recent economic disaster that would have been worse if Mr. Morgan hadn't intervened, several of the guests at an Astor house party lamented about all they'd lost in the stock market.

After listening to their diatribe through two glasses of Burgundy, I announced—to waves of laughter—"Too bad you've lost so much; the only thing I like about rich people is their money."

At the intermission of the season's ballet premiere, in response to a society doyenne's description of our Gutenbergs as the Pierpont

Morgan Library's greatest asset, I retorted, "The greatest treasure of the Pierpont Morgan Library is me," to a round of great guffaws.

Quips like this make me the toast of New York, and I am the recipient of the most coveted of invitations. And yet I know they talk about me behind my back, but I don't care. Gossip about my outrageous comments or my tipsy flirting or my increasingly expensive, brightly colored scarves distracts them from rumormongering about the one thing that matters—the color of my skin.

But speaking fearlessly does not yield the intimacy of connection, which is what I seek. In fact, I begin to feel like a circus performer, trotted out for the entertainment of the audience and expected to deliver a heightened act every time. Society wishes to adopt me into their ranks, not as an equal but almost as a pet, like the artists they sponsor and occasionally invite out.

This sensation is unsettling, even though I continue. I numb the discomfort by drinking too much wine. Mama notices, and she assumes the habit of waiting up for me, sometimes even hours after midnight, long after my sisters and Russell have retired.

"What are you doing, Belle?" she asks each time I stumble into the apartment. "I'm worried about you."

I wave her away as I move unsteadily on my feet until I drop onto the sofa. "Nothing. You know I need to do all this socializing for work, right? Parties and operas and theater, even intimate dinners and gatherings with the Morgan family. Isn't this what you wanted, Mama? For me to be rubbing shoulders with the Vanderbilts, the Carnegies, even the Morgans? Well, this is what it takes for me to be Belle da Costa Greene."

She gives me a hard stare before she turns away, and her quiet disapproval sounds louder than a scream. Her inquiries and condemnation continue apace until I can withstand it no longer. On the last weekend in May, I come home with a gift.

"I have a surprise," I say to my mother and siblings as we gather around the kitchen table for a late dinner. "I know how dreadful New York summers can be, so I've rented a two-bedroom lakefront cabin in the Adirondacks for eight weeks. I'm only sorry that your new job in Florida will prevent you from enjoying it, Russell."

My sisters squeal their delight, and even my mother looks happy. "This is wonderful," Mama says. "But can you get away for that much time?"

"Oh, no," I say. "This is for all of you. I have too much work to do at the library."

Her face clouds over, and I know she's worrying about appearances—a young single woman living alone in New York. But her concerns are vanquished by her joy over the summer escape. The next few weeks are ebullient as my family prepares for their vacation from the unrelenting heat and stench of the city. But no one is more delighted than I am that two hundred miles and two months will separate me from Mama's watchful eye.

The Sunday I send them off is the day Russell departs for Florida for his first engineering position; we are sad to see him go, but relieved he secured a position. When I return to the apartment from the train station, I celebrate the silence. I am alone.

Right away, I begin to plan all that I want to do over the next eight weeks. I want a life beyond work and its social obligations. I want the life that Bernard has stirred inside of me. I want something real.

The usual whirl of society events has ceased for the season, as the elite have decamped to their summer mansions and yachts. I take a trip to Princeton to see my old friends Gertrude and Charlotte, and after a fun but staid afternoon of reminiscing, on a whim I decide to contact two acquaintances from my school days at Teachers' College.

Katrina and Evelyn were as close to friends as I permitted myself during those years, but once I left for Princeton, we simply lost touch. Within a week, I receive a return note from Katrina with an audacious reply that sounds just like her. Her letter expresses her delight at my success and an invitation to meet her and Evelyn at a pub in Greenwich Village the following weekend. I haven't spent too much time in that part of the city, fast becoming known as America's bohemia, filled with New Yorkers who reject traditional socialization, preferring informality instead. As I make plans to meet my friends, I can almost hear Mama say, *Belle, inviting these young ladies into your life is like inviting a thief into your home to take your most precious jewels; you know you should have kept your door locked.* But Mama's imagined objections make me all the more determined to go. Haven't I made enough sacrifices on the altar of whiteness?

When I step into the pub on Seventh Street, Katrina and Evelyn are waiting for me. I beam at the sight of petite, red-haired, green-eyed Katrina next to Evelyn, her physical opposite in height and coloring, with black hair and blue eyes. As we order dark beers, I feel almost as out of place as I did at that first Vanderbilt ball. I take a cigarette from Evelyn when she offers, and I wonder if I fit in anywhere.

The pub is deafening with the animated conversations of groups of women alongside bands of men, so we lean in close, our foreheads almost touching. "So tell me about your teaching careers," I say.

My friends glance at each other, then laugh. "Teaching careers?" they sing together.

Katrina begins, "I abandoned that three months into my stint teaching second grade at the local public school. I couldn't tolerate the children, and I wanted to make a bigger difference—a splash, even—in the world." A wide grin takes over her small face, and she says, "I'm now an officer of the Woman Suffrage Party of New York."

"Wow," I say, wondering if she knows Rachel Costelloe.

"And I gave up the schoolchildren for a paintbrush," Evelyn says. She now paints all day, mostly portraits, and sells them at various shows every weekend in Greenwich Village.

I marvel at my friends' audacity in simply walking away from paths that had been laid out for them. "What did your parents think?"

"My father understood, but my mother was furious. She always wanted me to have a position that was proper and fitting." Katrina shrugs. "But I needed to do what was really in here." She presses her hand against her chest.

"It was the same for me," Evelyn says. "I certainly don't earn the money I would have as a teacher, but I'm happy."

"Have your parents come around?" I ask.

"Well," Evelyn says. "It's gotten better since I moved out."

"Me, too," Katrina echoes.

"You don't live at home?" I don't know what I find more shocking—the idea of Katrina as a suffrage leader and Evelyn as a painter or them living on their own.

"No, I live in the Martha Washington Hotel for Women, right around the corner," Katrina says.

"The what?"

"How can you not have heard of it, Belle? It opened not even five years ago, and it's a residential hotel that can house up to five hundred businesswomen. Not only do we have our own rooms and lovely dining areas, but the hotel has its own drugstore, tailor shop, millinery, manicurist, and newspaper stand, all run by women. The entire staff is female." She sighs. "It's heaven."

"I had no idea that such a place existed," I say.

"We don't advertise, but it's known among career women. In fact, the Interurban Woman Suffrage Council, which founded the Woman Suffrage Party of New York, has its headquarters in our building. I think you'd really love it at the Martha Washington, Belle. So many like-minded women."

As she explains her work in the women's movement, I'm reminded of Rachel, of course, which starts me thinking about Bernard, and I order another beer. Katrina's enthusiasm for the movement is as great as Rachel's, and I'm impressed with these formidable women. But even though I've read about the suffrage movement, I've not had the time or the exposure to develop a position.

Katrina continues, "I hope this doesn't embarrass you, but many of the women I live and work with look to you as an example."

"I've heard that before, but I'm not sure why women think of me that way."

"You are one of the most successful career women of our day, commanding thousands of dollars in the art world with the backing of one of the world's most powerful men. And, I'm guessing, without any pressure to marry and have children."

Her enthusiasm is infectious, and I find myself smiling. Even if she weren't so ebullient, I would be grinning at the idea of her utopian living conditions. Once I returned to New York, it had not occurred to me to reside anywhere but with my family. How free Katrina's life seems.

"Do you live there, too, Evelyn?" I ask.

"No, and I'm sure you've never heard of where I live," Evelyn says. "I have a room at the Trowmart Inn on Hudson. It's brand-new and though not as luxurious as the Martha Washington . . ." She pauses, glancing at Katrina. "It's just what I need and what I can afford."

"They both sound divine," I say, and mean it.

"I'd love for you to come to one of my shows," Evelyn says.

"And one of my rallies," Katrina joins in.

While they want to hear all about my world—especially, as Katrina puts it, "that rascal Morgan and how you manage to circumvent his notoriously philandering overtures"—I cannot stop asking about theirs. Besides living, working, and socializing on their own, they seem to be freethinking and dating often, giving me the impression that they are far more advanced than I am socially and sexually. How rich and full of purpose their lives seem, not to mention full of men of their choosing. And how bold, a description I'd previously associated with myself.

As we walk arm in arm across Washington Square Park and through the arch toward another pub, I think about the differences in our worlds. I act the part of the sophisticate and art expert among the country's wealthiest people, while Katrina risks all to bring the constitutional right to vote to *all* women, and Evelyn models a truly free existence as an artist. I feel simultaneously rudderless and inspired by these old friends.

I vow that we will see each other more frequently. Already they have shown me that life in New York City can be even freer than the one I've been living. Perhaps I should emulate their boldness, particularly with Bernard? Or perhaps I should use that boldness to do more for equal rights—and not just the woman's right to vote—than simply serving as a secret example of what a colored girl can be? Either way, change is coming for me.

It is past midnight when I return to my apartment that night, but I feel energized and inspired by my friends who are, in their own way, changing the world. But once I settle down inside my bedroom, I savor the silence and then reach for the two letters that I've yet to read from Bernard. These minutes alone with his words—of which there are many, as he's kept his promise and writes daily—have become the best part of my day in the five months since his departure.

My Belle, my dearest, dearest Belle . . .

I pause and smile. Bernard begins every communication this way.

What have you done to me? I cannot sleep. I cannot eat. I cannot even find pleasure in the art that adorns the walls of my home, I Tatti; paintings by Giotto and Veneziano do not compare to you. In all the world, in all this time, there has been no woman who has touched me like you, my Belle . . .

His letter goes on to tell me how much he has fallen for me, even though we've only been together on a few occasions. These proclamations do not seem overwrought or trite because I share his feelings. With each letter he sends me, I fall deeper under his spell.

I write to Bernard as well, but my duties prevent me from doing this daily, so I keep a running journal of sorts and post it to him regularly. After lingering over his letter, I crawl under my covers, pen and paper in hand, and write.

Did you like the miniature portrait of myself I sent to you? I know it's no Giotto but I hope it helps you imagine me in

Greenwich Village last evening at a pub with old school
friends, sipping beer and yammering away about the way
they're working to shift our society. They challenge me to
stretch and to become the best woman possible, to use my
unique position for a larger purpose. I want to be that woman
for myself, and I want to be that woman for you . . .

I pause, think of something that Bernard wrote me in his last letter, and then I continue.

Our relationship is like no other that I've ever known or
expected. It may surprise you that the arrangement that you
have with Mary suits me and my situation quite well. I am a
modern woman with a career of my own, and you do not
have to explain anything to me, my love. I am your Belle . . .

CHAPTER 21

The vibrant stained glass window in Mr. Morgan's study is open a crack, and a warm but refreshing breeze makes its way into the room. For a moment, I feel I can breathe as I sit across from Mr. Morgan with our card game of bezique spread across his desk.

The circulating air helps alleviate the stuffiness—whether it arises from the many layers of fabric, the cigar smoke wafting throughout the room, or the suffocation I feel from Mr. Morgan's mounting neediness.

I do not mind—indeed, I anticipate—the time and attention Mr. Morgan typically requires, particularly when it reflects my increased responsibilities both at the library and in society. But starting in the autumn after Bernard's return to Europe, Mr. Morgan began demanding me at his side in all aspects of his life.

It began with an "invitation" to a family birthday dinner for Jack— a surprise, as I'd never been asked to attend strictly family occasions. Initially, I thought he was simply being kind when he invited me, since I'd assisted with the planning, so I politely declined.

"You're family, Belle, but this isn't a gracious invitation. I'm *asking* you to be there."

I made an appearance because I understood what Mr. Morgan's *asking* meant—for reasons best known to himself, attending his family functions had suddenly become part of my job description. When I arrived, his family was welcoming enough, although their frowns told me my presence was as surprising to them as the invitation had been to me. This was the first of many private Morgan occasions where I didn't belong but attendance was mandatory. I became a fixture at more family birthday dinners, including those for the grandchildren, a small gathering for Louisa's anniversary, and even a harbor cruise for Anne's accomplishments with the Colony Club—and then my presence was demanded at the holidays as well.

This change has mystified me. I've wondered if he's rethinking our relationship, but never have we reverted from the professional to the personal beyond this inclusion. At every event, I've been introduced as his personal librarian, and that's how I've been treated. But what's become abundantly clear is that Mr. Morgan's need for me is growing stronger.

A shaft of blue light filters through the stained glass windows onto his desk, and with it, the breeze turns into an unexpected gust, blowing our cards off the table. I race around the vast study to gather them, and then painstakingly replace them in their original positions. Then I wait for the perfect moment.

As I play my card, I say, "I hear that a Hans Memling illuminated manuscript may be coming to market in the next few months." My tone is casual, as if I hadn't planned this comment for several days.

"You don't say," Mr. Morgan replies without looking up. He studies his cards before he makes his next play. His thoughts are with the game and not my words.

"Yes. I am excited about what it might mean for the reputation of the library to add it to our collection," I comment. Usually a reference to the library's standing makes him take notice, but he continues studying his hand.

I will not relent. "I believe that acquiring it might bring us one step closer to matching or even outdoing the British Museum and the Bibliothèque Nationale."

With those words, he looks up from his cards, and I've hooked him. "You do?"

"Yes," I say with a casual nod, "it would make your illuminated manuscript collection more complete than that of either the British Museum or the Bibliothèque Nationale—and those are the only collections that can contend with yours. Not to mention I do not think there are any other illuminated manuscripts by Hans Memling. You would have the only one."

I know the notion of having the only Memling of a particular type appeals to Mr. Morgan. The master of early fifteenth-century Netherlandish painting is famous for his altarpieces, which are of religious scenes, and for his portraits of his patrons. Mr. Morgan treasures the two Memling paintings he already owns. I am telling him the truth; it would be a tremendous coup to have Memling's only illuminated manuscript. The only untruth I utter is that I'm not entirely sold on the claim that the manuscript is indeed a Memling; I think it's more likely to be a Simon Bening. But that attribution wouldn't serve my current purposes.

He picks up his cigar, and puffs. "Hmmm," he mutters. "Does this manuscript have a name?" he asks.

I blush; I'd been hoping I wouldn't have to reveal that just yet. "Colloquially, it's known as the da Costa hours, because it is a book of hours once owned by the Sá family from the royal house of Portugal. Their emblem incorporates the da Costa arms."

He roars at the manuscript's name. "That's rich, Belle. Are you certain the lure of the manuscript isn't the link to your own family name?"

Oh, the layers and secrets behind that little joke. I turn the conversation back to the matter at hand. "Remember what adding Lord Amherst's Caxtons to your preexisting Caxton collection did to the library's prominence?"

He nods.

"We could do that again. Only this time, it would compound the library's preeminence manifold."

"God, I admire your courage," he says with a guffaw. "If only the men who worked for me had half your moxie, we could run rough-shod over the entire financial market. If only my son had half your fearlessness. Sometimes I think his wife, Jessie, has more . . . ," he adds, then allows the sentence to trail off. He doesn't need to finish it for me to fill in the blank; I've heard his views about Jack and his wife before. I've also witnessed too many exchanges in which Mr. Morgan prods Jack to daring courses of action with the company, only to wallow in his disappointment when Jack chooses the safer road.

"So, what's your plan?" he asks.

Staying casual, I say, "I've heard rumors that the manuscript will be offered at auction in London," and then I add, almost as an after-thought, "in a few months."

"And you are thinking that a trip to London to bid for it at auction is in order?"

"You are partly correct, sir. I would like to be in London at the time of the auction, but I'd like to try the same maneuver with the da Costa hours as I did with the Caxtons—purchase it before the auc-tion starts. I'd also like to visit Italy, not only to make some connec-tions there but to survey several potential acquisitions that aren't formally on the market."

He nods, and I smile until he says, "Think you might find the Caxton *Le Morte Darthur* there?"

My smile fades as he continues, "In the four years that you've been here, you've done a wonderful job in building my collection. I only have one complaint." I inhale, knowing what he's going to say. "Where's my damned Caxton, Belle? That is what I really want. You've known that from the beginning."

"I understand, Mr. Morgan, and it is my greatest desire to secure that for you. However, I don't think I should stop building your collection in the meantime." I pause. "I promise you that I will get it, but at the same time, this book will be an important addition, and the best way for me to acquire it is to go to London."

Finally, he says, "That trick with the Caxtons did indeed work." After a moment of thought, he adds, "I will grant your request for a trip to London and Italy—assuming you meet one condition."

"I will continue searching for the Caxton?"

"Do that, but that's not my condition."

It doesn't matter what Mr. Morgan wants me to do. I will do it so that I can finally see Bernard again. I have come to realize that if I'm to see him, I will have to travel to Europe. After nearly a year and a half, there has been no business opportunity for Bernard to travel to the States again. The moment has come for me to find a way to secure my journey abroad.

"Anything you want," I say, and mean it.

Perched on the end of my chair, I wait to hear Mr. Morgan's requirement for my travel. I watch him exhale a stream of cigar smoke so thick he must squint at me through it, until he says, "You must vow to me that the sole reasons for this voyage are the acquisition of this Memling and the possibility of acquiring some little-known Italian Renaissance treasures. That this trip isn't a ruse for a rendez-vous with that *Jewish* fellow, Berenson."

It is only when the fog of his cigar smoke clears that I see a glimmer of a smile beneath his mustache. Finally, I breathe. Is he teasing me? Still, I'm not sure, and my pounding heart keeps me on the edge of my seat. My voice is calm and unflustered as I manage to say, "Of course I am taking this trip for the purpose of securing the Memling and other paintings that will burnish your collection's reputation."

Mr. Morgan puts down his cigar and leans forward on his desk. "Belle," his voice is soft and his tone somewhat sad as he begins, "that Jew Bernard Berenson certainly isn't worthy of you, if indeed you have him in your sights."

For a moment, Mr. Morgan sounds paternal, as if he's ringing an alarm to protect me from something. Or maybe it's more possessiveness than protection. Is that why he constantly mentions "Jew" when he speaks of Bernard? Does he believe he can manipulate me, deter me from him because of what he suspects is Bernard's ethnicity?

There is no way for Mr. Morgan to know that his warning means nothing to me. He is speaking to Belle da Costa Greene, but Belle Marion Greener is the woman enamored of Bernard. Through our talks, through our letters, Bernard has touched me all the way down to my soul.

"I assure you," I begin. "While I'm in Europe, I will do whatever will benefit the Pierpont Morgan Library, and I will be entirely at your disposal the way I always am."

He peers at me as if he realizes that I still have not answered his question, and then he nods. "Not that I'm concerned, of course. Because no matter who you see or what you do, you are *my* personal librarian. You must always remember that you belong to me."

CHAPTER 22

My cheeks ache from smiling as our ship docks in England. I cannot wait until the familiar outline of the city materializes, and as I anticipate the museum and private collections unfolding before me and the animated intellectual conversations bubbling up alongside the artwork, I grow as excited as a child on Christmas morning.

My reunion with Bernard seems interminable in coming, and not only because it has been almost a year and a half since I've laid eyes on him. The ten weeks between Mr. Morgan's permission for my journey and my actual departure passed with aching slowness.

Mr. Morgan had set sail for his usual travel on the *Corsair III*, and without him to occupy all of my time, I filled my lunch and dinner schedule with art professionals, the only people in my set left in the city after the society folks fled. Not even Mama and my sisters were available to distract me because they were ensconced in the bungalow I'd secured for them in Tuckahoe. In between, I attempted to enliven my free time with a mix of friends and acquaintances I'd met through Katrina and Evelyn—writers, artists, political figures, and dancers, including Isadora Duncan, a new friend I admired for her defiance of social mores and insistence on living life on her own terms—but I still felt like someone was missing. No one could fill the void but Bernard, and I counted the days until my departure.

Now I was here.

"Mademoiselle Greene," Marie, the French maid whom I hired and who had agreed to accompany me on the trip as chaperone in lieu of Mama, calls to me.

I turn toward the diminutive, dark-haired girl, who not only assists with dressing me on this trip and at home in the many layers of slips, chemises, corsets, stockings, and garters required every day, but also practices French with me. "Oui, Marie?" I answer, as always trying to communicate exclusively in the language in which I need to gain fluency. After all, how can I evaluate French manuscripts if I must rely on another to translate?

"Voulez-vous inspecter les bagages?"

"Non merci, Marie. Je compte sur toi," I answer. There is no need for me to inspect our trunks because I trust her. How could I not? She'd agreed to the ruse of accompanying me for the entirety of my three-week trip, when, in fact, she would be spending much of the time in Switzerland visiting her own family. Although I have not explicitly told her that I have plans requiring freedom from escorts, she understands.

Taking a final surreptitious drag on my cigarette, something that has now become a habit, I join the other first-class passengers preparing to go ashore. Alongside Marie and a steward ferrying our trunks, I walk down the gangway to the busy harborside. Steam and fog conspire to obscure the people waiting behind the red rope at the base of the gangway. And the cries of hansom cabdrivers drown out the sound of the calls from family and friends.

I search through the faces, scrutinizing the line of people behind the red barricade. There I see a melee of working-class and upper-class people and, like the last time I visited London, an astonishing range of skin shades, even rivaling the variety I see on the streets of New York. But nowhere do I see anyone who resembles Bernard. A disturbing thought occurs to me. Is it possible that I've forgotten his face after a year and a half?

Just as this internal dialogue pauses, I see him. The fastidiously trimmed brown beard. The tiny circular glasses. The unique, brilliant gray-green gaze. He is beaming at me.

I turn to Marie. "Ah, there is my colleague, Mr. Berenson, who has agreed to take us to our hotel."

"Pourquoi vous ne parlez pas français, mademoiselle?" Marie is surprised to hear me deviate from our French.

In my excitement, I had forgotten, and now I can't be bothered. All I can think about are Bernard's words in his last missive: *My love for you is a journey that I hope will have no ending.*

Leaving Marie and the steward behind, I race to Bernard's side. Although I know it breaks every code of propriety and goes against Mr. Morgan's explicit prohibitions on this trip, I run into his waiting arms, where I am enveloped in his embrace. I know I can indulge in this behavior for a brief moment only—and even then, I can only get away with this because none of my New York compatriots are nearby—so I wiggle out of his hold and step back.

"Thank you for meeting me, Mr. Berenson," I say with a small smile.

"The pleasure is all mine, Miss Greene," he responds, not relinquishing my hand. His voice drops, and I must draw closer to hear. "I have waited for this moment for so long I'd begun to believe it would never come, Belle."

"I feel the same, Bernard," I answer in the same low tone.

"I cannot wait to show you off all over London, and then I hope you will let me introduce you to all my secret places in Italy. Just us two."

"Precisely as we wrote to each other?" I say with hope in my voice.

"Precisely."

"Then you know, from my letters, when we reach Italy and Marie takes her leave, I would like to show you my secret places as well," I whisper.

I receive the reaction I sought. The ever-confident, unflappable Bernard turns a vivid red, and he pulls me closer.

Like silly children, we stand staring at each other, with wide grins. It only ends because behind us, Marie clears her throat. A waiting steward is standing next to our four heavy trunks that must reach their destination.

Soon we find ourselves en route to my suite at Claridge's.

In the days that follow, I embark on an itinerary of Bernard's design. I delight in his guidance—it is my childhood *Venetian Painters* come to life—and emerge brimming with a new clarity about the way the international world of high-end art collecting works: the network of dealers and collectors and curators who dictate the marketplace, decide the popularity and availability of pieces, and influence the prices. Bernard gifts me with a new lens through which I see the art realm and my place in it. I feel a sense of belonging and purpose in my work with Bernard that Katrina and Evelyn feel in theirs. As we delight in art and each other, I think, *If only I could have him at my side always.*

Whether it is from the way our fingers brush as we both reach for the sugar at luncheon, or the manner in which he gently leads me through a door with his hand on my lower back, I long for more of him.

But we do not spend our time exclusively in the company of curators and dealers and experts and collectors. On the third morning, over breakfast in the hotel's restaurant, Bernard says, "I know you have a pre-auction appointment this afternoon, but I've made plans for us to have lunch today."

"I'll look forward to visiting whatever wonderful establishment you've chosen. You know that, outside of today's appointment, my time belongs to you." I pause. "And when we get to Italy, everything else will belong to you, as well."

Bernard is no longer surprised by my forwardness and matches my flirtations. When he leans toward me, I think he's coming closer to whisper a few suggestive words, but he says, "The special plan isn't a particular restaurant. It's the company we will keep. Mary is joining us."

His words shock me. "Mary? Your wife?" As if there could be another Mary.

"She's en route to Oxford for a work assignment and she wanted to see you," he explains, as if such a meeting is utterly normal.

She wants to see me? Whatever for? It had been one thing to be in Mary's company when my desire for her husband had been only inside my head and heart, but now that our feelings are acknowledged, I feel quite differently. But how can I say no? I am the one about to embark on an affair with *her* husband.

As I inhale deeply, I think about all of the strange pairings and unusual romances I have seen in Greenwich Village with Katrina and Evelyn. I've attended parties where men dress as women; I've met a trio, a man and two women, who consider themselves wed to one another; and even outside of the Village I learned of Boston marriages.

Leaving Bernard in the restaurant, I retreat to my room. I try to distract myself with a missive to Mama, but after every word I write, my thoughts return to the lunch ahead. Finally, after having written just two sentences, I put the stationery down. Not even a conversation in French with Marie can distract me.

I'm relieved when it's time for me to consider my attire; at least this will give me something to focus on. Marie laced me into my violet gown this morning, but I decide that I should wear something more demure. I don't believe I should be bold in my clothes *and* my behavior. I select a new gray gown; it's the most conservative I've brought. Marie sets to work fastening me into its dark folds.

My heart is pounding as I walk down the wide staircase to the hotel restaurant. From the bottom step, I spot Bernard and Mary sitting at a table on the restaurant's periphery. How long have they been there talking? I feel like racing back up the stairs, but before I can act, Bernard sees me and waves.

Both of the Berensons' faces are warm and welcoming as I approach them. Mary stands and opens her arms in greeting to me. Then she offers me a kiss on both cheeks. *How strange this is.*

"It is so good to see you again, Belle," she says.

"You, too," I say, hoping that she doesn't hear the trembling in my voice.

Mary and Bernard chat as we study the menu and place our orders, but I sit stiffly and find it hard to make a meaningful contribution.

Finally, Mary turns to me. "So, you'll be leaving for Italy in a few days?" she asks, as if we were making small talk about the weather.

I nod, because I don't trust myself to speak.

She asks, "Have you ever been before?"

This time I shake my head.

She glances at her husband and smiles. "I'm sure Bernard will show you a wonderful time."

My cheeks flush, and I cannot think of a single appropriate reply. I have sat with the Vanderbilts and attended parties with the Rockefellers and the Carnegies, and I work with the famous J. P. Morgan. Yet I have never felt so out of place in my life.

Although Mary and Bernard continue with their lighthearted exchange—talking of London restaurants and upcoming auctions—their discussion happens without me, except for the occasional shake or nod of the head. I feel like a harlot. It is all I can do to remain at this table. How can I possibly be at ease with the wife of the man with whom I'm in love? The man with whom I've planned a romantic trip *à deux* in Italy.

When the restaurant clock chimes twice, I am glad to have the excuse of my appointment to take my leave. "But you've hardly eaten," Mary says, glancing at my plate.

"It was delicious, but duty calls. Thank you so much for making time for me."

Mary stands when I do and embraces me. "I'm sure we'll meet again. Maybe next time in Italy?"

I am relieved that the lunch is over. But before I reach the doors to the restaurant, I hear Bernard's voice. "Miss Greene, please wait."

I pause and turn. "Yes, Mr. Berenson?"

"I'd like to accompany you to the pre-auction meeting," he says.

I wait for him to reach me before quietly asking, "Are you certain it is acceptable to Mrs. Berenson?"

"She encouraged me to join you, Belle," he says straightforwardly. "She finds you a remarkable and lovely young woman, and she wishes me the greatest happiness with you." It has to be my look of astonishment that makes him continue. "I know this must all seem very peculiar, but our relationship—though founded on respect and a shared passion for our work—is no longer one of romantic love."

His words fill me with relief. "This may sound peculiar to you, Bernard, but I am glad to hear it. Your arrangement with your wife and the sort of relationship you seek with me suits me perfectly, as I've written to you. It just feels a bit strange to be with you in her company."

When we step into the sumptuously decorated lobby of Bonhams' auction house, the medieval expert, a square-jawed, serious fellow by the name of Mr. Taylor, awaits us. I am glad Bernard is standing next to me. I have spent several days witnessing his art acumen and how our London colleagues pander to him; this is my opportunity to show him my professional savvy and prowess.

As we pass through the lobby into a narrow hallway toward the room housing the book of hours manuscript, I am fawned over by the staff. Inside the tiny space, I am surrounded by Bernard, Mr. Taylor, and his assistants. I slide on the white gloves that an assistant holds out for me and begin to examine the manuscript. It is organized like the typical book of hours, with the pages alternating between prayers rendered in gorgeous, rounded Gothic script and exquisite miniature paintings depicting scenes from the different seasons, then thoughtful representations of the rural labors necessary for each passing month. But it is the colors as vibrant as the day they were painted nearly five hundred years ago and the genius brushwork that take my breath away. Not surprisingly, memories of my father infiltrate my thoughts. *How Papa would adore this masterpiece and marvel at my proximity to it.*

I want this for the Pierpont Morgan Library.

"It is quite close in here," I say, fanning myself. I need to clear the room except for myself, Bernard, and Mr. Taylor. Playing upon the ever-present fear of a lady's fainting is a certain way of achieving my objective.

Mr. Taylor shoos the assistants out from the small chamber, and I return to my task. "Are you certain it's a Memling?" I ask without lifting my eyes.

Mr. Taylor chuckles as if I've made a joke. "If it was a good enough attribution for the esteemed Bernard Quaritch, I should think it is good enough for us."

By referencing Quaritch, one of the most preeminent booksellers of the last century, he hopes to silence me.

"I see the da Costa heraldry here"—I gingerly return to one of the book's first pages—"but as I'm sure you know, that page has several layers of paint, so we cannot say for certain when the coat of arms was added, and therefore we cannot attribute the royal Portuguese lineage to that emblem alone. Do you have additional provenance documentation?"

"Of—of—" Mr. Taylor struggles to get the words out. He seems unused to being challenged. "Of course, Miss Greene. Will you excuse me a moment while I retrieve those papers?"

I nod and busy myself studying a particularly charming miniature image of a man shearing sheep. *The bucolic scenes adorning the prayers are charming*, I think. As soon as I hear the door close behind him, I turn to Bernard. "Guard the door for a minute, will you?"

With a deep frown, he says, "What the devil—"

"Shhh." I tear the white glove on my right hand off and lick my index finger. Then I run it along the edge of one of the glorious painted scenes.

"Belle—" Bernard is horrified.

"If it's a forgery, then the pigment will rub off."

"But you could do dam—" he protests.

Keeping my gaze fixed on my hand, I shush him again.

I hold my index finger up to the light and rub it with my thumb. Examining my fingers, I see they are clean; no paint has rubbed off. "Good, good," I mutter to myself.

The door swings open, and Mr. Taylor reenters with a hastily assembled sheaf of papers in his hands. "Here we go, Miss Greene." I pretend to glance at the papers as he continues with his apologies. "Please allow me to walk you through the provenance documentation. I apologize that it's not assembled in as orderly a fash—"

I let him explain, frowning in concentration. At the end, I nod and say, "Would you accept twenty percent over the initial asking price? Right now, before the auction begins?"

Mr. Taylor gasps, and I hear a sharp intake of breath from Bernard.

The Bonhams' medieval expert stutters, "M-Miss Greene. That's not really done here. You might not realize that, being an American and all."

I stare at the man. "Really, Mr. Taylor? That isn't the sort of thing that's *done* in England? Then why was I able to preemptively negotiate Lord Amherst's Caxtons away from a London auction a year and a half ago?"

His eyes widen. "That was you?"

"That was me," I answer.

"I'd heard the rumors—we all did—but I didn't know they were true. Still, I am sorry, Miss Greene. I simply cannot breach protocol and sell it to you before the auction."

I stroll around the cramped room, circling him as if he were my prey, which, in a manner of speaking, he is. "Hmmm, I wonder how much the manuscript will fetch at auction when bidders hear gossip that it is not a Memling," I finally say.

"What do you mean? You would spread scurrilous rumors to acquire this manuscript?"

His indignation appears overdone, and in actuality, I'd anticipated this reaction. It is my turn to express shock and dismay. I force a suitable expression upon my face. "How dare you question my integrity! I would never spread *scurrilous* rumors. I would be merely sharing the truth with my fellow bidders. This book of hours is no Memling."

"What the—" His eyes narrow, and I see that he appreciates how I've boxed him in. Yet he hasn't settled on his reaction.

"The da Costa manuscript—a provenance I would not dispute, by the way—was not painted by Hans Memling or his school in the fifteenth century. It wasn't even painted by Gerard David in the early sixteenth century. It was painted by the Flemish illustrator Simon Bening in the mid-sixteenth century. And I have documentation to substantiate that claim." I slide out the papers linking the manuscript to Bening from my bag.

Mr. Taylor responds with unintelligible sputtering.

"It doesn't bother me a bit that Bening painted the book of hours. In fact, from my perspective and that of Mr. Morgan, it's a benefit. We quite admire Bening; he was the last great Flemish illuminator, after all, and highly regarded in his day. But I cannot say the other bidders will be as pleased. Most of the bidders will be there to secure a Memling for their collection. Or a David at the very least." I pause. "I imagine it would lower the price considerably when they learn that the da Costa book of hours is actually a Bening."

"What do you want from me, Miss Greene?" Mr. Taylor has recovered, and his voice is positively glacial. All his earlier solicitousness has been replaced by cold fury.

I keep my voice bright, as if we're chatting about a particularly favorable spot of weather. "I thought I'd been perfectly clear, Mr. Taylor. Shall I repeat myself? I'd like to purchase the da Costa book of hours today for the Pierpont Morgan Library, and I am willing to pay you twenty percent over the starting auction price."

I feel power surge through me. How many women have the opportunity to exercise their intellectual prowess and financial dominance—even if it derives from another—over a man? And the bigger question, one never far from my thoughts, is how many colored women have this chance? The sensation is exhilarating for so many reasons. And addictive.

We agree to terms, and Mr. Taylor excuses himself from the room to obtain the paperwork. Once we are alone, Bernard stares at me, shaking his head. "By God, that was masterful. I've never seen a negotiation handled with such murderous skill. And bloody bold," he says with a low whistle.

"If I don't take bold measures, then I won't get bold results. I'll be duped into buying a forgery, or I'll lose a valuable item to a competing bidder I've underestimated. My boldness is the reason the Pierpont Morgan Library collection is on its way to becoming unparalleled," I say without a shred of humility.

He pulls me toward the closed door, blocking the only means of ingress to or egress from the tiny chamber. Leaning me against it, he kisses me long and hard. By the time I break away, we are both breathless.

"I wish we were already in Italy," he says.

My heart is pounding, and my desire matches Bernard's. As longing surges through me, I say, "So do I."

Staring into my eyes, he whispers, "You are an extraordinary creature."

CHAPTER 23

We chance holding hands as we stroll down the narrow cobblestone streets of Verona. The touch of his finger on my bare palm sends shivers through me, and I thrill not only at the risk we are taking but at what the evening promises.

Bernard and I haven't dared to exhibit our feelings so openly until now. It is too dangerous. It is impossible for a man and a woman to travel together alone without raising eyebrows. The proximity of my maid Marie and the presence of colleagues delayed our intimacy while we toured the English capital, and we could not let down our guard even on the Orient Express, which carried us into Italy.

But now that we are in Verona, two hundred miles north of Florence, we can relax our vigilance. We have constructed our itinerary exclusively on these tiny out-of-the-way Italian towns so we can simply be two anonymous lovers.

I look over my shoulder and smile at Bernard. He appears lit from within in the glorious golden light of late summer. In this diffused sun, which warms but never sears in the late afternoon, its rays enlivening but never blinding, we enjoy the streets of Verona.

When we first arrived at the train station earlier in the day, Bernard suggested a carriage, saying the distance to our appointment was too far for the delicate heels of my shoes. But I insisted we walk, and I am pleased that I did. How else could I see the life of this bustling, crumbling, exquisite town firsthand? How could I inhale the pungent smell of its cheeses from the market outside the ancient, diamond-shaped city center—the Piazza delle Erbe—as well as the heady scent of incense wafting out from the numerous stone Catholic churches we pass? Without walking among the townspeople, how would I know that the locals' skin tone matches my own, supporting my claims of southern European heritage?

How else would I experience the sensation of returning home to a place I have never visited, with a man I feel I've known my whole life?

"Belle," Bernard says, pointing to a gap between two buildings, "cast your eye on the hills above the river Adige."

"By God," I exclaim as I glance across the town, which hugs the banks of the sinuous river to the nearby hills. "It's the background that Veronese and Antonello da Messina used in their paintings."

Art springs alive in the Italian town and hills. I linger at the landscape of undulating green and gold juxtaposed against ancient buildings, marveling at a sight that countless Renaissance artists strove to capture, and allow myself to be engulfed by the shimmering color. *Imagine*, I think, *when I was a young girl, entranced by medieval and Renaissance artwork alongside Papa, if I had known that one day I'd stand before the hills that inspired my beloved masterpieces. With the man who wrote the definitive treatise on the art so treasured by me and Papa.*

Bernard's finger trails down my arm, and I shiver. Tenderly, he says, "I hate to take you away from this sight, my love, but I must. Our appointment at the basilica awaits."

We rejoin our fingers as naturally as if we were an old couple. Strolling the remaining four blocks, we pass redbrick medieval structures interspersed by marble Renaissance buildings, set against a backdrop of crenellated castle walls. We walk in companionable silence toward the Romanesque church that is our destination: the Basilica of San Zeno Maggiore.

Passing through the bronze doors, we step into the nave and are bathed with the multicolored light that streams through the church's thirteenth-century rose window. Our heels clatter in the empty cavernous space. When we reach the altar, Bernard gestures to the famous Mantegna triptych hanging above it.

The first time I saw the triptych by Andrea Mantegna was in the pages of Bernard's book. Although I reveled in that reproduction, it does no justice to the actual San Zeno altarpiece, with its beatific, realistically plaintive Madonna holding the Christ child on her lap, encircled by singing cherubs and flanked by saints.

"When we gaze at this painting, Belle, we are staring across time, literally watching the evolution of Renaissance artists' understanding of pictorial space. Mantegna created perspective; he inspired Leonardo." He points to a few architectural devices and figures that diminish in size in the painting's background. "On one level, you still have the flat medieval two-dimensional depiction of certain key figures. Yet he created the illusion of a three-dimensional space. The beauty of these Italian churches inspired me to convert to Roman Catholicism."

There is such joy in his voice when he glances over at me. "Oh, are you crying, my darling Belle? You are the most enchanting creature." He pulls an embroidered handkerchief from his pocket and dabs at my eyes. "The same thing happened to me when I first stood before this masterpiece. It was at that moment—years ago, when I was still a young man living hand to mouth in Florence—that I loved this painting and the Renaissance oeuvre in a way that no one had in a long time. So many artists and their work had been forgotten. I also realized that by reintroducing this obscure Renaissance artist along with other talented painters and sculptors to the modern world, I might find a lofty place among wealthy art patrons and secure a position for myself in a stratum to which I had not been born. Much as artisans of the Renaissance had done. And much as you yourself have done. We are creatures of the Renaissance, you and I."

He takes both of my hands into his. "I believe this is one of the reasons you and I feel about each other the way we do. We are alike in many ways, some of which we don't mention." Pulling me even closer to him, he whispers, "I feel like we are having a *conversazione sacra* right now, just like the saints in the San Zeno altarpiece; what is this moment but a sacred conversation?"

The sound of someone clearing his throat interrupts us. It is the basilica's priest. He and Bernard exchange friendly greetings in Italian, and the priest gestures for us to follow him up the stairs to the altar. There, Mantegna's brushstrokes become visible, and I can envision the artist standing back to admire his work in this cacophonous space, alight with the inspiration that had been necessary to create the masterpiece.

We leave the basilica and take a carriage to our hotel. The day has been glorious but long, and we have special dinner plans. Inside the blessed coolness of the carriage, I rest my head on Bernard's shoulder, gazing at the Veronese sights that we pass. It is a moment hewn from the Renaissance itself.

The carriage comes to a rough halt in front of our hotel, where our trunks were sent earlier from the train station. Bernard steps out of the carriage first so he can help me, but as I attempt to slide across the carriage bench, something holds me in place. I look down and see that the hem of my navy-blue traveling gown is caught on a bench nail head. As I reach down to untangle it, I hear voices outside the carriage.

"Bernard! Bernard Berenson, is that you?" a heavily accented voice calls out in English. Then in French. "Monsieur Berenson?"

My head is still down as I hear Bernard reply, "Ah." His voice might sound hearty to the innocent passerby but I hear his alarm. "Imagine the odds of meeting you here in Verona, Monsieur Seligmann!" He shouts the name for my benefit.

Jacques Seligmann. No, no, no. How could we have the misfortune of running into the art dealer who knows us both so well?

As Bernard keeps Mr. Seligmann's attention, I direct the driver away from the hotel. While the carriage circles around Verona, I try to decide what to do. Bernard and I cannot be seen together in this way. The damage to my reputation, and to a lesser extent his, is incalculable.

After an hour of rambling through the Veronese streets, I ask the driver to return to the hotel. Once there, I am scared to step inside. Relief washes over me when I see Bernard rushing in my direction.

"How did you get him to leave?" I am sure Mr. Seligmann would have invited Bernard to join him and his entourage for dinner.

"I promised to visit him in his Paris gallery on my next trip to France. And consult him on a few pieces."

"I cannot believe that Jacques Seligmann, of all people, should encounter us here."

He nods. "I know, my beautiful Belle. But now we are alone again, and the night is ours. We will just dine here, at the hotel, so that we take no more chances."

I nod in agreement; all that matters is that we are finally alone. By the time we make our way upstairs, there is little room for patience. Our desire has been building for too long, hundreds of days that felt like thousands of nights, made more intense by our stay in London, where every day of forbearance felt interminable.

Bernard's lips are on mine before the door closes behind us, and to my surprise, his kiss is gentle, even soft, as if we now have those thousand nights back to explore each other. Then, as if he has spent all his gentleness on that one kiss, he sweeps me up into his arms and carries me through the sitting room and into the darkened bedroom, lit only by the gas lamp left on by the hotel staff. He lays me on the bed, pressing his body into mine, his desire apparent.

After a kiss deeper and longer than I think possible, his tongue begins a new journey, slipping to the soft space behind my ear before tracing a long line to the base of my neck. I can barely breathe as his fingers work deftly to undo the many buttons on my dress and then unlace my corset, all the while moving his lips and tongue along my skin. Suddenly, he lifts off my chemise, and I lie bare before him. He removes his glasses, then gazes at me. In a voice thick with emotion, he says, "You are so beautiful, my Belle."

I answer by pulling his lips to mine and placing his hands on my body. His fingers travel over me, caressing my breasts, my navel, and beyond. I shiver at his touch, and I begin an exploration of my own as I help him undress. When he is bare before me, I realize that a marble sculpture of a naked man, of which I've seen many, cannot capture the tactile allure of a real man. I touch him as he had touched me, until we are both out of breath.

His eyes glassy with longing, he hovers above me, hesitating. "Are you certain, Belle?"

"Please," I whisper into his ear. "I have waited too long."

As I'd dreamed about many nights over the past year, our bodies meld, each of us surrendering to the movement and emotion until our voices rise and drown out all other sound and thought. Then he utters something, "моя любовь," before collapsing on top of me. Moments later he rolls to the side, bringing me with him and wrapping me in his arms.

We breathe heavily for several minutes before Bernard kisses me and then whispers, "Belle?"

He doesn't need to finish his question in order for me to understand what he is asking. "Yes, Bernard. You are my first."

With those words, he holds me tighter, his arms a protective cocoon from the world, and I want to rest here forever.

"I didn't know," he says, with a tinge of guilt in his tone. "I didn't even suspect."

His words make my heart hammer harder against my chest as names roll through my mind. The names of the beautiful women that he's rumored to have bedded in the past, whispers I'd heard from society gossips during the Berensons' New York visit. How can I possibly measure up to a woman like Aline de Rothschild, also known as Lady Sassoon? How can I measure up to any of them?

He grows so quiet that I have to ask, "Did I disappoint you?"

His words come quickly. "No, my love." He kisses my forehead. "You could never do that. I just didn't know." He pulls me closer and rests my head against his chest. "You seemed a bit more—" He trails off.

Bernard doesn't need to finish. I understand. In order to take attention away from any questions about my ethnicity, I'd hidden behind my flirtatious behavior. Yet I hadn't fully considered the message that my coquettishness was sending; I'd conveyed a worldliness that was the opposite of my actual experience.

Our legs are tangled, and my thoughts are not quiet. "Bernard?" I ask.

He pulls me even closer. "It was beautiful, my love," he says, believing I seek more reassurance.

A shadow from the gas lamp's flames covers half of his face, and I ask, "It was wonderful for me, too. But—" I hesitate.

"What is it?" He strokes my hair.

"When we were making love, you said something that wasn't English. What did you say?" What I'm really asking isn't the meaning of his words but the reason he used another language in that vulnerable moment.

He presses his finger against my lips. "This is what I said." He kisses me again with even more passion than before, leaving me breathless. "That's all you need to know."

I curl into his embrace, and soon his soft snores fill the air. The gas lamp's shadows dance against the wall as I think on Bernard's words: *That's all you need to know.* I lie awake, satiated and unsettled at the same time. What language had Bernard spoken in the heat of the moment? And why wouldn't he answer my question?

These questions linger until the flame in the lamp burns out and the bedroom turns pitch-black. Who is Bernard, really? The words he'd spoken tonight sounded like Russian. Perhaps the label Mr. Morgan spat out is the truth. Maybe Bernard is a Russian Jewish immigrant and Bernard Berenson isn't even the name to which he'd been born but a name he assumed as he fashioned a place for himself in a world to which he didn't belong. Much like Belle da Costa Greene.

What a notion, I think with amusement. With a smile on my lips, I drift off into a contented sleep in the arms of Bernard Berenson, or whoever he is.

CHAPTER 24

SEPTEMBER 23, 1910
ORVIETO, ITALY

The early-morning light streams through the open balcony doors onto the desk where I have been writing for the last hour. The light has transformed from the gray-blue of dawn to the brilliant golden sunshine of mid-morning.

"Won't you come back to bed?"

Amid the tangle of white linen sheets and the matelassé duvet lies Bernard. His eyes look naked without his glasses, and they're heavy with sleep. And desire.

"I wish I could, my love. But I must post this letter to Mr. Morgan this morning." I tease, "You've kept me so busy over these last few weeks—by day with art and by night with your affections—I've hardly had a spare minute to write him."

Bernard groans. "Surely he can wait another day." When he holds out his arms to me, I am filled with longing and yearning, buoyed by memories of last night and the many nights before that. But none of those evenings are as memorable as our first night together—my first time ever—in Verona a month ago.

"Belle?" Bernard gently calls me again.

I am tempted. More than the quaint towns, the glorious landscapes, and the forgotten masterworks of Italy, I have enjoyed my nights with Bernard. Not to mention the occasional morning.

But if I don't finalize this long missive and post it before noon today—a Friday—I will add three days to its delivery time because of the weekend. Mr. Morgan hasn't received a report from me for over a week. Very soon, he will begin to wonder and maybe even worry. He could telegraph one of his representatives and set him on my trail.

Then Bernard says, "You know, I don't believe you've ever written me a letter half as long as that tome you're scribing to Mr. Morgan. And you get to see him almost constantly."

This has been a refrain on our travels. Why did I not write Bernard with the same regularity he wrote me, nearly daily?

"Well, he is my employer, and he does demand a regular accounting of my time when I am on a trip for him."

Bernard is quiet for a long moment. "I sense that you are keeping secrets from me, Belle. There is a certain reticence about you, a mystery I cannot solve even though secrecy is a language I speak. In some ways, it may well be the one in which I'm most fluent, and I suspect the same is true of you. And yet, I can't decipher you."

Why would a letter to Mr. Morgan bring Bernard to this conclusion, that I am hiding something from him? Or is he using this as an excuse to ask about gossip he's heard?

"How can you say that, Bernard?" I decide this is the best, and only, response.

No matter how close I feel to Bernard, how connected to him intellectually and emotionally, I will never divulge my secret.

I add, "With others, I always feel I am in the process of reassembling the sundry parts of myself to present the most pleasing whole, but with you, I am simply myself, complete and authentic. So you can imagine how your accusation makes me feel."

"It is j-just—" He stumbles over his words, a rarity. "You are uncommonly close to Mr. Morgan."

He sounds jealous, but perhaps he's kidding or simply backing away from his somewhat offensive assertion. Either way, I decide on a new approach. I stand, and as I allow my lilac silk dressing gown to pool around my feet, our eyes lock.

Leaning over him, I purr, "Are you envious of Pierpont?" I press my lips against his, but he doesn't kiss me back.

When I lean away, he asks, "Is that what you call him when you're alone?"

There is not a hint of humor in this display of possessiveness. It is so unlike the controlled Bernard he exhibits in public, unlike even the more open, but still restrained, Bernard he shares with me in the privacy of the bedchamber. Oh, how alike we are.

"Of course. When it's just us two, it's Pierpont and Belle." I laugh, trying to defuse his jealousy with a bit of the truth. Mr. Morgan does indeed call me Belle, but I would not dare call him anything.

In some ways, Bernard's envy is a relief. A jealous Bernard I can handle. A suspicious Bernard, I cannot. And recently, he's given me cause to be wary. During two separate intimate moments, he made troubling observations—*your hair is so different in the morning* and *your skin gets so dark in this Italian sun*—comments that sounded more like prompts for disclosure than innocent reflections.

Each time I'd been able to deflect his comment with a little laugh and a kiss, but I suspect he isn't finished. Consequently, at the moment I'm relieved to be facing jealousy rather than an inquisition.

"Don't toy with me, Belle," Bernard says, bringing my thoughts to the present. I realize that he's deadly serious. He cannot be teased out of this mood. His feelings are too intense and raw to withstand such joviality.

"I feel about you like I've felt about no one else," he says, "and I need to know what he means to you."

I sit down on the bed and run my finger along his cheek. "Mr. Morgan is my employer only, Bernard, a man to whom I'm indebted, as he has entrusted me with great wealth and power. He has my loyalty." I kiss him long and hard, which he returns. I break away only to tell him, "He doesn't have my heart. You must know that belongs to only you."

The edges of his lips curve into a smile, and when he kisses me back, I realize there will be no letter for Mr. Morgan today. I am lost. To Italy. To Bernard.

CHAPTER 25

At first, it is just my breasts, achingly tender to Bernard's touch. Then, two days later, it is abdominal pain coupled with an overwhelming wave of fatigue, just hours after awakening. I assume I've contracted an illness or eaten spoiled food, but then I try to remember the last time I had my menstrual cycle, which is usually very regular. It was over two months ago, before my arrival in Europe. I push the terrifying possibility out of my mind until I confront soft-boiled eggs at breakfast, excuse myself, and rush to the bathroom.

I am pregnant.

For a day, I keep the revelation to myself. What should I do? By the next morning, I realize I cannot answer that question. Not before I address all the other important questions first, most importantly whether there is any possibility of a life in which Bernard and I could have this baby.

I would need to give up my career; Mr. Morgan would never keep me on once he found out I am pregnant. I would have to leave my mother and siblings and New York City. Perhaps Europe's more flexible moral code and pockets of bohemian societies would be kind and welcome us. But I would have to anticipate society's and Bernard's reaction if the child did not share my lighter coloring.

If I chose to keep this baby, I would have to confess *all* to Bernard. He would need to know that I am a colored woman and that my real name is Belle Marion Greener. And I would need him in my life; society is unkind to unmarried mothers, whether they are white, colored, or black. While I know he loves me, does he love me enough to hear this? Can he love me through this?

When I am alone in the suite, I stand before the mirror and run my fingers around the tiny mound of my belly. I imagine my midriff swollen and full, with Bernard's arms around my shoulders. And then I envision us later, with a baby boy in my arms. A boy who has Bernard's coloring and my tenacity. A boy who is charming like his father, with ambition like his mother, and who has a love of the arts like us both.

The longer I turn my situation round and round in my mind, the clearer it becomes that Bernard's involvement is necessary to keep the child. I just hope that everything Bernard has said about his love for me is the truth.

The next morning, while we lie tangled in our sheets, I whisper, "Bernard, there's something I have to tell you."

He pulls me closer. "You can tell me anything, Belle. In fact, I wish you'd tell me everything," he whispers back with emphasis.

Burying my face in his shoulder, I say, "I think I'm pregnant."

His body becomes rigid, and he recoils to the opposite side of the bed. "This cannot be happening, Belle." His eyes are on the ceiling. "We cannot have a child."

I pull myself up and face him. "Well, we are. I am sure of it."

"I assumed you were handling it."

For a moment, I wonder what he's talking about, and then I realize he means some sort of contraceptive. That remark shocks me; how would I know about that? I was raised in a strict family that never would have contemplated premarital relations, and it isn't as if I have close girlfriends in whom I can confide. "No," I say. "I assumed you were. You are the experienced one in our relationship, after all."

In an icy voice, he says, "I told you I didn't want any children."

"You told me you never wanted to have children with Mary. You never said you were opposed to children altogether."

How can he take away this dream so quickly and heartlessly, without any heed for my feelings? I cling to my anger and disappointment, manifesting a coldness to match his. I know if I don't, I will dissolve into tears, and I cannot allow that.

When he stays silent, I continue, "But that is of no import, because I didn't plan this, Bernard. You must know that. I have my career to think about, among other things."

He abruptly sits up. "Surely *you* must understand that our situation will not allow for a child. Among other things, I am married, for God's sake, and Mary is my business partner on top of that. You're going to have to do something about your condition."

Me? Do something about *my* condition? He is every bit as responsible for this condition as I am.

I race to the bathroom. Sobbing, I lock myself in. I have told myself repeatedly that I do not want and could never have a chance at motherhood. Now that I'm pregnant, however, I feel a longing for a child.

Again, I try to calculate all the variables in this overwhelming equation. How can I make this happen on my own? Living in New York and continuing to work for Mr. Morgan is not an option. Even if my baby were fair skinned and I were able to preserve my identity as a white woman, the stigma of being an unwed mother would exclude me from the art and library world and bring shame upon my family. The downward social and financial spiral caused by my pregnancy and the consequent change in our circumstances could unmoor my mother and siblings from their white existence.

Could I return to Washington, DC, and live among my Fleet relatives in a community where my baby's complexion wouldn't matter? The dishonor of being an unmarried mother exists there as well. But even if it didn't, I have listened closely to my mother. Given the stranglehold that segregation and the white supremacists have over the South, I could not subject myself and my child to a life of suppression that is getting progressively worse.

The truth is, there is no place for me to go. As an unmarried colored woman, I would never be hired as a librarian or an art expert anywhere in America, and without Mr. Morgan's recommendation—which he would *never* provide if he found out I was pregnant by Bernard or anyone else—no one would hire me in Europe. With a child, I have no place and no one. Only Bernard's acceptance and support could have changed that, and he hasn't even bothered to come to the bathroom door to check on me.

I slide to the floor, bereft at Bernard's retreat. I grab a towel and scream into it, pummeling the cold hard tile of the bathroom floor with my free hand. What is so wrong with *my* blood that I'm not worthy of bringing a baby into this unfair world?

All I can think about are the words spoken to me more than two years ago, words I should have heeded. *You don't have the luxury of making mistakes, Miss Greene.*

CHAPTER 26

OCTOBER 12, 1910
LONDON, ENGLAND

I am torn in two by the pain. The agony of its slicing, stabbing urgency drives me mad, until I can't think and feel and be anything but the pain. The wave subsides, and I'm relieved to learn that it hasn't wholly subsumed me. In the void left in its wake, fragments of memories—or dreams, perhaps—enter my consciousness. Gazing at gilt-haloed Madonnas and saints, red-tiled roofs, and glorious sun. Laughing as we dodged friends of Mr. Morgan's in Ravenna by slipping out the back door of a trattoria. Watching sheets of rain cascading on narrow Venetian streets as the great city square before St. Peter's becomes submerged in a rising tide of water. Listening to the rhythm of Baudelaire being read aloud as I drift off to sleep underneath crisp white bedsheets in an ornate Italian bed. Strolling hand in hand in the sun-dappled light of Murano island near Venice, where men blow glass of vivid blue, red, and gold into a dizzying array of shapes, as if by magic.

What is dream, and what is real?

I hear voices, and I strain to open my eyes. A blond woman in a white dress wearing a white hat like a nun's wimple stands next to a man in a thin white cotton coat over a standard-looking gray worsted wool suit. I narrow my eyes, but not too much. Every movement brings pain. But I wonder, *Who are these two? Where am I?*

"Miss Greene, can you hear me?" the man asks in a British accent; there is nothing Italian about this pale, thin creature. He reaches for an object that dangles around his neck. I know the name for this medical device, but the word stays lodged in the recesses of my brain, refusing to reach my lips. Ah yes, it's a stethoscope. The man must be a doctor. Am I in a hospital? Why?

I part my lips, try to speak, but all I hear is an animalistic grunt. Was that me? I wish I could search the room for more signs to guide me, but I can't even lift my head from the pillow. Still, I know I must try to make myself heard again; I must make this doctor and nurse understand that the pain has not driven away my consciousness completely. Willing my vocal cords to make an intelligible sound, I try again. But all I hear is that guttural noise. Could that really be coming from me?

I strain, attempt to move my head off the pillow, but then the world fades to black.

When I awaken, it takes only moments this time to determine where I am. And as I try to move, every limb in my body feels impossibly heavy. I try to lift my right leg, then my left, to no avail. My hands and arms are leaden; only my fingers gain any distance off the surface of the bed. But I am grateful for one thing—the pain has subsided.

"Miss Greene, it is good to see your eyes so clear and lucid this morning."

The voice comes from my right. When I turn my head, I realize it is the same nurse as before. I try to speak before the darkness comes again, but my throat and mouth are bone-dry. Finally, I'm able to croak out, "Water, please," in a voice that doesn't sound anything like my own.

"Certainly." The nurse, a model of efficiency, reaches for the glass of water sitting on the table next to me and brings it to my lips.

As I sip from the glass, I glance around the sterile hospital room, watching as the nurse stands and rings a bell. She then adds, "You had us concerned. You've been suffering from an extraordinarily high fever for two days now."

Two days? I've been in this bed, largely unconscious, for two days? What am I doing here in England? The last clear memory I have is boarding the train from Venice with Bernard's friend, Mrs. Ethel Harrison, heading for London.

Ethel Harrison. Bernard. Venice. London.

Memories flood me and fill in the blanks. I know why I am here. The recollections cause a heaving, racking sob to emanate from my throat, and a different sort of agony descends upon me. Suddenly, I'm sobbing. My tears feel hot upon my cheeks, and I cry until I cannot catch my breath.

"There, there, Miss Greene." The nurse lays a consoling hand over mine. "There is no need for you to be concerned. You're through the worst of the infection. Your fever broke not two hours ago. You'll be right as rain in no time, once you get your strength back."

How can she say that? Would I ever be "right as rain" again? After what I'd just done? After what Bernard encouraged me to do, what I agreed to?

When my cries don't stop, the nurse offers, "Should I fetch your friend for you? She's just down the hallway speaking to your doctor."

I have to pause for a moment, to recall who she's talking about. Then I nod, realizing she must mean Ethel, who is really Bernard's friend first. But after all she's done for me these past few days—here in the hospital and the travel from Italy to England before that—I suppose she's proven herself to be my loyal friend, too. My eyes feel swollen and sore, and I allow myself to rest. Just when I close my eyes, I hear the door creak and the clatter of heels—definitely not the soft pad of nurse's shoes—and my eyelids flutter open. Over me, I see Ethel's mournful brown irises staring down.

"Oh, Belle," she breathes, sounding relieved, "it's so good to see your eyes open and a pinch of color back in your cheeks. We have been worried sick."

"We?" I do not remember anyone accompanying us to London from Venice, but that doesn't mean we didn't have another companion. My memory is operating in fits and starts.

"Bernard and I." She lowers her voice. "We are the only two who know—" She struggles for the right euphemism. "Know about your procedure, of course."

I blink at those words. "Is Bernard here?" I want more than anything in the world for him to hold my hand and tell me everything will be all right.

But will it be all right? The stain of my actions—our actions—lies heavy upon me, and I think about how it would feel to meet his eyes, knowing what we've done and wondering whether I would have agreed if my real identity had left me another choice. But regardless, he *should* be here, especially after the illness that's befallen me on the heels of the "procedure."

"No." She hesitates and glances at the floor. "He's still in Paris. He hasn't been able to make it to London." She looks up, and there is a bit more cheer in her tone when she adds, "But I've been keeping him updated by cable, and he sends his love."

I sense that Ethel, a kindly woman with a long history of friendship and loyalty to Bernard and Mary, has made up this latter mention of Bernard's affection.

Hasn't been able to make it to London or didn't want to come? If Bernard truly feels the depth of emotion for me he professed in all of his letters and in Italy, then nothing and no one could have stopped him from boarding the next ship to London to see me. Particularly since he is both the cause of my condition and the impetus for the procedure. His absence speaks volumes to me. It seems the relationship to which I felt inextricably intertwined has become unraveled. Or perhaps it was never the relationship I believed it to be.

I will have to proceed on my own. "Is everything—" I fumble for the correct word. "Taken care of?"

Ethel asks, "You mean your condition?"

I nod. No one, it seems, can bring themselves to say the word "abortion." Not even me.

"Yes." She nods. "Your condition was addressed by the procedure. They think the infection that followed might have been prompted by the 'liver pill' you took in Venice." She shakes her head. "Which didn't work."

The words "liver pill" bring a rush of fresh memories. Now I recall the terrible torrent of events that began when Bernard and I first arrived in Venice nearly two weeks ago. Once I told Bernard about the pregnancy and the options appeared narrow, he summoned the loyal Ethel, and as I sat, a specimen between them, my status was quietly discussed with a disturbing amount of expertise on both Bernard's and Ethel's parts. I agreed to the initial step, and somehow Ethel procured the abortifacient "liver pill" from a sympathetic Italian physician. While retching ensued, my "condition" remained.

The morning after I took the unsuccessful "liver pill," Bernard mentioned "the next step," a euphemism that sent sickening chills through me. At first I refused to discuss the details of what this "step" would entail; from the whispered conversations I'd overheard over the years, it seemed far more barbaric than swallowing a simple pill. Only when my silence yielded firm reminders from Bernard about what we'd agreed to—reminders that demonstrated to me his unwavering commitment to end the pregnancy—did I relent. It was then when he shared that I must travel to a special clinic in London where my "condition"—never my baby—could be permanently addressed and that Ethel, not Bernard, would accompany me on this journey. Bernard told me for the first time that he needed to be in Paris for business. *Coward*, I thought but did not say aloud.

"Belle?" Ethel interrupts my terrible recollections. "Did you hear what I said about the infection?"

"Yes," I hasten to answer, even though I hadn't been listening, "the infection was caused by the 'liver pill.'" I pause, then ask the question that I must have answered. Even if I loathe the response. "Will Bernard be coming to London from Paris?"

Ethel hesitates. Then she draws her chair closer to my bed, and her hands form a prayer-like triangle. "Belle, I am so terribly sorry, but I just received a telegram. Bernard sends his regards, but he will not be able to come to London after all."

CHAPTER 27

Belle, Belle, don't leave us!" Ellen Terry cries out, gesturing for me to rejoin the group of old New York friends like Ethel and P. G. Grant and new acquaintances like Ellen, a legendary English actress with whom I'd been sharing a few glasses of champagne. But I wave her away, laughing.

"I need a breath of fresh air." The bar is crowded tonight in the first-class lounge, one of the centerpieces of the *Oceanic*. Launched in 1899, the White Star Line ocean liner is sumptuous in every detail, from the frescoed gilt dome that soars over the dining room to the masterful wood paneling and brass finishes in the staterooms—and the first-class lounge is no exception. Mr. Morgan would approve; after all, through his holding company, the International Mercantile Marine Company, he is one of the owners of the White Star Line.

"But *you* are the breath of fresh air, darling," Ellen retorts. Ellen had been standing next to me when we boarded. Soon she was introducing me to her friends and arranging for us all to meet up at the bar. After two glasses of champagne, she declared that we two were the only somewhat avant-garde souls on board and that we *must* be inseparable for the duration of this voyage. Actresses certainly make friends easily.

Lifting the flute of champagne to which I've been holding tightly, I toast the group from afar. "I'll see you at dinner!"

I wander among the other passengers strolling on the deck. Spotting an empty corner at the railing, I claim it for my own, watching as the English shore recedes into the far distance and becomes an indistinct smudge against the darkening sky and sea. How I wish my last days with Bernard and the past weeks in London could fade from view so smoothly. All I want is to return to my old self.

Bernard. *Even the thought of his name wounds me afresh.* For weeks, as I recovered in London, we scribbled bittersweet, mournful letters to each other of what might have been. There were some letters hopeful for the future, attached to gifts of Fortuny nightgowns and Parisian perfumes. In some ways, these were the most painful. Each missive contained promises that soon he would cross the English Channel to see me.

But he never came. By the time I boarded the *Oceanic*, I was angry. I told him as much in my parting missive:

> *How could you be only hours from me and yet stay away, offering excuse after excuse? How could the man I loved—the man to whom I'd given myself—behave in this way, especially given the loss and suffering I'd just endured? How could you do this to me?*

The question I didn't write, but certainly thought, was, *How could I let him?*

I push away from the railing. Only a few people still mill about. I suppose most have retired to their cabins to rest and dress for dinner. My heels clatter as I cross the wood-planked flooring, and just as I'm about to enter the hallway where my stateroom awaits, I bump into a familiar but unexpected figure. Anne Morgan.

"Anne?" I exclaim.

"Belle?" she replies.

"Now don't sound so surprised to see Belle here, Anne. You knew she'd be on board," Bessie Marbury, who stands at Anne's side, interjects. She uses her big, booming voice, one that matches the largeness of her physical presence. I've come to know and enjoy the famous theatrical and literary agent. She is a force to be reckoned with in her chosen fields. She represented Oscar Wilde's work before his death, which means she's fearless and cares little for society's scorn. Representing the brilliant plays of George Bernard Shaw is another mark in her favor. And finally, she seems inclined to like me even if Anne and Elsie de Wolfe have negative feelings about me. We give each other large genuine smiles. I note that Elsie, the rumored third in their Boston marriage, is absent, and I wonder at her whereabouts; I rarely see them separately in social settings.

Bessie gives me a warm embrace, bellowing, "Wonderful to see you, Belle."

"Lovely to see you, too, Bessie." With a cordial nod, I add, "You as well, Anne. Did you two board in Paris? Mr. Morgan mentioned that you have been at the Villa Trianon these past months."

But I hadn't known Anne was on board the very same ship as I am, headed back to New York. Mercifully, Anne has been less of a regular presence in the library due to the chasm between her and her father's political views, particularly Anne's public support for the female garment workers, a cause that enrages her father.

"That's right," Bessie answers, while Anne gives me only a lukewarm nod. "And what a glorious time it was. We ended our stay in Paris, of course."

"Ah, how was Paris?" I ask, leading the women out of the narrow hallway and onto the more spacious deck.

"Magical, as always. Divine food and even more divine theater," Bessie answers for them both. She is one of the few people whose forceful personality makes Anne seem less than commanding.

"How fortunate for you both."

"Paris wasn't part of your itinerary on this trip?" Bessie looks surprised.

"Only briefly. I spent most of my time in London meeting with curators and dealers, and then a month in Italy, assessing artwork for the library's collection. Unfortunately, I only had two days in Paris en route to Italy."

Bessie wags her finger at me, then Anne. "You'll have to convince that controlling Mr. J. P. Morgan to loosen up your schedule to accommodate more time in Paris."

Glancing at Anne, I say to Bessie, "Honestly, I have no complaints. I had a glorious time traipsing through some tiny Italian towns."

Anne finally chimes in, "Where did you go, Belle?"

While this question would be natural in a typical conversation, Anne and I do not have a history of engaging in typical conversations. Ever. This is the first time in a while that she has even acknowledged my presence. I answer cautiously, "I visited the better-known towns first, of course, like Florence and Venice. But I found the smaller locales—Verona, Ravenna, Siena, and Orvieto—to be the real gifts."

"How did you discover these towns?" Anne asks.

Anne's curiosity is uncharacteristic when it comes to me, so I choose my words with care. "I had an exceptional guide."

Anne glances at Bessie with a triumphant little smirk. "I bet you did, and I'm guessing I know who that guide was."

My stomach lurches. This is the trap she was trying to set with her seemingly innocuous questions. Of all people to know about my time with Bernard—maybe even my relationship with him—Anne would be the worst. She has already speculated about what she calls my tropical roots. What will she do if she believes she holds two secrets about me?

"Belle," Bessie says, with a disappointed glance at Anne, "what Anne is alluding to is the fact that we had dinner with Bernard Berenson in Paris two nights before we boarded the *Oceanic*."

"Oh?" I decide that I will not offer up anything to them—not a single detail and not a single emotion—that Bernard has not already given them. I am furious with Bernard that he might have shared *anything* about our time together with Anne Morgan. He knows how rocky my relationship is with her.

"And he mentioned that he gave you some advice about what towns to visit in Italy," Bessie says.

"He did." I admit this small fact, waiting to see what else will be added.

"And that, when his schedule allowed, he stopped in a couple of the towns as you toured them to share the art highlights," Bessie continues.

"He *is* the world's foremost expert on Italian Renaissance art. His guidance was very useful." I force a smile.

Anne exclaims, "He must have been more than a tour guide. It seems you broke his heart."

Despite my intention to remain calm and reserved, I blurt out, "*I* broke his heart? I cannot believe he said that."

Bessie shoots Anne a scolding look. "He didn't say that, Belle. Bernard hinted that he found you irresistibly alluring during the brief time you spent together and that the world seems a bit . . ." She pauses, searching for a word. "Dimmer since you left."

In a loud voice, Anne says, "I find it hard to believe that showing you around some churches and museums for a few minutes would leave him so despondent."

Bernard despondent? For a moment, I don't hear the insinuation in Anne's remark. But then her implication becomes clear.

Rather than reacting defensively, I decide to use the artifices that serve me well in the social sphere. "I cannot help it if my charms disarmed him," I say with a toss of my scarf. "There was no intentional coquetry, but men will see what they want to see."

Bessie guffaws, a decidedly unladylike sound. But then everything about Bessie is unladylike. "So true, Belle, that most men don't realize the foolishness of their views. Didn't Shakespeare say, 'A fool thinks himself to be wise, but a wise man knows himself to be a fool'?" She shakes her head, and then says, "Anne and I tried to convince Bernard to join us on the *Oceanic*—some bracing ocean breezes and the indulgence of the ship would perk him up, we told him—but somehow he knew you'd be on board and said you wouldn't want to see him."

I doubt that Anne's invitation to Bernard to come aboard the *Oceanic* was innocent. Perhaps she planned on taking evidence of the romance back to her father, breaking our unspoken agreement to keep what we think are each other's secrets.

It is some solace that Bernard realizes how terribly he's disappointed me—and that he's suffering. It would be unfair if I were suffering alone.

"I cannot imagine what he was talking about," I reply.

"Ah well, there's no accounting for the views of men," Bessie says. "I think it's time to retire to our stateroom, don't you think, Anne?"

The two women are sharing a room? It seems that Bessie has unwittingly provided me firm evidence that Anne, Bessie, and Elsie are indeed in a Boston marriage. Such information could transform rumor into fact.

"You go on, Bessie. I am right behind you," Annie says, her eyes fixed on me. She waits until Bessie is gone to speak again. "Bessie is being diplomatic. It was clear from Bernard that you two had quite the affair. You were supposed to be in Europe for work, not for love. I wonder how my father would feel about that."

I know exactly how Mr. Morgan would feel. He would hate that I deceived him, especially when I promised the trip had nothing to do with Bernard. Hate that I allowed Bernard—of all men—to capture my attention. And hate that anyone has diverted my attention away from him.

I have no choice about what to say next. "I wonder how he would feel about you sharing a stateroom with Bessie Marbury. The space is large and opulent, but I do think there is only one bed."

Anne's jaw clenches. "You think you're so clever with your little threats, but don't forget that the tally is in my favor. I now know two of your secrets, while you only know one of mine."

I shake my head and force a laugh. "Anne, I really don't know what you are talking about. I have nothing to hide."

"I'll be watching you, Belle. My father may be blind to your wiles and deceptions, but I am not."

This threat should scare me, but strangely it emboldens me. This is the pettiness of a rich spoiled older sister who is lashing out at her treasured younger sister, the one who gets too much of Daddy's love. Anne doesn't see me as an employee but as part of the family. And by now, I feel certain that while I suffered mightily at Bernard's hand during these travels and could not hold on to him at the end, Mr. Morgan and I share an unbreakable bond. I will not let anyone or anything take that away from me.

CHAPTER 28

DECEMBER 14, 1910
NEW YORK, NEW YORK

I press my fingertips against my temple, trying to stop the room from spinning. A voice says my name, and I try to focus upon it through the swirl of the chandelier lights and the bright colors of the ladies' gowns. Placing my hand on the wall behind me, I steady myself in the main vestibule of the Century Theatre, designed to resemble the Comédie-Française of Paris, where the celebration of its opening rages on all around me, and I've been raging right alongside it.

"Are you quite all right, Miss Greene?" the man with the beautiful azure eyes repeats.

Who is this man again? His name dances around the hazy periphery of my memory, but I cannot summon it up. I do know the gentleman waving at me from across the room, however. He's Giulio Gatti-Casazza, the Metropolitan Opera director, so I wave back.

The man continues to stare at me, and I know I need to say something. "I'm fine. It's just the noise in here." I hear myself speak but my words sound off. Am I slurring?

"Ah yes." He glances around the vestibule. "The acoustics in here are rather challenging for a theater, don't you think? And the conductor seems a bit—manic, doesn't he?" He keeps talking, but I cannot keep my attention fixed on his words.

The space remains packed with people, although the crowd has thinned quite a bit since I arrived a few hours ago. Still, many of New York's rich and powerful remain, several of whom are benefactors of this grand theatrical project. But where is the propriety of the rich tonight? Usually, even at the most elaborate of affairs, people speak in hushed, decorous tones, all the better to hide any untoward comments or behavior. Not tonight. The voices are loud and thick with alcohol and competing with the echoing orchestral music led by a conductor who has perhaps had a little too much Burgundy.

I giggle at my own observation, until the man says my name again. "Miss Greene, I think maybe it's time for you to retire for the evening. That last glass of champagne seems to have gotten the better of you." He points to the champagne flute I'm holding.

"No, the night has just begun." I laugh, swallow the last of the bubbly, and hand the flute to a passing waiter. A colored waiter.

The waiter takes my glass and hands me another. Then, I do something I've never done in my life as a white woman—I look the colored man straight in his eyes. He holds my gaze, and I know that he sees right through me. But I do not look away, the way I always do, the way Mama has taught me to do. I hold his glance and smile as if I'm daring him to speak, daring him to tell this room filled with the best of New York's *white* society what he knows.

For the first time in my role as a white woman, I have no fear, because nothing could be worse than the way I already feel. What could be more terrible than the guilt and pain and loss I've been experiencing for the last month?

But the waiter does not speak. He gives me a simple, respectful nod, and then continues around the theater, offering champagne to the revelers.

"Miss Greene, are you certain you should have another glass?" my companion asks. "I think you may have had a bit too much already."

I shrug. "Usually too much of anything is bad—except champagne. Too much champagne is just right." I laugh as I take a few more sips, and when the man laughs along with me, I think how enticing he sounds.

"It's getting very late, Miss Greene. Perhaps it's a good hour for us to part?"

I raise my eyebrows, and once again, I try to remember his name. I know this man, I've seen him across auction aisles and ballrooms alike, but his name is somewhere inside this champagne glass. "Well." I lower my voice and step closer to him. "I'd go anywhere with you."

He takes my glass and extends his arm. I'm grateful because I feel dizzy. As we proceed toward the entryway, a servant races toward us with our coats, and the man helps me into my fur-edged wrap. I turn to wave to the other guests as we exit the theater, and as I step over the threshold, I trip.

"Whew!" I exclaim, clutching his arm.

"Are you all right?" he asks, looking me over. "I think you'll be fine."

"Yes, because I'm with you." The December air is chilly, but I feel warm as I hold on to him. I try to rest my head on his shoulder as we stroll toward Central Park West, but it takes too much energy for me to keep my balance.

If I cannot have any more champagne, at least I can go home with this man. I can't remember his name, but that is of little matter. All I want to do is feel something with someone else tonight so that, by morning, maybe I'll feel nothing of Bernard.

The gentleman raises his hand, and a carriage appears; it must be his own, not one for hire. With effort and his support, I step up into the luxurious interior, sliding across the upholstered bench to give him enough room to get inside. But he only nods, taps the side of the carriage to signal that he's ready for its departure, and says, "It was good to see you again, Miss Greene. Please give Pierpont my regards."

"We aren't going home together?"

His eyebrows rise. "I don't think so. You're a lady who's had a little too much champagne, and I'm a gentleman. You'll feel better in the morning by heading directly home."

"I want to feel better tonight," I say.

Despite himself, he chuckles, "Good night, Miss Greene."

The last glass of champagne takes hold of me, and I reach for his hand. "What's wrong? Is my dark blood showing through?"

He frowns as if my words are nonsensical, and then nods to the driver. When the carriage jerks away from the curb, I lean back with a sigh, give the driver my address, and then close my eyes, trying to stop my stomach from churning. This is not how I wanted this night to end. I wanted to be with a man who could make me forget the man I can't get out of my mind.

Within minutes, I reach our apartment. As I step down onto the street, I feel the frigid temperature, and it keeps me steady on my feet. Until I try to tiptoe into the apartment, where I stumble into the entryway table, sending letters ready for posting skittering across the floor. "Damn," I mumble. Picking them up is no easy feat in the tight corset necessary for my beaded burgundy evening gown.

Even though we've moved into a more luxurious apartment, Mama still has a bedroom door that creaks. "Belle, is that you?" she whispers, pushing her graying hair out of her eyes. "Are you all right?"

"I'm fine, Mama."

"You look like you've had too much alcohol." She glances at the mantelpiece clock. "It's after two o'clock in the morning. That is too late for an unmarried woman to be out." She risks, "And without a proper chaperone."

From the moment I stepped back into my family's apartment from the *Oceanic*, Mama has been trying to wrap the cords of convention back around me. "Mama, you know that socializing is part of my work and—"

"What happened to you in Europe, Belle?"

She's asked me this question a few times over the past several weeks, so I'm not surprised. "Nothing, Mama. Just buying art for Mr.

Morgan," I answer, trying to keep my words articulate and my stance steady despite that last glass of champagne I downed.

"Don't be smart with me, Belle." Her tone is sharp. "You've been different since you returned home. You seem . . ." She pauses, hunting for the right words. "Distracted and restless. Even reckless."

Reckless. That is how I feel because I can't tolerate a single quiet moment to overtake me. If I allow that, I will be overcome with thoughts about Bernard or, worse, my baby.

It is impossible, however, to banish Bernard since we reestablished our correspondence, just weeks after my return. It began with a one-page letter with the words *My dearest Belle, I adore you.* My heart quickened, but it was with my head that I responded, in a letter without a salutation: *Bernard, It appears you are much better at saying those words than living them.* I continued with a litany of all I'd suffered and the responsibility he bore.

Yet he continues to write, continues to profess his adoration, and while my mind demands that I remember the truth, my heart prefers to recall the year that we spent building up to those days in Italy when I discovered the power and wonder of his love.

Finally, I respond to my mother's observation, "Actually, the party-goers tonight said I looked different as well. But they said I've never looked better." I am desperately trying to keep my words clear and my voice steady; it won't do to have Mama know how drunk I am.

"Don't you dare trot out your party quips to me, Belle. They might work on those foolish society folks, but I know an attempt at deflection when I see one." Her beautiful eyes brim with judgment and anger. "Did something happen on the boat?"

On the *Oceanic*? I almost laugh aloud thinking that something unpleasant might have occurred on that bastion of fun and forgetting. My most displeasing encounter was with Anne, and after the first day, I made sure I saw her only from afar. Otherwise, I joined fully in the merriment.

"Of course not, Mama. You've been on that voyage. It's nothing but food and frolic."

She shook her head. "Something happened, Belle. On the *Oceanic* or in Europe. I know it."

Her persistence makes me pause, makes me almost want to tell her because I feel like I'm going to burst. Mama had been my confidant until my trip, and I'd believed that Bernard would become that person, that he could come to know the real me. But he has wounded me, changed me. He will never be my intimate; I don't think he can even be my friend.

I say, "A few late nights doesn't mean a thing. You're being silly, Mama." I shrug off my coat and toss it onto the sofa, where I settle. Sitting is better than standing if I'm going to continue this conversation; it'll help keep the room from spinning.

"I am not talking about the parties, Belle." Her voice is softer now. "I'm talking about your drinking at those parties. I'm talking about the late nights, every night. I'm talking about you waking up sick and tired and unfocused when you leave the apartment. I'm talking about all the risks you're taking."

For an instant, the image of the colored waiter flashes through my mind and then my words—"dark blood." What was I thinking? But I cannot admit this; I cannot alarm Mama.

"Staying out late at a party that I must attend for reasons of my work is hardly a risk." I close my eyes and massage my temples. At this point, all I want to do is go to sleep.

"Getting intoxicated at one of those parties with your so-called friends and letting slip your actual heritage is a risk none of us can afford, Belle. Being unable to perform your job at the Pierpont Morgan Library because of your nightlife affects your entire family. Can't you see that?"

The true reason for Mama's concern makes me seethe. I am thirty-one years old, and I have borne this burden of financial responsibility and my true ethnicity for my entire adult life. "When have I ever been unable to perform my job—or my duty to my family?"

She raises her eyebrows and takes in my rage. Her voice is calmer when she asks, "Have I ever told you about the years your father and I spent in Columbia, South Carolina, when he was a professor?"

I am stunned. Not only at the quick change in her focus but that she has mentioned my father. I shake my head; of course I know that he was a professor, but I know nothing about their early years together.

She lowers herself next to me. "Your father was such a dashing man and so full of promise. When we married in 1874, I was happy to leave the comfort of my parents' home for South Carolina. It felt like a romantic adventure, traveling by train and carriage with him at my side. I had never been that far south of the Mason-Dixon Line. We wouldn't have dreamed of it before the war, when free coloreds were regularly snatched up and sold to plantations. But after the war ended, laws were passed that protected us. Your father and I were naive enough to believe that the country had really changed.

"A year before our marriage, Richard was hired as the first colored professor at the newly integrated University of South Carolina, in the state capital of Columbia." My raised eyebrows make my mother add, "Now before you get any ideas about grandeur, this capital was a dirt-road city with wooden buildings, a college, and aspirations well above its station or the state's political willingness, as it turned out. The campus itself was a touch more impressive, but only a touch.

"It had twelve expansive brick buildings that faced each other across a pretty grass lawn, all tucked away behind a seven-foot-tall brick wall. That wall made me feel a bit safer, I confess. As we rode in the carriage from the station to the campus, we received icy stares from the white Southerners, while the coloreds were almost as bad with their curious gapes."

Her face softens. "Those were heady times at first, Belle, I can admit that now. We dared to relax our guard. Your father was full professor of mental and moral philosophy, as well as a librarian. We shared an attractive duplex residence with the white chemistry professor William Main and his family."

I almost want to stop Mama right there; I have so many questions. But I say nothing, sobered and spellbound by Mama sharing these facts—a woman who never wants to revisit her history.

She continues, "It was a remarkably cordial living arrangement. Your father had a certain amount of prestige, given his Harvard background. But over time this changed. Local conservatives were furious that their white boys were . . ." She pauses for just a second, and I see that she's trying to control her anger. "Sitting next to colored ones in a classroom taught by a colored professor. Their sentiment began to foment up the chain to the state legislators. Your father couldn't ignore what was going on. He jumped into the fray. He went to meetings between faculty and state legislators. He organized church gatherings and rallies.

"It was there that he became known for his speeches on the subject of civil rights, particularly advocating for the Civil Rights Act that his friend Charles Sumner introduced just before he died."

"Papa was friends with Charles Sumner?" Mama's words stun me. How could Papa have been friends with the famous senator from Massachusetts who'd fought for the civil and voting rights for freed slaves after the war?

"Well, of course," Mama says. "Your father was friends with most of the men involved in the civil rights movement at the time. Frederick Douglass. Booker T. Washington. W. E. B. DuBois. Well, when he wasn't having disputes with them over how best to secure equality, that is."

A few weeks ago, I'd read an article about a new civil rights organization, the National Association for the Advancement of Colored People, and W. E. B. DuBois was listed as one of the founders.

Her eyes are no longer on me but in the past. "Even though the Civil Rights Act that President Grant signed into law was weaker than we wanted, and even though we knew that fury over the university's integration was growing, we were still optimistic that the spirit of the act to protect all citizens in their civil and legal rights would triumph. We were still hopeful, still happy."

Mama speaks in terms of "we," as if she were involved, as if she and my father were the sort of partners I never witnessed them being in their marriage. Again, I am stunned. Of course, I knew of my father's work, and I understood that it was the reason for the demise of their marriage. But I'd always believed that Mama had been on the other side. Not that she hadn't wanted rights for colored people in America; I just thought she'd always felt it was pointless to fight, since equality would never happen against the backdrop of white supremacy.

I feel as if I'm looking at Mama with fresh, understanding eyes.

"That was also where your father fulfilled one of his lifelong dreams. He enrolled at the university's law school. And while his professional life was expanding, I became pregnant and gave birth to our first child." When she pauses for a moment, I wonder if she will say his name. "Little Horace." Mama's eyes well up with tears.

We'd heard whispers when we were young, about a child born before Louise. But the hushed conversations ended whenever we'd walk into a room. And Mama had never mentioned a baby out loud.

As I listen now, my hand moves to my belly in empathy over the lost child. I don't let it linger, though; once I realize what I'm doing, I drop my hand.

"It was as if darkness descended upon us all at once. Horace died when he was only nine months old. He was such a wee little thing, sickly from the start, and we had to bury him right there in the campus cemetery. If I hadn't already been pregnant with Louise, I might have just curled up in a ball and died. Especially with the news your father brought home every evening." Her voice is just a whisper now. "The conservative Democrats were growing more powerful in South Carolina, all over the South, really. So were the Ku Klux Klan. Colored people were being murdered at rallies. Your father's life was threatened several times. He ignored the danger and continued his speeches, particularly around voting time. The white people couldn't bear to see a proud, articulate, strong colored man among their ignorant white masses—and they certainly couldn't stand equal rights for people they considered no better than a pack of mules.

"Your father fought hard for the Republicans to stay in power in the legislature and governor's office," she says with pride, "but they lost to the Democrats, who made short work of dismantling Reconstruction. The integrated doors of the University of South Carolina closed within weeks. It was going to be turned into a small whites-only private men's college.

"As we rode out through the university gate into the city of Columbia on that last day, I saw how much every white person we passed hated us. And I felt it too . . ." She pauses, as if she needs another breath before she can continue. "As they spit in our faces and threw garbage at our backs. We were lucky we weren't lynched.

"Your father and I lived through a brief, fleeting time in history when equality might have been possible. But racism and fear rose up within white people and eradicated that possibility when they were asked to stand side by side with the colored people. It was in that moment that I could see the future clearly. Our tiny, accomplished colored community would soon be gone. The lofty postwar ideal of integration would disappear along with it. There would only be black and white, two races separated, but certainly not equally.

"I recognized this long before your father comprehended it or accepted it, Belle. I knew his work would be futile. When we moved to New York, there was only one choice, only one decision that could be made." Her gaze shifts from the distance where the past lives to my face, to the present. "Our only hope would be to live as white."

She stares at me with hard eyes. "If you do not want to tell me what happened while you were in Europe, Belle, that is your prerogative. But I need you to understand the risks you are taking and the danger in which you are placing your family. Because if the truth about your identity is revealed, and your family's along with it, we will all become colored again. And you don't want to go back to being Belle Marion Greener, I promise you that."

I am stunned into silence by my mother's story. I feel grateful that she has shared this critical part of her past with me, but I realize that this has not been about sharing her interior life with an adult daughter; this is a mother's cautionary tale. This isn't about history; this is about the future and what my world will be if I dare to fly too close to the sun. Of all the "suggestions" she's issued to me, of all the warnings she's given and I've lately resisted, this one registers.

She rises, turning her back on me as she closes her bedroom door. I sit and allow her words to sink in. Embedded in what she told me is another message: living as white is not what she wanted to do, but what she felt she *must*. She pretended to be part of a people who had threatened my father, almost run my parents out of town, raised the specter of lynching, only because she had to. She became one of them even though she'd been a proud member of one of the most prominent colored families in Washington, DC; she'd adored being a Fleet. She gave up the identity she'd loved to live among people she abhorred, *only* for the betterment of her children.

I push myself up from the sofa, steadier now as Mama's story and her revelations have sobered me. I recognize her sacrifice, and I accept the necessity of this choice for all of us. I will take heed.

CHAPTER 29

APRIL 20, 1911
NEW YORK, NEW YORK

Since my conversation with my mother four months ago, I allow her mandates to guide my existence, on the surface at least. At my work-related social occasions, I monitor my drinking, and with Mr. Morgan, I am the essence of propriety. When I allow myself my small rebellions, I modify my late nights and behavior, so when I join Katrina for a few women's rights rallies or Evelyn for Greenwich Village poetry readings, I am home early and my actions are only that of a spectator. Even with the new friends in my circle—the actresses Mary Garden, Ellen Terry, and Sarah Bernhardt—I enjoy their independence and discussions of their sexuality vicariously, never revealing my own indiscretions, even the more recent ones.

Sometimes I wonder why I take any chances at all. Wouldn't it be safer to concentrate my efforts solely on the library and the social engagements necessary for that work? But I find that when I allow any moment of quiet into my life, thoughts of Bernard fill that void. Even though I read the loving letters he continues to send and I keep the gifts of artwork and gowns he continues to post, I must do whatever is required to harden my heart against him. The occasional evening of caresses at Alistair Barron's apartment or a session of kissing with Samuel Yardley in an empty box at the opera help fill any chinks in my armor that might be open for Bernard. I cannot allow myself to hope that some new version of Bernard will appear instead of the real man I know him to be.

And in the past few weeks, I've undertaken a new endeavor that has consumed me mightily, one I hope will seal my fate forever with Mr. Morgan and assuage Mama's fears for good. In this critical enterprise, mercifully, there has been no room or time for thoughts of Bernard.

"Belle!"

The sound of my name startles me from my musings. Normally, I am at Mr. Morgan's door before he even begins to yell for me, but I have scurried to his side seventeen times already today.

This morning has presented unique challenges. Three of Mr. Morgan's four mistresses are in town for the season, and he's assigned me the unpleasant task of keeping them separate when their visits overlap—which has occurred on three distinct occasions today, and it's just approaching noon. All this on the morning of one of the highest-profile auctions I will ever attend, one where I hope to procure a much-anticipated item.

"Belle!" Mr. Morgan bellows again. "I know you're in there! You are not only insulting me, but you are offending my dear guest, Lady Johnstone."

I perk up at the name. Lady Johnstone is the only one of Mr. Morgan's four mistresses that I actually respect. Sharp and intelligent, she and I have bonded over several lunches at the Colony Club. Lady Johnstone's inside knowledge of art and culture intrigues me, as my inside knowledge of Mr. Morgan intrigues her.

To ensure that I am presentable for Lady Johnstone, who is always impeccably groomed and dressed in the latest Parisian gown, I smooth my hair and rise from my desk. I've just begun to organize my notes for the Hoe auction tonight. Every person of importance in the manuscript part of the art world is in New York for the sale of the book collection of Robert Hoe, and I have to be prepared. Yet I cannot offend Mr. Morgan or Lady Johnstone, even though much is at stake this evening.

Tonight is more than just another crucial auction for me. Tonight, I will finally be able to do what Mr. Morgan asked me to do on the day of my interview. Tonight, I am determined to take away the auction prize, the one I finally located after months and months of sleuthing. The one I tried without success to secure before the auction even began tonight—the rare William Caxton edition of Thomas Malory's *Le Morte Darthur*, the incunabulum Mr. Morgan has had me seeking like his own Holy Grail.

Striding into Mr. Morgan's office, I call out my greetings. "Good morning, Lady Johnstone! If I had known you were in the office, I would have raced out immediately instead of hiding in my study, pretending I couldn't hear Mr. Morgan."

We laugh at the absolute impossibility of anyone ignoring Mr. Morgan.

He says, "Can you please entertain Lady Johnstone for a moment while I meet briefly with King?"

"It would be my pleasure, sir."

He stands up from behind his desk. "Lady Johnstone, did I tell you that tonight, Belle is going to bring me my treasure?"

"Yes"—Lady Johnstone smiles—"you told me last night and again this morning."

"Did I? I must have forgotten in my excitement."

"I will do my best to win it for you, sir," I assure him. Again.

"Doing your best is wonderful, Belle, but securing me my Caxton is necessary."

When Mr. Morgan leaves the room, I smile at Lady Johnstone. "He's very excited about this Caxton. He's been waiting a long time."

She nods. "You know he doesn't want to attend the Astors' affair with me tonight, don't you? He's been making these comments about the auction as a means to excuse himself from the Astors' and go with you instead. I've had to hold firm, and insist on his attendance."

"I would not presume to know anything about what Mr. Morgan wants to do, Lady Johnstone."

She laughs again, a melodious chiming sound. "If anyone has any certainty about Pierpont's wants and desires, it is you, Miss Greene." Despite the laughter, I hear a darker undertone in her voice. "He would much rather be at the auction with you than at this soiree with me."

"I do not know about that. But if that's true, it's only because he's been longing for this particular Caxton for years."

She begins to pace around the room, running her finger along the spines of priceless tomes, dislodging them from their carefully arranged positions. "Do you know what Pierpont said about you last night, Miss Greene?" Her tone has shifted, and she is no longer looking at me when she asks the question.

I'm not certain that I want to know, but I give her a small chuckle. "No, I cannot even imagine what he might have told you about me. Doubtless I give him many reasons for complaints."

She stops and there is not a hint of laughter about her now. "He told me you were the most important person in his life."

Her words surprise and flatter me, but still, I wave my hand in the air dismissively. I must. "He was joking, no doubt. It is only because we are about to land an important volume that I was even on his mind."

"There was no humor in his voice, Miss Greene. There was only respect and admiration."

After all these months of knowing me, does she perceive me as a rival when there is no reason? It has been years since Mr. Morgan and I shared one of those intimate moments. Long ago, we decided, without discussion, that a relationship between the two of us would never be. So why is this coming up with Lady Johnstone now? Does she sense something undetectable to me?

Before I can get an answer, the office door opens, and I jump as its ornately carved edge nearly grazes a medieval book of hours that is out of place on the shelf due to Lady Johnstone's interference. Mr. Morgan's booming voice overtakes the room. "Well, Belle. It is time for Lady Johnstone and me to depart." His voice is lower, softer, when he adds, "But I know you will do a fine job facing the jackals at the auction on your own. I will see you in the morning, and I expect to see that Caxton in your hand."

Lady Johnstone's smile has returned. For the moment, at least, she will be the most important person in John Pierpont Morgan's life.

Before the auction commences, I stop off at home to change into a more striking ensemble, a vivid sapphire Fortuny gown that Bernard sent me. Pushing him away doesn't mean I can't put his presents to good use.

This year I purchased two adjoining apartments in a doorman building on the corner of Fortieth Street and Park Avenue. It is within easy walking distance to the Pierpont Morgan Library. Each has a separate entrance, but they connect in the middle with a single door that I alone can unlock. It is my attempt at an autonomous life, the sort that Katrina and Evelyn have. I delight in decorating my side with new, light-colored, streamlined furnishings alongside the artwork Bernard has gifted to me, like the Piero della Francesca painting. On evenings that are free from social engagements, I adore reading on my own sofa amid my precious books and artwork in the quietness of my own space.

When I'm inside the parlor, I hear Mama and my siblings squabbling in their larger apartment, but I ignore their quarreling. The time for the auction is near, and I can't risk becoming embroiled in a lengthy conversation or debate. I live close because of propriety's demands, but it does not mean I must act as though we share the same space. And tonight is too important to my family's future to be weighed down by the pettiness of the present.

Once I arrive at the auction house, I am guided to an aisle seat in the third row, as I now prefer, next to Alfred Pollard, the British Museum's head of print and rare books. Alfred has become a colleague and friend since my first visit to London. We make small talk about the other auction-goers and flip through the catalog as the hundred or so chairs reserved for bidders fill up. As the lights dim and a hush settles on the crowd, my heart flutters in anticipation.

As usual, the auctioneer opens with a highlight of the sale, in this case a rare Gutenberg Bible. I'd asked Mr. Morgan about his interest in this item, but he demurred. "I have too many damned Gutenbergs." This gives me license to focus on the other bidders as the auctioneer starts the process.

I assumed that two or three of the usual players would bid for the Gutenberg, and that the Metropolitan Museum would secure it. I was incorrect. A new competitor has entered a field typically populated by well-known players.

"Who on earth is that?" I whisper to Alfred, as the bidding grows close to fifty thousand dollars, an unheard-of sum for a Gutenberg.

"I believe that's Henry Huntington."

I recognize the name. "The California railroad tycoon?"

"The same."

"Arabella's nephew?" The familial relationship to my social acquaintance, the collector Arabella Huntington, becomes clearer.

Alfred's whisper drops to a near indiscernible level. "Some say that Henry is in love with Arabella, and that he is pursuing her now that his uncle—Arabella's husband—has passed away. It is said that he believes the way to her heart is by populating her walls and shelves with masterpieces."

"The nephew in love with the aunt?" Even though I have seen quite a few unconventional pairings in my day, including me and Bernard, I am aghast.

"That's the rumor."

I eye Huntington. "If he keeps this up, he'll drive up the price of the other auction items to unnecessary levels."

"By God, I hope he stops with the Gutenberg, because if he does what you suspect, he'll price us out of the market."

Alfred and I wait and watch. My prediction proves correct. Item after item, Henry Huntington swoops in and outbids the competitors. It seems that almost every object is of interest to him, whether book or artifact, medieval or Renaissance.

By the time *my* Caxton reaches the auction stand, I am ready. Sitting upright, my neck elongated like a swan's, I face the auctioneer with an unflinching stare, and he nods in recognition before he begins.

"On the stand we have an extremely important example of rare incunabula. This volume, entitled *Le Morte Darthur*, by Thomas Malory, was printed in 1485 by the famous printer and publisher William Caxton. The book recounts the legend of King Arthur and the Knights of the Round Table and their quest for the mythical Holy Grail. There are no other copies, just a few single pages torn from a lost volume." He inhales, then calls out in a distinctive singsong voice, "Do I have an opening bid?"

Before I can raise my hand, the auctioneer calls out, "I have fifteen thousand dollars. Do I have sixteen thousand?"

I am astonished; no one opens the bidding at such an exorbitant level. It must be Mr. Huntington. I raise what has become my signature red scarf since the Boston auction. "Twenty thousand dollars." A gasp ripples throughout the crowd.

Mr. Huntington and I continue in this high-stakes tit for tat until all other bidders fall away, and the level reaches forty-five thousand dollars. The auctioneer resumes bidding in five-hundred-dollar increments, and we match each other. I admit I'm nervous. Mr. Morgan told me that I could spend any amount to get this prize, but I never thought I'd get close to fifty thousand dollars.

"Forty-six thousand," I bid with a flick of my scarf.

"Forty-seven thousand," Mr. Huntington replies.

"Forty-seven thousand five hundred."

The room is quiet, and for a long minute, he does not answer. "Forty-eight thousand," he finally responds.

"Fifty thousand dollars." I signal to the auctioneer and my competitor that I *will* have this item. It is not an amount that I ever expected to say, but I'm determined to secure Mr. Morgan this coveted treasure.

I wait, assuming that Mr. Huntington's fifty-one thousand dollars will arrive any second. But I continue to wait, until a small rumble sounds out across the room. His silence registers among the people.

"Sold!" the auctioneer cries out, "for fifty thousand dollars."

My heart doesn't stop racing, and I'm thankful that the Caxton was offered at the end of the auction, as I don't know how long I could have remained still while other items were sold. The position of the Caxton may have been the reason Huntington dropped out; perhaps he'd reached the last of his allotted cash for the auction. When I rise, I am bombarded by a sea of congratulations for securing one of the evening's treasures. I'm giddy with success—until I step outside.

Throngs of reporters gather on the steps of the auction house. I assume they're waiting for the victorious Mr. Huntington, who, aside from my Caxton, absolutely dominated the auction. But not a single journalist seeks the railroad tycoon. As they all call out to me, I flinch inwardly. With the exception of the *New York Times* profile that faded away with relative speed, I have avoided publicity.

"Miss Greene, Miss Greene!" Reporter after reporter yells out my name. I've been approached by newspapers before, but nothing like this.

I struggle to make out the queries, and then hold up my hand. "Gentlemen, one at a time, please."

The first reporter says, "Evening, Miss Greene. I'm Mr. George Thaw from the *New York Times*, and I want to start out by thanking you, miss. We are delighted that one of our own New Yorkers—and a beautiful young woman at that—triumphed at auction. We wouldn't

have wanted that California collector to steal all the prizes away from
our city."

A cheer breaks out across the crowd as the upright mustachioed
men who'd sat alongside me at the auction continue down the stairs
past me, looking alarmed. Publicity is not seemly in the stodgy art
world.

Their reactions convince me I should seize this opportunity no
matter the risk. As always, I hide in plain sight by standing firm and
speaking boldly.

"Thank you, Mr. Thaw, for your kind words. I, too, am delighted.
If wealthy collectors like Mr. Huntington prevail in obtaining all
available treasures for their personal collections, then they remain
outside the purview of scholarly study. We can't have that. The rare
book I purchased on Mr. Morgan's behalf today will not only stay in
New York, but will also be available for academics at the Pierpont
Morgan Library."

More cheers resound from the crowd of reporters. I feel triumphant as I stand before them, a colored woman in their white world.

CHAPTER 30

Even though it is nearly ten in the evening, I return to the library to complete some work I'd abandoned in order to attend the auction. And I want to place the long-awaited Caxton *Le Morte Darthur* on Mr. Morgan's desk so that it will be the first thing he sees when he sits on his lion's throne tomorrow morning. This is a victory for us both, although of two very different sorts.

But when I walk past the security guard into my office, Mr. Morgan is sitting at my desk, overpowering my diminutive chair with his girth.

I smile as I pause just inside the door. "I am surprised to see you here, sir."

"How could I not stop by to congratulate you, Belle? Not only did you secure the precious Caxton for me, but I hear you are the toast of the town."

How did he already hear? "I did manage to procure the Caxton."

"That's an understatement, by all accounts. You managed to grab the Caxton away from a scoundrel, who thinks he can march into my town and take all the treasures away from me."

"I am glad you're pleased."

"Pleased? That's an understatement. How many years has it been, Belle?"

"Five, Mr. Morgan."

"Is that it in your hands?"

"Yes." Beaming, I walk to his side and present it to him. While he turns the elegantly written pages and studies the decorations and illustrations, I watch and wait.

"You've done it, Belle," he exclaims. "This calls for a toast."

He rises to pour us drinks from the array of liquors I keep on my sideboard. "I understand there will be write-ups in every major newspaper tomorrow."

My goodness, how does he know that? I suppose he's got a network of informants everywhere.

"Really?" I venture a bit warily as we touch crystal glasses.

"About your triumph, yes, but also about you. The beautiful, young, brilliant librarian to Mr. J. P. Morgan who prevailed at auction and captured the Caxton. It's an American success story. That's not all," he continues, "it seems your fame will extend beyond New York. The articles about you will appear in London and Chicago."

I take a deep breath. My father has been living in Chicago. Uncle Mozart shared this with me in one of the letters he sends me every six months or so, although Papa isn't typically mentioned:

> *I also want to tell you about your father. I hadn't heard from him in a couple of years, but he reached out to me last week. He is writing and he lectures periodically, but he is struggling to find meaningful work as a lawyer or scholar. For reasons I do not understand, he's been ostracized by his friends in the political realm. Life in Chicago is not easy for him, but his cousins continue to do all they can to support him financially and emotionally. I know it is difficult for you to hear about his Japanese family, but they have not joined him here . . .*

The thought of Papa reading a newspaper article about me is thrilling, if nerve-racking.

Mr. Morgan interrupts my thoughts. "I only wish I were younger, Belle," he says before he lifts the glass to his lips again.

I tilt my head. "Why is that? You're at the peak of health and the pinnacle of your power."

"It would give me longer with you." His eyes are sad, his tone sentimental.

I'm surprised and quickly deflect, trying to lighten the moment. "Stop teasing me."

"I'm not teasing," he says, his eyes intense and unreadable before he looks down into his crystal glass.

The office is silent as he finishes his whiskey and then returns the glass to the sideboard. When his eyes find mine again, the longing I see in them leaves me breathless. As he approaches, I do not back away, even when he is so close I can smell the whiskey on his breath.

He lifts his hand, and his fingertips trace the side of my face. "Belle"—his voice sounds thick—"I want more time at your side, to experience the world alongside you."

Then, he lowers his head toward mine, and our lips touch in a surprisingly tender but ardent kiss. When we break apart, we stare at each other, searching for answers in the other's expression. Then, his lips curl upward, releasing the tension between us.

"Oh, Belle." He takes a deep breath. "I don't know."

I am not certain how to respond, so I fall back on playfulness. "Should we?"

"Could we?" he replies. There is nothing lighthearted about his tone; he is in earnest.

Is Mr. Morgan asking whether we could be lovers? To act upon this attraction would risk everything else we are to each other. We are more than colleagues; we are partners, a joint force in the art world. In our shared passion to make the Pierpont Morgan Library the best, we are closer in some ways than friends and family. We are parent and child. We cannot sacrifice the whole in favor of the one part that will end badly.

I chuckle nervously. "No, we shouldn't, we couldn't." For five years, I've seen women cycle in and out of their places in his world, and I care about Mr. Morgan too much to become ensnared in his harem. My position needs to remain firmly fixed.

His eyes grow stormy and I wonder if I have offended him. But then, the darkness passes, and a wry smile peeks out from beneath his mustache.

"That is exactly what I was going to say." When he leans toward me again, his lips aim for my cheek, where he bestows a chaste peck.

I exhale in relief as he leaves. But I notice that his shoulders are sagging. For the first time, he looks small. When I hear the thud of the heavy bronze doors shutting, I wonder what I've done. No one rejects Mr. Morgan. Even though we both agree that this is the right choice, should it have been him who made the final decision? Will I live to regret my words?

CHAPTER 31

The relationship between Mr. Morgan and me has changed. Exactly when and why has this happened? Was it the kiss? Could that one act have sparked the slow burn of this shift? When did our hours of daily banter, which alternated between pleasant and challenging, transform into disagreeable, jealous interrogations and overt cross-examinations? When did we stop discussing manuscripts, medieval artwork, and the legacy of his library and, instead, start talking about me? When did he stop asking me to read to him or play cards?

Maybe it wasn't the kiss. Perhaps it started a few months later when I became more sought after on the heels of the Caxton acquisition and the rumors grew about my supposed romantic relationships. Or was it this past April when we heard the terrible news about the *Titanic?* He was a part owner and was meant to sail on that fateful maiden voyage from England to New York. We both knew people who died among the fifteen hundred souls lost. Does all his clinging and jealousy stem from his fear that death is marching toward him, as it does for all mortals?

Hints of our former relationship tease me from time to time. For a few resplendent weeks in December of last year the discovery of a rare cache of priceless treasures lying in a farm in Hamouli, Egypt, brought us together. When we received a letter asking whether we wanted to acquire fifty early Christian Coptic manuscripts, I knew we had to own them. They predated other Coptic Old and New Testaments by nearly two hundred years. After long days of conversation, Mr. Morgan agreed. He understood, as did I, that this assemblage of manuscripts could turn the Pierpont Morgan Library into an international center for orientalist and biblical studies.

He turned the final decision and negotiation over to me, and I acquired the manuscripts for a price of forty thousand pounds, which was significantly lower than the sixty thousand pounds they had asked. We rejoiced together. But as soon as the manuscripts arrived later that month, he turned jealous and suspicious again.

I hear him rustling papers in his office, and I tense. I have been so deep in my own thoughts that I didn't hear him return from a lengthy luncheon with Lady Johnstone, the only one of the four mistresses who remains, and even her status is tenuous.

Once a favorite of mine, she has gone from friendly to wary to downright hostile, and in light of Mr. Morgan's aberrant attitudes, I do not blame her. My only solace is that he is leaving soon for a trip to Egypt that will remove him from the Pierpont Morgan Library for a blissful few months.

"Belle!"

I march officiously into his office just moments before he bellows again. Lady Johnstone is standing next to him, her hand resting proprietarily on his shoulder. She's wearing a becoming pale pink gown with a spray of glittering diamonds around her long, elegant neck; together they look like they've dressed to have their portrait taken.

When I enter, she leans down to kiss his cheek, then says, "I'll leave you to it." She straightens herself and glares at me. "To her," she scoffs.

Once we are alone, Mr. Morgan gestures toward the chair before his desk with his cigar, but then he goes quiet for a long moment. I position my silver pen over my tablet and ask, "Did you call me into your office to discuss the cataloging of items to be returned to the Victoria and Albert Museum?" The British tax laws have been favorably altered recently. It makes sense to bring Mr. Morgan's London collection home, and I've been overseeing that monumental process.

"Who did you lunch with today?" he suddenly barks.

He never used to ask me these kinds of questions. I existed for him alone, so he did not concern himself with my activities outside the Pierpont Morgan Library and its business. Not until that night. Not until that kiss.

Might things have been better if we'd taken that kiss further?

I answer him with the truth. "No one. I ate lunch alone."

"I find that hard to believe." After a puff on his cigar, he sends a large smoke ring in my direction. It encircles me, making me feel as if there is a noose around my neck.

"If I'm not dining with an art colleague, I eat at my desk. That is my usual habit."

He snorts in disbelief. "You expect me to buy that you did not lunch with one of your admirers? Say, William Gibbs McAdoo, president of the Hudson and Manhattan Railroad?"

"No, Mr. Morgan." I sigh. He's asked me several times about Mr. McAdoo, a gentleman who has taken an unreciprocated fancy to me. "I have never dined alone with Mr. McAdoo. In fact, I haven't laid eyes on the gentleman for over six months."

Mr. Morgan's inquiries have begun to sound like Bernard, whose tone in his letters has shifted from how much he adores me to forever accusing me of romantic entanglements. Bernard and I haven't seen each other in years, and if the rumors are to be believed, *he* is the one who is currently traipsing across Europe with his new mistress. It is ironic and painful that the only person with whom I've behaved with full licentiousness accuses me of scandalous behavior with others.

"What about that upstart young banker? The Cuban fellow, Harold Mestre?"

Another young man who has shown interest. While I'd never

admit it aloud, I'd found Mr. Mestre's attentions flattering and even allowed myself to indulge in light physical intimacy. His youth and vivacity are appealing, and I'd even feigned acceptance to one of his many proposals. For a brief time, I'd imagined that marriage, and even children, might be possible with the olive-skinned stockbroker, whose skin tone mirrored my own. But that elusive link I feel with Bernard is absent with Harold, and anyway, what would happen to my family if I ceased working as Mr. Morgan's personal librarian— to their lifestyles, their expenses, and their tie to their white lives?

"No, Mr. Morgan. I did not have lunch with Mr. Mestre."

He puffs on his cigar but doesn't send any more smoke rings my way. "I suppose I should be appeased by the fact that many of your lovers are in Europe."

Now I have many lovers in Europe? When he has not authorized a trip to Europe for years? "What are you talking about?"

This reference, however, to European men is a new tactic. "I hear that Charles Read of the British Museum is quite taken with you. He calls you his 'Little Belle,' apparently."

How could he think I would ever be interested in Mr. Read, who'd been supportive of Mr. Morgan's decision to remove his art and book collection from England against public outcry over the treasures leaving the country? The lovely Englishman might fancy me, but the idea of us as a couple is laughable. "Mr. Read is not, nor has he ever been, of romantic interest to me."

He puffs on his cigar again. "So, there is no truth to the rumors that you're in love with Mr. Bernard Berenson either?" He gives a half smile. It's the same smirk he doles out to the competitors he's quashed.

This is the first time Mr. Morgan has mentioned Bernard in a very long time. Without blinking an eye, I say, "Mr. Berenson and I are acquainted with each other, as you know from the visit he and his wife made here. But I have not seen him for several years." I hope my voice sounds steady.

"Then why does that particular rumor surface over and over?"

Recognizing that it is time to fend off his onslaught, I parry with a touch of humor. "I've also heard the rumor that I'm your illegitimate daughter several times, but that doesn't mean it deserves more credence than if I'd only heard it once."

But Mr. Morgan is unmoved.

Centering himself behind the desk, he stares at me for a moment before he says, "If you are planning on deserting me—to marry or for any other reason—then you should know that will be the last day I set eyes on you. And it will certainly be the last penny I spend on you."

From my earliest days as the Morgan librarian, I have always been "his" Belle. But this is not any kind of loving possession; this is a threat, one that has both financial and emotional impact.

I understand how much Mr. Morgan has done for me. After six years, he has more than tripled my already high salary. I earn as much as some doctors, which has afforded me and my family a fine life. I need to reassure him I'll remain at his side for however long the seventy-five-year-old tycoon has left to live. But it is time for more than reassurance; we need to speak plainly.

"What happened to us, Mr. Morgan?" I attempt to keep my voice steady. "You lay out what you will do if I desert you, but most of the time, it feels like you don't want me around anymore. Is it because I—" I stop before I ask him about the night of the Caxton auction.

He glares at me, his expression as hard as his heart has been toward me. "What were you going to say, Belle?" His question is a challenge, as if he dares me to ask about the kiss. Did he take my words that night as a rejection? Does he not understand that it is because I genuinely care for him that I wanted to preserve what we had?

When I stay silent, Mr. Morgan says, "You are the one who is thinking about leaving me." Then, his voice becomes self-pitying. "Have you given no thought to how much I've given you? How much you mean to me?"

"How can you not understand how much you mean to me? How

much this"—I gesture around the room—"institution that we are building together means to me? You of all people, you see me in the library and in your office from eight o'clock in the morning until eight o'clock every night, and sometimes long after that. So how can you possibly think that I am here for any reason other than what we create together? And how can you think I would ever consider leaving?"

I think I've convinced him, but then he says, "If you leave me, I will write you out of my will."

For Mr. Morgan to threaten me with the specter of his will—an inclusion that has loomed on the horizon for many years through regular hints and innuendos, though I've asked him for nothing—is despotic. Is that all he thinks of me? After what I just said? Is that all he thinks of my commitment to our work and his legacy?

"Perhaps you've begun to believe those god-awful profiles on you in the *Washington Post* and *Chicago Daily Tribune*—that you're the perfect society girl and serious scholar rolled together. But you"—he bangs his fist on his desk, exhibiting an anger toward me I've never seen before—"are *my* personal librarian. I made you into who you are today. You are nothing without my bankroll, and don't you forget it."

Fury rises within me. How dare he? I've always acknowledged Mr. Morgan for the chance he took on hiring me and the trust he's placed in me. I've thanked him for what he's done. But I have done my part, too. I have worked long and studied hard. Day after day, I've done his bidding to build this institution. For him to assert that the entirety of my success and that of the Pierpont Morgan Library is attributable to his money alone is appalling. I am both furious and deeply hurt. And something much, much more. Embedded in Mr. Morgan's words is an unconscionable sentiment that I can no longer ignore.

"You cannot treat me like something you have bought and paid for." My voice quivers as I speak. "Like one of your manuscripts. Or—" The rest of the words hover on the tip of my tongue, begging to be released. *Or a slave*, I think over and over.

Yes, I have lived my adult life as a white woman, but when I lay my head down at night I am as colored as the first enslaved African men and women who landed in this country three hundred years ago. After all my father has done to fight for equality, after all my mother has given up to ensure that I had the best opportunities, I will not permit myself to be spoken to as if I am owned. Not by Mr. Morgan, not by anyone.

His eyes narrow. "Why not? The way I see it, I already own you."

Even though I'm shaking, even though I want to scream, even though my heart pleads for me to cry out, I rise slowly and stand before him calmly. "You can buy a great many items and objects with your gold, Mr. Morgan, but you cannot buy me."

Then, for the first time, I walk out of his study without being dismissed. I am still shaking when I return to my office, fighting tears that I will not shed. He spoke to me as if he were the master and I was the— I stop my thoughts there. I cannot allow myself to think the unthinkable.

CHAPTER 32

APRIL 1 AND 10, 1913
NEW YORK, NEW YORK

I accept the telegram from the delivery boy, and for a moment, I'm tempted to leave it on the pile of correspondence on which it's been placed while I tend to an urgent negotiation. But then I remember the telegram I'd received only five days before, informing me that Mr. Morgan had contracted an illness while traveling in Cairo and had been taken to a hospital in Rome for additional treatment. Even though I'd been told he was expected to fully recover, I feel pulled to open the telegram. What if it contains news about his health?

I reach for the letter opener, and slice open the envelope. Squinting at the nearly illegible scrawl on the telegram, I read:

> *Mr. J. P. Morgan died in Rome on March 31, 1913.*
> *Arrangements are being made to bring him home.*

The telegram drifts from my hands to the floor, and my tears are instant. How can this be? Through my watery eyes, the unimaginable words stare up at me from the crimson-red carpet.

"He cannot be gone," I whisper.

We were everything to each other. I'd known that, but now that he is gone, I feel the truth of it as I haven't before. For him, I was the daughter and son he never had, the confidant he'd always sought, the business and art partner who'd boldly advocated for his goals, and the lover he'd dreamed about but held in abeyance. For me, he was the father I'd lost, the companion with whom I could discuss the day's minutiae, the business mentor who'd supported me beyond my wildest dreams, and the lover for whom I longed but could never have.

I swipe my tears away. I must stop. Much will be required of me in the days ahead, and the Morgan family must not think me unfit for the tasks. I must honor Mr. Morgan as I know he'd want and tend to dear Junius, who will mourn him as much as I do. But soon, the time will come for me to face alone the unthinkable—living in this world without him.

A few days later, I am standing beside Mr. Morgan's family and friends and colleagues. The sun shines on the harbor, catching the tips of the waves in a playful dance. But the air is bitter cold and the wind brisk, unusual for April. This is the chatter on everyone's lips, a distraction that unifies all of us who have gathered. I listen to the refrain but don't chime in. My grief has broken me.

A horn blasts across the harbor. The *France* is finally approaching after an hour delay, fulfilling its final mission for its once-powerful owner. It is bringing him home, to the city he reigned over like royalty, to the Pierpont Morgan Library, where he had found his intellectual and spiritual home.

As the *France* inches closer, I am lost in my own thoughts, completely unable to fathom a life without Mr. Morgan at the center. Joyful memories of him flash through my mind. Sitting in his office and reading his favorite Bible stories to him. Surveying the guests at a party, deciding which of our "enemies" to dismantle next. Witnessing the pride on his face when I strode through the library with the Caxton *Le Morte Darthur* in my hands.

Remembering that last night leads me to wonder again, how could he leave me with the terrible fight between us left unresolved? Months of travel have passed without any reference to it in our letters, and now, we can never speak again. I will never be able to give him my apology, and I will never hear his.

The weight of that is crushing me. I work to console myself. Death is always a harsh taskmaster, and it serves no one for me to succumb to despair. In that moment, I resolve to bury the memory of our last conversation forever. Mr. Morgan gave me so much that I treasure, and I have always known that he treasured me. It can only diminish his life to remember the angry, despairing man he became in the last months of his life.

Making that decision is a great relief. It allows me to remain strong at the sight of the ornate casket being carried down the gangway and loaded into the waiting horse-drawn hearse. Mr. Morgan's body is being transported to the Pierpont Morgan Library, where it will lie in state.

Once it is out of our sight, we release a collective sigh. Jack then turns to me. "Belle, I'd like you to ride with us in the family carriage to our home."

Anne's eyes widen. "The occasion is for family only, Jack," she interjects.

If I'd thought that her disdain for me would lift now that her father is gone, I was wrong. Anne, it seems, will continue to battle me for a place in her family—and perhaps even in her family institutions.

"What is Belle *but* family, Anne? She spent more time with Father in these past years than anyone else, and he always insisted that she attend every family function, even the small ones," Jack says.

"Father isn't here anymore, Jack, in case you hadn't noticed."

I watch as he winces.

"Jack," I say, "it is really no trouble. I have my own carriage here, and I'd planned to have it take me directly to the library anyway. I don't have much time to prepare before we open the doors to the public tomorrow, and I want to be at the library when your father arrives today." The viewing of John Pierpont Morgan must be commensurate with his stature as an important American figure.

"Why don't I ride with you, Belle?" Jack offers.

"I don't want to take you away from your family, today of all days," I say with a glance at Anne.

"Nonsense. You are family, too, and the carriage can take me to my house directly after it drops you at the library."

"That would be lovely. I'd welcome the company." I see the loathing in Anne's eyes as Jack climbs into the carriage alongside me. I can almost hear her vowing that she will not allow another Morgan man to get tangled in my web.

She needn't worry that I'll take Jack away from her. Jack has many admirable qualities—a strong marriage and family life, as well as patience, among others—and these will keep him from the sort of unique intimacy that Mr. Morgan and I experienced. But there's another distinction that no one would suspect. The famously ruthless financier operated his collection out of a pure love of art and beauty, while Jack plans on managing it based on value. I am worried that Jack plans to dismantle his father's legacy.

But Jack and I do not discuss these issues now. The loss sits between us like a third person in the carriage, heavy and dark, and impenetrable. The carriage lurches as we pass brownstones, office buildings, bustling sidewalks, and crowded streets as if it were a typical day in New York City. Without thinking, I say aloud, "It seems impossible that all this can exist—that New York can continue on as normal—without him. He *was* this city."

"Belle," Jack says, his voice thick. Turning toward him, I see that his eyes glisten with tears. "We will make sure that he lives on in this world. You and I."

Once at the library, I wait on the steps for the hearse. As Mr. Morgan is brought inside, I keep my focus on preparing the rotunda with wreaths of red and white roses. I stay awake until nearly dawn, ensuring that every detail is perfect inside this magnificent, gleaming institution that we created together.

Returning home only to bathe and change into a fresh black dress, I am ready when the mourners line up to pay their respects. At ten o'clock, they enter, and for hours, hundreds of people pour into the library, slowly circling the rotunda and the casket to say farewell to the legendary tycoon. Mama, my sisters, and my brother are among them, as all have benefited tremendously from Mr. Morgan's largesse. Thousands more will be honoring him across the country, with flags flying at half-mast and Wall Street closing for the day. I survive two days of public viewing by saving my sorrow, knowing that when I lock up the library at seven o'clock in the evening on the second day, my grief will come.

When I finally close the fortress-like bronze doors and face the casket, it is just me and Mr. Morgan. I have even dismissed the security guard so that I can be alone. I stand at the foot of the coffin, close my eyes, and place my hand on the polished wood. The words from our last conversation seep into my mind, and I want to say, *I'm sorry*, but I shake my head and push that away.

Instead, I rush into Mr. Morgan's office and gather his Bonham Norton Bible, turning to the last verse I read to him, months before in a rare tranquil moment between us. It hadn't been one of his favorite biblical stories, but a passage he particularly admired. And as I review the words, I find them to be strangely appropriate for this moment.

I take a breath, and as if Mr. Morgan were sitting in front of me on his lion's throne, I begin: "Let not your heart be troubled, ye believe in God, believe also in me." Reading the entire twenty-eight verses of the scripture, I gingerly close the Bible when I reach the end. I bow my head and allow my grief to fill the rotunda, praying silently and sobbing to myself. I hope the words give him solace, wherever he is.

Tomorrow, Mr. Morgan will be honored in a fifty-carriage procession including not only family but also government officials and distinguished citizens, and there will likely be thousands of citizens lining the sidewalks to watch the mournful parade pass. But tonight, it is just us two—as we have always been, and as I would always like us to be.

CHAPTER 33

AUGUST 14 AND SEPTEMBER 8, 1913
NEW YORK, NEW YORK

This is my summer of mourning. I move through my days in the library pretending that Mr. Morgan's office is not as empty as I feel. When Jack starts to appear at the library, I catch glimpses of him at his father's desk, and it unsettles me. The physical resemblance tricks me momentarily into thinking Mr. Morgan has returned, but then I remember and realize—no one else can truly fill his lion's throne.

Compartmentalizing my sadness, I try to forge a relationship with Jack beyond the familial one I've shared for years. It is challenging, and I try to mask my despair and address the list of inventorying and valuation tasks he's assigned me; I need him to know that he can rely on me. Although he finds the occasional painting or manuscript compelling—the Gutenbergs in particular—I know he doesn't connect with the art in the same way that Mr. Morgan did. Rising financier that he is, he thinks of the collection as a set of assets. His father's mission for the library—my mission as well—was not based upon economics; it was based on a passion for art and the desire to create a collection unchallenged in breadth and importance among

European and American institutions. How will I keep the Pierpont Morgan Library's holdings intact in the face of Jack's inclination to parcel the items off and sell them in chunks to the highest bidders? Is this what will become of Mr. Morgan's legacy? And me?

By August, I'm so fraught with nerves and grief I allow myself a respite while my mother and siblings retreat to the Adirondacks once again. I accept the invitation of one of Evelyn's friends to spend two weeks on the North Shore of Long Island, possible only because Jack and his family are away. Nancy opens her parents' estate to us, and seven of us—including myself and Evelyn—have our own rooms in the ten-bedroom mansion. In this beautiful, sprawling, gray-shingled manor overlooking the bay, the women read, draw, and paint, and I spend the bulk of my days writing in my journal, exploring my thoughts, and trying to adjust to a new world, one without the existence of J. P. Morgan. Perhaps one without a role at the Pierpont Morgan Library.

Occasionally, I study the letters that Bernard continues to send, which have increased in number since the death of Mr. Morgan. After his initial expression of sincere condolences, he has returned to declaring his adoration for me: *I cherish you, my dear Belle, and wish for the day when I will hold you in my arms again.* His sentiments do little to move me; though I still long for the man I believed Bernard to be, I have no desire to be with the man he truly is. I wonder if I'll ever find again the sort of connection that I shared with either Bernard or Mr. Morgan, however fleeting.

Days of solitude thinking about Mr. Morgan and my future leave me feeling wistful and troubled, and the evenings of revelry with the other women staying at Nancy's house are a much-needed balm. We gather inside in front of the large stone fireplace on comfortable sofas, playing bridge and chatting and laughing until the sky becomes midnight blue. One night after several glasses of wine, Nancy tells the sorrowful story of her great-great-aunt Estelle, who'd died in this house one hundred years earlier, and we agree that we can feel her presence. From that night onward, we each call out to her when we retire for bed: "Good night, Estelle." I am the only one who also whispers, "Good night, Mr. Morgan."

On my return to New York, I discover that neither my grief nor my worries have lessened over my sunny holiday. When Jack returns a few weeks later, I hope that an onslaught of work will help dislodge or soften my sadness and concerns. But within the week, Jack summons me to his office in a tone so serious I become quietly panicked. Did he decide on his summer travels to sell off the library collection and dismiss me along with it? What will become of me—and my family—in the wake of Mr. Morgan's death and Jack's very different perspective on art and manuscripts?

Jack gestures for me to enter but does not speak as I settle into my usual chair. I try not to think about how strange it looks to see Jack behind the desk. He puts on his spectacles, then carefully unfolds a document and holds it up to the lamp on his desk. I am immobile as I await his verdict.

Jack flips from one page to the next, finally clearing his throat and saying, "Belle, I've asked you into my office to discuss my father's will."

The will?

"I'm certain you won't be surprised that my father specified that the Pierpont Morgan Library and all its contents pass to me."

I'd assumed as much, even though no one said so explicitly. "I'm not surprised in the least. Your father always believed you were his natural successor at the library." I pause. "He often spoke to me about how he was certain that you'd bring the library the international acclaim it deserved."

"Did he?" His eyebrows rise in surprise.

I nod, feeling little remorse at my exaggeration.

"That's nice to hear, Belle. As I'm sure you know, my father and I did not always have the . . ." Here he hesitates, fumbling for the correct word. "Smoothest of relationships. Although I respected him greatly and loved him dearly."

"He felt the same way about you," I say, and we smile at each other. It must have been—and still must be—so exhausting to be the son of the great J. P. Morgan. It was hard enough just being his librarian.

He signals that we are returning to the business at hand. The will. Flipping to another page, Jack says, "There are two provisions that specifically address you."

"Me? Two?" I am surprised. Although Mr. Morgan made references to his will from time to time—usually in a threatening fashion— I never had a sense that I'd actually receive anything of consequence from him.

"Yes, the first provision specifically directs me to maintain your employment for a term of at least a year." He glances up. "My father didn't need to spell that out, Belle. I had every intention of keeping you on."

"Thank you." I look down at my carefully folded hands in my lap. I don't want Jack to see that my eyes well with tears of happiness and relief at the two messages Mr. Morgan has sent me through his will. First, even after our argument, Mr. Morgan trusted and forgave me enough to make this provision for me in his will. Second, I can see that he wanted me to guide Jack to the goal we'd shared; Mr. Morgan knew I'd need this time to convince Jack of the importance of the collection itself and the significance of keeping it together with me at the helm.

He pauses. "There is a second provision, a financial one. You have been left the largest personal bequest aside from the family members." I hold my breath, not daring to imagine an amount. "My father wanted you to have the sum of fifty thousand dollars."

"Fifty thousand dollars?" I am stunned. It is close to fifty times what the average person earns in a year. It is an inordinate amount of money, and the sum will provide my family and me with financial security for life. Most of all, it was a warm and generous act. Mr. Morgan could have inserted all sorts of codicils to ensure that I'd take care of the library just as he would have wanted or that I would only receive the money upon a host of contingencies. But instead, he has given me the freedom to live the life I choose.

"It is much deserved, Belle," Jack says, and I don't bother to hold back my tears.

My step feels light as I walk home. I have new hope and purpose that I haven't felt since Mr. Morgan died. I burst through the door connecting my apartment with my family's. I was not expected, but I know they'll make time for me and utter no snide words about my absence. Mama, Teddy, Louise and her husband, and Ethel and her husband are gathered around the dining table, and they all greet me with warm hugs.

It has been so long since I sat down to a meal with my family. My siblings have married and built careers and lives quite different from my own. Russell, who'd returned from Florida, is an engineer in New Jersey, where he and his wife have a home. While my sisters are still both teachers, Louise's husband is looking for a job as a speech therapist, and Ethel's husband is searching for a job to do just about anything.

Teddy is just months away from getting her teaching degree and has grown more confident, even as she has become more enchanting in appearance. Given that both of my brothers-in-law are out of work, everyone lives here in the apartment until their situation changes. It is a good arrangement; the men fuss over Mama, which she enjoys, although there's nothing she'd enjoy more than the security of her sons-in-law's employment. Even though she doesn't say it, I know she doesn't like the family being so fully dependent on me.

As Mama places a high pile of chicken and potatoes on my plate, I pull up a chair and say, "I have some news."

"What's that?" Mama asks as she continues to serve my sisters.

"Mr. Morgan provided for me in his will."

At first, they all stop and stare at me. Then, all at once, my sisters and Mama begin talking. Among their voices, I'm able to discern Mama's question. "He included you in his will?" She sounds as astonished as I felt.

"What do you guess his gift might be?" I ask, looking between my mother and my sisters.

"He would leave you what you love," Mama says. "A Renaissance manuscript." She nods definitively.

"No!" Teddy jumps in. "I think he left you three Worth gowns and jewels to go with them."

"That's what I was thinking," Louise chimes in.

I chuckle at their guesses, knowing that my sisters hope for gowns and jewels so they might get my castoffs.

"So, who's right?" Teddy asks, her eyes shining with excitement.

"None of you."

"What is it, then?" Teddy asks, tapping her foot in an impatient gesture I know all too well.

I draw out the news. "He left me—fifty thousand dollars."

My sisters scream, but Mama jumps up from the table to embrace me. "Oh, Belle," she says. "I'm so grateful that Mr. Morgan thought to take care of us."

Then Mama rejoins my sisters, and they erupt in squeals and hugs. Now, even my brothers-in-law have stood and joined in the celebration.

"With that much money, I could afford to get that pink dress at B. Altman's!" Teddy cries out.

"With that much money, you could afford a house to go with the dress!" Louise shrieks.

They clasp hands and jump up and down, while my brothers-in-law stand smiling. Mama steps back and looks on, beaming. They've come to expect me as a source of money. How comfortable they've become on the back of my work.

I sink into my chair. Not only do they express no gratitude toward me, but they also fail to acknowledge the loss that accompanies this windfall.

A single tear streams down my cheek just as Mama glances in my direction. She races to my side, kneeling by my chair. "I'm sorry, Belle. We've been thoughtless in not thanking you."

My sisters and brothers-in-law stop their celebration.

"That's not it, Mama, although a 'thanks' would be nice."

"What is it, then?"

"I miss Mr. Morgan, and I feel lost without him. Everything I have—we have—is due to him. He could be difficult and possessive, but he made me into who I am."

Mama squeezes my hand tight. "Mr. Morgan was a powerful and generous force in your life, and through you, in our family's life. But make no mistake about it, Belle. *You* made yourself into the person you've become. He gave you the opportunity, but every bit of your success belongs to you. You are Belle da Costa Greene."

CHAPTER 34

With Jack's October departure for his annual sojourn to England comes a welcome reprieve in work, particularly from the pressure to educate Jack on the value of keeping the library collection intact. But what I told my mother a few months ago is still true. I feel lost. In the wake of Mr. Morgan's death, I am awakened to what I feel is a new darkness and a growing recklessness.

I miss Mr. Morgan, and his death opens up the door to other grief in my heart that I've never let myself fully acknowledge before. Behind that door, I see Bernard and my baby alongside my father. In the space that the work reprieve grants me, I find myself longing for all of them—Mr. Morgan, Bernard, motherhood, my father—knowing that reunion can never be.

I try to assuage that longing with words. I read through Mr. Morgan's treasured Gutenbergs, looking for him in the glorious script, the vivid illustrations and decorations along the paper's edges, as well as the language of the Bible itself. I write to Bernard, trying to understand the soul of this man with whom I connected like no other and the heartbreaking decision to not have our child, while staying distant from him to protect myself. I seek ways to connect with my father through his writing. I analyze his essay "The White Problem," which challenges and confuses me. Then I turn to writing I think would please him—*Harriet, the Moses of Her People* by Sarah Hopkins Bradford, the autobiography *Narrative of the Life of Frederick Douglass, Up from Slavery* by Booker T. Washington, and from the Pierpont Morgan Library's own collection, an early edition of the poems of Phillis Wheatley, an eighteenth-century former slave who wrote beautiful but conflicted poetry about slavery.

When this isn't enough, I seek more reading to help me understand my father, his decision, and its impact on me. Nothing was more important to him than what was happening in our own country, events that I've sometimes ignored as I pursued my own individual success. I study a broad swath of the newspapers, imagining Papa's fury at President Wilson's decision to take a hammer to racial equality and authorize segregation within the federal government. I envision a smile on his face when he learned about the work of colored women like Ida B. Wells, Mary Church Terrell, and the twenty-two young women from Howard University, members of a colored sorority, Delta Sigma Theta, who joined thousands of others in the Women's Suffrage Parade in Washington, DC, despite the fact that they weren't wanted. While I am impressed with the work that's being done, particularly by the colored fraternities and sororities, and feel pulled to the cause, I wonder how I can help. Living as a white woman, could I ever participate in this important work for colored people? Or should I abandon my false identity and launch into the fight for equality? I feel like there's no real place for me inside my father's world—or in the white one—and I am adrift.

As a woman, I refuse to be defined by a man," Katrina says, and I watch as the table full of women in serious, somber-colored blouses and skirts nod in agreement. An onlooker in the restaurant at the Martha Washington Hotel might think the other women look dowdy compared to me, in my stylish teal dress and a matching scarf that has become somewhat of my signature, but in actuality, they are leading far more independent, radical lives than I am.

"Exactly," another woman responds, the one with the wiry red hair that refuses to be tamed by her bun. "Especially since most men think a true woman is a pious, submissive wife!"

"That doesn't fit any of us," Katrina says.

"Not at all. We are autonomous individuals who deserve our own political identities," the redhead continues.

Then Katrina and the other three women begin speaking together. "We hold these truths to be self-evident: that all men *and* women are created equal . . ."

They hold up their cordials in a toast, and although I lift my glass to join them, I feel disconnected from them. When Katrina asked me to join her and three of her friends for cordials and desserts, I jumped at the chance to quell my restless mind and seeking heart with numbing drinks and distracting conversation. I didn't expect that the discussion would drive me deeper into my own sense of isolation from the world.

When Katrina sees my expression, she whispers, "We were just reciting a part of the Declaration of Sentiments from the Seneca Falls Convention." I feel even worse. Shouldn't I have known that? *How out of touch with the critical issues of my gender and race I've allowed myself to become*, I think. My independence seems self-focused and in name only; am I just a fraud?

"Excuse me, ladies, can I offer you another drink?"

I look up at the colored waiter. I wonder if I have more in common with him than the white world in which I pretend to belong. But when I smile in empathy with him, that little bit of kindness takes him aback, and whether it's my grin or my appearance that confuses him, I can tell he's one of the few colored who do not recognize me for the imposter that I am. He's used to being a black man invisible among white people.

"M-Miss, would you like another cordial?" he stammers as Katrina and her friends burst out in laughter at something else I don't understand.

"I would," I say to him. Then, leaning close, I say, "Thank you for your service."

He pulls away from the table, confused by my compassion. "Um, I'll get you that drink," he says, scurrying away as if my goodwill is a white person's trap. *How terribly sad*, I think.

When a white waiter returns with my drink in place of the colored man, I know that I must stop behaving so recklessly, as if I'm going to make a decision about my race right here at the Martha Washington Hotel. There must be some other way I can appease my restlessness without risking my identity. At least for tonight.

Taking a long, final sip of my drink, I get ready to say my farewells, when three young men approach our table. "May we join you?" a lanky blond man asks the table, while his two dark-haired friends wait.

Katrina hops up and squeals. "Charles, what are you doing here?" She introduces us to her brother, and the three men join our group. Even though Katrina and I knew each other during our school years, I don't recall meeting her brother.

One of the darker-haired fellows sits at the end of the table in the chair next to me, and after a long period of awkward silence in which I decide to order a third drink, I ask him about the book he's carrying.

"*The Souls of Black Folk*," he recites the title. "Have you read this?"

"By W. E. B. DuBois," I say.

"You've heard of him?"

My lies begin. "No, not really," I say as images of my father flash in my mind. Then I add, "Just a little," in case something I know slips out.

"Do you know that this man right here"—he taps the book—"was the first colored man to earn a doctorate from Harvard?"

My eyes widen. "No," I say, "I didn't know that." In this moment, I feel a surge of pride and long to tell him about the first colored man ever to graduate from that esteemed school. But I say nothing about Papa as the young man continues on about his love for this book and his hopes for racial equality. I can't risk it.

"Reading this has given me such insight into what it's like to be black in this country. How black people must have two sets of eyes all the time, two fields of vision that are totally incongruent because they have to be mindful of how they see themselves, but that is most likely completely the opposite of how the world sees them. So it's like walking this balancing act," he goes on.

I am amazed at how this young white man has captured so much of that book and my life. As he continues talking, the words he speaks sound like my father's, and even though they are emanating from a white man's mouth, they are just as earnest. *Incredible*, I think, *men of two different colors saying the same thing.* This white man was born in a place of familial prosperity, but still yearns for equality; my father's longing stems from a place of survival. It gives me hope.

But after I finish my fourth drink something else happens—no longer do I see my father in this young man. I see and *feel* Bernard. With this thought, I realize I must leave. As I start to say my good-byes, Katrina directs the young man with whom I've been talking, "Jonathan, help Miss Greene secure a carriage home, will you?"

He escorts me through the elegant lobby outside. No carriages are in sight, so we stroll toward the park, where occasionally they form a queue. His arm slides through mine, but instead of maintaining the usual polite distance, I lean toward him as my last drink makes my head spin. He is surprised when I stand on my tiptoes to kiss him. His return kisses are sloppy and his hands clumsy, but his inexperience doesn't matter to me. I am searching for one thing—a connection, however fleeting, to anchor me.

Jonathan takes my hand and leads me to a nearby building. I wait while he unlocks the door and then we silently walk up one flight, entering a single room stacked high with books. I realize Jonathan must be a student, and I wonder about his age as I glance at the simple furnishings—a desk, a bed not much larger than a cot, and a small round table pressed up against an icebox, a stove, and a tiny sink. In this moment, however, I don't care about his age or his decor.

When he reaches for me and starts to unbutton my dress, I try to surrender to the feeling. We lie on the bed, and I allow him to undress me. But the kisses and the caresses do not give me what I need—to fill the void with definitive *meaning*. I sit up on his bed and push him away. Without speaking another word, I slide on my undergarments and gown and leave, never even saying goodbye.

I rush into the night, finally staggering into my apartment with a throbbing head and a broken heart. I cannot remain in this restless darkness. I must find answers to the questions about who I'm going to become now that Mr. Morgan has passed away, how to be Belle da Costa Greene, maybe not authentically but completely. As I lie in my bed, I turn this conundrum round and round in my mind. Then, in an instant, I know what I must do. In order to move forward, I must go back.

CHAPTER 35

DECEMBER 4, 1913
CHICAGO, ILLINOIS

The hotel restaurant, filled with dozens of rectangular tables with black tablecloths and white overlays, is empty save for the maître d' and an old gentleman at a table set for two. Where is he? The hour is correct; we formalized it in one of the letters we've exchanged over the last month.

But then, I look more closely at the elderly man in a charcoal-gray suit.

When he stands and in a low, melodious voice says, "Is that really you, Belle?" I recognize his voice. His curly hair and beard are now a shock of white, but his aristocratic features—the long, thin nose and finely chiseled cheekbones—they are all the same.

"Belle," he says again and stretches out his arms, as if asking for permission to embrace me. I start to shake when I am pulled into the familiar warmth of his arms. I haven't been held like this since he left.

The way Papa says my name is special; he draws it out and it sounds like the refrain of a song. To him, Belle is not simply a name but an expression of his feelings for and about me.

"Sit, my sweet girl." He takes my leather overnight satchel and pulls out a chair for me.

I slip off my coat. It is winter in Chicago, and the breeze was bitter on my walk.

As we both take a seat, we smile nervously at each other. The white linen overlay on the table stretches between us like an unnavigable ocean.

Finally, Papa speaks. "Belle, you cannot know how I've longed for this day."

Sobs overtake me. I have missed my father through the years, but it is only at this moment that I realize the pain of his absence is more than emotional, it is physical. The ache for him has been ever present, and now it rises up from inside me.

He is first to cross that ocean. Leaning across the table, he clasps my hands.

"Papa, I've missed you terribly." My face is wet, and I withdraw my hands to retrieve my handkerchief and dry my eyes and cheeks.

As if he'd been waiting for me to regain my calm, the waiter approaches. We scan the menu quickly and place our orders, a simple chicken soup for me and lamb chops for Papa. We are both eager to be alone.

"Seventeen years," Papa says and shakes his head. "I can't believe seventeen years have passed us by. I am so grateful you found me."

"Uncle Mozart has been keeping me abreast of where you've been as much as he could. He was the one who gave me your address."

"When I received your first letter, well—" Again, he shakes his head. "I've been keeping up and following you, too."

"You have?"

"Of course, and I'd always wanted this day to come, but I didn't dare hope."

"There is so much that we have to catch up on, where do we even begin?"

"Start wherever you want. I can't wait to hear everything."

I launch into a spirited recitation of what my sisters and brother have been doing. "Well, do you remember how Louise and Ethel were inseparable as kids?"

He nods.

"Nothing's changed. They have found a way to live together in an apartment—with their husbands." I decide not to mention that they're all living together in an apartment I pay for, with Mama and Teddy. No need to insert troubles into our reunion.

When Papa leans back and belly laughs, I am taken back thirty years, to the dining table where we all gathered for dinner and Papa sat at the head, entertaining us with stories that filled our home with laughter.

"So, Russell isn't there?"

"No, thank goodness," I say, and we laugh together. "He's also married, but he and his wife live in New Jersey. He's an engineer and as steady and as solid as you raised him to be."

He nods, but his smile fades and I regret my words. Russell was still a young man when Papa left; Papa had started to raise his son, but he certainly didn't finish. He didn't complete that task with any of us.

His face brightens again when I tell him about Teddy. "And then, there is Teddy. Oh, Papa, she is so lovely and will be finishing up Teachers' College soon."

He asks me for a few details, and we chat, but I don't broach Mama. And while I share my siblings' spouses' names and professions, I have omitted their ethnicity. No need to talk about race yet.

Then Papa asks me about my own career. I place my spoon down in my bowl. "Papa, there is not a day that goes by when I don't think of you. Every time I've held something in my hands, like the Sweynheym and Pannartz copy of Virgil." Papa releases a low whistle before I continue. "I've wished I could share the moment with you. One time, I even had a chance to go deep behind the walls of our favorite place—"

He interrupts excitedly. "The Metropolitan Museum?"

"You remember?"

"How can I ever forget the weekends when you and I would spend a whole day there?" The idea that those memories remain with him fills me with peace and warmth.

He continues, "Belle, you've traveled all over the world collecting these rare manuscripts, and I've loved hearing about your conquests. But I think it was that article in the *Chicago Daily Tribune* that made me the most proud. When you won the Caxton *Le Morte Darthur?* What a triumph!"

I smile, but say nothing. The memory of that auction is a highlight in my life, and it would have stayed that way if I hadn't returned to the office that night. But I try not to think about that and continue sharing with my father the smaller particulars about my work. He is glowing as I describe the manuscripts I handle daily and the world-class groupings I've assembled and the other glorious collections I've explored.

"What success you've had, Belle! The papers hardly capture your scholarly achievements. To be able to study and collect rare books and precious art for your life's work. It's a career I would have pursued if it had been open to me after Harvard. What a gift."

"It's a gift you gave me. *You* were the one who introduced me to the beauty of art and the importance of the printed word and its history."

"I am so pleased you were able to pursue what you loved. I just wish—" He stops and lowers his eyes.

"What, Papa?"

When he looks up, he's smiling, but the joy doesn't reach his eyes. "I wish I'd been there with you, been there for you. I wish I'd been able to stay by your side, and not end up in Russia, where I started a new—"

I know he's about to say "started a new family," but I don't want us to be distracted with talk about his Japanese family when our time is so limited. So I quickly interrupt him by saying, "No, no, Papa. There's no need for wishing. You planted the seeds for my career."

"Well, it's you that's cultivated them. It's more than any colored girl could ever dream of, and it's more opportunity than would have been available to me as a colored man."

I tense at his use of the word, glance around to make sure he wasn't overheard, but then I stop myself. There isn't another soul within earshot, and no one knows me in Chicago.

As he notices my reaction, the smile that he's worn since I arrived fades. He pushes his plate away and leans back from the table. "But that's the price, isn't it? Pretending to be someone that you're not." His tone carries no judgment. "When I saw your picture in the *New York Times*, I was so proud of you. But I was also profoundly sad. I realized that to achieve one dream, you had to forsake your core identity. Changing your name is easy. Changing your soul is impossible."

"You don't approve, do you?" I lean forward. This is what I've always wanted to know, the question I've always wanted him to answer.

He gives me a rueful chortle. "It is not a question of approval. Our society forced you to make that choice. And that is a travesty. There were no good choices for you or for your mother. It is not for me to judge the decisions you have made."

He has every right to judge. Papa is as fair as Teddy, and he could have lived our life. Instead, he sacrificed everything to live authentically as a colored man.

"Since Mr. Morgan died, I feel so lost, Papa. And I wonder if I would feel this way if I'd made a different choice." He nods in understanding. "I wonder sometimes if the sacrifice I made to have this success is worth it." It is a relief to confess my doubts out loud.

"My darling Belle." Papa reaches for my hand and squeezes it. "You are more authentic than anyone I know. You have lived the life that was meant for you; it's just that you had to do it as a white woman because of racism." He sighs. "I wish you knew about the time, a brief time, mind you, when a colored man or woman could stand tall and thrive, regardless of the shade of their skin."

"I know, Papa. Mama told me about your professorship at the University of South Carolina. Those must have been promising days. Full of hope."

His expression is wistful. "I hope it helped you to understand why I couldn't abandon the fight for equal rights. But I also want you to understand why I left."

I had made so many judgments about Mama and I'd been wrong. Now I'm glad Papa will have the chance to tell me his story.

The waiter clears our table, giving my father a few moments to collect his thoughts. Once we are alone, Papa begins. "When I walked out of that door, I wasn't sure what I was going to do, but I knew I couldn't live in two worlds. It was impossible for me to pretend to be white, to live as the father of a white family and to continue to fight for racial equality. The only way to genuinely protect my family was to continue to actively argue and battle for our rights. I wanted to give you all a brighter future."

We order dessert, and my father slips into his professorial voice. "Reconstruction made us equal. Discrimination was against the law. And the federal government protected us.

"But when the Supreme Court overturned the Civil Rights Act, segregation began its journey to legality, and there was no protection. We lost our freedom, but I didn't lose my hope. I thought we could have the ruling modified. I believed it would be a battle, but one we could win." He shakes his head. "But it's been much harder than any of us thought."

"Even though it's been difficult, you've been fighting on the right side, Papa," I reassure him. "You have so much to be proud of."

"Perhaps," he says. "But this is a political battle we're fighting, and sometimes the leaders fight among themselves. At the moment, I am bereft of my old allies. I sided with Booker T. Washington because I admired how he strategized with business owners and politicians. But the tide has turned, and Willie DuBois is now leading the movement. I admire Willie, especially his plans for the National Association for the Advancement of Colored People. They are intriguing. But for some reason, I make him nervous, and because of that, I've been in the wilderness, separated from the life that I know." My concerned expression must be upsetting to him, because he tries to perk up and paints a smile on his face and adds, "But I've done some good writing here."

I nod when he mentions his paper "The White Problem," but I remain quiet. He sounds so much like the orator papa that I remember, and I don't want to interrupt.

"I argued that the problem between the colored and white races wasn't due to some kind of inherent flaw in colored men and women. It was the result of the bigotry and racism that white people had toward us. I presented proof of the heights to which colored folks could fly if untethered from racist bindings. I listed hundreds of colored men and women from the Revolutionary War through to our present day who had made astonishing strides in the arts, science, politics, business, literature, even the military.

"There was a time when your mother had the same beliefs. Early in our marriage, she was as certain as I was about those words 'all men are created equal.' However, once she stared racism in the face, that was all she could see. She couldn't see promise, she didn't have hope; she felt that primal urge to protect her children, and *that* I understand." He pauses, and I wonder if my father has his own regrets about leaving. But then he says, "I still believe. I still believe that someday there will be equality in this country. That someday there will be a new civil rights act, and a new president and Congress to enforce it. That everyone will be able to follow their dream, regardless of race. That those words about the equality of men in the Declaration of Independence will be true."

I hear his hope, although it is hard to envision this future. While I am inspired by the young women and men in colored colleges who are following in the steps of my father, my daily encounters are what influence me the most. The newspapers are still filled with reports of beatings and lynchings. I see countless colored men employed at the lowest levels as hotel workers and day laborers, as well as the colored women working as hotel cooks and dressmakers. It is honest work, but they are not treated with dignity in their positions, especially when I hear racist views being bandied about in the high-society circles in which I travel. All of this makes it impossible for me to see what my father envisions.

I shake my head. "I wish I had your hope, Papa. I want to, but I don't." I pause, thinking how much my words are like the ones Mama said to Papa all those years ago. "That's why I'm so conflicted. I *know* this life that I've lived is false at its core, and while I yearn for another, I'm afraid because of the world we live in." I blink away the tears forming in my eyes. "I hope you're not too disappointed in me."

His voice is soft when he says, "No, Belle, I could never be disappointed in you. I'm only disappointed that, in order for you to have this life, you have to pretend to be white. I'm fighting for a time when you could have your same life *as* a colored woman."

I wipe away the tears that I can't hold back. "I find myself at a crossroads. I have the liberty to strike out on my own path. Perhaps more authentically—"

"Your own path," he repeats. "Is it the bequest Mr. Morgan left you that provides that liberty?"

The news was announced in the papers a few months ago, so I'm not surprised he knows. "In part. But I've also been considering what to do next in my career, my life."

"Are you going to leave the Pierpont Morgan Library?" He sounds surprised.

"That's what I don't know. Mr. Morgan made provisions in his will for me to stay."

"Do you still love the work? Do you feel that you're making a valuable contribution to the world? Building a legacy that will benefit more people than just yourself, your mother, and your siblings? Does your path have *meaning*?"

"Yes, in answer to all your questions. My plan is to turn the Pierpont Morgan Library from a private library into a public institution so that thousands and thousands of people will see the beauty and significance of the early written word—the importance of reading and books as a great equalizer among humankind. But I'm not living my life openly as a"—my voice drops to a whisper—"colored person.

And I'm beginning to wonder if I should be." I pause and ask Papa the question directly: "Should I come forward with the truth so I serve as an example, as you have done? As you wrote about in your paper?"

He sighs. "Belle, all I've ever wanted for my children was the opportunity to soar, no matter their heritage, and to live a life of *meaning*. That has been my fight. But in our current society with our current laws, it's enough that you succeed, that you are able to follow your passion in your work, that you leave a legacy that will benefit the multitudes—one day, even the colored multitudes. It breaks my heart to say it, but right now, I do not think you can have both."

I am astonished. This is not the guidance I expected from the man whose life has been dedicated to equal rights. When I arrived in Chicago, I believed I'd leave it with the mandate to own my ancestry, a path I'd begun to consider as a viable option for me.

"Proceed with your work and your unique mission, Belle, and continue to accomplish great things. This is not the time to change course. You are one of the most important librarians and art historians—and one of the most successful self-made women—in this country, and what's most important now is that you leave your own legacy. The one you described to me."

There are confused tears in my eyes, tears of relief and astonishment and a modicum of disappointment. I'd expected that Papa would help me open a new door; I'd imagined that with his counsel, I would reinvent myself. But he has closed the door instead. He has just given me permission to continue to thrive as Belle da Costa Greene.

"One day, Belle, we will be able to reach back through the decades and claim you as one of our own. Your accomplishments will be part of history; they'll show doubtful white people what colored people can do. Until that time, live your life proudly." He gives me a smile full of love and warmth. "I'm so proud of you."

I squeeze Papa's hand. Then, I close my eyes, savoring his words and absorbing his hope.

CHAPTER 36

DECEMBER 10 AND 22, 1913
NEW YORK, NEW YORK

I will myself to stay impassive as I wait in the lobby of the Belmont Hotel. *As cool and serene as a marble statue in the Greek and Roman section of the Metropolitan Museum of Art*, I think, *and as incapable of feeling.* That's how I will look, and that is how I will feel. Cold and numb.

Then I see him. He is strolling down the grand staircase with Mary. When they approach, I reach out to her first.

"How lovely to see you again," I exclaim, as if the meeting had been arranged by the two of us.

"Belle, you look more beautiful than ever," she says, generous with her praise as always.

"As do you," I say, although this is untrue. Mary appears heavier than I last saw her, and her skin has a clammy, slightly sickly pallor. Has she been ill? Bernard hasn't mentioned it in his letters, but then he rarely discusses her.

Bernard wears an elegant, well-tailored gray suit. His eyes are as bright and intelligent as I remember, and his hair and beard are still dark and close-cut. When he draws close to me for a welcoming kiss, the heady scent of him is overwhelming.

Our meal is friendly, and we fill one another in on our travels and stories of mutual friends. I can hear myself talking comfortably in a way that my unsophisticated younger self never could. I am not the same woman as the one Bernard bedded in Italy.

When I regale them with the story of my wildest contretemps in Greenwich Village, some months ago—a rowdy night in which a strange mix of my suffragette friends, artistic companions, and I almost got into fisticuffs with a group of hooligans—Bernard practically spits as he says, "Such company is beneath you, Belle. You deserve better than a motley band of singers, musicians, artists, and activists fighting for a cause that doesn't make sense."

I directed the conversation to my Greenwich Village endeavors knowing it would antagonize him. I wanted him to see that we now inhabit utterly different orbits and have not a thing in common, that there is no reason for our paths to cross in any way other than professional.

"I think I can decide for myself what company is beneath me," I say with a pointed glance his way. Then I light a cigarette. "Anyway, don't be so narrow-minded, Bernard. Those women are carving out a new, independent life. One that doesn't require men."

Mary lets out a devilish chuckle. "How intriguing," she says.

I continue. "We are going to have to get used to new ways of thinking—in the way we conduct our lives and the way art is created as well." I hope he understands that I am sending him a message; I'm not only talking about bohemians or art the likes of which I saw in the 291 gallery.

"What do you mean?" A scowl appears on his face.

Blowing a smoke ring toward the ceiling, I say, "Surely you can read the tea leaves that nonobjective art will become mainstream. We will have to find a way to welcome modernist art on walls alongside our beloved Italian Renaissance masters. Won't you be going to the Armory Show while you're here?" The exciting—and shocking— Park Avenue show shook up the staid New York art world when it opened earlier this year. It features a thought-provoking exhibit of impressionist, fauvist, and cubist works, including striking pieces by Paul Cézanne, Vincent van Gogh, and Marcel Duchamp. The experience of seeing those utterly new perspectives on landscapes and portraiture had been just as exciting as sitting next to Teddy while we devoured the thrills and shocks of *The Last Days of Pompeii* in one of the new picture houses.

It is at this tense moment of intellectual and artistic disagreement that Bernard excuses himself. As he walks away, Mary slides her chair closer to me, and quite against her usually deafening volume, half whispers, "May I speak frankly with you, Belle?"

What can I say but yes?

"I know things ended badly when you and Bernard were last together."

I inhale, wondering how much she knows.

She continues, "But I also know you two still have feelings for each other. He sets aside hours a week to write you and eagerly reads your letters. He's been counting down the days until he saw you. And since we arrived, he's been preening for you. There is no one who can replace you. Please give him a chance, Belle. If you're not ready now, perhaps when we return from Boston next week?"

How strange to be discussing my former lover with his wife. How wrong. "I'm not certain I can do that, Mary."

"Belle, I don't think you realize the effect you had—and continue to have—on Bernard," she presses. "You managed to scale the wall around his heart that he built in his youth as a means of surviving a world filled with prejudice for people like him. It was difficult for him, a young boy from Lithuania living in Boston. I'm sure he's told you the stories."

I smile, but I do not tell her no.

She continues, "But that wall is no longer there because of you. You got to him, and when you left, he was devastated. Even once we both returned to Italy weeks later, he could neither eat nor sleep, spending hours just gazing out the window. I encouraged him to go after you, but he said you were too upset because he didn't come to London."

Could she possibly understand just how much agony her husband subjected me to?

She continues, "He stayed in Paris because he didn't know how to handle that much emotion, but since then, Belle—"

I interrupt her. "I hardly think he's been pining for the past three years, Mary. I've heard he's been consoling himself with his new friend, Edith Wharton."

Mary winces at the mention of Edith's name, but her discomfort doesn't stop me. I add, "Along with others." I do not want Mary—or Bernard—to think me naive any longer.

"Belle, you of all people know that other women and other men"— she gives me a long stare that lets me know they, too, have read the gossip columns and heard the rumors—"can serve as a means of distracting you from your real emotions."

She clasps my hand, holding it tight in hers. "Edith doesn't mean anything to him. But you do. Promise me you'll give him a chance?"

As Bernard sleeps, I stare at him, saying a small thanks for Mary's generosity and wisdom. Not only because I am here with him now, but because these last three days have allowed me to understand Bernard and the role that I want for him in my life.

When Mary and Bernard returned to New York three days ago after a week in Boston, I allowed Bernard first to accompany me to the new Shubert Theatre, where we saw the George Bernard Shaw play *Caesar and Cleopatra*, and next to an afternoon strolling through the halls of the Metropolitan Museum. On those two occasions, I had an epiphany. I realized that I did not have to erect the barricade around myself that I'd built for my first meeting with Bernard and Mary, because I no longer had to protect myself from him. In his presence, I no longer felt the same sway of emotion and longing for him; it had been replaced by a companionable rapport based on our shared worldview as outsiders in an insular realm, a deep respect for his intellect and artistic knowledge, and laughter.

Now, as I stare at him with his hair tousled, I can truly see him as if for the first time, for the flawed human that he is. A man fearful of intimacy, because he's been living behind a persona that he's created to protect himself from the ostracism he's undoubtedly felt since his youth and certainly during his adult years. Because of that, he cannot allow anyone to get close, not even me. I'd suspected this since Mr. Morgan's reference to Bernard as a Jew, a suspicion that was reinforced with the Russian words Bernard uttered during our first night together. But not until Mary mentioned the prejudices that Bernard suffered as a child because he was Lithuanian did I know for certain he wasn't the Boston-born-and-bred Brahmin that he pretends to be.

Doesn't Bernard realize that he is the only one who believes his Jewish heritage is a complete secret? Not that I can fault him for trying to hide his identity, even if the repercussions of being discovered would be less significant than they would be for me. That is a horror I can't allow myself to fully imagine.

Bernard's eyes flutter open. "Good morning," he says and then kisses me.

I enjoy the feeling of his lips on mine, but these days with Bernard have proven I'm free of his sway. I am free, although that freedom does not mean that I want to bar him from my life completely. I will invite him in and enjoy him—including his skill as a lover—on my terms.

"Can we really manage it?" I untangle myself from the bedsheets and sit up in the bed.

His eyes crinkle at the corners as he wraps his arms around me and bestows feather-like kisses on my neck. As I close my eyes and tilt my head, once again I think about how grateful I am to be in his bed.

By the time we had dinner last evening, just us two in a private room at Delmonico's, I was ready to let him seduce me with art, as he had before. Over Burgundy and oysters and filet mignon, I allowed him to lure me in with his confession about the few modern painters he admired, Gustav Klimt among them. I permitted him to woo me with his languorous descriptions of Klimt's brushstrokes and his use of gold leaf and mosaics. And I succumbed to his seductive descriptions of how Klimt captured the erotic female form in his art.

By the time dinner ended, I was ready to return with him to his room at the Hotel Webster. There, I enjoyed his skills and charms, realizing that he understood my body and my physical needs as no one else. As I succumbed to his touch and his whispers, I felt I was returning home. But this time, even though I ended up in his bed, I knew I would never be hurt—romantically—by Bernard again.

"I think we can manage it," Bernard finally whispers in my ear. "I don't see why not." His fingertips tickle my bare back, and I shiver.

I have to shift away from him so that I can speak. "I'm not certain that any couple has successfully undertaken this challenge before."

"But we are not just any couple," he says, taking a long curl that trails down my back and wrapping it around his finger.

"I suppose that's true."

"I will write you daily so our connection stays strong, and you will write as often as the Pierpont Morgan Library allows. I enjoy those journal-like letters that you send. They make me feel as though I'm with you all day. You can talk of your modern painters, and I will confess that Mr. Klimt's work has a special appeal to me. His use of gold is almost Renaissance-like, after all." We smile together. Bernard and I have enjoyed our passionate conversations about the changing art world.

"That seems reasonable," I say. "You won't feel jealous of my work when I can't match you letter for letter?"

"I promise."

"And when we are together, we will be fully committed to one another."

"Exclusively." He springs the curl free from his finger and reaches for another.

"But when we are apart, we will be free to pursue our passions—whether they take the form of work or pleasure," I say.

"As you have insisted," he says, reminding me that he argued for a firmer commitment between us. I refused. Pointing out that expecting fidelity in romance had only caused us strife and insecurities—both private and voiced in our letters—in the past, I argued for something entirely new. And he had relented to this more flexible arrangement.

"Any other course will be doomed to failure," I maintain, as I had several times.

"And we don't want failure," he says, kissing the small of my back. "We will exist on letters and—"

"Rendezvous," I finish for him and fall back into his waiting arms.

CHAPTER 37

The heavy bronze doors to the library close loudly. Who could it be? I am alone here, save for the security guards, and my calendar contains no appointment for the afternoon. In fact, I'd cleared my schedule so I could prepare for Jack's return from Europe tomorrow.

Rising from my desk, I stride across my office toward the rotunda, just in time to bump into Jack. "What a pleasant surprise," I say. I'd planned to work all afternoon and evening on the outstanding items for my morning meeting with Jack, as the previous days had been spent in Bernard's company. Now I worry Jack will want to plunge directly into business matters for which I'm not fully prepared. "I didn't expect you back at the library until tomorrow morning."

"The *Oceanic* just docked, and Jessie and I knew we had to come to the library straightaway to see you." His eyes twinkle underneath his heavy, dark eyebrows. For a moment, he is the image of his father. My heart clenches at the resemblance.

I focus on the situation at hand. The Morgans needed to see me? As soon as they disembarked from their annual stint in London? The news will be either stupendous or disastrous.

"Your father used to do the same thing," I tell him, my tone bittersweet at the memory.

"I know," he says with a pat on my hand. He understands how hard Mr. Morgan's passing has been on me; this shared grief binds us together. "For much the same reasons that we do so today, I'm guessing."

I hear the clip of Jack's wife's delicate step across the rotunda. Her sweet face, still pretty if a little matronly after four children and over twenty years of marriage, peeks into my office, and she beams. The couple, Anglophiles to the core in their manner and interests and not only because they'd lived in London for many years, are devoted to each other. After Mr. Morgan died and Jack became a fixture at the library, I witnessed how involved Jessie was in every aspect of his life, providing him with firm and definitive guidance and support when needed. She fills the hole in his heart left by his father's judgment.

"Oh, Belle, we are so delighted to see you." Her voice bears a tiny English accent after so many months abroad, and in her deep blue traveling dress with its striking silhouette, she must be wearing the latest London fashion.

"I'm pleased to see you both. Three months away is too long," I say as we embrace.

"Were your ears burning while we were away?" Jessie asks, with a sparkle of her own in her soft aquamarine eyes.

"No more than usual."

"Your name was on everyone's lips in London."

"My name?" I am surprised. I haven't been to London for nearly three years. Surely more scintillating things have transpired in the meantime.

"Oh, yes," Jack chimes in. "All the men in the art and book world told us how highly they think of you. Curators, dealers, experts—well, they seem to be unanimous in their view that you created a marvelous collection for my father here at the library."

"How lovely to hear. You know it means the world to me that I honored your father—during his lifetime and now," I say.

"Oh, Belle, there was even one dinner in which Charles Read half threatened to steal you away from us. I do believe he'd like to bring you to England to work for him at the British Museum," Jessie exclaims.

I'm flattered that the highly esteemed keeper of the Department of British and Mediaeval Antiquities would express such an interest in me, even if it was just dinner party chatter.

"He wasn't the only one, Belle," Jack says, all seriousness. They glance at each other, as if they'd rehearsed this exchange and he was now prompting her next line.

Jessie's face is now somber as well. "We can't have that, can we, Jack? We must keep our Belle."

I look between the two of them, wondering what is going on.

"So I—we," he says with a meaningful glance at Jessie, "have been thinking. You've been very clear in your desire to keep the Morgan collections intact, which we understand and appreciate, as it was my father's goal as well. And while we still feel that we need to address my father's somewhat objectionable and problematic practice of keeping as much as two-thirds of the family financial capital in artwork, perhaps we don't have to divest the collection here at the library. It seems the Pierpont Morgan Library is considered to be quite important, especially in its holdings of rare books and manuscripts."

"Really?" I blurt out. Of course, I've been pleading for this for months. It only took a roomful of lofty British men to convince him that I was right.

"Yes. We will have to sell off certain portions of father's holdings, many of which were never held here at the library, some of which predated your role as librarian even."

My body tenses. Even though I don't actually own any of the objects in the library or Mr. Morgan's homes or on loan to museums, I feel a certain sense of pride and ownership about them. I say a silent prayer that the items dearest to me—those incunabula and manuscripts that together tell the history of the written word and its power to lift humanity—can be spared the guillotine. "Which items do you have in mind?"

"I studied the inventory you prepared while we were in London, and the Chinese porcelain collection currently on display at the Metropolitan Museum of Art seems like a natural first to go."

I exhale slowly, hoping my relief isn't audible. These four thousand pieces, many Ming dynasty vases among them, are indeed exquisite, but were largely a project of Mr. Morgan himself. While I wish Jack could preserve it intact for Mr. Morgan's sake, the collection is too vast for one family, even for one museum, in truth. During one trip to the museum, I had the misfortune of seeing some of the pieces packaged away in a basement storage room because even the Met didn't have the space to properly display the collection in its entirety. "That's a logical choice, sir. I believe they could fetch up to three million dollars."

His eyes widen. "Well, that amount would go a long way to pay the tax authorities."

"Any other initial thoughts?" I want to prepare myself if Jack is targeting any other item of particular value to me.

"The Fragonards?" he asks.

In 1902, Mr. Morgan had purchased Jean-Honoré Fragonard's masterpiece, *The Progress of Love*—a series of eleven painted panels, commissioned by the last mistress of Louis XIV, which celebrate the different stages of love—and created a room to house them in London. I have never seen them, and have no particular feeling about them. Consequently, I'd be relieved to see them on the sale list over some favorite treasures. "Another fine choice. I'm guessing we could get in excess of a million dollars for them."

He lets out a low whistle, and then says, with a broad smile, "Are you pleased, Belle?"

"I am overjoyed," I say, and mean it. The Pierpont Morgan Library's collection—the legacy Mr. Morgan and I created together—will remain intact. This is a key step in creating the larger *meaning* I discussed with Papa.

Jack and Jessie smile at my reaction, and then he says, "I'm glad to hear it. We'll maintain the core collection here. The books and the manuscripts, the treasures you deem most important."

My cheeks hurt from smiling. While I'll lament selling off any piece of artwork Mr. Morgan and I acquired together, the thought that I will be able to keep much of the library's collection feels like deliverance. "I cannot thank you—"

"Jack, Jessie! Where are you?" a familiar voice cries out, interrupting me.

"In Belle's office!" Jack calls to his sister.

With her unmistakable, plodding footsteps, Anne storms into the room. "I went over to your house to welcome you home, but I heard you came here first. Whatever for?"

She doesn't bother to greet me as she bestows lavish hugs upon her brother and sister-in-law.

"We had some good news to give Belle, and we didn't want to wait."

Anne turns to glare at me, as if she's just noticed I am also in my office. Even though her eyes are on me, she speaks to her brother. "It couldn't keep until tomorrow? You've just got off a transatlantic voyage."

Jack's smile is firmly affixed. He is pleased with his plan, and that's what he's thinking about. Selling off the art will amass the money he needs to pay taxes and keep a more liquid estate and business. Maintaining the library largely unscathed will allow him to retain the Morgan reputation in the rarefied world of collecting.

He explains to Anne that the library will survive, and my place as the guardian of the books and manuscripts as well. "We will keep Belle at the helm. It will be a fitting tribute to Father. You know what brought him the deepest pleasure was reading the voices of the past. Collecting the books, touching the letters and the documents."

Jack is right. It's that intimate conversation with the past that provided the connection between Mr. Morgan and me. Each book in the library contained a world of personalities and stories and history.

We shared an insatiable curiosity. The deeper we each read, the more we would understand about this world we live in, and the more questions we had.

I wonder if Anne is contemplating whether there is any way around her brother's decision. But she knows the will leaves this decision entirely up to Jack. Her father's bequest to her was an unfettered three million dollars and no power, but lack of authorization has never stopped Anne.

Strange that she's so quiet. Does this reticence signal a rage so intense she dare not voice it in front of her brother?

Sensing a brewing awkwardness, Jessie steps in and guides Jack away. "Well, darling, we've delivered the news. Should we return home and ready for dinner?"

"Yes, my love," he replies. Then, he turns to his sister. "Are you coming?"

"I'll be there, but I'd like a word alone with Belle first."

After a flurry of farewell embraces and expressions of gratitude, we are by ourselves. I've seen her only four times since the funeral, and on each occasion, she let me know that her father's death changed nothing. She always made her disapproval abundantly clear.

"I won't pretend that I like you, Belle," Anne begins. "I think you had my father wrapped about your little finger, and I don't like what you turned him into during his final years."

My heart is pounding, but I eke out a laugh. "Anne, I think you know that *no one* could manipulate your father. He was a force of nature, and I was simply hired to do his bidding."

It is Anne's turn to laugh. "Don't take me for a fool, Belle. Somehow you found a way to bend my father to your will, when no one else could."

I suddenly understand why Anne loathes me so much. It isn't that I'd occupied the bulk of her father's time; Anne had a busy life of her own that left little space for him, in truth. It was her conviction that I had the power to influence the great man—something she was never able to do, whether it was her fight in the movement for the woman's right to vote or her support of the women workers striking for better factory conditions in the great Shirtwaist strike three years ago.

"But that has no bearing on what I want to tell you." Her generous bosom expands as she takes a deep breath. Clearly, whatever she needs to divulge weighs heavily upon her. "I understand you've become friends with Bessie," she says in a softer tone.

"I don't know if I would say we're friends," I answer. "We've run into each other on several occasions, and Bessie is always cordial."

"Did you know my father hated Bessie?" The switch in her tone and the direction of this conversation is surprising. She doesn't give me time to respond before she continues. "A couple of years before he died, she was up for the French Legion of Honor," Anne explains, and despite the sadness in her tone, I hear her pride. "It was for her work representing French playwrights. It was an award she clearly deserved, but my father made sure she did not receive it."

This is something I did not know.

Anne says, "It was his way of punishing her for his suspicions about me and about our relationship. He blamed her and wanted to punish me for not being the daughter he wanted. For not being Juliet or Louisa." Her devastated expression tells me more about her love for Bessie than any proclamation could have.

I am stunned by this news, but I shouldn't be. Mr. Morgan's code of morality was strict and old-fashioned, even if his behavior was not. He would never have tolerated such supposedly aberrant behavior from one of his children. It was unthinkable.

For a moment, I flash back to the day when I almost confessed about my race when I mistakenly thought that Mr. Morgan had discovered my deception. Hearing this story of Anne and Bessie makes me wonder what he would have done if he'd learned the truth and that information became public. What sort of punishment would he have exacted upon me? I know now that I would not have escaped unscathed.

I have new questions. If Mr. Morgan knew about Anne, why did she allow me to threaten her with what I thought was a secret?

She answers my questions before I can even ask them. "If you had said something to him about me and Bessie—told him that we shared a stateroom, for example—he probably would have felt he needed to take further action, not wanting the truth about me to become public. I couldn't bear for Bessie to be punished even more for my sins."

"I'm sorry, Anne. I didn't know."

Without acknowledging my apology, Anne continues, "Even though he and I did not see eye to eye, I loved my father. No matter our falling-out, no matter what he thought about me."

"He loved you, too." I feel as though I must say this to her. And it is true; he loved her in his way.

After a pause, she says, "I suppose so. He did leave me enough money to go about my life and support my causes without ever having to marry, and I am indebted to him for that."

I nod.

"Anyway, Bessie thinks I've got you all wrong. For the most part, I disagree with her, of course." Here, she gives me a half smile.

Is she teasing me, or does her smile carry a different message?

Her smile turns into a sigh. "There is one thing I do know, Belle. With the public disparity in our political and social views, I cannot keep the flame of my father's legacy alive, even if I wanted to." She pauses. "But you, with your expertise and your loyalty to his vision, you can."

My eyes widen.

She takes a deep breath before she continues, "So, I want you to know that I support you as the librarian for the Pierpont Morgan Library." And then, with a smirk, she adds, "No matter who you really are."

Even though I shouldn't ask, even though everything inside of me tells me to let it end right here, I must know. "How did you find out about me?" I ask. "Who or what gave me away?"

She pauses, and an apologetic expression appears on her usually stern face. "Until this moment, I only suspected. You just confirmed it for me."

My breath catches in my throat. What have I done? Was all of this chatter just bait so I could fall into her snare and confess my real heritage? Did she just lure me in to destroy me?

Her voice softens. "Don't worry, Belle. I know how painful it is to be judged by a construct of society that doesn't make sense and because of that, have to live with a painful secret. Neither of us has been able to live openly as our true selves, and I'm sorry for the role I played in threatening you with your hidden identity. I hope we can keep our secrets from this point on."

Although Mr. Morgan is no longer here, I suppose Anne would want to keep her private life private, just as I need to protect my own secret from an unforgiving world. Even though I have much more to lose, I smile back at her. "Yes, Anne. Our secrets are safe with each other."

CHAPTER 38

OCTOBER 14 AND DECEMBER 2, 1916
LONDON, ENGLAND

Miss Greene! Miss Greene!" the reporters call out as I walk down the gangplank to the shore.

My escort from the *Liverpool* waves them off, but they are persistent. "Miss Greene, what are you here in London to buy?" "Miss Greene, what does the Pierpont Morgan Library have its sights set on this trip?" "Miss Greene, the *Evening Sun* just declared you the most successful career woman in the world. How does that title feel?" "Miss Greene, will you be working with Mr. Morgan on his war efforts while you're here?"

Don't the London newspapers have more pressing matters than my arrival? Their country is at war in the greatest conflict the world has yet seen, one that President Wilson inexplicably refuses to enter. Surely the reporters have any number of war-related stories to cover, although it is flattering to know that my success as the head of the Pierpont Morgan Library registers on this side of the Atlantic.

A motorcar awaits on the dock to take me to Jack's city house, after which it will deliver my trunks to Claridge's, where I managed to get a suite on the strength of the Morgan name, despite the hotel room shortage. Jack has summoned me from New York to evaluate and potentially purchase rare books, which are flooding the city during the war. And I was happy to comply, no matter the risks in transatlantic travel after the Germans torpedoed the *Lusitania* last year and no matter my mother's near hysteria over my voyaging to war-torn Europe. London offers not only immersion in its still-bustling art world but also Bernard. He has promised to travel from Paris, where he is holing up for the duration, to London to meet me. Even after our almost three years apart, warmth courses through me thinking of him again.

How different our London reunion will be, I think. In New York we'd agreed that I would have the liberty to pursue work and other men if so inclined, while he would provide me with the safe haven of his trusted advice, laughter, and affection. I believe it to be as close to a real union as I'll ever have—especially since he no longer holds any power to devastate me.

The motorcar slows as we approach Prince's Gate, where the town house Jack inherited from Mr. Morgan is located. This is one of two homes Jack and Jessie own in England, the other being the lavish Wall Hall mansion and estate in Hertfordshire, which they use for shooting and extravagant parties. I know little of the Prince's Gate town house, but it is rumored to be spectacular.

The front door opens before I can even lift the knocker on the surprisingly modest exterior. I'm underwhelmed by the facade and the entryway. But when the briskly efficient servant directs me to the drawing room, I am awestruck at the space. Here Fragonard's masterpiece, *The Progress of Love*, covers the walls, and the entire room has been decorated to pay tribute to its magnificence. I see why the paintings are so celebrated as I study each panel; I am particularly drawn in by the depiction of the final stage of love, the calm pleasure of a stable union as represented by the exchange of love letters. Do I find this painting particularly appealing because it so deftly captures the sort of relationship Bernard and I now share?

Jack finally peeks his head out from an adjoining room, and then bounds into the room, albeit with a fraction of his prior energy. Last year, while in England, Jack was attacked by a German sympathizer who'd learned of his financial support for England and France, quite against Wilson's orders on neutrality for American citizens. While he has recovered rather well and it hasn't cowed his involvement in the war effort, I am relieved that his injuries have not dampened his ardor for the library either.

"How have I been functioning without you in London this past month?" he cries out with a laugh, after we embrace.

I laugh along with him, thinking of something I wrote Bernard about Jack: *Sometimes I wonder if I've sold him too well on the merits of the library and of yours truly. When he's in New York, he almost never departs from the library, just like his father, and my role as his partner in art and finance leaves me little time for anything else.* Of course, I never describe to Bernard the myriad ways my relationship with Jack is unlike the one that I shared with his father. Obviously, I have no paternal feelings toward him, but more importantly, although Jack and I are closer in age, no flirtation passes between us. There is no unacknowledged longing. The many complicated layers have been reduced to a simple collegial accord. Jack has no need for me to fill the void in his heart—as I had for Mr. Morgan—because Jessie is there already.

He gestures around the gilt-laden drawing room, where every fabric, every piece of furniture, and every decoration has been chosen to glorify the paintings. "What do you think of the Fragonards?"

"It's impossible to believe that these masterpieces will be removed from these walls and sold. I can't imagine that they'll soon be sailing across the Atlantic and hanging in some other mansion. They seem to belong here."

It is the melancholy in my tone that makes Jack say, "But we did agree that they could be sold without impacting our other important collections, didn't we?" He is not really inquiring but reminding me of the conclusion we'd previously reached. In fact, I've already begun the long dance of discussions about their sale with the Duveens and a few other dealers.

I nod. True to his word, Jack has involved me in all his decision making about the future of Mr. Morgan's art and manuscript collections. Among other matters.

He signals for me to sit in the pale aqua Louis XIV chair as he lowers himself into its match. As we face each other, I think how tired he looks beneath the dark bushy eyebrows and heavy mustache. Is it the war alone that's taking this toll upon him? Is he still recovering from his injuries? Or is the dispersal of his father's belongings dredging up heavy emotions?

"The number of rare manuscripts and books on the London market is breathtaking, Belle. I cannot begin to sort through the possibilities," he says, and I observe an overeagerness, almost like greed, in his expression. People are desperate for funds in wartime. Is his desire to partake of this bounty opportunism? But how can I judge, when I am planning on reaping the spoils of war alongside him?

"That's why you have me," I say, pushing those thoughts aside.

"Indeed." He sighs. "And a relief it is."

Jack slides me a handwritten list. "These are the dealers I've already met or who have sent me letters describing attractive manuscripts and rare books."

I pick up the paper and review it. The names on the list are familiar; in fact, I've dealt with many of them in the past. I realize that I am fortunate with Jack; he feels no embarrassment in acknowledging my expertise in authenticating the provenance of and pricing these items.

"I'll set up meetings with each of them straightaway. Please be assured that I'll handle it from here," I say.

"I have absolute confidence in you."

Keeping my eyes on the list, I ask, "Should I sail to Paris after I've made my way through all that London has to offer? There might be a hidden cache of illuminated manuscripts waiting there." I think how delicious it might be to take in the Parisian sights with Bernard, outside the purview of Jack, whose anti-Semitism, which I'm sure was passed down from his father, makes him naturally disposed against Bernard. I keep my ongoing relationship with Bernard secret from Jack as a result.

"I forbid it, Belle," he says flatly.

I'm taken aback. This little outburst is so unlike Jack's steady and predictable nature.

He notices my reaction. "Belle, I'm sorry. It's hard for you to comprehend how dire the situation is in Europe. The news we get in America is insular and self-focused, and so you wouldn't know that travel is extremely risky and inadvisable, even if you could obtain the necessary paperwork and special permits. By God, you've got to get permission from the local police to travel to the countryside from London these days."

Jack is not finished. "Listen, Belle, I want you to undertake the library's business, and the moment you're finished, sail home. Soon enough, America will be in this war, too, and I don't want you anywhere near the danger. Travel is not impossible right now, even with the war, but I think it should be considered impossible for you. You are too precious to risk."

I nod. I feel sure that Jack is right about this new reality. But if I can't go to Paris, will Bernard be able to travel to London? What will the impact of this red tape and bureaucracy be? And why hasn't Bernard forewarned me about the danger and delay? Shouldn't he be worrying about my safety as much as Jack is? Is it possible that the war has affected Paris to such an extent that Bernard couldn't have even informed me in advance?

I am tired, but I suppress my yawn. For the last six weeks, I've been out late too many nights and consumed too many glasses of fine wine. War hasn't halted the high life in London; instead, it seems to have fueled it. I simply cannot appear vulnerable in any way, even with simple exhaustion. The Duveens will be on the lookout for any chink in my armor.

Why am I more wary of the Duveens than the dozen or so others I've met with over the past weeks? What is it about their manner and bargaining style that puts me on edge? I have no choice but to work with the ingratiating pair. They hold too many exclusives on desirable items—making it impossible to access certain objects without them—and represent too many crucial clients with huge collections for me to avoid them. Still, they leave me cold and disconcerted, no matter their reputation of exceeding cordiality.

I stare at the clock above the mantel in the parlor of my hotel suite and pace as the stylishly narrow skirt of my burgundy gown catches at my ankles. Why are the Duveen brothers late? Anger is building inside me. On some level, I recognize that it isn't the Duveens with whom I'm furious, but Bernard.

Week after week, he has offered me a litany of excuses for his failure to come to London. Train strikes and coastal military maneuvers and torpedo threats for ships crossing the canal. Although I understand there may be truth to his justifications, not everyone feels as he does. The esteemed dealer Jacques Seligmann traveled from Paris last week without incident to try to woo me into leaving the Pierpont Morgan Library and joining his business. Bernard's elusive behavior reminds me too much of his absence during my last, dark days in London. I've been a fool thinking that Bernard and I could create a singular relationship. And while he doesn't have the power to wound me any longer, he has retained the power to spark my rage.

The door knocks with an authoritative rap. As the maid opens it, I compose myself, and then calmly ask, "Do you always keep your clients waiting?"

Immediately deflated, Joseph and Henry Duveen freeze. For all their games and the web of spies they purportedly have planted in the homes of the wealthy and their rival dealers, I find them remarkably easy to unsettle. Perhaps it is because they are so very English, so very unprepared for the unexpected.

"We are terribly sorry, Belle," Henry, the elder of the brothers, rushes to apologize. "We try never to keep clients waiting."

"How about lady colleagues?" I use an impish tone to further confuse them.

"You are certainly our only lady colleague, and if a military convoy hadn't rolled down the street in front of our motorcar, we would never have been late." As he bows, Joseph takes my hand to lightly kiss it.

Does he imagine courtliness will win me over? I should think he would know better by now. "I suppose I cannot blame you for the war, can I?" I retort, and they chuckle, a little nervously to my mind. *Good, nervous is how I want them.*

I sit, nodding at the brothers to take the seats across from me. Waiting while the maid collects their hats and coats along with their drink orders, I sip at a glass of sherry to blunt my fraying nerves.

The brothers lower themselves onto the settee across from my chair, and I raise a topic I'm guessing they won't expect. They are used to the ritual of pleasantries. "The Fragonards were looking especially lovely when I saw them the other day."

The brothers give each other what they think is an unobtrusive glance. "I thought we were here today to discuss manuscripts," Joseph says.

While the Duveens have a trove of manuscripts and rare books to sell me, we both know the real prize is the commission they could make on the sale of Mr. Morgan's Fragonards and any other artistic masterpieces we choose to let them broker. If I hire them.

"All in good time." I take another sip, relaxing as the amber liquid warms me inside. "I thought we'd start with the Fragonards, since I know your real plans are to represent the Morgans in their sale. Should they decide to sell them and should I decide to hire you, that is." They need to know I understand their strategy and true goals, and I want that to factor into the prices they'll offer me for the manuscripts at their disposal.

Joseph clears his throat, and says, "Since we've decided to eschew the formality of discussing the manuscripts first, perhaps we should also discuss the decision by Mr. Morgan the younger to sell the family collection of Chinese porcelains. We would welcome the opportunity to represent the Morgans in that sale, too."

Although I am taken aback, my face remains blank. How did the Duveens know we'd decided to sell the porcelains next? Jack has never taken to Asian art, and since they didn't complement the objects we were keeping, we'd agreed we'd find a buyer for them after the Fragonards were sold. But he hadn't told anyone, except maybe Jessie. And I hadn't told anyone—except Bernard.

At that realization, fury rises within me. How could he? I had trusted Bernard. I'd believed him to be my confidant, with whom I could safely share my worries and my secrets if not my love. After we reconnected in New York and in our subsequent long exchange of letters, I'd shared my apprehension that Jack would dismantle the library and sell the books. When Jack decided to keep the library largely intact and enlist my help in selling certain pieces of art, I'd shared my thoughts on which objects should be sold. Why would he have shared my secrets with the Duveens, of all people?

But I can't allow myself to fixate on that now. Joseph interrupts my thoughts. "You know, Belle, if you select Duveen Brothers to assist in the sale of the Fragonards or the Chinese porcelains or any other item you may wish to divest, it could be financially beneficial for you."

Joseph isn't making any sense. "What are you talking about?" I ask.

Henry takes a turn. "We would be immensely grateful to be chosen as the dealer for all of the Morgans' important sales. So grateful that we'd be happy to share our commission with you."

Now I'm the one who is unnerved. "Why on earth would I do that?"

He shrugs as if the answer is self-evident. "Don't you deserve to make at least a portion of what the dealers make? Especially since you are doing most of the work and not receiving a commission? As an

employee of the Morgans, you only get a salary, not a cut. And it's
not like you're an actual Morgan and adding the purchase price to
your coffers."

"That is unethical," I say. The Duveens want me to enter into an
arrangement with them whereby I'd agree to sell all of the Morgans'
artwork through them—to clients of their choosing—for a part of
their sales commissions. This would mean that the Morgans would
not necessarily get the highest prices for their artwork because they
would all be sold to Duveen customers, rather than the highest bidders. If I did this, my loyalty would be to the Duveens, not the
Morgans—something I would *never* contemplate.

"It is more common than you might think, and there are other
agreements as well. In fact, your friend Mr. Berenson has a beneficial
arrangement of his own. For years, he's been authenticating important
Italian Renaissance paintings for us, and when we sell the piece, he
receives a portion of the commission."

"No," I say, shaking my head. How could this be true? Even if he
only authenticates artwork that he truly finds to be worthy, the scheme
stinks of self-dealing. If the art community learned of it, the arrangement would destroy Bernard's reputation as *the* unbiased Italian Renaissance expert. I can't even contemplate the possibility that he might
authenticate pieces that don't merit his attention.

"Oh, yes, Miss Greene. We have had this arrangement with Mr.
Berenson for some years." Henry looks at his brother. "Although our
understanding may have run its course, and we may have to cut Mr.
Berenson loose. I think we all know that the Italian Renaissance business isn't what it once was—so many other sorts of artwork are gaining
popularity instead—so we may not need his services any longer."

I now understand why Bernard betrayed me. He'd been in league
with them for years, perhaps the entire time I've known him. And by
offering them information about me and the Morgans, he was trying
to prove himself valuable at a time when he'd outlived his usefulness.
If he could provide them with the Morgans' plans, then perhaps they
wouldn't end their lucrative arrangement with him.

Even though I feel like I might be sick, I stand up. Staring at the two swindlers playing at English gentlemen, I say, "I work only for Mr. Jack Morgan. He has my full and exclusive loyalty. Now"—I gesture toward the door—"if you will let yourselves out."

I leave the parlor and enter the study. Choking back a sob so the Duveens cannot hear it, I collapse on a chair. The true nature of my loyalty isn't the only thing made plain today in this encounter with the Duveens. I have finally seen—and allowed myself to acknowledge—the depths of Bernard's treachery. Is no one what they seem?

CHAPTER 39

DECEMBER 10, 1916
LONDON, ENGLAND

I watch my stack of trunks roll down the Claridge's hallway on a trolley, and I trail in their wake. When will I next see London? By then, how will the English capital be altered by the war? Can I wash from my memories of this once-adored city the scenes of disappointment that transpired here? At least I know I'll return to New York professionally triumphant if not personally.

My trunk overflows with rare and priceless incunabula and manuscripts. Those I cannot fit in my allotted luggage will arrive in the Morgans' bags in a few weeks. This time in London—meeting with dealers and collectors, scooping up books before they came to market, luxuriating in the last vestiges of London decadence—has been productive and enjoyable only because I refused to wallow in thoughts of Bernard once I sent my final letter to him. I know the mourning will come on board the *Liverpool*, and only there will I allow it to flow freely. Until we reach New York, that is, and then I must slip into the role I've designated for myself and inhabit it fully.

In my final, parting missive to Bernard, I'd written:

How could you take the affection I shared with you and
abuse it so willingly? Refusing to come to London, not once
but twice, during my time of need, and then bartering my
secrets for your own gain? Was any of it ever real, Bernard?
Or were our trysts always arranged for your personal profit?
I thought, at least, we had an understanding and trust
between us.

I am only grateful that I never shared my real secret with him. What might he have done with the knowledge that Belle da Costa Greene was born a colored girl? Held an auction? Sold the secret to the highest bidder?

Two uniformed bellmen scurry to my side. "Miss Greene, your motorcar to the harbor is loaded and waiting for you, ma'am."

Slipping the men a tip, I follow them to the idling Rolls-Royce. I wrap my fur around my shoulders, and just as I'm about to step up and inside the gleaming silver motorcar, I hear, "Belle!"

Turning, I catch sight of a man racing toward me. It is Bernard.

"Belle, don't leave!" The ever-respectable Bernard is screaming so loudly I can hear him over the street din of horse-drawn carriages, motorcars, bicycles, and motorized buses. "Please talk to me!"

Should I bother? My decisions about Bernard have already been rendered, and I do not worry that his sentiments will sway me. I did not have any desire for a grand love affair with Bernard when I set out to see him in Europe, but I did expect the behavior of a trusted friend, at least. The betrayal I received in place of trust has hardened my heart against him forever. Does he deserve even a second more of my time? No. But I decide I want to have the last word.

Instructing the driver to wait, I stride over to Bernard, where he stands forlorn on the sidewalk in front of Claridge's. His forehead is damp with sweat despite the December cold, and he is panting. I enjoy his public discomfiture and I wish one of his precious English colleagues would step outside and witness *this* Bernard.

"Have you come to answer my questions?" I ask with more calm in my voice than I feel.

"I'm sorry?" He looks perplexed.

"It's a little late for apologies, don't you think?"

"Oh, Belle." He appears crestfallen, but I doubt every emotion that flits across his face. "There aren't words for how terribly sorry I am."

"Try." No amount of effort on his part will change my mind, but I'd like to watch his efforts. At least he's not pretending that he didn't tell the Duveens my secrets, because that's one battle I don't feel like fighting.

He shakes his head. "I don't know why I told the Duveens about the Chinese porcelains. It was a mistake, a moment of weakness. But it was the only one." His face appears earnest, but I know it's willful oblivion. A reluctance on his part to acknowledge and own his culpability.

I hold back a laugh. "Do you really think you betrayed me only one time?"

His eyebrows rise. "I swear I didn't tell them any other details about the plans you and Jack have for the art collection."

"Betrayal takes many forms, although disclosing my secrets to the Duveens is certainly one. An unforgivable one."

His frown shows that he is confused, but then, his eyes widen before he asks, "Do you mean Edith Wharton? Or Natalie Barney?" He names the expat Parisian literary salon host with whom he's rumored to be involved. "We agreed we could see other people when we weren't physically together, Belle."

"Oh, I don't care about them." I wave his words and their names away with a swat of my hand. "And the fact that you do not know what I'm talking about makes me all the more certain of my decision. The particular betrayal I'm talking about is abandonment."

"Because I . . . I . . . didn't come to London?" he stammers. "If you believe that I did not come because I do not care about you, you are wrong."

"Do you mean this time? Or when you refused to come the first time, when I was horribly sick after the abortion?"

He flinches at the word, as I have done many times through the years when I think about what I did. But why should he be spared the reality of our actions? "Please don't offer any more empty rationales for your decision not to come this fall—after all, Jacques Seligmann was able to make the trip—or your refusal to do so six years ago. I know precisely why you chose to stay away."

He tries to grasp my wrist, but I pull it away. "I did not come— then and now—because I love you too much. You are the only woman who has managed to get truly close to me, and I've been afraid I'd lose everything for you. You just don't understand."

"I understand perfectly, Bernard. You've already gotten everything you wanted from me; in this case, every useful bit of information about the Morgans and their plans. And you are too self-serving and too uncaring to even be a friend, never mind a lover," I say, keeping my expression placid.

I begin to walk away from him and he grabs my arm. "Belle, I beg you to listen to me," he pleads. "You are the love of my life."

Those words make me pause, quite against my resolve. Despite all his failings and all his deceptions and his pathetic pleading, Bernard was my first, and perhaps only, love and knows how to pull at my emotions. I remind myself of who he really is—and how he can never be anything meaningful in my life—and my determination returns. I remind myself that I am free.

"Please remove your hand from my arm, Bernard," I say, but he will not let go.

As I try to jerk away from him, the Claridge's doormen witness my distress, and race to my side.

"Move away," they say, standing on either side of me. Together, they peel Bernard's fingers off me, then hold him back while I hasten to the Rolls-Royce and climb inside. I do not glance back at the scene, and instead, I ask the driver to depart.

The engine roars, but still I hear, "Belle! Belle!"

For a moment, the driver hesitates, but I say, "Please, go on."

With a nod, he drives the motorcar away from the hotel. Even though I can hear Bernard call my name, I keep my eyes fixed on the road ahead. I will not look back.

CHAPTER 40

The stones crunch underfoot as I make my way down the long, winding path to the gravesite. Even though the sun feels as if it's smiling, the long walk through Cedar Hill Cemetery is sorrowful.

I note the familiar headstones of the Hawleys and Seymours, monuments to the venerable blue-blooded families permitted burial rights here. Several minutes pass before I see the peak of the mausoleum jutting out over the crest in the path. Only as I make my way down the small hillside does the rectangular tomb of the Morgan family come into full view.

The raised Morgan name is crisp as ever on the granite surface. However, the grass surrounding the grave is ragged, and there are no flowers marking the tomb. At first, I'm taken aback, but then, I suppose I usually visit the monument on March 31, the anniversary of Mr. Morgan's death, when the site is prepared for visitors.

But I need to visit with him today. Because this is the only suitable place to mourn the death of my father.

I settle on the stone bench across from the monument. Tears come unbidden, and I do not even try to stop from sobbing. My father died on May 2, over a month ago, but I have only now heard the news about his fatal cerebral hemorrhage in a letter from Uncle Mozart.

Poor Papa did not even have one of his children in attendance at his funeral. The man who spent his life battling for equality—and sacrificed much for that fight, including his first family—deserved more than we gave him in the end. Did his Japanese family even know about his death?

After we left each other that day in Chicago, we promised to see each other again. I'd harbored fantasies of future afternoons with him at the Metropolitan Museum of Art, but I didn't dare ask him to visit me in New York, and I'm certain that in the years that followed he never considered asking me.

Once he gave me his blessing to hold on to my white identity for a life of meaning, I suspect we both knew that we'd never see each other again. Belle da Costa Greene could never be seen with Richard Greener. The glances that I still suffered through, the rumors I still heard, would have turned into front-page news if my father and I were discovered together. Simply being in my father's presence in front of the wrong person in New York would have exposed me, my siblings, and Mama.

"I've lost you both now, Mr. Morgan. You and Papa." Saying aloud the nature of my loss yields more tears. After all, I cannot speak these words to anyone. "Mr. Morgan, I know our relationship was more complicated than that of father and daughter. Especially after that night of the Caxton auction." I stop there. As when he was alive, I do not mention the kiss we shared. "But before that night, you encouraged me like a father, supported me like a father, believed in my capabilities like a father. As a result, I owe much of what I've become as an adult to you."

I think about the words I want to say next. "But Papa knew the other side of me, the colored part I had to hide from you." I pause, because I'd like to think that Mr. Morgan can hear me, and if he can, he needs time to digest this information. He may not like it. But I must continue as if he does. "Papa knew the little colored girl I once was. He nurtured me, and I owe just as much to him, if not more." I sniffle as the tears recede, and then I have a thought.

My last memories of church are from childhood, when the whole Fleet family would pile into carriages to attend services at the Metropolitan Baptist Church with the Reverend Robert Johnson. Our churchgoing rituals stopped once we moved to New York. But there are remnants of Sunday school lessons in my mind, and I like to believe that a beautiful hereafter awaits us after all of the turmoil on earth.

"But now, I have to navigate without either one of you to create the legacy I owe you both."

Once again, I stop and search for the right words, the specific question. Because now, I need Mr. Morgan's help and guidance. "But how can I pay my debt to you and Papa if I cannot get Jack on board? While he has been wonderful in supporting me as the head of the library and keeping our manuscript and book collection intact, he is the gatekeeper to this final decision—to make the library a public institution. If the library is kept private, how can I keep my promise to Papa to live a life of meaning, to impact larger society for good?"

I sit silently for a moment. *Perhaps I am being greedy.* Shouldn't it be enough that I've risen to become one of the most influential people in the art world and built such a magnificent collection? It certainly would be satisfactory for Katrina and her friends who've successfully advocated for the Nineteenth Amendment and the right of women to have professional careers. The height I've achieved is almost unmatched among women, and I take quiet satisfaction in that.

As I sit in front of Mr. Morgan's grave, I know that somehow, someway, I've got to bring Jack around. Is a direct appeal to Jack the right tactic? I've hinted and lightly cajoled, which yielded his agreement to allow in the occasional scholar, club, or lecturer. Yet that's still far from converting the library into a *public* institution, where outsiders can enter regularly and without specially granted permission, where regular people can revel in the magnificence and significance of the early written word. Like Papa taught me. No, the reticent

Jack recoils from bluntness; that is not the right approach, it will remind him too much of his father.

I stroll around the monument, warming myself in the sun. I wonder for the hundredth time since my meeting with Papa if he and Mr. Morgan ever met. It wasn't until after my trip to Chicago that I began to really study my father. I read more of his writings; I researched his history and his travels. I learned about the work that he and Mr. Morgan did on the Grant Monument Association in the 1890s. Papa served as secretary, and his work was his full-time paid job, while Mr. Morgan was on the board, with very few responsibilities other than fundraising. But even with that, how strange it would be if Papa and Mr. Morgan—whose lives as a colored equal-rights activist and a white tycoon, respectively, never should have intersected—had actually crossed paths? And not only in the hereafter?

The tie between parent and child is unbreakable, despite the sort of relationship they actually shared. The manner in which Papa continues to affect my life bears that out, and I imagine that it must be true of Jack as well.

And with that thought, suddenly I know what I must do.

I have been approaching this in the wrong way. I've been trying to appeal to Jack's sense of art. But that has not moved him. What I must do is appeal to the larger Morgan heritage, the dynasty that Junius Morgan established in banking and that J. P. expanded into a corporate finance empire that dominated Wall Street and industry and that Jack has now turned into a global enterprise.

"The Pierpont Morgan Library as a public institution," I say aloud, as if I'm practicing my presentation with Mr. Morgan and my father first, before I pitch it to Jack, "will continue the family custom of honoring its predecessor."

Yes, Jack will want to do this out of a sense of tradition if not emotion. In this way, by honoring his father, Jack will actually be honoring his lineage. Just as I will be honoring my own father and my own secret ancestry.

CHAPTER 41

JUNE 26, 1922
LONG ISLAND, NEW YORK

Y ou seem miffed at the Pierpont Morgan Library's purchase
of certain gilt-laden gospels from the Earl of Leicester?" I
ask, unable to keep the hint of a smile from my lips. Mr.
Paul Tennant is about to step into my magnificently laid trap, right
here at a party on the veranda of Winfield Hall, at the Woolworth
mansion on the Gold Coast of Long Island, New York.

"It does seem that cultural treasures are leaving England more
quickly than they are coming in these days, treasures that belong in
England, to England. And they are exiting in the hands of Americans," Mr. Tennant says, his British accent heightening.

"You've made an interesting observation," I say, as if I'm actually
considering his preposterous argument.

The men and women gathered around us—a Phipps, a Vanderbilt,
and a Frick among them—nod, and Mr. Tennant nods, his hands
folded in righteous indignation, along with them. As I'd hoped.

"But do England's cultural treasures really belong to England?" I
ask. "Did England actually create the treasures that you are so upset
to see in American hands? Are they part of *English* heritage? Let's
consider your precious Elgin Marbles, for example. If I'm not mis-

taken, in the early eighteen hundreds, Lord Elgin took the statues from the Acropolis in Athens to London, and Greece has been asking for them back ever since."

Mr. Tennant's mouth opens and closes, but before he can form a single word, I say, "Would it surprise you to learn that the Earl of Leicester's precious gospel books that you're so concerned about actually came from Belgium?"

Mr. Tennant storms off, and I am left with an assemblage of surprised, but amused, fellow guests. "Oh, Belle, you always have a keen observation at the ready!" Amy Phipps Guest says with a chuckle.

"Only because I'm provided with so much material!" I reply, and the group erupts into laughter.

My yellow chiffon skirt twirls around my ankles as I spin around to have my champagne glass filled by a passing waiter and bump into Jack. "What a surprise!"

Even though Jack's two-hundred-and-fifty-acre island estate, Matinecock Point, is only a few miles down the Gold Coast of Long Island from the Woolworth mansion and he and his wife had undoubtedly received an invitation to this event, I never expected to see him. He feels comfortable only at the library or in the company of his immediate family—small talk and party banter are not his forte—and he declines to attend most social occasions. In America anyway.

"Well, the Woolworths have a prizewinning rose garden, and Jessie was determined to compare her flowers with theirs. It's a neighborhood rivalry," he says with a draw on his meerschaum pipe.

I've become so adroit at reading Jack's mannerisms over the years that I can tell by the way he fiddles with his pipe that he'd rather be at Matinecock Point, reading Rudyard Kipling or doing crossword puzzles.

"No one's roses can compare with Jessie's," I say. "Or her tulips or her daffodils for that matter."

"I assured her of that, Belle, but you know as well as I that my wife is quite the determined woman. She wouldn't listen to my protests, so here we are."

"Her tenacity is one of many reasons why I like her so much."

He nods. "You share that quality, Belle, and perhaps it's one of the many reasons I like *you* so much. The shelves of the Pierpont Morgan Library would be emptier without it." This is the closest Jack has ever come to flirtation. Unlike that of his father, this coquetry—if it even merits that label—is utterly innocent.

"Should we join Jessie in the gardens?" I ask.

"I wouldn't want to take you away from your admirers." He glances at the group keeping a place open for me in their circle.

"Nonsense." I wave my hand. "There's no one I'd rather talk to than you and Jessie."

He gestures toward the gardens. "Lead the way." We stroll around the wide veranda, past the hundred or so guests still mingling.

We chat about the extravagance of Winfield Hall, the main building on the Woolworth estate, and I realize that another, recently built structure of the Woolworths might provide me with the opportunity to have the conversation I'd planned earlier this month, when I was in the cemetery.

"I understand that the Woolworths built an astounding mausoleum for themselves at Woodlawn Cemetery. Apparently, it is modeled after an Egyptian pyramid, complete with sphinxes, pillars with hieroglyphics, and enormous bronze doors decorated with pharaohs. Quite the tribute to their family."

"You don't say," he replies, though he doesn't sound very interested.

"Do you have any ideas about how you'll honor your family?" I say, and Jack looks startled. I feel uncomfortable pressing on, but I know I must proceed with this line of argument or lose this chance. "You know, next March will be the tenth anniversary of your father's death."

He glances at me, but we don't slow our pace, making me grateful for the ease of the shorter skirts currently in fashion. Finally, he says, "It's hard to believe that much time has passed."

"I know." I sigh. "Some days, when I'm at the library, I feel like he's still there." I'm surprised tears still burn behind my eyes after all this time. Especially since I am the one who brought up this topic as prelude to an enormous request. But then, maybe it's my own father for whom I'm crying; he has been gone for only six weeks.

He says, "I know what you mean. I feel him, too. I suppose he was always larger than life, so we shouldn't expect death to eradicate him from our existence."

"Well put." I pause, and then ask, as if just making conversation, "Have you thought of how you'd like to pay tribute to your father?"

For the first time, his steps slow. "What do you mean?"

"Your father erected the Morgan Memorial at the Wadsworth Atheneum in honor of his father, Junius. I assumed you had something similar planned." Then, I ask, "How would *you* want to be remembered?"

My question surprises him as I'd intended. Death has stretched its claws toward him in the past couple of years. Two years ago, in April, while Jack and his family were attending services at St. George's church near Stuyvesant Square, an anarchist stepped into the church, and while the ushers were taking up the offering, the man shot and killed Dr. James Markoe, the family friend and physician of the Morgans. Later, reports suggested that the intended target was Jack. Then, only five months later, a horse-drawn carriage pulled up in front of Jack's offices and set off an explosion that extended half a mile and killed thirty-eight people, including several Morgan employees. Jack's own thirty-year-old son Junius, who worked in the Morgan offices, narrowly escaped death. Jack was supposed to be in his office that day, but at the last minute had decided to stay at the library.

Jack finally says, "I haven't thought about it," but I cannot imagine that is true.

"I believe your father thought about it. I think he knew exactly how he wanted to be remembered."

"He didn't leave any instructions, Belle."

I stop walking and stare at him. "In his will, your father stated that he wanted his collections made 'permanently available for the instruction and pleasure of the American people,' and that only 'lack of the necessary time to devote to it has as yet prevented my carrying this purpose into effect.' I didn't object when you decided it was best for the Morgan fortunes overall to sell some of your father's best items to the Fricks—like the Fragonard room or the Chinese porcelains or the Rembrandt portrait—or to donate thousands of objects to the Metropolitan Museum or the Wadsworth Atheneum. If we don't preserve the collection left—the manuscripts, books, and drawings at the library—and make them 'permanently available for the American people' as he set out, then the terms of your father's will won't be met. And he won't be remembered as he wanted."

Jack shakes his head. "I think you're reading into the will and—"

"Am I?" I dare to interrupt my employer. "Or is it convenient for you to ignore his plainly stated wishes because they took the vague written form of a request, not an outright mandate?"

His face reddens at my words, but this is a conversation that must be had. I cannot allow Mr. Morgan's legacy to go unfulfilled, not only because of Mr. Morgan but because of what my father challenged me to do. I will not let either man down.

"Jack, you know what your father wanted. It's time to let go of the Morgan as your private library. It's time to turn it into what it was meant to be—a public institution in honor of your father."

CHAPTER 42

MARCH 28, 1924
NEW YORK, NEW YORK

I am sitting at my desk, where I have arranged myself before a pile of letters with a fountain pen in my hand when the reporter arrives in my office. I want to keep this conversation short, which is why I am signaling how busy I am.

I have continued to deny all press access to me, including the *Ladies' Home Journal* last month. But I have weighed this request from the *New York Times* to profile the Pierpont Morgan Library and its lady directress and deemed it worthy.

Samuel Bennett is the name of the journalist. He strides into the room, all blunderbuss and confidence. But then I see that he's little more than a boy, with the fresh, pink skin of young adulthood and a scraggly ginger mustache. I gesture for him to sit in the chair before me. How small and inconsequential he seems compared to the great man—both figurative and literal—who, from time to time, positioned himself in my guest's chair.

"Miss Greene, thank you for taking the time to meet with me." He holds his pencil above his pad in the quintessential reporter pose.

Even after all these years, I can't allow this journalist to shine his light too brightly. The world is expanding and getting smaller at the same time. With the invention of the radio and the expansion of newspapers and magazines, I am more concerned now than I've ever been before that someone, somewhere, might learn the truth.

In this charged racial landscape, news that the head of the Pierpont Morgan Library was a forty-year-old black woman would decimate everything, would change the world for all of us. As I'd admitted long ago, Mama's concerns were right.

While the end of the war has brought great economic growth and widespread prosperity to the country, racial tensions have escalated throughout the nation. Lynchings by the Ku Klux Klan are continuing, as are race wars and massacres of colored people in cities like Tulsa, Oklahoma; Rosewood, Florida; and even my beloved Washington, DC, as Mama predicted long ago. The most terrifying part of all of this is that the federal and state governments have endorsed these mounting racist sentiments by rejecting anti-lynching bills like the Dyer Act, despite President Harding's support, and by adopting despicable legislation like Virginia's Racial Integrity Act, which prohibits interracial marriage and defines "white" as one with no trace of blood other than Caucasian. No, in this environment, I can take no unnecessary risks.

Nothing distracts like the gilt of priceless artwork. I stand and ask, "Would you like a tour?"

"That would be another great honor." He rises alongside me, and together we stroll from my office and into the lobby, but not before I point out my gleaming walnut-lined walls and richly painted paneled ceiling as well as the medieval portrait busts and porphyry urns that sit atop my mantelpiece.

Once we're in the library proper, I introduce him to the awe-inspiring thirty-foot ceiling, veritably dripping with gold leaf and paintings of historical figures and signs of the zodiac, and three floors of bookcases bursting with precious volumes. I lead him to the table and cases where I've arranged for a sampling of the library's treasures to be on display—the Gutenberg Bibles, the collection of Caxtons, as well as key portions of the Hamouli Coptic manuscripts—and as I do, I experience the strangest sensation. I feel as though I'm leading this reporter through the path of my own life, as marked by the manuscripts I've acquired and artifacts I've secured.

Mr. Bennett exclaims at all the proper moments and seems awe-struck by the Gutenberg Bibles. But I can tell he's waiting for the perfect opportunity to spring his list of questions upon me. If I can conduct the actual interview while we are surveying the paintings and manuscripts, I believe I stand a chance at evading the more sensitive inquiries.

"You may feel free to ask your questions as we tour the library, Mr. Bennett. You needn't hold off until the end," I offer, as if motivated by courtesy and grace alone.

"That's awfully kind, Miss Greene. I am on a deadline."

I am about to launch into a description of our key acquisitions over nearly twenty years, when Mr. Bennett interjects, "What education prepared you for a position of this magnitude? Did you have formal training in these different fields? In some ways, it seems as though you were more of a curator or dealer than a librarian."

The question is logical and perfectly acceptable, but it catches me off guard. It's the exact question my mother prepared me for the night before my interview with Mr. Morgan all those years ago.

I flash him my best disarming grin, the one I've used for decades as I've practiced misdirection. "There was no better education for this incredible position than the training I received as a librarian at Princeton University in its rare books department."

As he scratches this down in his notes, I change the topic and turn his attention to the Caxton volumes on one of the viewing tables. I regale him with the colorful stories of their acquisition, well-known in art circles but new to the public. It is another tactic I've developed over the years, distracting my audience by dazzling them—whether through an outlandish remark, an outrageous dress, or a good tale.

"How has the Pierpont Morgan Library changed as its status has gone from private collection to public institution? It is a tremendous accomplishment and, of course, a great gift to the people of this country," he adds as we stroll into what was once Mr. Morgan's study, but which has been Jack's library office for over a decade now.

"Yes, it's been described as the most meaningful cultural gift in American history." I beam every time I think about the establishment of the library as a public institution—my long-held dream come real, a legacy come to life. "Ah, you likely know, the process began when Mr. Jack Morgan very generously transitioned his ownership of the library and its holding to a board of trustees with an endowment. Then, courtesy of a special act of the New York legislature, this marvelous place became a public reference library with research purposes, and an art gallery," I explain. We go on to discuss the slate of programs I have planned for the library, as well as an upcoming exhibit of the letters and manuscripts of the founding fathers, such as George Washington, all open to the public.

I finish the tour of Mr. Morgan's study. The vibrant fifteenth- and sixteenth-century stained glass panels inserted in its tall vertical windows certainly deserve Mr. Bennett's notice, as do the inlaid walnut bookcases, the alabaster chandelier, and the stunning Renaissance triptychs and portraits by Hans Memling, Macrino d'Alba, Perugino, and Lucas Cranach, among others.

As I must, I draw his attention to the portrait of Mr. Morgan. I purposely ignore, however, a newly acquired painting that hangs near Mr. Morgan's immense walnut desk.

"May we take a photograph of you?" he asks a bit sheepishly as we finish his questions.

"I suppose," I answer, making no effort to mask my hesitation. I am no stranger to portraits. Over the years, Paul Helleu, René Piot, Laura Coombs Hills, William Rothenstein, and even Henri Matisse sketched or painted pictures of me. But those were for my personal use. Not for the public gaze.

"Do you have any particular place you prefer?" he inquires. "There's no shortage of gorgeous backdrops," he muses, and then leaves me to consider while he summons the photographer who's been waiting outside.

As he steps back into Mr. Morgan's study, I realize the perfect location for a fitting portrait. It will certainly be a risk, but it feels worthy and appropriate. Even necessary.

When the photographer arrives, I position myself as he sets up his equipment. I stand between Mr. Morgan's lion-footed desk and a portrait I recently advised Jack to purchase. This painting, entitled *Portrait of a Moor*, was painted at the end of the sixteenth century by Domenico Tintoretto's workshop and ostensibly depicts a Moorish ambassador to the Venetian court, resplendent in official garb next to a white package with wax seal, emblematic of his diplomatic role. While the brushstrokes are masterful and the portrayal breathtakingly lifelike, these are not the reasons I urged Jack to acquire it. The subject of *Portrait of a Moor* is of a darker man, a man who looks exactly like Papa. It is my homage to the two men who supported my climb to this peak, having their emblems sit side by side for the ages. Now, with this photograph, my official portrait will include the symbols of them both—Mr. Morgan's lion-footed desk and *Portrait of a Moor.*

After thirty minutes of taking shots, the photographer finishes and packs up his bulky camera. Mr. Bennett pulls me to the side. "Miss Greene, I hope you don't mind me asking you a personal question." Before I can agree or disagree, he continues, "There have been rumors, and I wouldn't be a good journalist if I didn't ask you about them. Did you and Mr. Morgan ever have a more intimate relationship?"

His face is flushed with embarrassment, and I imagine that his superior insisted he ask the question. I know I should be irritated or offended as befits a lady, but in actuality, I'm amused.

"I apologize for asking. I know it isn't really appropriate—"

I interrupt the stuttering young man, and say with a smirk, "If I were your average librarian, I might be offended, but I've never been average at anything."

"So—" He waits for my answer.

"Suffice it to say that we tried," I answer, laughing. *How Mr. Morgan would have enjoyed my bawdy response.*

He is flustered and confused, as I can see he isn't certain if my answer is a yes or a no. "Ah, okay." But he recovers quickly, and asks, "One last question, if that is all right with you, Miss Greene."

I nod my acquiescence, although I hope it conveys my lack of enthusiasm as well. That last question *should* have been the finale, and I've given as much of myself as I feel comfortable during the course of this interview.

"Can you share your personal plans with us?"

Finally, and for the first time, he has posed a question I am delighted to answer.

"For the rest of my days, I will be perfectly satisfied and honored to serve as the Pierpont Morgan Library's lady directress."

EPILOGUE

The charred corner of a letter drifts from the flames into the hearth. Even though I know the singed edges will be hot, I grab for it in an effort to rescue it from the flames. But before my fingertips reach it, I stop myself. Why would I stop this endeavor to destroy all my records? It isn't as if saving the letters will restore the people memorialized in them. And I can allow nothing to blacken my legacy.

Can pulling Mama's messages from the flames return her to my side, where she lived her entire life until she died almost ten years ago, leaving me truly alone for the first time in my life? While we had our challenges in my early years, I released that animosity when I returned from Chicago in 1913, and my mother and I forged a closer relationship. While Papa held beautiful dreams of equality for us all, Mama saved me—and all my siblings—from the segregation and racism in America, freeing me to fulfill that early promise Papa saw in me.

Will maintaining the sole letter I have from Papa re-create him, gone over twenty-five years now, and his hopes for true freedom along with him? Would I really want the man who had given me so much to return to this world, one that's moved away from the early promise of equality he experienced as a young man in the Reconstruction era? The America I inhabit is the antithesis of the society for which he worked, even though groups like the National Urban League, the National Council of Negro Women, and the Congress of Racial Equality have protested the laws of segregation and inequality. If he saw our segregated country and the unabashed white supremacy that continues in our midst, his heart would shatter. Even though colored and white soldiers fought side by side in the war, the black military returned home to Jim Crow laws that have kept colored people in a persistent state of social and economic inferiority. Lynchings are still common, segregation is the practice, and discrimination keeps colored people from getting better education, better employment, and better homes. The despair would be too much for Papa to bear.

Would saving the long, elegantly written letters that Bernard sent me for years from Europe restore the love we felt for each other? The girl I once was and the man I discovered him to be can never reunite and re-create that fleeting passion. No matter the unusual bond we once shared for all those years, we are too altered, too shattered, to return to those innocent days. And anyway, I needed to break the bond of that flawed love in order to soar.

Finally, I think of the man who made the greatest difference in my life. If I retrieve all of Mr. Morgan's personal letters from the fire, will it conjure him up again? While I'd give anything for another laugh or fight or heated game of bezique with him, the business realm he left behind is so changed and regulated that the titan of finance could no longer reign as he liked—without any oversight or accountability. How on earth could he survive that alteration? And what about the fear inside my heart that, if Mr. Morgan were to return, I would discover that he felt the same way about colored people as he did about Jews?

No, the preservation of these letters will do nothing to restore the people I love or animate my memories of them. Preserving my records will only serve to provide the racists of this world a reason to destroy the legacy I've worked my whole life to build and for which I've made countless sacrifices—the only contribution that will outlast me—the Pierpont Morgan Library, my gift to the people of this world.

I push the errant letter back into the flames with the brass poker and stoke the fire again. But as I do, Papa's words surface in my mind, and a rogue wish sparks within me. What if Papa's hopes came true? What if our society could transform and evolve in the manner he dreamed about? Could there one day be a world in which we have new governmental leaders and new laws that would grant equality to all of the citizens of this country? Could our society change such that we would walk among each other, live with each other, and perhaps even love one another, no matter the color of our skin? And if that day did come to pass, would someone, someday, reach back in time to discover my story and proudly claim the real me, the colored personal librarian to J. P. Morgan whose name was Belle da Costa Greene?

Historical Note

We have endeavored to share the life and legacy of Belle da Costa Greene as accurately as possible, even though we have written a fictionalized version of Belle and her world in *The Personal Librarian*. We attempted to anchor her narrative in the available facts. Given that Belle was a fairly well-known public figure—as was J. P. Morgan and, to a lesser extent, Belle's father, Richard Greener—there was rich material upon which to draw.

Thus, the depictions of Belle herself, Richard Greener, Genevieve Fleet, J. P. Morgan, Jack Morgan, and Bernard Berenson, as well as more minor characters based upon real-life individuals, hew closely to the known details. We also strove to capture as authentically as possible the historical context in which Belle lived: her upbringing, her career as the Morgan librarian and curator, her social life in the upper echelons of Gilded Age society, her dabbling on the fringes of the bohemian and suffragist worlds—and, most importantly, we tried to imagine and portray the sacrifices and strains of her passing as white in a racist society hostile to African Americans.

Sometimes, when necessary for the pacing of the story or the narrative arc of the book, we have taken liberties with historical dates and details. For example, we refer to the scandal involving the shooting of Stanford White of the famous architectural firm of McKim, Mead & White in a chapter that takes place in January of 1906 when, in fact, the murder took place several months later. Similarly, we referenced the wedding of New York society figures Marjorie Gould and Anthony Drexel in a scene dated March 1908 but the wedding occurred in 1910. The Armory Show took place in New York City in February and March of 1913, but we suggested it was still ongoing in December 1913. For the exhibit at the 291 gallery, we compressed the Rodin and Matisse shows into one show taking place in May of 1908 when, in fact, there were two exhibitions in 1908. In addition, we imagined certain Gilded Age parties, like the summer soiree at the Woolworths' Gold Coast mansion; while fictional, they were all modeled after other such lavish affairs. Regarding the sale of the famous series of paintings entitled *The Progress of Love* by Jean-Honoré Fragonard, we have Jack Morgan considering selling them in 1913 when, in fact, Henry Clay Frick purchased them in 1915. The timing of the Pierpont Morgan Library's purchase of the painting *Portrait of a Moor*, which hung in Mr. Morgan's study, took place in 1929, not 1924, and it is only speculation on our part that the similarity between the subject and Belle's father prompted the acquisition.

From time to time, we faced gaps about the nuances of certain relationships, not uncommon when dealing with women's histories and records. Often such records weren't considered worth preserving until recently. Additionally, Belle's story was challenging because she was determined to keep the more private aspects of her life hidden. In these instances, we structured the story around the research, and in the gaps, we made logical extrapolations.

As one example, Belle's romantic relationship with Bernard Berenson is well documented; however, the intimate details of that relationship are not known. We had to make important inferences about key events, such as particulars about their courtship and affair in America and Europe, and the manner in which their status as outsiders knit them together. Certain letters and dates point to Belle having had an abortion and its long-lasting impact on her, but the details are not documented. Heidi Ardizzone, author of Belle's wonderful biography, *An Illuminated Life: Belle da Costa Greene's Journey from Prejudice to Privilege*, and one of the few historians to look closely at her life, suggests that it did happen, and we took fictional liberties from there. Also, Bernard had a long working relationship with the Duveens, and recent scholarship points to some practices Belle might have found objectionable, so we envisioned an impact on Belle and her business dealings. We admit to taking significant creative license with regard to the rousing conclusion to Belle's relationship with Bernard. In real life, their connection lasted for decades, but we perhaps chose to end the relationship as we wished Belle had—and hope she would approve of our dramatic imaginings.

With other profound relationships in Belle's life, we made similar suppositions based on our understanding of the context and characters. For example, with J. P. Morgan, the vast amount of time he and Belle spent together has been documented by many people connected with the famous financier, as have the sorts of activities and social occasions in which they engaged and their overall closeness. But we didn't know the *full* extent of their relationship—neither its apex nor its nadir—despite the many rumors that circulated about them and the fact that Belle herself was quoted as saying, "We tried!" in response to a question about being Morgan's mistress. So we spun out a textured, complicated relationship, rife with the sexual tension we imagined *must* have been present given their personalities.

Similarly, in Belle's relationship with her father, we don't know the extent of her youthful connection to him, although there are reports about their affection for each other and their shared interests, so we envisioned what might have been. We also didn't have any confirmation of what happened in their later years, after Richard had left Belle and her family for foreign travels and another family. However, when we read in Heidi Ardizzone's biography of Belle that she took a strangely timed trip to Chicago—a trip that had no business purpose—we felt certain that she must have met with her father, who was living in Chicago then. And so we conceived of the reunion with her father that Belle so richly deserved.

Along those lines, when we learned that Anne Morgan had never warmed to Belle as Jack Morgan and his other sisters had, we contemplated creating a challenging relationship between Anne and Belle, one in which they were each hiding secrets about their identities. The speculation around Anne's sexuality that existed even during her lifetime—fueled by her relationship with well-known lesbians Elsie de Wolfe and Elisabeth Marbury as well as her refusal to marry and her politics—influenced this decision, as did the opportunity to explore the societal pressures on both Anne and Belle to be other than their authentic selves.

We also had to consider how people of African descent would have been addressed during the early twentieth century as well as how Belle would have thought of herself. What we discovered was that the term "colored" was used prominently during the time period early in the novel—particularly with respect to people of mixed heritage—as well as "black," and then those terms evolved into references such as "Negro" as the law and perceptions changed in America. As Belle aged in the novel, we initially utilized the more era-appropriate word "Negro," but as we considered it, we felt that Belle would probably not have used the term "Negro" in thinking about herself. In addition, while these kinds of cultural issues were being addressed and changing in society, Belle was not a part of that change, and we felt that it would have been difficult for her to see herself and others like her as anything except for the term that she'd grown up using, which was "colored."

For a deep dive into any of these subjects or historical individuals, we recommend many nonfiction books and writings, including but not limited to *An Illuminated Life: Belle da Costa Greene's Journey from Prejudice to Privilege* by Heidi Ardizzone, *The House of Morgan: An American Banking Dynasty and the Rise of Modern Finance* by Ron Chernow, *Bernard Berenson: A Life in the Picture Trade* by Rachel Cohen, *Uncompromising Activist: Richard Greener* by Katherine Reynolds Chaddock, Richard Greener's own essay "The White Problem," and *Stony the Road: Reconstruction, White Supremacy, and the Rise of Jim Crow* by Henry Louis Gates Jr. We also suggest a review of the Morgan Library's excellent publications as well as a tour through the incredible institution.

While we adored writing about Belle's panache in society—her witty quips and her eye-catching fashion, as well as her sometimes outrageous behavior—we also faced an enormous challenge. Given the very intentional lengths that Belle went to to destroy her letters—leaving behind only her business correspondence and her missives to Bernard (which he'd promised to destroy but failed to do and which did not discuss Belle's race)—we had a very limited record of how she *felt* about passing in the racist world in which she lived and conversations emanating from those feelings. Needless to say, she did not talk publicly about her heritage for the same reasons. Clearly, Belle did not want her real identity discovered, not a surprise given the racism of her times and her legitimate concern that if her background became widely known, her accomplishments at the Pierpont Morgan Library would be eviscerated.

So when we began writing about Belle's interior life, in particular her feelings about living as white, we entered the realm Marie often describes as the space between the pillars of the architecture formed by the facts—a space where we used a blend of research, personal experience, fiction, and logical extrapolation—to reach Belle's inner self. We also relied on Victoria's own experiences as an African American woman and her family's experiences, in particular those of her grandmother, who was fair and often passed when necessary. Drawing on this familial experience—and pairing it with research based on historical instances of passing, as documented in books such as *A Chosen Exile: A History of Racial Passing in American Life* by Allyson Hobbs—we hope we did justice to Belle's struggles and brought to life the terrible injustices and pain that racism and segregation have exacted upon individuals and the United States as a whole.

Our country had a chance at racial equality in the years after the Civil War—an equality that Richard Greener and his family briefly experienced and for which he advocated his entire life—but white supremacy and segregation rose up in reaction to those efforts. We hope that *The Personal Librarian* explores not only the incredible life and legacy of Belle da Costa Greene but also the sacrifice and suffering that the African American population has endured as a result of the horrific response to the promise of equality—then and now. More than anything, we hope *The Personal Librarian* inspires discussion about these important issues, conversations that will foster understanding, compassion, action—and ultimately change.

Marie Benedict's Author's Note

This is not my ordinary author's note. But then *The Personal Librarian* is not my usual novel. I had no idea that writing a book about Belle da Costa Greene, personal librarian to J. P. Morgan, creator of the Pierpont Morgan Library's famous manuscript collection and a woman with a life-altering secret, would change me. That in bringing Belle to life, I myself would awaken and gain a sister in the process.

I first discovered Belle years ago, when I was a different person living a different life. I was a commercial litigator in New York City, working for one of the world's largest law firms, and I was terribly unhappy. I knew I wasn't engaged in my life's purpose, and the Pierpont Morgan Library became one of my refuges during those dark days. Strolling through its jewel-box interiors, I could pretend that I was a historian or an archaeologist or an author unearthing the hidden past—the life I longed to live, rather than the life I was living.

On one of those afternoons, I found Belle. The discovery didn't emerge from an informational plaque about her role at the Pierpont Morgan Library or an exhibition about her contributions or even the display of one of her portraits; such references were not highlighted at that time. No, I learned about Belle from a passing docent, who took a few moments from her busy schedule to describe this astonishing woman and, in so doing, offered me a new lens through which to view the Pierpont Morgan Library, its collection, the time in which it was created, and much, much more.

Belle haunted me for decades, especially once I began digging deep into her background. I learned that her father, Richard Greener, the first African American graduate of Harvard, had been a prominent advocate for equality in the decades after the Civil War, particularly for the Civil Rights Act of 1875. An act that affirmed the equality of *all* people and provided for equal treatment in public transportation and public accommodations for everyone. An act that the Supreme Court overturned in 1883 and, in so doing, undermined much of the Thirteenth and Fourteenth Amendments, which banned slavery and guaranteed equal protection of the laws, respectively. As a result, Richard Greener's daughter was forced to hide her true identity. In order to become the most successful career woman of her day, she lived as a white woman. What must it have been like to be Belle da Costa Greene? I couldn't help but wonder, and I began contemplating writing a novel about her.

However, I recognized I couldn't write this story by myself. In penning previous books, I'd been able to imagine the lives of many other women with varied origins and experiences, but I knew I could not conjure Belle alone. How could I possibly conceive of what it would be like to be an African American woman in the years immediately after the Civil War—when slavery was supposedly abolished, but white supremacy, Jim Crow laws, and lynchings were actually on the rise? And how could I take that one step further and envision what it would be like when that woman tried to pass as white, especially when it had been her father's dream to fashion a world where all people could live freely while openly celebrating their heritage? Not only would such an exercise be presumptuous, but Belle deserved to have her story told by an African American author.

The years passed, and sometimes I could almost hear Belle tapping her foot, waiting impatiently as I left the legal profession and began writing about other historical women. Then one day, I started reading *Stand Your Ground* by Victoria Christopher Murray. In the pages of this compelling, important award-winning novel about the shooting of a Black teenage boy by a white policeman—told from the perspectives of the boy's mother and the wife of the policeman—I hoped I'd found my partner.

I could not wait to meet this incredible author who had crafted such a nuanced, crucial examination of race from two very different perspectives. But I was also a little intimidated. What would Victoria be like? Would she really want to work with me on this book? After all, she had her own bevy of projects lined up as well as endless work travel, and I worried that she'd find me audacious for even attempting to tell Belle's story. Who did I think I was?

However, from our very first conversation, I felt connected to this brilliant, warm woman. We learned how alike we were in some ways, both striving oldest daughters, eager to please our parents with traditional success yet yearning for another path. Not unlike Belle. Together, I hoped we could excavate Belle from the detritus of the past and share the astonishing contributions of this critical woman, along with the history of the post–Civil War era, an era in which America attempted equality but white supremacy rose up. Luckily for me, Victoria agreed to be my writing partner, and we embarked on this mission.

Writing Belle's story with Victoria—after dreaming about it for so many years—was a joy, and I often thought about how fortunate I was in her partnership and burgeoning friendship. When we finalized our first draft and hit the send button to our wonderful editor, I thought we'd brought Belle to life, and the unjust, racist world she inhabited along with her. I thought that I'd come to fully know Victoria in the process. I didn't know that I was just beginning.

Our edited manuscript arrived along with the coronavirus and quarantine. Victoria and I had the time and the technology (thank you, Zoom!) to talk in person nearly every day, sometimes for hours a day. While these long conversations initially focused on the hard work of revising *The Personal Librarian*, they quickly shifted into a sharing of our personal experiences, both with the pandemic and with the issues of discrimination we were exploring in the pages of our book. And when the racism always lurking in our society—since long before the days we write about here—reared its ugly head so incontrovertibly with George Floyd and Christian Cooper, and people took to the streets in protest despite the pandemic, those discussions became intense and intimate, and our friendship deepened.

Honored by her trust in me, I listened as Victoria shared her experiences with racism, the sort of daily degradations she suffers as well as the larger, bolder acts perpetrated on her. My heart clenched as she told me of her own parents' attempts to change systemic racism with their involvement in the civil rights marches of the 1960s and 1970s, and as she described the segregation that her grandparents endured during the years of Jim Crow laws, which sometimes necessitated that her fair-skinned grandmother pass as white. My heart ached as Victoria and I witnessed the horrific white supremacy running rampant in our society right before our eyes—terrifyingly similar to the incidents we discovered in our research and wrote about in the pages of our book—and I found myself growing furious on behalf of Victoria and Belle.

It wasn't only our book that changed in the editing process; I did, too. Victoria generously offered me a lens through which to see the world, and it altered me, and continues to do so. I'd always believed myself to be a proponent of equality for all, but my conversations with Victoria made clear how little I knew about the struggle and about myself. As I listened to Victoria, I realized how removed I had been, how protected by my own white privilege I really was. And how much I had to learn and how much I had to *do*. For Victoria—my partner, my friend, and my sister—and for all our shared humanity. And for Belle.

Victoria Christopher Murray's Author's Note

"What is Liza thinking?"

That was my first thought when my literary agent (who is amazing) sent me a proposal to work with another author. Collaborating wasn't new for me; I'd worked with ReShonda Tate Billingsley on six novels, and I loved writing with her far more than writing independently. So I was always open to this type of opportunity.

But this project was unusual because of the author. Marie Benedict was a *New York Times* bestselling author who'd written wonderful stories of strong women whose names had been lost inside the folds of history. I was impressed, but I couldn't figure out why a historical fiction author would want to work with a contemporary writer like me.

Because I couldn't wrap my head around that concept, it took me a while to even read the proposal. It just didn't make sense; it wasn't a fit.

And this is why reading is fundamental.

Because once I finally read *The Personal Librarian* proposal and found out who Belle was, I was fascinated for so many reasons. An African American woman helped J. P. Morgan build his massive art and manuscript collection, but no one knew she was Black? Her life, before I'd even studied more about her, seemed like the lives of so many of the grandparents and great-grandparents of my friends, whose lighter skin was the mark of one of the most heinous acts of slavery. In my family, my grandmother (whose complexion was so light that my younger sister Cecile once asked about pictures on our mantel—"Who is that white lady?") shared her own stories of occasionally passing out of necessity or to make life easier.

I knew Belle from my own familial experiences. I knew the pain of the decision she made to leave behind her heritage, and then the fear of exposure that came with that choice. I could imagine how every day, once she walked outside her doors, she had to put on an award-winning performance, but then at night, when she returned home, took off her "costume," and laid her head down, she was still Black.

I wanted in—I wanted to be part of this project and bring Belle da Costa Greene to life.

The proposal was only the first hurdle, though. Next, I had to meet Marie. Embarking on a project like this meant that we would spend hours together. I was prepared for that, but was Marie? Would we have the chemistry to endure all the time, all the effort, all the work, that was in front of us?

Our agents set up the call for us to speak. I said, "Hello," Marie said, "Hello," . . . and that was it. I think we were two, maybe three minutes into the call before we were more than potential cowriters; we were already friends. By our third or fourth call, we were finishing each other's sentences. By the time we met in person, we were sisters.

For the next few months, we worked tirelessly, spending hours on the phone planning each chapter, bringing Belle to life. We finished writing the first draft of the manuscript, and at the end, all I could say was that the entire process was amazing for me. I loved working with Marie. She taught me so much about writing history. I became a champion researcher as I searched and searched to discover one hidden fact after another about Belle. My biggest challenge was the flowery dialogue of the early twentieth century. There were times when I just wanted one of the characters to say, "Are you kidding me, dude?"

Clearly, that wouldn't have worked, but it didn't matter. Because whenever I gave up and wrote something like that, Marie followed with what we began to call her magical historical brush. I'd write something like "'That's what's up, Belle,' J. P. Morgan said." And Marie would change that to "I feel like we should be heralding you with a ticker tape parade, Belle." (Okay, maybe it wasn't that bad, but it was close.)

Once we turned in our manuscript, I knew I had a friend for life. What I didn't know was what was ahead for me and Marie. I had no idea that a pandemic would leave us both stranded in our homes, revising the manuscript. I had no idea that we would spend even more hours than before together, just about every day, working on our story. I had no idea that we'd have to continue working right after we watched a man murdered in the streets of Minneapolis. I had no idea that as a disease threatened our bodies and civil unrest challenged our souls, Marie and I would bond far beyond the experience of writing together.

Our country in disarray was the background music as we, a white woman and a Black woman, talked through our emotions of what felt like our country crumbling around us. Marie checked on me every day, giving me an outlet for the outrage that burned within me, although just as many times I had to be that outlet for her. We created a safe space between us as we discussed the history of Black America, the history of white America, and the hope that one day these two Americas would converge into one.

All of those thoughts, all of those emotions, spilled into Belle's story because so much of what we were experiencing in our society as we wrote was what Belle wanted to avoid by passing as white more than one hundred years ago. She didn't want the color of her skin to be used as a weapon against her, an excuse to keep her relegated to the lowest jobs, the worst neighborhoods, with little possibility for a better life.

Writing *The Personal Librarian* has been a life-changing experience for me, and I am so grateful for this opportunity. There couldn't have been a better time, there couldn't have been a better project, and, most importantly for me, there couldn't have been a better person to navigate through all of this with than Marie Benedict. I don't know what the writing future holds for us, but what I do know is that I have a new sister for the rest of my life. And my hope, my desire, is that everyone who reads this story will feel the emotions and experiences that we tried to pour onto these pages and they will come to love Belle da Costa Greene as much as we do.

Marie Benedict's Acknowledgments

Belle da Costa Greene captured my imagination and heart years ago, but her essential and timely story—as Victoria and I discovered and then let unfold in *The Personal Librarian*—would have remained as hidden as Belle's own identity during her lifetime without the support and championship of so many. As always, I must begin with my own personal advocate, my brilliant and generous agent, Laura Dail, without whom this book would not have been possible. I am incredibly thankful for our wonderful editor, Kate Seaver, whose desire and passion to share Belle's story was evident from the very start and who has guided this book beautifully. The amazing folks at Penguin Random House have our endless gratitude: Ivan Held, Christine Ball, Claire Zion, Jeanne-Marie Hudson, Craig Burke, Anthony Ramondo, Jin Yu, Lauren Burnstein, Dache Rogers, Natalie Sellars, Michelle Kasper, and Mary Geren.

However, without the constant and unwavering love and support of my boys—Jim, Jack, and Ben—none of this would have been possible. And without my talented and phenomenal partner, friend, and sister, Victoria Christopher Murray, *The Personal Librarian* would not have come into being at all.

Victoria Christopher Murray's Acknowledgments

This project started to come together even before I became involved. I am so grateful for my phenomenal agent, Liza Dawson, for seeing this opportunity and knowing how amazing it would be for me. And that was just the beginning. From the moment Marie and I spoke with Kate Seaver, we knew we wanted to work with her as our editor. Thank you, Kate, for believing in Belle as much as we did and for taking this journey with us. To the team at Penguin Random House, all I can say is *Wow*. When this novel was just a thought, everyone saw our vision and shared our excitement. Thank you to all: Ivan Held, Christine Ball, Claire Zion, Jeanne-Marie Hudson, Craig Burke, Anthony Ramondo, Jin Yu, Lauren Burnstein, Dache Rogers, Natalie Sellars, Michelle Kasper, and Mary Geren.

I cannot complete this without recognizing the most important people in my career—the thousands of readers who've been with me on this twenty-year journey. Thank you for being excited about *The Personal Librarian*, and I hope you come to love Belle as much as I do.

And finally, to Marie. What can I say about you? I thought I was meeting a new writing partner, but I got another sister instead. I will be forever grateful to Belle da Costa Greene for that.

The PERSONAL LIBRARIAN

Marie Benedict and Victoria Christopher Murray

While we hope you've enjoyed *The Personal Librarian* and the experience of immersing yourself in Belle's story, we also hope you agree with us that this novel contains so much that we all need to discuss. Even as we were writing it, we drafted questions for you to consider and then revisited them many, many times as the story evolved and we got to know Belle and her world more intimately. The day-to-day struggles Belle faced as an African American woman passing as a white woman in a racist world were challenging in and of themselves, but the repercussions on her emotional and personal life were every bit as important.

We understand that our readers come from different backgrounds and will see Belle's story and our questions from many perspectives. Our dream is that *The Personal Librarian* will be embraced by book clubs from the full range of those different backgrounds, and that readers will connect to Belle and learn from her experiences as we have. In addition, we think it would be wonderful if book clubs could have the transformational experience that we had when writing this book. Thus, we hope that book clubs will reach out and join together with other clubs, bringing together readers from a broad range of backgrounds, ages, and experiences to share in the discussion of Belle.

This guide is simply that, a guide that aims to spark conversations that will foster connection, action, and, hopefully, progress toward equality.

Questions for Discussion

1. How might you explain Belle's rise to such breathtaking heights in society and her profession at a time when women—especially African American women—faced such blatant discrimination and exclusion? Did Belle possess certain personality traits that yielded this incredible outcome? If so, what are they? What sorts of outside influences contributed to her ascent?

2. In some ways, Belle's parents had somewhat unique experiences or backgrounds for African American people during this time period. What kind of reaction did you have to her parents' histories? How might those histories have impacted Belle, even when she had not been told the details of her parents' pasts?

3. How did you view Belle's relationship with her mother? Do you think Belle resented her mother, or did their relationship change over the course of the book such that they came to a place of understanding? If so, what was Belle's turning point with her mother?

4. How would you describe Belle's position among her siblings? How did you feel about her relationship with them and her responsibilities to them?

5. What sort of reaction did you have to Belle's relationship with her father? Do you think Belle ever felt deserted by her father in the same way her siblings did? Why or why not?

6. What sort of pressure do you think Belle might have experienced from the rumors about her true ethnicity? Do you think J. P. Morgan heard the rumors? Do you think he knew she was passing as white and decided to ignore it, or do you think he was unaware of her heritage?

7. What do you think *really* happened romantically between Belle and J. P. Morgan? Do you agree with the portrayal in the book?

8. How would you describe the attraction between Belle and Bernard Berenson? What were the attributes that drew them together and, ultimately, forced them apart? How did you feel about their relationship—and Belle's ability to have a partner and family of her own?

9. What surprised you the most about Belle's life? About her time period?

10. How familiar were you with passing before reading this novel? Has your understanding of the reasons and sacrifices behind it altered after reading about Belle's life?

11. What sacrifices did Belle make by choosing to follow her mother's path? What advantages did she gain?

12. Before reading this book, were you familiar with the Civil Rights Act of 1875 or the efforts toward equality that occurred during Reconstruction? Did you have any understanding of what transpired in the years after Reconstruction? What might have happened in the United States in the decades that followed if the Civil Rights Act of 1875—along with the many efforts at equality that occurred during Reconstruction—had not been overturned?

13. How do the racial issues and events in the book relate to events happening today?

14. In the end, do you think Belle was happy with her choices and decisions? Do you think she would have done anything differently?

Photo by Anthony Musmanno

Marie Benedict is a lawyer with more than ten years' experience as a litigator. A graduate of Boston College and Boston University School of Law, she is the *New York Times* and *USA Today* bestselling author of *Her Hidden Genius*, *The Mystery of Mrs. Christie*, *Lady Clementine*, *The Only Woman in the Room*, *Carnegie's Maid*, and *The Other Einstein*. All have been translated into multiple languages. She lives in Pittsburgh with her family.

CONNECT ONLINE

AuthorMarieBenedict.com
AuthorMarieBenedict
AuthorMarieBenedict

Photo by Jason Frost Photography 2020

Victoria Christopher Murray is a *New York Times* and *USA Today* bestselling author with more than one million books in print. She has written more than thirty novels, including *Stand Your Ground*, an NAACP Image Award winner for Outstanding Literary Work (Fiction) and a *Library Journal* Best Book of the Year. She holds an MBA from the NYU Stern School of Business.

CONNECT ONLINE

VictoriaChristopherMurray.com
VictoriaCMurray
VictoriaChristopherMurray
VictoriaECM